JENNIFER ROBERSON

KARAVANS

DAW BOOKS, INC.

DONALD A. WOLLHEIM, FOUNDER

375 Hudson Street, New York, NY 10014

ELIZABETH R. WOLLHEIM

SHEILA E. GILBERT

PUBLISHERS

http://www.dawbooks.com

First Paperback Printing, April 2007
1 2 3 4 5 6 7 8 9

DAW TRADEMARK REGISTERED
U.S. PAT. OFF AND FOREIGN COUNTRIES
—MARCA REGISTRADA
HECHO EN U.S.A.

Printed in the U.S.A.

I dedicate this to my uncle and to my aunts, with love,

Sam Hardy
Molly Hardy
Clare Witcomb

and to the memory of my mother

Shera Roberson

AFTER SO MUCH TIME, his voice, the words, came hard. He had been—*other*—for time out of mind.

"I," he said. And, in shock, repeated it: "I."

Other words, more words, came back to him. Words that, strung together, shaped identity. He knew those words. And knew himself, when he had not for an endless time, immured in darkness.

"I . . . am . . . man."

A man. He was.

Human.

"I am man. I am *a* man."

The emphasis was important.

"I am a man."

He crowed victory, no longer mute.

He was a man.

Was he not?

Around him the world shuddered. Darkness bled into light. Nausea took him. Bile burned the back of his throat, occluding a sob.

So close.

So close to . . . elsewhere.

So close to home.

"I am a man."

He was. Had been. Was born so.

Man. Male. Mortal.

He remembered, *remembered,* after a space—for time out of mind—when he could not.

"I am," he said aloud, seeking solace, seeking strength.

But darkness wrapped its fingers around him. Darkness took him up, as if to inspect him more closely. His head filled, and his eyes. His ears. His mouth and his nose. He choked on it.

Darkness.

Darkness dangled him by the scruff of his neck, as if he were vermin caught by a dog. Darkness smelled him. Shook him. And then, with a twitch of negligent hand, darkness discarded him.

He fell. And fell.

When he landed, when he had recovered breath enough to speak, strength enough to move, he sat up. Light. In place of darkness, light. He saw. He smelled. He heard. He felt. He *tasted.*

"I am a man," he said. And, "Home."

He stood. Balanced. Began to walk.

To humankind. To home.

To anywhere other than where he had been.

Alisanos.

Human?

Was he?

Could he be, after dwelling in Alisanos?

He stopped walking. Stretched out his arms, and gazed upon them. Began to tremble.

At the end of his arms, in place of his hands, were—*other.*

He screamed.

Human?

No.

Not he.

Screamed and screamed and screamed.

ILONA AWOKE ABRUPTLY to the sound of a scream resounding within her skull. For that moment of shock, the initial instant of confusion caused by a sudden awakening out of deep sleep, she heard it. And then realized the sound had not been a true scream but merely the futile attempt of her sleep-fettered body to cry out. She had managed at most a moan.

Her wagon was dark. She had dropped the oilcloth sides of the roof canopy and blown out the last lantern hours before. The karavan encampment, wagons gathered within a sprawling grove of wide-crowned trees at the edge of a haphazard tent settlement, still slept, save for the occasional yip or bark of a dog, the restless wuffling of picketed draft animals, the ceaseless metallic scraping of insects known as nightsingers.

She lay awake in the narrow cot beneath the roof ribs of her tall, high-wheeled wagon, recalling the scrambled flashes of dream-born images. Confusion, mostly: scarlet lightning, a roaring wind, black skies, steaming rain, the glimpse of a woman's profile, a Hecari warrior with war-club raised, a karavan turning back. None of it made sense.

Ilona closed her eyes and rubbed the lids with her fingers, stretching them out of shape. Jorda, the karavan-master, had never turned back in all his years on the roads throughout Sancorra province. His reputation was for always getting his people where they paid him to go. It made no sense that Jorda would turn back.

Voice hoarse from sleep, Ilona chastised herself. "You read *hands*, remember? Reading dreams is not your gift."

But she could not shake the images, the memory of panic. Red lightning, a roaring wind, black skies, a woman, inexplicably steaming rain, and a karavan turning back.

Not Jorda's karavan, then. Perhaps nothing more than a dream construct, false images conjured from the back of her mind.

Ilona turned onto her side, resettling blankets over her upper shoulder. She was a diviner, yes, but the omens and auguries she read lay always in a human palm, not in images fed to her in the darkness. Her dreams were merely dreams, albeit some more dramatic than others. Nightmares, however, only rarely plagued her.

But she could not remember experiencing the violence of

such dreams on the day before the karavan was to leave. Usually those dreams were filled with the minutiae of departure, the nagging concerns that she might forget some chore, neglect to pack things she needed for the journey, be not quite ready when Jorda gave the order to the karavan to follow him out of the grove. It didn't matter that she had been with Jorda for years and on numerous trips; she always worried something would be lost or forgotten in the confusion of departure.

Ilona sighed and stroked a strand of hair out of her face. Diviners were not immune to such omens as she read in hands. If she had time the next day, perhaps she could consult with a dream-reader in the tent settlement. It would do no good if one of Jorda's three karavan diviners ignored her own future while she read those of others.

THOUGH RHUAN WAS a karavan guide, a man hired to ride out ahead of the column of wagons to scout the safety of the roads and water holes, that duty also included providing protection to the folk joining Jorda's karavan. In the nights immediately before departure, he and Darmuth, the other guide, rode the perimeter of the grove in which more than thirty wagons had gathered. The draft animals, mostly horses and a few mules, were tied or hobbled close by; the remuda, the small herd of extra riding horses kept for Jorda and his two guides, and the draft teams used by the three karavan diviners were picketed farther away with the horse-master keeping an eye on them. It was not unheard of for thieves to sneak among the wagons, hoping to find a few items they might later sell. Rhuan and Darmuth prevented that.

He rode his favorite horse, a handsome cream gelding boasting a black-spotted rump and a splattering of larger black spots spreading across the balance of his body. In the darkness of the grove Rhuan couldn't see Darmuth, but knew he was present. And knew also that Darmuth, because of a duty never spoken of among the humans, would be watching *him* as much as he tended the welfare of the karavan.

Though lamps and lanterns had been blown out hours before, a ruddy glow emanated from dying cookfires scattered throughout the grove. Jorda was not the only karavan-master who camped his folk here; there were times when the wagons outnumbered the trees. But it was late in the season, and only two karavans remained. Sennet was leading his out in the morning; Jorda's departure was set for a day later.

Without warning, Rhuan's flesh prickled. He felt the hairs rising on his limbs, at the back of his neck. The ratcheting of the nightsingers abruptly stopped. From under one of the wagons a dog lifted its voice in a howl; neighboring dogs joined it in a wailing threnody. Within moments Rhuan heard sleepy voices testily calling out to quiet the noise, some threatening punishment, and one by one each dog fell silent.

The night felt *heavy.* Rhuan reined in. His skin itched. An accompanying shudder ran the length of his body. But he made no attempt to rub or shrug away the annoyance. Instead he slipped off his horse, dropped the reins so the spotted gelding would, as trained, remain in place, and walked to the nearest tree.

Rhuan knelt beside the gnarled roots that broke through the soil. Still the nightsingers held their silence. He placed his palm against the trunk.

Those in the settlement who knew him, or knew *of* him, also knew he wasn't human, but Shoia, a man born of a race from a far distant province, a race never seen before in Sancorra. But though it was no secret he was Shoia, Rhuan refrained from exhibiting all of his gifts. It was one thing to be the subject of much speculation about what a Shoia could do, and quite another to be feared for his abilities. He desired the trust of the humans, not their wariness. A guide's effectiveness would be lessened if his charges feared or distrusted him. It was important they not witness this communion between man and tree.

But it was dark beneath this tree, farthest from the fires,

and he was shielded by the horse, who dropped his head to seek out the sparse sprigs of grass that had withstood a barrage of wagon wheels and hooves. Rhuan spoke softly, using the language he'd known from birth but never spoke among the humans. Darmuth would understand it, but then he was no more human than Rhuan; and Brodhi, Rhuan's kin-in-kind, spoke it as well. But Brodhi, mercifully, was absent. This was a private moment.

Beneath his palm Rhuan felt the roughness of bark; more deeply, the thrumming of vibrancy and life in the heart of the wood. The elderling oak was not yet on the verge of death. With grave respect Rhuan sought that life, sought the sentience, an awareness that humans could never understand.

He jerked his hand away, hissing. His palm tingled unpleasantly. It was not the oak, he knew; elderlings did no harm, but could be conduits for danger. Their roots ran deep below the surface, cognizant of things unknown among men. Rhuan felt the prickling awareness bestir the hair on his flesh again, answering the first faint precursor. Change was coming. A change so profound it would touch even earth and sky and sun. Humans would suffer. Humans would die. His body knew, even if his own sentience instantly denied the truth. Certainly Darmuth knew as well. But Darmuth had said nothing. He left it to Rhuan to discover for himself.

Alisanos was coming.

Rhuan rose. The horse raised his head, ears flicking forward like sharp-tipped sentinels. The animals sensed it. The trees knew it. And now he banished denial and allowed himself to admit the truth. Because by admitting that truth, he might be able to save human lives before Alisanos took them.

If the humans permit me. Rhuan took up the dangling rein and swung it over the gelding's neck. *If they* **believe** *me.*

Chapter 1

"I NEED MORE BONES," Hezriah declared. "You must bring me another body."

It was stifling inside the undyed, soiled oilcloth tent. He'd have rolled up the sidewalls in hope of catching a stray breeze except his job was not the kind people wanted to see on their way to market. His was the kind of job no one *needed* to see, either, because it was the prosaic and thus tedious side of the augury business. For all there was magic involved—at least, for the legitimate diviners who truly did converse with the gods—no one wanted to see how the ingredients required by the magic were assembled. Just the end result.

They want to see the flesh on the body, and breathing, not the bones underneath. Hezriah smiled, liking the turn of phrase; most appropriate for his line of work. *I should write that one down.* "Well? Have you a body for me?"

A bead of sweat rolled down the heat-flushed cheek into the wiry beard of the other person in the tent. His hireling, Merriq. "Brought you one last week, didn't I?"

Outside, someone shouted, hoarse-voiced; the bonedealer caught three words in ten. Something about a moonsick man. Not his business; he had no time for such folk as lacked a proper mind. Deepwood bait, such folk. Their bodies and brains were cursed, not fit for augury.

"That was a child, Merriq. Not enough bones there to fill but a partial order." Something stung his cheek; he slapped hard, gritting his teeth. The dead insect tumbled to the hard-packed dirt floor covered by a hemmed sheet of black-dyed canvas, slightly sun-rusted. Dusty footprints marred the surface: his own, and Merriq's bigger, booted feet. "Cursed horseflies," he muttered. "Should all be sent to Alisanos." Though, come to think of it, more probably they had come *from* the deepwood; all demons and devils did, be they in human form or other. Hezriah scowled anew. "Have you anything due in from the anthills?"

"Day or two," Merriq answered stolidly. "Still too much meat on the bones."

"Well, that will do for Dardannus." Hezriah nodded, briefly calculating how long the Kantic diviner would tolerate the delay without reducing payment or looking elsewhere for a supplier. Practitioners of the Kantica did not count patience among their virtues. "But I need another body as soon as possible."

"Do you want me to kill someone?"

He grunted. "No, no. Let them die on their own; I have ethics, and I respect the law—unlike some I could mention, named Eccul! But surely you can find someone crossing over the river in one of the alleys, can't you? Or someone murdered for not paying his debts?" The latter happened frequently among bad wagerers and drunkards.

The hireling's massive shoulders hitched. "I can poke around."

"Good. Do so. Or Eccul will have my clients." Hezriah sighed, aware of a sense of oppression not entirely due to the heat and close confines; there were plenty of other bonedealers who could take over when he failed. Eccul was merely one of many, if more annoying than most. "Any Shoia in danger of dying?"

Merriq shrugged. "Not many in town *to* die. Not that they ever do."

Hezriah scowled. "There's Rhuan. Disgustingly arrogant young man. Surely someone will kill him soon." He brightened. "Or possibly Brodhi? I saw him earlier, come in from the road. He was heading for Mikal's tent. Do you think someone might kill him there? Brodhi isn't well liked. In fact, I don't know of *anyone* who likes him."

"No one will kill Rhuan *or* Brodhi," Merriq declared. "Shoia can't die."

"Oh, certainly they can die." Ludicrous legends annoyed Hezriah. "You simply have to kill them seven times."

"In a row?" The hireling snapped his thick fingers: *click-click-click.* "Like this? Seven times?"

"How should I know? I've never seen a Shoia die even once." The bonedealer slapped at another bite, this one upon his neck. "Cursed horseflies!" He wouldn't mind them so much if there were a divination denomination that used dead horseflies for augury, because then there would be profit in his misery, but he was aware of none. *Perhaps I should invent one, like the charlatans do.* "Go on, then. See what you can bring me. Find Arbath—probably drowning himself at Mikal's or spending himself in a whore—and take him with you. Two of you will serve better than one. Just haul the body out to the anthills as soon as possible, so the ants can do their work." Thinking, he chewed at his lip as Merriq turned away, then tacked on the ritual promise: "find me a dead Shoia, and I'll triple your wages."

The hireling, halfway through the tent flap, glanced back over his shoulder. Light eyes above the gray-threaded reddish beard were grimly amused. "I find me a dead Shoia in town, and you can sell *my* bones for the Kantica. Shoia look after their own." He paused, grimacing. "If any bones are left."

The tent flap settled behind Merriq's departure with a melodic rattle as strings of charms were disturbed. Bird bones. Vermin bones. Rabbit. The skull of a cat. Suspended on thin, knotted twine interspersed with brass, colored glass, and clay beads, hollowed bones pierced to let the wind through. Ordinarily they made a pleasant sound to ears familiar with the song. But just now the noise reminded Hezriah that if more bodies were not to be found soon, he'd likely lose a customer or two.

"Eccul will be digging them up from the graveyard, despite the punishment for it, and cut out the rest of us entirely," the bonedealer muttered; Eccul, after all, had no ethics. He took the easy way, rites and permissions be damned.

Shaking his head, Hezriah squatted on black canvas before the flat sheet of heavy green-gray stone—the bonedealer's anvil, it was called in the trade—and returned to the work interrupted by Merriq's arrival. He took up the hammer—a smooth, round, purplish river rock bound by leather onto a sweat-stained wooden haft—and began smashing the heavy thigh bone to pieces. Chips and splinters would show up against the black fabric flooring, so the attrition rate was negligible.

"Horse will do for now," he murmured, smashing away, "but I'd rather have a Shoia."

Shoia bones were a bonedealer's lottery. They made the best auguries for the Kantic diviners, who found omens and portents in the bones themselves prior to burning, and in the ash after. But Shoia bones generally remained housed in Shoia *flesh*, which was, predictably, not particularly amenable to dying for anyone's sake, let alone a bonedealer's. Or even a Kantic diviner's.

There was Rhuan. And there was Brodhi. Hezriah didn't personally know of other Shoia, here in the settlement or anywhere in the world. And both were currently in residence, though as likely to leave soon. But Merriq was right. No citizen who knew what they were would attempt to kill either Rhuan or Brodhi. Not even Eccul, who had no ethics; Eccul dug up bones, but did not stoop to murder.

Hezriah glowered. *Yet.*

No, only a stranger might attempt to kill a Shoia, and even if it was true they could die—after six other deaths first—no one knew how to keep count.

Except probably the Shoia themselves, who very likely wouldn't tell.

Hezriah wondered briefly if Brodhi knew how many deaths Rhuan had left, or if Rhuan knew Brodhi's count. He'd heard a story that Rhuan had been killed here in the

settlement before he hired on as a guide for Jorda's karavan, but no one knew if it was true. At any rate, neither
Rhuan nor Brodhi showed any signs of dropping over dead
on their own.

"Cursed Shoia," Hezriah muttered, wishing them to Alisanos along with the worthless horseflies. "The world
would be an easier place if they died just once, like everyone else!"

But Shoia did not die just once. And there were numerous tales of how various murdered Shoia, rousing back into
life, avenged themselves on their killers.

"Seven times. Seven times dead, dead for good. *Then* I
could have the bones."

The bones, and everything else. He could dole out the
body to various divination denominations. Teeth, hair,
nails, certainly the entrails. Plus other bits and pieces.

But Hezriah would be a very wealthy man even if all he
got were the bones. The practitioners of the Kantica were
supremely generous when it came to buying Shoia bones.
Everything else was gravy.

BRODHI WAS AWARE of others eyeing him as he
strode into the ale tent. It never stopped, the watching. Oh, those grown accustomed to his race, to his presence among them, had learned to mitigate to some degree
the overt fear, the perverse fascination, but none of them
was ever entirely successful at obscuring their fervid interest. They wondered, he knew, how Shoia magic manifested,
how it worked, and what it felt like.

In truth, magic didn't feel like anything in particular. It
resided within his bones and blood the way breath lived in
his lungs, the way his heart beat: steadily, unceasing, wholly
unremarkable. It *was,* nothing more.

But they were human, and thus, like children, attracted
by that which they could not understand. By that denied
their kind.

"Brodhi! The usual?"

He glanced across at Mikal in his traditional spot behind a plank of adze-planed and waxed wood resting atop two ale barrels. The human was big, broad, missing an eye and two of his teeth, but his comfortable equanimity was always present. His opinion of his customers was shaped only by behavior, not by race. Or the presence of magic.

"Yes." It was close inside the faded green tent, redolent of unwashed humans, of ale, of dirt, of redleaf chewed and spat. With due deliberation, unrushed by his audience, Brodhi unhooked the heavy silver badge at his right shoulder—a leaping horse surrounded by a flattened circle—and unslung the rich blue mantle of his rank. Summerweight wool, lacking the heft of winter-weave. He tossed it across the nearest unoccupied table, though only an instant before the table had hosted two men. But they had, of course, vacated immediately upon recognizing him—or what he was, if not who. Men, mortals, either hated or feared his kind. Occasionally both. Either response resulted in a swift retreat from Brodhi's immediate vicinity, lest he be minded to protest their presence.

Or, he reflected, recalling his kinsman's comment, perhaps they merely *disliked* him. Trust Rhuan to know; humans were his hobby.

Brodhi never protested when it came to humans. They were what they were; dealing with mortals required no small amount of patience, but he had learned that even before arriving in Sancorra province.

Though Rhuan, upon more than one occasion, declared Brodhi claimed no such thing as patience. But then Rhuan was nothing even approximating something—or some*one*—to be trusted in his opinions, even if he was close kin.

By the time Brodhi reached the crude bar, threading his way through the spittle-fouled dirt aisle amid low mutters of protective invocations, Mikal had poured his ale. Foam mustached the rim of the dented pewter tankard, then spilled over in a lazy, tendriled beard. Brodhi took the tankard, comfortably cool in his hand, tested the foam with his tongue, inhaled the heavy, bittersweet tang, then drank down several deep swallows. A common beverage, human ale, but immensely satisfying in its own way after days spent on the road breathing dust more often than air. Ale was his one willing concession to human habits and affectations.

At least of those concessions and compromises that his service did not require.

"News?" Mikal inquired in his deep, slow voice, wiping down the plank with a tattered clump of burlap. Big, divoted knuckles sprouted wiry strands of black hair.

Brodhi took another generous draft, then employed a very human gesture to rid his upper lip of foam: He backhanded it away. "News," he agreed, and everyone in the tent fell instantly silent. They had been specifically waiting for what he had to say.

News. It was the coinage with which silver-badged and blue-mantled couriers purchased ale and food on the roads through the provinces. Though his myriad tightly woven braids were weighted with the flat, hammered brass and silver rings that were the currency of the world, they remained threaded on thin leather thongs plaited, Shoiastyle, along with beads, into his waist-length copper-colored hair. For him and his like, who was Rhuan, the rings were ornaments, not coinage.

"Well?" Mikal asked, dark brows drawing together.

Brodhi pitched his clear voice, trained to override even the raucousness of drunken revelers, though none here reveled. They waited.

"The war," he said, "is over."

Tension sprang up among the humans. There came a stirring in the tent. He heard a derisive mutter that mentioned old news not worth hearing; someone else hissed the man into silence.

Brodhi merely glanced over the tent's occupants. "The war is over." This time with a slight emphasis on the final word. "Sancorra of Sancorra has been executed."

Save for sharp, startled inhalations, all remained silent and still. Indeed, *this* news was unquestionably fresh. Fresh as the blood of the province's former lord. Brodhi himself had seen it spurt but a matter of weeks before. Senior couriers were required to witness all such executions, so their news was accurate and untainted by rumor.

"Therefore the Hecari of Hecari says," —he paused and deftly assumed the remembered inflections— " 'If you wish to make war with me, you shall have to find a new lord. The one you had now lacks a head, and is therefore unable to help.' "

Silence was palpable a moment, then was replaced by the faint, familiar sounds of men reaching for and chanting over protective amulets. Brodhi smiled derisively as he heard the chiming, the clicking, the rattling, the rustling, the muted whispers of renewed invocations. He wore no such thing, trusting to himself rather than to the various false godlings humans worshipped.

Brodhi tossed back the rest of the ale, then set the mug down with the soft thunk of metal on wood. Even Mikal was stunned.

Sancorra of Sancorra has been executed.

He looked upon them even as they looked at him. Expressions were slack with shock, or twisted by worry. Grimy hands clutched amulets and charms strung around throats, wrists, waists. He noted how lips moved, mouthing prayers and petitions. In the doorway, suspended from the ridge pole, a string of bones and beads and feathers stirred in the faintest of breezes. Mikal's own charm against the hazards of the world.

This time Brodhi spoke for himself, not in trained courier cadences. "You knew he would do it. It was war, and no one is better at waging it than the Hecari of Hecari, who has, with his armies, already overrun three provinces. Only a fool—or a dreamer—could believe it would fall out otherwise. Sancorra was fortunate to have lasted as long as he did." He eyed those present, marking the stolid resistance of humankind as their faces closed against his words. He did not take pity on men such as these, mortal and unimportant, but he did offer simple intelligence. "Accept defeat," he advised, "and you may survive. The Hecari of Hecari is neither a patient man, nor a merciful one."

It was as clear a warning as he would ever give. It was

suggestion. Simple observation. They would take it as they would, as they were inclined, depending on their substance. But of one thing Brodhi was certain: they would blame *him*. It was illogical to do so, and wholly bootless; as courier he was sworn to neutrality, trained to divulge no opinion while on the road. But he brought word, and often bad. He was the messenger, and thus proxy for whomever the others disliked, distrusted, feared.

He was in from the road now, the message delivered. He could now state his own opinion. This settlement, this haphazard assemblage of flimsy oilcloth structures that existed on no maps because it was too new and undoubtedly impermanent, was his final stopping place. Now the province knew.

Sancorra of Sancorra was executed. The war was truly over.

The Hecari warlord, called Hecari of Hecari in the fashion of the provinces, was a ruthless butcher, a man proved capable of any atrocity. His victory here was complete, as it had been in the other three neighboring provinces. But while Sancorra *the man* had lived, even in defeat, hope for Sancorra the province survived. Now hope would die. It made lordship easier for the man who had wrested it—and a province—from a popular hero.

A hero without a head.

Because Brodhi knew the humans needed to speak, to curse, to threaten, to complain, to argue over which of their myriad gods might yet save them—and that they would do none of those things in his presence—he calmly collected his courier's mantle and exited the tent.

They were all of them fools. Any man was, who put his trust in a lord rather than in himself. Better to trust no one at all, unless he be enemy. Then one knew where one stood.

But humans were weak. Were fallible. Humans *dreamed*.

Chapter 2

*T*HE SETTLEMENT, SUCH as it was, existed because there was water, and also because it was temperate in climate, provided lush pasturage for a thousand head of live-stock, and groves of trees for wood and shade. It existed also because the people of a province had arrived to depart, and departure required an appropriate gathering place. A place of farewell. A place of ending as well as of beginning.

Tents. Hundreds of them, oilcloth and wooden poles, spread across the land like a creeping tide. Dyed every color and pattern imaginable: solid, patchwork, peak-roofed, sun-faded, rain-streaked, poked with holes or in-tact; the door and ridge poles painted or carved with protective glyphs.

Audrun, sitting inside a high-sided wagon with her tow-headed, blue-eyed children—they took after their father, not her, with her dark gold hair and brown eyes—supposed once there had been but a few tents, and likely lined up in simple straight rows along either side of the road, just up from the modest river attended by groves of trees. But time and other arrivals had expanded those rows into a flood tide, blots of colored oilcloth interconnected by tangled, skeinlike canyons of foot-packed pathways. People thronged those pathways, weaving in and out and around the tents.

It was a true settlement, but impermanent. People remained because other people departed. It was a gathering place of refugees, both ending and beginning. The old life discarded. The new life embraced.

Or the new life dreaded.

Davyn had called it the "jumping-off point." Here, her husband said, was where everyone *jumped off* the main road through Sancorra province to the individual routes that would lead to their destinations.

Strange, Audrun reflected, shoving a fallen strand of hair behind an ear, that the act of departing a war-divided land united it. Surely the gods would take pity on them all and decide to keep the people whole; could they not see what it was doing to Sancorra province?

But the gods had not spoken of such things; the gods had, in fact, suggested by silence, by lack of intercession, by speaking to no diviners of any denomination despite thousands of rituals and rites over the months of war, that this was what they intended. Even the diviners had been baffled, for their own auguries predicted victory.

But there was no victory, save for the enemy. Thus the province had been sundered. Sancorra of Sancorra surrendered his holdings—and his life. The enemy held the province now, and many had determined in rage, in sorrow, in loss, in bitter admission of defeat, that they could not bear to see worse done to their land than had been done already. It was best to go.

Just—*go*. Elsewhere. Away. Where the enemy did not rule. Where the enemy did not take their pasture lands, their fields, their crops, their gardens, their wells; where the enemy did not overprice such things as a family had to have, so that they could afford no better than the meanest portions of what they themselves had grown; where the enemy did not dictate how they should serve the warlord-cum-king, be it by taxing them into starvation or taking their sons for its armies. Nothing remained for them in this homeland. It was time they found another.

But oh, it was difficult to leave! More difficult than she had *dreamed*. Audrun felt the roots of her heart being torn out one by one, ripped from fertile ground until waste was left in its place, a rupture of the soul. She did not hate, she did not wish vengeance, she did not curse the enemy with every breath, did not buy the time of diviners to find an answer for why her people had lost. But she acknowledged the terrible pain of the ending of what she knew, of what she had known all of her life. What she had expected to know forever.

Moreover, had she believed it possible that they would leave their home, she would have taken the herbs to keep herself from conceiving. Four children already, and now another in her womb. No, she would have done better to take the herbs, no matter what the moonmother might have said, though it pained her to consider that she would have missed seeing the tiny face, missed counting the delicate fingers and toes.

And yet it was the unborn child that had caused her husband to decide the time had come to leave, to depart the lands she and Davyn had tilled into bounty, the house he had built into comfort, the room where all of their children had been conceived and born. Tangible things, precious things, but altogether impossible to uproot and pack away for the journey. Only such things as clothing, utensils, tools, the makings of a new life could accompany them.

And memories.

But her memories of *this* place would be forever tainted, colored by the knowledge that *this* place existed only because their province was destroyed. Because *this* place had been, before, nothing but a road winding through the valleys, one particular mile of it very like all the other miles.

That road, this place, this wagon, was now both present and future. And she detested all of it.

THE AGING, DYED oilcloth had faded over time from crimson to a streaky reddish-orange. But the Kantic priest rather liked it; the hue imparted a pale and peaceful roseate glow to the interior of the tent. Dardannus supposed someday he should have the tentmaker make him another—in trade for a favorable augury, no doubt; the tentmaker did not grasp that true divination was not always auspicious—but for now he was satisfied. And the white of the bones, hung along all the tent poles—chains of curving ribs, a spine strung on gold wire, dangling tibia and femurs, a necklet of phalanges, intermixed with a pleasing array of beads, tiny mirrors, clay eyes, and artifacts—looked so nice against the color.

He smiled briefly, then bent to take up a scattering of costly ivory-colored splinters from the copper bowl on the rug beside his low, cushioned bench. He murmured softly to them, invoking the blessings of the gods in the tongue of the Kantica, and carried the fragments in his cupped hands to the center of the wooden table.

"Hold them," Dardannus said quietly.

The woman sitting on the other side of the table, heavy legs folded upon a green cushion, jerked her hands back from his offering. "Hold *Shoia* bones?"

"They impart nothing to you," he soothed, "but they must know you. Let them taste your scent, the texture of your hands, the gentleness of your touch."

She was unconvinced. Lavetta had been a regular follower of the Kantica for several months, but she was timid, unwilling to surrender herself to his guidance. It had taken some time to turn her away from false diviners, but at last she had agreed to see what omens he might find for her in the Kantica. Surely the auguries *Dardannus* studied would be more positive than those she had experienced with the charlatans. He was the greatest Kantic diviner in the settlement.

Lavetta declared, "You didn't make me hold all those other bones."

She was wary. Dardannus quietly set his handful of fragments down upon the crimson cloth, which had not been exposed to the elements and thus was not faded. Against it, the bones were pearlescent.

It was a sad little pile of nothing much recognizable; small bones such as fingers and toes, and fragments of larger burned more quickly, so small pieces, chips, and splinters were best, unless one worked a Great Augury, in which whole bones and a bonfire were used. In this case it was the ash Dardannus needed, not the actual bones. And the fire was ready; he need only set the splintered pieces into the flame and let it do its work. In time the bone would burn down to grit and ash, and he could read the resulting omens.

"It shall be as you say, Lavetta. Perhaps when you have fully accepted the Kantica. . . ." His voice trailed off.

Her mouth sagged. "You mean you won't read them for me unless I hold them?"

"There are different rituals associated with different bones," he explained, "just as there are different gods. The others required less of you. These require more."

Lines appeared in her brow. "Why are Shoia bones so different?"

"Better to ask why are the Shoia themselves so different." He kept his tone soothing. "One may see deeper, and farther, with Shoia bones. The Shoia themselves live much longer than ordinary men—indeed, it is often said they can never die—and thus their bones are richer. By using them, I can see farther into your own life, Lavetta. Instead of a mere echo of the gods, I may well hear them shout."

Her painted-on eyebrows arched up in startlement. "About me? Why would the gods shout about me?"

He reached across and briefly touched the back of her hand. "Lavetta, you must never doubt your own value in this world. It is true you have encountered hardship in your life—"

"Four dead husbands and no wealth to show for it? I should say so!"

"—but even the most afflicted may gain the true peace of the afterlife," he continued, ignoring the interruption. "One merely needs personal worthiness so that when one's spirit crosses the river—"

"That's what I want!" She was suddenly less sharp. She was human again, and small, reduced in body, heart, and soul, and terrified that her afterlife would be worse than her life. "Oh, yes . . . I want so much to be worthy! I want—I want to know that I'll go to a better place when I cross the river, not to . . . not to *that* place."

"Alisanos?" He spoke the name intentionally, without fear, though Lavetta paled and made a ward-sign against it, grasping the amulet around her throat. "I think you are in no danger of such a fate, Lavetta. You are but a poor widow attempting to make do with such as the gods have given you."

"And what *else* do they intend to give me?" Tartness had returned. "Another husband who can die?"

A tedious woman, Lavetta. But she always paid on time; for that, he forgave much. "Perhaps. Or perhaps a husband with whom you may someday, many years from now, grow old." Lavetta was already in middle age and heavy-bodied with it, but a little harmless flattery soothed many. "But only Shoia bones will allow me to look deeply enough, to see far enough to bring you the answer you seek."

She peered at the pile of bone splinters from beneath frowsy graying brown hair. "Just—hold them? That's all?"

"Briefly," he told her. "Then I shall burn them, and we shall know your future—"

But Lavetta's potential future ended abruptly as someone flailed at the oilcloth, attempting to find a way in through the canvas. A man's voice, raw from shouting, *still* shouting; scrabbling hands finding the slight gap between flaps to rip the fabric aside. He stood hanging on the cusp between light and dark, with the yellow glare of the sun behind him and the rose-tinted pallor of the tent before.

"Send me back." His voice was a harsh, crowlike caw, as if words came hard to him. His mouth opened in a rictus of effort. "I thought I was a man . . . I thought—" He drew in a trembling breath, released the words on a lurching rush. "Tell me how to go home!"

 LERIN HELD OUT a sienna-colored clay cup. "It's a bitter brew, and for that I beg your pardon, but most effective this way. I have made it somewhat stronger for you than for the usual client, as you will naturally have shields in place." Lerin smiled; she was a handsome woman in late middle age, hair gone to gray, but the smile lighted her face into youthfulness. "You've done this before, if not with me; you know what is to come."

Ilona, accepting the clay cup with its pungent herbal tea, shook her head as she lifted the cup to her mouth. "I've never sought a dream-reader."

Lerin's dark brows arched over blue eyes. "Never? And you a diviner yourself?"

Ilona swallowed some of the bitter drink. "My dreams have never been the sort that needed reading." Disbelief still shadowed the older diviner's eyes, so Ilona clarified. "For me, dreams have simply been something that occurs when I sleep. I've never attempted to sort them out for meanings."

"Then you have closed off a part of your soul."

They knelt upon the rug-strewn floor of Lerin's tent. It was a small tent, but cozy and comfortable. The usual collection of beads and charms dedicated to various gods festooned the main pole. Lerin's cookfire was out of doors; inside, she relied upon a small oil-filled brazier to heat her teas and potions.

Ilona accepted the reproof with chagrin; she would have said the same herself, had Lerin come to her.

"Nightmares?" Lerin asked.

"Occasionally." Ilona sipped more tea. "Not often enough to concern me."

"Then what brings you to me?"

Ilona drew in a deep breath. "What I saw last night . . . the images seemed to be of a *future* time and place, not a jumble of memories or suppositions. I felt that clearly. They were vivid, disturbing, and they awakened me from a sound sleep."

Lerin nodded. "A presentiment."

"This is Jorda's last trip of the season," Ilona explained, "and he's late departing. You would think I'd dream of all the tasks that need to be done hastily, instead of what I saw." With effort, she drank down the dregs of the bitter tea. "The dream felt—different."

The dream-reader reached out and took the cup from Ilona's hands, smiling slightly. "Well, we shall discover what you saw, and what it means. I see the tea is working; do you feel relaxed?"

Ilona was aware of a lassitude sweeping through her body. "I feel as if I might sleep for months!"

"Oh, no. Sleep comes after." Lerin made a gesture. "Lie down there, if you please, on your back."

Ilona followed instructions and settled upon the pallet made comfortable by cushions and blankets. She stretched, hearing subtle cracks of tense muscles. "If nothing else, my back will be improved before we rattle it to pieces again upon the karavan roads!"

Lerin set the cup aside and knelt at the head of the pallet, settling long, dark skirts. "I will place my hands on your brow, like so." Ilona felt the cool fingers resting against her skin. "I will draw the dreams out from hiding, but you will have to guide me, Ilona. Find the images you saw, those that disturbed your sleep. Place them at the forefront of your awareness. If they are mixed with other dreams of no consequence, I won't be able to give you an accurate reading."

Ilona wasn't certain she could unwind the pertinent dreams from the others, particularly since she had been told to do just that. Her subconscious was recalcitrant that way. But as the tea worked through her body, she let it also invade her mind.

"Good," Lerin said softly. "Call up the dreams, Ilona. Remember them as clearly as you can."

"They're just fragments," she murmured, eyes drifting closed.

"Fragments are merely pieces needing someone to put them together into a whole. As you read hands, so I read dreams. Trust me, Ilona. Let go, and bring those fragments forward."

Crimson lightning. Steaming rain. Howling wind. Hecari. A karavan, turning back. A woman in profile.

Fragments. Moments. Nothing more.

"Let go, Ilona." Lerin's voice was soft. "Let them become *my* memories."

Ilona exhaled. She let the memories of the dream, the tangled skein of images, leave her mind and enter Lerin's.

Chapter 3

"*I* WANT TO GO HOME," Torvic announced, leaning out of the high-sided wagon so far his elder sister snatched his tunic and yanked him back down.

By rote, Audrun answered, "We must go on, Torvic."

"I want to go home," Megritte echoed; as she would, as expected, because she followed Torvic's lead in all things. She was four. He, at five, had the sagacity of age.

Torvic also had the stubbornness of their father. "I want to go *home*."

And it was Ellica, fifteen, the eldest girl, who said what her mother longed to: "There *isn't* any 'home' anymore, Torvic! The Hecari stole it all!"

"Hush," said Audrun. "Not here." The enemy's ears were everywhere.

Gillan, the oldest son, heir-in-waiting to whatever they might make of the new land, knotted a sixteen-year-old fist into a hank of Torvic's tousled fair hair. "Be still, sprat. Do you think Mam needs to hear such talk? Da said to wait here, and be still. So—*be still.*"

"I *am* still," Torvic retorted, very carefully not moving at all so he wouldn't actually be lying. "But I can talk. Da didn't say I couldn't talk!"

Ellica muttered, "Da should have."

Megritte, whose braids were loosening into freedom, tried a question of her own. "When are we going home?"

"We're not!" Torvic snapped, transforming his own reprimand into one for his inferior. "Didn't you hear Ellica? Didn't you hear Mam?"

"Oh, stop." It amazed Audrun most days that she had birthed such headstrong children, since in her youth she had been praised for her kindness, sweetness, and grace. Now, queasy, hot, weary, and completely bereft of such things as kindness and grace, it meant nothing but extra effort to control her equally hot and weary children. "I haven't the patience for this. Your da will be back soon; until then, be still. Be *quiet*," she persisted, seeing the look in Torvic's eye. It would last perhaps the count of ten fingers, she thought, before someone spoke again. And she couldn't blame them. They had been on the road for days, either cramped in the wagon or walking alongside it. There had been no time for leisure, and no settlements offering other children to talk or play with. As difficult as it was for her to uproot her life, it was worse for the children. They had no voice in the matter.

Upon approaching the tent settlement, Davyn had halted the wagon yards away from the outskirts, carefully not infringing upon it or the dusty, tree-cradled area where departing karavans gathered. Both settlement and karavan area were a matter of paces away, but the wagon nonetheless remained isolated, clearly part of neither tents nor karavans.

Before Davyn went off to find a karavan-master, he and Audrun rolled up and tied the yellow-painted oilcloth sideflaps stretched over the curving roof-ribs so they might benefit from fresh air, but he made it plain they were all to remain inside the tall-wheeled, closely packed wagon containing what was left of their belongings. Not to set foot, Davyn warned, on the ground without his say-so.

Immediately after his father's departure, Torvic asked his mother what they were to do if they needed to pee, at which point Gillan reminded him that they, as males, need only aim over the sideboards. This observation resulted in cries of disgust from Ellica and Megritte, and a reprimand from Audrun.

Though she might have preferred that option herself, in place of the chipped crockery pot shoved under one of the narrow cots.

Now they sat and fidgeted amid bedding, furniture, foodstuffs, pots hanging from roof-ribs, and clothing trunks, with such farming implements as they retained attached to the exterior sideboards, tailgate, or hanging beneath the floorboards of the huge, high-sided wagon. But what Davyn hadn't considered in his attempt to keep them safe was that this settlement, with its floodplain of colored tents, offered such enticements for bored and curious children as Audrun had never seen.

Megritte asked, in the smallest of her voices, "Where did Da *go?*"

"To see the karavan-masters," Gillan answered, "so he can find us room in one of the karavans." He waved an arm in the direction of the nearby grove of broad-crowned, thick-trunked trees where wagons and livestock waited. "They're over there; see them? Those are the karavans, meeting up with the karavan-masters."

"Horses," Megritte observed, peering through dust at the mass of conveyances and beasts some distance away. "*We* don't have horses. We only have fat old oxes."

"Ox*en,*" Torvic corrected. "Don't you know anything?"

But the "fat old oxes" were not so fat anymore. Their journey from the family's home in the midst of the province to this place at its edge had worn the fat away. And it concerned Davyn, who knew they needed strong, healthy oxen to get them overmountain.

"Can I go see Da?" Megritte asked.

"No," Ellica said sharply. "We're all to wait here. Da said so."

Megritte voiced what her mother very well knew all of them wondered. "Why?"

"Because," Audrun said succinctly, intending to leave it there; then relented because she had detested that answer herself in childhood. "Because we know nothing of this place, or the people in it."

"Bad people?" Megritte asked.

Torvic, being Torvic, brightened perceptibly. "Is there danger?"

"Might be," Gillan observed, affecting his father's drawl.

Audrun smiled at him, marking how he grew more like Davyn each day, gaining height and width of shoulders even as his voice broke. But she directed her words to Torvic, offering a lesson, though she doubted he would learn it. Not today, not here and now. "But there is also the chance of getting lost. Can you count all those tents? Can you see from one end to the other? Could you find your way along all the twisted pathways? Would you know how to find the wagon if you got lost?"

"I'd ask," Torvic answered promptly.

"Ask who?" Ellica was definitely peevish. "We're strangers here, Torvic. No one knows us. They don't even know Da or Mam. Who could you ask that would know?"

Torvic put his chin up. "Diviners," he declared. "They know everything."

Audrun touched her belly, glancing at the nearest roof-rib with its dangling thong of colored beads and bone-carved charms. They had not seen a diviner in all the weeks on the road. Davyn would make sure the spells were renewed for the wagon and oxen before they left, and the omens read, but she would like to find a moonmother who could tell her whether the child was healthy and whole.

And whether it would live. Whether all or any of them would live, on the road winding along the dangerous edges of the deepwood.

Audrun shivered again. They were near the borderlands, Davyn said. Alisanos. Too near, she believed. She felt it in her bones.

"Diviners know everything," Megritte echoed.

"Then *I* want to know," Ellica challenged, "who I'm going to marry."

Torvic made a sound of desperate derision. In that, Gillan joined him.

Audrun blessed their innocence, that the most important thing in their lives just now had nothing whatsoever to do with a journey along a road so close to Alisanos, where devils and demons lived.

IN HIS VIOLATED tent, the Kantic priest and his female client gaped at the disheveled man standing before them whose trembling, outthrust arms so clearly beseeched their aid. Lavetta, swearing by a god she supposedly no longer worshipped with her conversion to the Kantica, leaped up clumsily, overturning Dardannus' table in her attempt to escape. The diviner heard the faint clang of copper bowl against upended table leg and the anguished protest rising from his own throat as the bone fragments tumbled in an ivory shower to the carpeted floor. He rolled from his bench, wincing as a knee pressed against a knucklebone; he found it, gathered it up, began collecting the others with immense care, as if they were precious gems.

For the Kantica, they *were*.

"Please—send me home!" The stranger's voice, issuing from blackened lips and a spittle-fouled beard, was a harsh, rasping wail.

With more agility than Dardannus expected of her, heavyset Lavetta bent, ripped one sidewall from the ground, wholly heedless of the damage she did to hangings, spell-charms, and artifacts—many of which came down in a tangled disarray of string and beads, cascades of mirrors, wood, and wire—and ducked under it, shrieking about Shoia bones and moonsick men.

Furious, Dardannus glared up from his costly fragments long enough to mark the stranger's greasy, matted hair and beard, the blood-rimmed eyes, the soiled clothing. The man *reeked* of ordure. And of something else, something more . . . alien.

Anxious to recapture his priestly dignity and aplomb, Dardannus summoned his most deep and dramatic tones.

"Would that I could, I'd send you this moment to Alisanos itself!"

With a garbled outcry the stranger stumbled forward, fell to his knees before the overturned table. He was shuddering as if beset by palsy, hands reaching out again toward Dardannus in supplication. "Now! *Now!*"

And then Dardannus noticed that the fingers were not fingers at all, but claws. Thick, black curled claws, turned back onto themselves so sharply they cut into the flesh of the man's wrists, which were themselves scaled and a sickly purplish-green.

The priest nearly vomited.

A man with claws and scales was no man at all.

I thought I was a man, the stranger had said. As if he once was. As if he knew he was no longer.

Dardannus swallowed back the bile of fear and horror. In frantic haste he snatched up the nearest bone still dangling from his tentpole and waved it threateningly. *"Away!"*

"Please." Claws shook and rattled. "Show me the way home."

The Kantic priest heard the fear rising in his own voice. He squashed it with anger. "Find it yourself." He wielded the scapula, wishing it were a bit more substantial. "You were there once already . . . find it yourself!"

The grime-smeared face crumpled. The man was sobbing as he rocked on his knees. "I don't know how. Once I did, *once* I did, when it took me—but I am lost now, *lost . . .*"

Emboldened by the stranger's obvious feebleness—and feeble-*witted*ness—Dardannus decided the scapula was less effective than simple human force. He set the bone down, hesitated to summon the will to put hands upon the filth of madness, then snatched handfuls of the man's dirt-crusted tunic. With a grunt of effort, he hauled the body to its feet. "Your home's not here," he wheezed, stiffening his arms as he swung the man to face the tent flaps. "Look for the deepwood *elsewhere!*" And shoved.

The man was gone. Oh, not entirely; but he was now outside the tent. Dardannus heard the broken sobs and continued pleading. For that matter, he still *smelled* the man; but no, that was the reek of effluvia left in the madman's wake even as he staggered away.

For a long, long moment, Dardannus stood frozen in place. *From the deepwood?* Breath tangled in his chest. *He was once a man—* But clearly, so clearly, no longer. *He has claws—he has* claws—

Dardannus gagged, swallowed bile. Aloud, he whispered in horror, "Alisanos took him . . . *changed* him . . ."

But the stink of the man remained. It abruptly transformed the experience from one of horror to one of entirely mundane resentment. Easier to deal with. "Holy gods," the diviner murmured in disgust, then transformed the words into a prayer. "O most holy gods, Mother of Moons, I petition you to cleanse my tent of this taint—" He turned again to the task of collecting the bits of bone he had dropped when snatching the scapula from the ridge pole. "—so I may serve you in purity—"

Even as Dardannus bent, the door flap was pulled aside yet again, rattling the few remaining charms. One of them fell, clacking against those already tumbled upon the rugs. "In purity?" an amused voice asked. "Or in profit?"

Dardannus spun around so quickly he nearly lost his footing in the rucked carpet and the trap of his own overturned bench. He caught himself before falling; it would have been most painful to land atop a wooden leg. "*Mother of Moons,*" he gasped, noting the red hair, brown eyes, and the wealth of coin-rings and beads woven into Shoia braids. Then, in shock, "Rhuan?"

"In the very flesh." The tone was mocking, as usual; Dardannus recognized it easily. Rhuan was infamous within the settlement for his ironic tongue. "Not what a Kantic priest would prefer to see, I understand, flesh not being in your purview, but I rather prefer it this way. Now—" coppery brows rose, "—show me these Shoia bones Lavetta was shrieking about."

"That man!" Dardannus toward the tent flaps behind Rhuan. "That man was—he *is*—an Alisani demon!"

"Who? That moonsick fool I saw staggering away?" The Shoia grinned; incongruous dimples appeared. "I think not."

"He had claws and scales! In place of fingers and flesh!" The grin faded abruptly.

"He did!" Dardannus insisted. "He came in here begging for me to send him back to the deepwood."

The mocking was banished now, as was the laughter. "What did you tell him?"

"That I couldn't. I don't know how."

Rhuan's voice was cool, bereft of its usual lightness. "You know *precisely* where the borderlands are, Dardannus. We all do." Then added, dourly, "For the good of our lives."

The priest felt a knot in his lungs. Tension. A tinge of fear. The Shoia wouldn't forget what Lavetta had said about the bones. "I told him he could go back without my help. He came from there . . . he can find his own way back!"

"Maybe he can't," Rhuan observed mildly. "If he's a human once taken by Alisanos and now escaped, he may not have mind enough left to find his way anywhere." His expression was pensive, turned oddly inward for a man everyone knew as someone who laughed even when he killed.

Or so Dardannus had heard.

The priest straightened his robes. "It isn't my responsibility to see him back to the deepwood." Then he cursed himself for providing the Shoia a very neat opening.

"Ah. Yes." Rhuan didn't miss the opening. Rhuan, they said, missed very little. "Your responsibility lies with bones, not moonsick old men—or even a poor fool who's escaped Alisanos. Therefore I propose we discuss that responsibility." He was smiling again, with an edge to it Dardannus didn't know how to interpret. "Show me the bones, priest. Then tell me where you got them."

Dardannus summoned his flagging willpower and forced himself to breathe. It wasn't easy. His lungs wanted not to work, and his throat threatened to close. Inwardly he chastised himself as he held out bone splinters in his upturned palm, offering them in silence. He was a *diviner*. A *Kantic* diviner. He had no business being frightened half to death.

But he had never witnessed a living Shoia inspect Shoia bones.

Rhuan took, then rolled, the fragments in his hand, as if tasting them with his flesh. His face was impassive, schooled out of its habitual mocking smile into a smooth mask of implacability. Dark copper-tinted hair was bound back into a thick complex plait of beaded subsidiary braids, slicked away from a face that was, Dardannus realized uneasily and abruptly, alien. And yet it *should* be alien, that face; Rhuan was Shoia. Shoia were not human.

The priest's lungs still wished not to work, and his throat felt tighter than ever.

Even Rhuan's skin was colored copper. Oh, it was normal flesh, warm as a human's—Dardannus had felt the touch of slender fingers when Rhuan took the bones from his own trembling hand—but there was a faint coppery cast to the flesh, as if the sun tanned him differently. And just now, strangely enough, that flesh seemed stained a bit darker.

Dardannus shifted uneasily. It was the light, surely. His crimson tent was weathered to that faded, streaky orange-rose. It merely cast an odd glow across the Shoia. Probably his own face was colored oddly as well.

Then Rhuan looked at him, looked into his eyes, and the skein of logic was undone. The skin *was* darker. The eyes, usually a warm cider brown, contained the faintest flicker of red.

The priest drew in a sharp, tight breath. He knew little enough about Shoia, and likely less about Rhuan or his kinsman Brodhi, though the latter was not known for violence. But rumor had it a man might die by Rhuan's hand and never know he was dead as he fell down upon the ground.

And then the Shoia's skin was not darker, and his eyes merely brown. It was Rhuan again, odd and oddly dangerous, but *familiar* Rhuan, with the familiar skin tones, the *over*familiar—and annoying—

irony in his voice. "Be free of your fear, diviner. These are not Shoia bones."

Dardannus nearly gasped. "Not—?" And then realized it was very likely best not to show disappointment and outrage over being cheated of Shoia bones before a Shoia.

Yet Rhuan seemed to understand very well what the priest was thinking. Smiling faintly, he tipped his hand and let the fragments fall in a wispy shower to the disordered rug. "Be free of your fear, Dardannus—and also with your tongue. Who sold you these as Shoia bones?"

"What—" He cleared his throat, firming his voice. "What will you do to him?"

Rhuan's smile sweetened. "Talk to him."

Dardannus was again aware of all the rumors he had heard, all the tales both large and small, born of fertile minds, and possibly some truths.

I am a Kantic diviner. The gods themselves will aid me. Even a Shoia may not gainsay a god.

Dardannus met that smile with one of his own. And lied. "Hezriah," he said calmly; Hezriah had been charging him more of late, and it was time to teach the bonedealer a lesson about such things. "Hezriah sold me those as Shoia bones."

Chapter 4

Shouting caught Audrun's attention. Still wagon-bound, still trying to keep the peace among fractious children, she glanced up from irritated contemplation of a new snag in her road-stained skirts. It took but a moment to find the individual from whom the noise issued: a ragged, bearded man staggering out of the tents. The children, like hunting hounds—no doubt grateful to have something upon which to fix their attention—drew themselves up into a tensile awareness, staring.

People near the tents scattered away from the man like chicks from a flapping apron, mouthing prayers, clutching at protective amulets, and making various ward-signs. The man's arms were outstretched, yet his hands were cocked upon themselves at the wrists as if useless, not reaching, not grasping, making no motion beyond an odd, helpless gesture of pleading, of loss, of futility.

Megritte was round eyed. "Who's *that*?"

In dramatic tones, Torvic announced, "An Alisani demon come to get you, if you don't behave!"

Audrun reprimanded him automatically, but did not take her eyes from the staggering stranger. He was close enough that she could see his tattered tunic and leggings, matted hair and beard. Was he besotted on ale?

Megritte, deciding her brother told the truth regarding Alisani demons, shrieked piercingly.

Ellica winced visibly, clapped her hands over her ears. Audrun very nearly mimicked her, so shrill was her youngest daughter's tone. But she had no time to do anything but watch the man warily, half fascinated, half fearful, and hoping very hard he would not see them.

But he oriented himself on the sound of Megritte's shriek. Audrun saw him look. Saw him *see*.

And then, mouthing silence, he began to stagger directly toward them.

Megritte shrieked again, more loudly yet. Audrun took her into her arms, letting the girl bury her head against a pregnancy-tender breast, and hissed at Torvic to get down, to *sit* down at once; at Gillan and Ellica to move away from the sideboards.

She badly wanted her husband there, but he was not. It was up to her to protect them all. And so she finally unstuck the clinging Megritte, forcefully handed her over to Ellica, and ordered all of them to get out of the wagon at once.

Ellica gasped. "Get *out?*"

"Go to the tents," Audrun hissed. "Not far, but get away. I'll come fetch you when it's safe." She clambered over the sideboard nearest the approaching man, seeing no sense in remaining cornered in the wagon. "Haste, now." And when they hesitated, "*Gillan. Ellica.* Do as I say."

Audrun turned back to face the stranger. She heard her children moving—the rasp of cloth, the clanking of hanging pots stirred by movement, the hitch of bodies over the side, the murmured complaints and questions from Torvic and muffled sobs from Megritte—but did not see them, did not watch them go. They were children, not fools; she trusted them to look after themselves until she could gather her lambs again. Best to send them away from the wolf while she played guard dog.

The man stumbled closer. His damp, reddened eyes were fixed on her. He appeared not to see the children at all, which suited Audrun. She clutched the wagon with one hand and tugged her tunic and skirts into order with the other. It was habit, to face all things in life with such tidiness and competence as could be managed.

ILONA OPENED HER eyes. She felt an absence in her mind, the lack of a touch on her brow. It took her a moment to focus on the oilcloth roof. Lerin's tent.

Memories returned. "Are we finished?"

"Yes. You may sit up."

Ilona did so, turning her body to face Lerin. "What did you see?"

"I saw a storm like no other, with killing winds and rain. I saw a karavan, and Hecari warriors. I saw a woman."

"Was there enough for you to read?"

Lerin's smile was of brief duration, merely a wry twitching of her lips. "If one knows how. A portion should be clear even to someone not a diviner: a storm is coming. But that is not why the karavan turns back; there is an even greater threat that causes that."

Ilona shook her head. "Jorda has never once, while I've been with him, turned a karavan around."

Lerin made a slight silencing gesture, counseling patience. "That may be. But in the future—a week from now, a year, a decade—he shall do so. The Hecari?" Lerin shrugged. "It should come as no surprise that you might see one or many in your dreams. They are a plague upon the land, consuming Sancorra day by day, and you have seen them among the karavans."

Ilona nodded; she had seen far too many Hecari as she traveled the roads with Jorda. "What about the woman?"

"Little to see," Lerin replied. "A profile, tawny hair no more. She is a stranger as yet, but will come to be known to you, come to be important."

Part of Ilona was frustrated by the information. It told her very little. But she supressed her impatience; surely there were times when the clients she read for felt the same. "Is this woman to be a client of mine?"

"I think that likely," Lerin said. "But in profile, it was difficult to see enough to recognize her, and her hair was loose beside her face. I can only tell you that *a* woman will bring great change—"

Ilona's brows rose sharply. "You said nothing of a change before."

Lerin ignored the interruption. "—to your life, to the world, or both."

She struggled to keep her tone courteous. "But you can't tell me when any of this will ocur. This storm, turning back, or the woman's arrival?"

"As you said, they were fragments." The older diviner spread her hands. "I'm sorry, Ilona. I wish I could tell you more; I don't mean to be vague with obscure predictions, like a charlatan. But you do know enough from this to recognize the moments when they arrive in your future."

Nothing more remained to be said or done. Ilona inclined her head in brief thanks, diviner to diviner, as she rose, and paid Lerin in the coin used among all diviners: The promise of a reading when Lerin desired one.

Slipping through the tent flap, Ilona looked into the skies. A bright, brilliant blue, and cloudless. It was not a day for a storm of any sort, she felt, had it crimson lightning and steaming rain, or merely the kiss of moisture on her hair.

Briefly she shook out her skirts, then set off toward the karavan grove. But ahead of her on the winding footpath she saw a familiar back. "Rhuan!" She hastened to catch up. "Rhuan—wait."

But as she reached him, as he swung around to face her, Ilona discovered that it wasn't Rhuan after all. The expression was much more severe than she had ever seen Rhuan wear, feckless as he was; and every line of the body bespoke irritation.

Embarrassment heated her face. "Oh—Brodhi. Forgive me; I thought you were Rhuan."

His eyes, like Rhuan's, were brown. But there was no amusement, not even resignation in them. Brodhi's tone was clipped and cold. "We are not so much alike that we should be taken for one another."

Embarrassment faded. "But you are," Ilona said mildly. "Particularly from the back."

"I am taller—"

"A finger's width, perhaps."

"—and my braid pattern is much different."

"Brodhi," she began patiently, "no one in this settlement knows anything at all about the ritual braid patterns of the Shoia. Almost no one in this settlement knows anything at all about the Shoia, period, except for what Rhuan has told us; the Mother knows *you* never say anything about yourself." She waved a hand to forestall the bitter reply she saw forming in his eyes. "But of course you're correct: why should you share anything about your race with ignorant Sancorrans?" Ilona bestowed upon him a sweet, insincere smile. "Excuse me; I have duties at the karavan."

She brushed by him and stepped back onto the footpath, reflecting that perhaps she should not have provoked him, but Brodhi annoyed her. That he felt himself far superior to the Sancorrans had been plain from the first day of his arrival in the tent settlement, having added it to his courier route. She asked Rhuan once why his cousin was so different from him in temperament; Rhuan merely said they had vastly different sires, and that Brodhi had been so since their childhood.

Ilona shook her head as she strode down the footpath. There were not enough years in a person's life to waste any of them on bad moods and attitudes.

BRODHI GRITTED HIS teeth as he watched Ilona march away. He knew her only by sight; he did not trouble himself to share the company of the karavan-masters and their hired diviners. He found himself feeling bested in their exchange, that she had dismissed *him* rather than the other way around. It was a feeling that left him disgruntled. Annoyed, he turned on his heel to resume walking, then halted abruptly. He had to. Or risk tripping over a child.

That child looked up and into his face. He saw the rich blue of her eyes, the pale hair and lashes, the clarity of her skin. Human skin. Fragile skin. Brodhi could see her spirit through it.

In a high, thin voice she asked, "Will you help us?"

And then others were there: an older boy, an older girl; a boy not much bigger than the smallest child, who had spoken. Four hatchlings, loose without supervision.

"Go home," Brodhi said.

Four very similar faces blazed into the redness of shock and indignation. Well, that was not unusual; his own skin took on varied tones dependent on his mood.

"Go home *please*," the elder girl snapped. "Or is courtesy beneath you?"

"Ellica," the oldest boy murmured, though he was no happier. He simply hid it better.

Courtesy *was* beneath him. But amusement wasn't. Brodhi smiled.

The youngest, the tiny girl, was unperturbed by undercurrents. "Can you help us?"

"He won't," the sister said, no more polite than he. "He's Hecari. Why should any of *them* help us?"

It shocked him into speech. "Hecari! I?"

The older girl glared. "Well, aren't you? Who else would be so rude as to give us orders?"

He glared back. "I am not Hecari."

It was now the youngest boy's turn. "Then what are you?"

"Torvic, hush." The older boy, perhaps fifteen or sixteen, reached down to gather the little girl into his arms and settle her on his hip in practiced motions. "Come. We'll find someone else."

But they had, against his will, managed to intrigue him. Before they could leave, he asked, "Why do you need help? And where are your parents?"

"Our da is at the karavan grounds," the older boy answered.

"And our mam," the girl—Ellica?—interjected, "is the one who needs help. There's a moonsick man who won't leave her alone."

Brodhi's curiosity evaporated. "Well, then go find a moonmother. She'll look after him."

"And what about our mam?" the youngest boy demanded. "What if he hurts her?"

"Why should he harm her?"

The littlest girl, tucked into her brother's arms, declared, "He's a demon."

Brodhi's brows rose. "Oh, now he's a demon? First he's moonsick, now he's a demon? And I am Hecari?" He looked down his nose at all of them. "Such judges of others as this should be trusted to know the truth?"

The small one stared piercingly at him. "You're *mean.*"

"Megritte!" The oldest boy turned a shoulder even as the elder sister stepped between them, as if to defend her kin.

Brodhi said, laughing, "That much at least is true," and went on his way.

The whims and entertainments of human children were beyond his comprehension. This clutch was new in town; likely one of the resident children had set them on him. It was one of their favorite tricks.

Unfair, he thought in passing, to use the innocence of the youngest in such tiresome games as this.

AUDRUN, HER SPINE set against the sideboards and hands flattened on the wood, could smell the stink of the stranger, could mark the yellowing of broken teeth bared between blackened lips. His eyes were brown, the whites veined with blood. Grime compacted in the seams of his face.

"*You* have a wagon," he blurted hoarsely. "Oh, Mother of Moons . . . will you take me there?"

He didn't sound moonsick. Just weary. Audrun, now that

her children were safe among the tents, dropped one hand to shield a belly not yet showing much of the unborn infant. Stiffly, she moved along the wagon, hitching now and again on implements roped to the sideboards, to the rump of the nearest ox, who was patently unconcerned with filthy, stinking strangers. She eased her way farther until she felt the yoke.

The man followed, wavering on his feet. Ill, or drunk, or moonsick. Perhaps all three. "Will you take me there?"

Nervously she asked, "Take you where?"

Such a radiance of hope and longing she had never seen in a face. In that moment she was not afraid of him, but stunned.

"*Home,*" he rasped.

Now she stood at the ox's head. They could not afford to lose the wagon, did not dare let this man somehow take from them all they had left in the world. Her children were safe. Now she must guard the wagon. "I don't know where your home is."

His outstretched hands trembled. "Alisanos."

Audrun recoiled so hard she fetched up against the ox. She was vaguely aware of the warm bovine breath issuing from broad, moist nostrils, the butt of a heavy head as it pushed against her spine.

"Alisanos," the man repeated. "Please . . . will you take me home?"

No one in the world wished to go to Alisanos. Unworthy folk were sent there by the gods to be punished, but no one willingly went into the deepwood. Only—

Then she saw the hands he extended, and the breath left her lungs in a rush.

"Home," he whispered, as Audrun's concentration split into tripart strands of frenzied thought.

She gripped the amulet around her neck and prayed every prayer, made every petition she had ever prayed and made to the gods, relying on them now; saw in her mind's eye where the wagon was in relation to the nearest of the tents; realized she and her husband would have to consult

diviners as soon as was humanly possible, paying exorbitant fees, lest the taint of the stranger's madness stain them
forever and make *them* unworthy to cross the river into a
safe and happy afterlife.

The three portions of her mind braided themselves
abruptly into a tight plait of certainty. The gods would protect her and her children against the condemned soul. They
were worthy.

Emboldened by faith, Audrun tangled nimble, unwavering fingers in a series of warding signs. "Go away."

The man, weeping, turned from her. Audrun watched as
he made his staggering way back into the tent-city. Where
she had sent her children.

Time to fetch them back. But Audrun waited until the
stranger was lost to sight amid the tents. Then she gathered
up her skirts and ran, avoiding his path as she made her own.

HEZRIAH THE BONEDEALER, bent over his
stone "anvil," looked up sharply as the sun-rotted
door flap was yanked aside so violently the oilcloth tore.
His mouth sprang open to remonstrate, then clamped itself
closed. He found himself on his feet, hammer clutched in
his hand, with no memory of rising. The nape of his neck
prickled as he saw the beads, the braids, the face.

"I beg your pardon," the Shoia said formally, making a
vague and imperfect attempt to sort out the ruined tent
flap. Then he turned his full attention on Hezriah, who felt
his mouth go dry. Only this morning the bonedealer had
been hoping someone would kill Rhuan. And now here he
was. Alive. And presumably uninterested in dying.
"Bones," Rhuan said calmly. "Shoia bones. I understand
you're selling them."

Hezriah had never actually spoken to Rhuan before,
though certainly he had spoken *about* him. Everyone did.
"N–no."

"No?"

He managed it more definitively. "No. I'm not." Hezriah was aware of the hammer's weight dragging at his shoulder. He closed a hand around the string of amulets hanging about his neck. "What would you have me swear on?"

Rhuan smiled, ignoring the multitude of protective amulets. "Your life?"

"I've *never* sold Shoia bones." He would, had he any, but he told the truth. He had sold no Shoia bones.

Rhuan continued to smile. "Have you sold any bones *as* Shoia bones?"

"That's deceitful!" Hezriah gasped.

Rhuan gazed at him in the closest thing to amazement Hezriah had ever expected to see in the alien face.

"That's unethical," the bonedealer went on. "I am an honest man making an honest living. Ask anyone."

The Shoia's brows hitched themselves higher. "Anyone?"

"Well, not Eccul. Eccul will lie. Eccul has no ethics. *Eccul* would sell Shoia bones, or bones *as* Shoia even if they're not."

"Eccul would."

"Yes."

"Who's Eccul?"

"Eccul is—" But Hezriah did not finish. He caught the glint of a knife in Rhuan's hand as he spun in place, braids flying. It seemed to the bonedealer that the Shoia somehow *melted* into position, confronting the man who came flailing through oilcloth, tearing down the remains of the tent flap. Startled into response, Hezriah swung up his stone hammer.

The arrival, in soiled, crusted clothing, wavered on his feet in Hezriah's damaged tent. Blackened lips parted the matted nest of his beard. "If I sell you some bones," he rasped, "will you take me to Alisanos?"

Hezriah gaped. He clenched the haft of the stone hammer even harder, but it dropped to his side. Rhuan seemed startled, murmuring briefly to himself in a language the bonedealer didn't know.

What Rhuan muttered then sounded very like a curse.

The stranger's bleary eyes fixed on the Shoia. His face turned a sickly shade of green beneath the film of grime. *"You,"* he blurted. More quietly, in startled disbelief, he repeated, "You." Then cried out an eerie, descending note of anguish and denial. Of ending. Of grief.

The collapse was slow. Disjointed. As if the bones within his flesh failed piece by piece. He fell forward heavily, face down. Hezriah, shocked to utter silence, heard the dull, wet crunch of the skull as it smashed itself against the stone block.

Hezriah, dropping his hammer, heard also the rasp of breath through his own constricted throat. He was sick with shock and fear. A dead man lay in his tent. But worse . . . the man's murderer stood right before him. Looking at him.

"You." Hezriah unintentionally echoed the dead man. His lips felt stiff as other words he meant not to say came forth from his mouth regardless. "You killed him."

The Shoia blinked in unfeigned surprise. With ostentatious resignation, Rhuan displayed his knife. "Do you see any blood?"

Hezriah knew he was likely dead anyway, after what he had witnessed. "Spells." He licked his lips, closed a hand around the amulets at his throat. He spoke because he could. Because he needed to, in the face of such disaster. "You killed him with a spell."

"I don't do spells."

"You're Shoia."

"I don't *do* spells." Rhuan scowled, parsing out his words with infinite care and emphasis. "*I* don't do spells."

Hezriah couldn't believe he had the courage to speak so bluntly to a man who had just committed murder. Without, apparently, getting any blood on his knife. "He looked at you. He recognized you. And you killed him."

"He *died*," Rhuan emphasized; and there was a vast difference. "Why would I kill this man? . . . Except perhaps to rid the world of a truly disgusting stench." He waved a hand before his face. "That is remarkably foul."

Hezriah had not thought before in terms of Rhuan re-
acting like a normal man to such things as bad odors. Or
that he, who had just murdered a man with unseen spells—
perhaps he had merely *wished* it; who knew what Shoia
could do?—could speak as if he intended no harm to the
human witness.

The bonedealer glanced down at the body. He stared,
stared harder, and felt sickness again in his belly, renewed
prickling on his neck. "His hands."

"His hands?"

"They aren't. Hands." Hezriah pointed, trembling.
"Look."

Rhuan looked. He frowned. Then knelt and peeled back
the filth-encrusted tunic sleeves, unveiling forearm as well
as fingers. Which weren't fingers at all, but claws, thick,
long, black claws twisted back against wrists clearly *scaled,*
not fleshed. Scaled a sickly purple-green. "This is the man
Dardannus mentioned."

"Alisani," Hezriah breathed. Naming the dead. The
demon.

Rhuan looked up. "Now do you believe me?"

Jerkily, he nodded. Maybe he wouldn't die after all.
Rhuan had not killed this *thing,* and thus Hezriah had witnessed no murder. Merely a demon's death.

Or the death of a man who had been born human, but
had been altered by the deepwood.

No one killed such folk. Not even Rhuan, Hezriah believed, no matter what anyone said about him. Because
then you acquired the dead's damnation. You were banished to the deepwood, never allowed to cross the river
when you died, to become like—this. Hezriah felt sicker
than ever. He wanted ale. He wanted to leave. He wanted
to leave to *find* ale; or perhaps something even stronger.

Rhuan, still kneeling, rubbed absently at his brow with
the carved butt of his horn-handled knife. "Best go get
Kendic." He sounded regretful as any human. "I'll stay
here with the body."

Hezriah nodded stiffly. Kendic would want to know.
Kendic was head of the Watch, such as existed.

"Now," the Shoia suggested pointedly. "Or do you want this poor dead fool to remain here all day, stinking up your tent?"

Hezriah did not. He went.

Chapter 5

GRANDMOTHER MOON LAY in wait for the sun to dip beneath the horizon, surrendering day to night. The west was ablaze. Ilona, squinting against the brilliance, ducked beneath pierced-tin lanterns dangling from the carved, curving ribs supporting the domed oilcoth covering of her wagon sitting amid the karavan grove not far from the ocean of tents. She had taken up the rugs, beaten them, and was sweeping out the painted floorboards when a shadow fell across her line of vision.

She glanced up: a man. Tall, thick in the shoulders, yellow of hair and beard, blue of eyes. Ilona read him at once even without seeing his hand, merely by marking the set of his shoulders and the tension in his face.

Standing at the top of the folding steps, clutching her broom, she opened her mouth to give him the ritual greeting of a hand-reader. Then realized that was not his goal. "Yes?" Ilona, like anyone else, had to rely on verbal answers in such things as were unconnected to the rite of divination.

Even his tone reflected weariness. "I have tried all of the karavans, asked all of the masters. None of them will take us. Someone sent me here . . . but your master also says there is no room." Belatedly, color staining his face, he added, "My name is Davyn."

"Ilona. Hand-reader, though that you know from the glyphs." She gestured briefly, indicating intricate symbols painted onto oilcloth and plank sideboards as the faintest of sunset breezes stirred charms and chiming bells suspended from the roof-ribs over her head. Regret pinched. "It's growing late in the season," she explained, as if it would matter. "Most of the karavans have gone on already. Now those folk who were late to decide all wish to leave at once." She reflected the last was not particularly tactful; likely he had been late to decide as well. But when left to herself as a woman, not a hand-reader, her tact often departed.

He nodded, seemingly unoffended. "Is it—is it me?" He lifted a broad hand and displayed his calloused palm. "Something here?"

"Ah, no." She blurted it without thought, looking away at once from the hand; brushing her head, charms rattled, bells chimed. Ilona had learned there was often pain from seeing only portions of the truth. Either she did a full reading, or she did none.

But he took it badly, color peeling away. "Is it so terrible?"

Ilona turned back sharply, attempting to rectify what she had begun so badly. "No! Oh, no—I'm sorry. That isn't what I meant. Please . . ." She glanced aside, then made a warding gesture. "Turn your hand away. If you wish a reading, certainly I will do one. But I dare not even see you sideways."

That baffled him. "Sideways?"

Ilona set aside her broom. It was difficult explaining to those who were not gifted with the art. "If you see a man sideways, you know very little about him. Yet you may judge him by what you see, and judge him wrongly. Therefore to be certain of who and what he is, you should see *all* of him." She paused, looking into his tired face for comprehension. "Would you buy a horse without looking at its teeth?"

"Ah." That he understood; she saw the faint smile. It altered him tremendously. There was some handsomeness in him, beneath the worry and weariness. "I have a family.

Four children, and my wife is to bear another. We have decided to go overmountain to her grandmother's land in Atalanda province. Yes, we decided late—*I* decided late—but should we be punished for it?"

That, too, pinched. "It isn't punishment," Ilona told him honestly. "It just *is.*" She knew that was no help—once more her tongue failed her outside of a reading—and tried yet again. "It isn't *required* that you join a karavan. If the road is well-traveled—"

But his face had gone white. His mouth was taut. "Too close." He clipped his words. "Too close to the—borderlands."

Ah. That, she understood. No, they dared not go on their own; and only one road went so close to the borderlands. It was folly to risk Alisanos alone, lacking the protection gained by sheer numbers and the presence of Jorda's three diviners.

Ilona drew in a breath. To break the moment, to change the tone, she sat herself down on the doorstep of the wagon, arranging the split tails of the knee-length leather tabard worn over baggy, summerweight trousers. She rested feet in scuffed boots upon the next to last wide rung, asking with carefully calibrated inquiry, "Might you go elsewhere?"

It brought pain, that question. "My family has always lived in Sancorra province. I can conceive of no place I would rather be ... except now. After all that has happened." He gestured futilely; she understood completely. *Hecari. War.* "But my wife's grandmother came from Atalanda province. My wife has blood-kin there, if distant. We would do best to go where we have blood than where we have none."

Ilona tried once more. "Wait here, then. Until next season. You would have your choice of karavans next year." She gestured expansively. "There is pasturage, game, water ... you could do worse."

He was a man of simple dignity and immense pride. But defeat—by the enemy, by refusals of the karavan-masters—had worn away his substance. He was not yet desperate, but self-control was fraying. "I haven't the means to wait a year. And the diviners have said the child should be born in Atalanda, if it is to be worthy of the gods' protection. The journey will take time. We must go soon."

She asked it because she had to. "Why did you come to me?"

He spread his palm and looked into it. "I wondered—I wondered if it was me. If something *in* me . . ." His voice trailed off as he lifted his head to look at her again, hand falling slack at his side. "I don't know. I saw you, sweeping. Your motions . . ." He shrugged. "Your coloring is darker than hers, but, well, in motion, you reminded me of my wife."

Ilona felt the coil of regret tightening in her belly. How she hated this! "I'm sorry. If Jorda has said there is no room, then there is no room."

The man nodded. "I know." He managed a faint, fleeting smile that left nothing of itself in his eyes. "I know."

She watched him turn and walk away. A tall, wide, sturdy man. A man of substance, and certain to be judged worthy when it came his time to cross the river, for all he had no wealth. And like so many others in Sancorra province, he had lost everything to the Hecari.

Ilona shut her eyes. She could not change fates. She could only read them.

AUDRUN WENT IN search of and found her children inexplicably huddled behind a brown-dyed tent in the midst of the settlement. They gazed at her with identical wide blue eyes. It never failed to strike her how similar they were, despite dissimilarities in height and gender. Davyn was bearded now, and weathered, but she saw him again in the faces of his children. She wondered idly if the new baby would share Davyn's coloring and thus that of its siblings, or, at long last, her own dark gold hair and brown eyes.

Smiling, she said, "Come back to the wagon."

Kneeling by the tent, they were stiff as wooden dolls

with jointed limbs. Megritte, eyes stretched wide, whispered loudly, "We saw a demon!"

"He killed that man," Torvic added, fascination overriding his younger sister's tone.

Audrun frowned and looked to her eldest for explanation. "What man?"

Ellica and Gillan were not prone to childish excesses like Torvic and Megritte, but they too looked stricken. "The man who came to the wagon," Gillan explained faintly.

It stunned her. The man had not left her wagon all that long ago. "He's *dead*?"

Torvic, clutching tent ropes knotted to thick wooden ground pegs, thrust out a pointing arm. "He went in there. He went in there with the demon."

Skepticism made it difficult to maintain an even tone. "The demon went into the tent with another demon?" Audrun glanced briefly across the footpath, then before her children could answer she made up her mind to contain the tale before it grew lengthier and even less believable. "Never mind. We are going." She caught her youngest daughter's hand in one of hers and clasped the other over Torvic's skull, swiveling it to aim him. "Move. *Now*."

They knew that tone. They moved.

Megritte, seeming pleased to surrender her demon-watching responsibilities, asked, "Did Da find us a karavan?"

"I don't know. Torvic, stop twisting! But if we don't get back to the wagon someone may well steal it—Megritte, stand up on both feet; you're too big for me to carry!—and then we'll have no need to join a karavan at all."

Her children continued to ask questions all the way back to the wagon, and Audrun continued to insist there were other far more interesting things to discuss in the world though she was not at that moment, in view of a dead man, murdered or no, certain she knew of any.

And then the wagon was there before them, and so was Davyn.

"Bless the Mother of Moons," Audrun sighed, releasing

her two youngest to run to their father. "And bless those who have more patience than I—and more children!—for they are truly the worthiest among us."

Then she saw Davyn's eyes, even as he smiled and pulled his two little ones up into his arms, and Audrun realized a new home overmountain lay farther away than ever.

BRODHI, FREE ONCE more of meddlesome human children, continued his journey along one of the maze-like pathways among the tents, and sensed the presence, as always, before he saw its progenitor. He stopped. He summoned patience. He did not turn. "Yes, Darmuth?"

Laughter, if soft. Then the other slipped around from behind, sliding into his path. Neatly blocking him.

A short, compact, smooth-skinned man of indeterminate age was Darmuth, with feathery pale brows and eyelashes, and a head shaved all over except for one coarse silver-haired plait low on the back of his skull. It was clubbed on his neck, wrapped with a length of red-dyed leather thong. His eyes were light gray, very like winter water. He wore a simple black leather tunic with the sleeves chopped short to expose muscled tattooed arms, shell-weighted leggings, and a vulgar purple silk sash doubled around his waist. The hilt of his knife, jutting from the tooled sheath tucked into the sash, was black-and-white striated horn, the pommel intricately carved.

"I've lost him, Brodhi."

Irritably Brodhi countered, "You never lose him. You can't. You've just let him wander off."

The man grinned. "You refer to him as if he's a pet."

"Not *my* pet." Brodhi resettled the bright blue courier's mantle hanging off his left shoulder, feeling the tug of the wrought-silver badge pinning it to his long-sleeved leather tunic. He hid impatience; Darmuth would keep him here, if he saw it. "Perhaps a leash might serve."

The man cocked his head. "Have you seen him?"

"Not lately." Brodhi shrugged idly. "He's here somewhere. Or so I've heard."

"Rhuan's *always* somewhere," Darmuth noted. "Too many 'somewheres.' I do lose track."

Brodhi wasn't amused. "You do no such thing."

"All right." Darmuth's vulpine grin flashed; his canines were slightly pointed, and he had invested in a brilliant green gemstone that was drilled and set into the left one. "I actually wanted to visit with you. It was an excuse."

Though surrounded by tents, Brodhi was aware that, as usual, the footpath he inhabited had emptied of people. They found other ways to go where they wished to go rather than share a path with him if they could avoid it.

Or—he brightened a moment—perhaps it was *Darmuth* the humans avoided. In his way, Darmuth was more exotic and unique—and threatening—than a Shoia.

"It was no excuse." Brodhi folded his arms, mantle rippling. "What is it?"

"Ferize," Darmuth answered. "How is she?"

Brodhi suppressed all emotion. He held his face expressionless. "Ferize is—Ferize."

"When did you see her last?"

"I don't remember."

One of the feathery brows rose. Darmuth could mimic Brodhi's arrogance, even to capturing the intonations of his voice, which annoyed Brodhi no end. "Surely you do."

"A month ago. Two months, as the humans reckon time." Brodhi shrugged again, putting more indolence into the motion. "Possibly three."

Darmuth shook his head in mock admonition. "A man should be more attentive to his wife."

"I am as attentive as I need to be, for such as Ferize." Brodhi smiled easily, flicking supple fingers in a human gesture to suggest departure. "Go away, Darmuth. I don't like you."

The tattooed man laughed. "You don't like *anyone*, Brodhi. Not even your wife. Not even your own—" He paused. "What do the humans call them? Cousins?"

Dryly Brodhi said, "Rhuan makes it supremely difficult for me to like him, Darmuth. You know that."

"Well, he is difficult," the other conceded. "But he isn't my cousin. Nor my kin. Nor even my *kind*. Therefore *you* should tolerate him better, being blood-bound."

"That I tolerate him at all is a miracle unto itself," Brodhi pointed out, "and if we were *not* blood-bound—or kin at all, for that matter—I wouldn't tolerate him in the least."

Darmuth grinned. The green gem sparked. "So difficult to believe you are related, you and Rhuan. One can hardly credit that your father and *his* father, born themselves of the same parents, could sire such decidedly different sons upon—"

"Never mind," Brodhi interrupted sharply, who didn't like to discuss such things with anyone, let alone with Darmuth. Perhaps especially with Darmuth, who knew more about Brodhi and Rhuan than anyone in the world.

Except possibly for Ferize. Who was, after all, Darmuth's kin-in-kind.

"But I should like to contemplate this," Darmuth said brightly, gemstone glinting. "We know what will become of you both if you don't succeed in your tasks. One would think you'd be in accordance, as you desire the same things—"

Brodhi cut him off with a sharp, silencing gesture. "But we don't. We want entirely different things, Rhuan and I." With sustained effort he regained his fraying composure. "It is a mark of how deeply different we are, Darmuth. In tastes *and* temperaments."

"Perhaps." Darmuth tilted his head slightly. "Perhaps not."

This time the gesture of dismissal was not a human one. "Go away, Darmuth. You and I are not blood-bound, nor kin-in-kind."

The shorter man inclined first his head, then folded his body upon itself in a parody of abject submission. "Spare me, I beg you. Be not unkind to your inferior."

The word Brodhi spoke was not even remotely polite.

Darmuth, laughing, unfolded his powerful body and took himself away.

ILONA KNEW THE stride even before she saw his face. She heard the muted rattle of fringe bearing beads, rings, and shells swinging from the outer seams of his amber-hued leggings and tunic. She glanced up from the low table set just outside the rear steps of her wagon. "You're late. Quite late. *Extremely* late."

Rhuan slowed, then stopped altogether. He came over to where she sat upon her cushions laid out on her rugs, surrounded by glowing pierced-tin lanterns hanging from wrought iron crooks driven into the ground, the low laquered table modestly hiding her knees. "I know." He quirked an eyebrow, marking her preparations and professional posture. "Business poor tonight?"

"Not after Jorda speaks his piece to the people of his karavan. Then they'll all come. I am simply preparing."

He winced. "Am I that late?"

She nodded. "He's threatened to slit your throat already. Darmuth suggested he not, as you are occasionally useful. He was looking for you earlier, too."

"I was talking to the Watch."

Ilona smiled archly. "Drunk again?"

"I'm never drunk," he retorted. "No. About a dead man."

She tended her table, straightening rich silks and embroidered velvets, placing charms, carved stones, and blessing-sticks in precise arrangements. "Did you kill him?"

He was as aggrieved as she had ever seen him. "Why does everyone think *I* killed him? I don't kill every individual who crosses my path!"

"Only most of them." She was comfortable bantering with him. He made it easy. "Rhuan—Jorda truly is unhappy. We're to leave at first light."

"*That* late," he muttered. "I thought we had two more days." He shook his head; the gold and silver rings threaded loosely through multiple braids clattered faintly against his beadwork. "All right. I'm going."

"Who died?" Ilona called after him.

He turned back, hesitating. "Some poor man who stumbled into Alisanos, then found his way back out again."

She chilled. Stilled. "Was he—?"

"—human?" Rhuan's expression was grim. "Not anymore."

Ilona felt her belly clench up into a hard knot as Rhuan left. She murmured a prayer to Sibetha, the god of hand-readers, then expanded it to any god who might be moved to take pity on a human who went into the deepwood. Most never returned. Those who did, died.

Rhuan hadn't killed him. He hadn't needed to.

No wonder he looked so grim.

By habit, Ilona spread her left hand. But she read nothing in it. No hand-reader could divine future or fate from his or her own flesh.

She gathered up the blessing-sticks and, closing her eyes, began in a quiet murmur to tell over their representations, invoking goodwill and good fortune. The man's death was a very bad omen for the night before departure. She would have to consult Jorda's other diviners to see if the potential events set into motion by this one involved the welfare of the karavan. Jorda would have to be told as well. He might wish to put off departure for a day or two so she, Melior, and Branca could test the auguries, which would disturb him; he could not afford to wait much longer. It was late in the season already. Once the rains began, the roads would be nearly impassable.

Meticulous preparations were always required before a karavan departed. Countless rites and rituals conducted by Jorda's three hired diviners promised protection for his clients. But now even more, and more elaborate, preparations were needed.

Ilona stroked the satiny finish of the ancient blessing-sticks, feeling the incised, time-faded glyphs. Her lips moved automatically through the chants and prayers.

Though her voice was little more than a thread of sound, she knew the gods would hear.

That a human should escape Alisanos was very bad indeed.

Bad to lose them in the deepwood. Worse to get them back.

Chapter 6

AUDRUN WAITED UNTIL the family had eaten, until Davyn agreed to take the children for a walk before bedding down—he had, after all, been absent for most of the day—then wrapped herself in an enveloping shawl and, beneath the risen crescent of Grandmother Moon, marched over to the karavans encamped in the grove of trees at the eastern edge of the tent settlement, not far from where Davyn had halted their wagon. Her husband had told her which masters he had seen and their various explanations for why they would not take them on; the last one, she felt, was an excuse, not an explanation. So she went there.

It was all confusion at the various encampments. She threaded her way through the sprawling mass of trees, cookfires, livestock, and wagons, and asked so many people to direct her to the karavan-master that Audrun lost count. Probably none of the directions were wrong, but the master was never where he had been by the time she arrived. If she didn't know better, she'd believe he was avoiding her. But at last she found someone who knew, who pointed at two men nearby and said the taller man was the karavan-master, the other was his senior guide. Audrun thanked the karavaner and marched over. Each step closer fed a growing desperation.

The karavan-master, she discovered upon arrival, was a remarkably large man with a beard the color of glowing hot coals and wiry russet hair pulled into a single thick braid. In the muted glow of multiple campfires scattered like brilliant flowers, his eyes were clearly green, and as clearly angry. He turned from his guide impatiently as she halted beside him.

In the face of his annoyance, Audrun found her own, laced with anger. "How dare you?" she demanded. "How dare you turn us down because we have *oxen?*"

The guide, a dramatic sort, she noted, in multiple orna-mented braids and fringed, amber-hued leather leggings and shirt, seized upon the opening. "You turned them down because they have *oxen?*" he echoed. "Jorda, how could you? How dare you?"

The karavan-master, bearlike, swung a huge cupped hand, as if intending to cuff. The guide, laughing, skipped neatly out of the way, bead- and clasp-strung braids flying.

Audrun knew it was rude to accost the master in front of his own employee, but she hadn't the time to be polite. "My husband has spoken with every master here. No one will take us on. But *they* had the courage to say they were full. You made our oxen your pitiful excuse."

His voice was very deep. "Oxen are slow."

"But steady," she retorted. "Dependable. More depend-able than horses."

"And slow," he repeated.

She could not help the sharpness in her tone. "What, do you intend to *race* along the roads? Is there a competition for which karavan arrives first?"

The anger in Jorda's eyes died out, but she had very clearly annoyed him. Audrun didn't care. She had an entire family with which to concern herself: her personal karavan.

"It is the end of the season," the master told her coolly. "Pace does matter. Earlier in the year, your oxen would have been welcome. But now . . ." He shook his head. Sil-ver rings in his ears glinted. "It's the truth, not an excuse."

"We are going overmountain," she said steadily, unde-terred. "To Atalanda. The road leading there breaks off from your route, yes?" So Davyn had told her when she questioned him more closely; she wouldn't be made a fool of. "We won't be with you all the way. Only part of the way. And isn't it true that when a karavan first sets out that it requires days for all the wagons to sort out their places? Some horses are faster, some are slower."

"Of course," the guide broke in cheerfully, displaying unexpected dimples, and earned a glare from the master. "I've known it to take the better part of a week."

"Rhuan," the big man growled, "you had best go find Darmuth. *He's* doing his job."

"And the better part of my job doesn't begin until tomorrow."

The hand came up again. "The better part of your *life* may never begin at all!"

The guide, Audrun saw, was not in the least cowed by the noise. "What about the Sisters?" he asked. "You took *them* on, after swearing you never would."

Audrun seized on that. "Sisters?"

Jorda was staring at his guide as if he had lost his mind. "I can't do that!"

"Why not? She says they are desperate—" The guide glanced at Audrun. "Are you desperate?" He nodded as *she* nodded; they were. "Desperate," he repeated, as if that settled it.

"My husband has offered to work as well as pay," she told the master firmly. "We are neither destitute nor helpless; and I have a son as well, old enough and big enough to do his share. My daughter and I can take on mending and cooking, and the younger ones—" Audrun broke off, aware the big man was staring at her in alarm. "What is it?"

"How many of you *are* there?"

"Six," she answered. "My husband, four children, and me." Then she amended. "Seven, actually. But the littlest one has conveyance already."

The karavan-master blinked at her in bafflement.

It was the guide who understood. "She's in whelp." He was grinning. "Jorda, you *can't* tell a pregnant woman she isn't welcome."

Jorda scowled. Audrun had the impression he wished to say he very well *could* tell her she wasn't welcome, but for some reason he didn't. "These Sisters," she began. "Perhaps we could help them? If they are women without men of their own, my husband could aid them, even my oldest son."

The guide was laughing again, teeth showing. Jorda appeared to be on the verge of choking. "I can't do this," he muttered. "Rhuan, even *you* would not have me do this!"

"What is it?" Audrun repeated.

The guide, for a change, offered no comment. He merely assumed an expression of supreme innocence that Audrun, thanks to having children, recognized as entirely feigned. Cider-colored eyes glinted.

Jorda rumbled another growl, then turned to her stiffly. "They are indeed women without men of their own," he said, with precise enunciation, "because they have *everyone else's* men. They're Sisters." He said it more plainly still as she gazed at him blankly. "Sisters *of the Road*."

It meant nothing to Audrun. The guide said helpfully, "He means they are whores."

Audrun's mind went blank. She felt the emptying of sense, of comprehension. She wondered vaguely if she were supposed to be angry, to feel insulted; and if she felt neither, was she then abnormal?

She heard the big man move, a slight shifting of the massive body. She became aware that his eyes were genuinely sorry, but also wholly relieved. Apparently this was a better excuse than oxen being too slow.

"This is acceptable," she heard herself say.

Jorda's mouth parted the thick beard. "What?"

"They are acceptable. Your terms. We will go behind the Sisters." She kept her tone very even. "Of the Road."

He blinked at her, brow furrowing. The karavan-master, she realized, did not believe her.

"The war," Audrun said, summoning dignity, "has changed everything. One makes shift where one must. Where we lived, it was very bad. My husband—" She paused a moment, to recover her composure. "My husband lost every member of his kinfolk. Father. Mother. Three brothers. Two sisters. Their children. There is no one now of his blood. Only my kin survive, and they are overmountain." Briefly her hand cupped the slight curve of her belly beneath voluminous skirts and long, unbelted tunic. "We sought the advice of fourteen different diviners. All of them said the same. This child must be born in Atalanda, if it is to survive at all." She raised her chin, the better to meet the suddenly sharp green eyes. "Sancorra is defeated. We can do nothing here. But we can do *everything* there."

BRODHI HEARD THEM even before he entered the couriers' common tent. Timmon, Bethid, and Alorn. Laughing, as usual, telling impossible tales of impossible adventures and equally impossible sexual encounters, insulting one another with impunity, insulting those who would never hear the comments to know they were the butt of jokes. Nowhere were couriers different. He didn't know if they were hired for it, or gained the vulgar camaraderie upon the road.

It was dusk, and the interior of the tent was accordingly dim. Brodhi slid silently into the tent before they realized he was there. Bethid lay sprawled on her narrow pallet, one leather-gaitered leg cocked up as she grinned up at the glyph-carved ridgepole overhead. Her short-cropped fair hair was mussed into upstanding tufts and spikes, her dun-colored woven tunic stained. She had tossed her blue courier's mantle across the foot of her pallet, though Timmon and Alorn had resorted to crude iron hooks depending from the ridgepole. Timmon and Alorn themselves sat upon a spread blanket in the center of the tent, throwing bone dice.

The two young men were intent upon their gambling. It was Bethid who saw him first. "Brodhi!" She sat upright. "We weren't expecting you back so soon."

He availed himself of the nearest empty hook and hung up his mantle after shaking it out briefly and making certain the heavy silver badge stayed pinned. The jesting had died. So too had the insults.

Timmon and Alorn exchanged glances. The dice were scooped up and tucked away into a hidden pocket. As one the male couriers rose and went to the entry flap. Timmon stepped through, murmuring something Brodhi didn't catch; Alorn hesitated and briefly turned back. "Bethid? Want to come? We'll go down to Mikal's."

"In a moment." She jerked her head to suggest he go on, then tugged at a loose gaitered boot, tightening leather straps. "You could *try*, Brodhi. Learn the dice games. Play a few throws. Let them think you're human."

He sat down upon the nearest open pallet and began to undo knots in the leather thongs cross-gartered over his own gaiters. "Why should I pretend to be something I am not?"

Bethid waved a dismissive hand. "You know what I mean. Let them think you don't hold them in contempt."

Brodhi glanced at her in mild irony. "But I do."

"*So much* contempt," she amended, scowling at him. "Is it so difficult to accept everyone for what they are? To let them maybe like you?"

"Difficult? No." Gaiters undone, unwrapped, he set them neatly beside the pallet on the earth floor. "Infinitely impossible."

Bethid emitted a rising growl of frustration as he tugged off his boots and put beside the gaiters. "*You* are infinitely impossible!"

Suppressing a faint smile, Brodhi watched in silence as she rose swiftly, stamping her right foot more deeply into the loose boot. She shot him a sharp, annoyed glance, which he turned away with the implacability that warded him against too much human intimacy.

Yet of all the couriers Brodhi served with, Bethid was the one he was willing to tolerate. Occasionally.

"I'm going for ale," she said. "This is your last opportunity. Will you join us?"

He shook his head.

Bethid shook hers and departed.

When she was gone, clattering the charms and blessing-sticks suspended at the door flap, Brodhi stretched out his lean length upon his pallet. He folded his hands across his abdomen and closed his eyes. *"Ferize?"*

It took but a moment for her to answer. *"Yes?"*

Startled pleasure kindled that she was so close after days of absence. *"The primaries are done with you?"*

"Until next time."

"Where are you?"

"Nearly there. Do you wish me to hasten?"

"No."

She was silent a moment, tasting him. *"What is it, Brodhi?"*

He smiled openly. Bethid would have been shocked. *"What it always is."*

"Humans are not that bad, Brodhi." Ferize's tone had a bite to it. *"Weak, yes. Flawed, yes. Exasperating? Always. But tolerable."* She paused. *"If one is himself tolerant."*

He grinned, baring teeth. *"My breeding suggests that is not my temperament."*

"Your temperament," she replied, *"is gods-awful. But it is a reflection of your sire's, so I suppose you come by it honestly."* And then she laughed the warm, ringing, joyous laugh that heated all his flesh, even when he was most displeased with her.

"Ferize?"

Absence was her reply.

A wave of loneliness engulfed him, startling in its magnitude.

Perhaps he should have told her to hasten after all.

ILONA ACCEPTED PAYMENT from her latest client with thanks and a brief blessing. Payment was not required—she and the other two karavan diviners were in Jorda's employ—but few clients were comfortable walking away without giving her something for her time. She had learned to accept anything: a coin, a charm, a length of cloth, even a chicken. Some gifts she kept, others she passed along to someone in greater need.

The sun had set following Jorda's karavan-wide meeting to explain to everyone how the morning departure would be undertaken. He also warned them of the possibility of encountering Hecari on the roads, parties of them demanding a "road tax." As Ilona expected, many of the people immediately afterward sought the words of the karavan diviners, hoping to learn if the departure was auspicious, and she had been quite busy. Now she was alone, freed from questions and outthrust hands; she began to pack up her clothes and cushions, to blow out the hanging lanterns. But Rhuan arrived in the middle of it, and so she stopped.

Candlelight and sunset glinted off his beadwork and ornamentation. For a moment Ilona was swept back to the night she had first met Rhuan in Mikal's tent three years before, when she had been mourning Tansit, one of Jorda's guides. Then she had wanted to give the Shoia neither time nor attention; but he had died not long after, only to awaken with her kneeling beside him in one of the dark footpaths where he had been murdered, thinking to guide his spirit across the river once she read his cooling hand to know his people's ritual. It had been more than startling to witness his revival, until he explained how it was Shoia could survive six deaths. She had witnessed one, but Rhuan never told her how many others he had experienced. That, she had learned, was a Shoia's self-defense.

When Rhuan paused and told her where he was going, and why, casually explaining his errand was duty-related, she scoffed. "I can't believe Jorda agreed to that."

"He did."

But Ilona knew that expression, even if gilded by the ruddy purple hues of sundown. There was more to the story. With Rhuan, there always was. "What did you do?" She blew out the candle in a hanging lantern, stirring the pierced tin into motion. "*This* time?"

His tone was matter of fact. "Helped someone who needed it."

Her laugh was a breathy blurt of skepticism. "To ride with the Sisters?"

"Not *with* them, precisely," he hedged. "Behind them."

"Eating dust."

"That was the choice. The woman made it. I merely . . . assisted Jorda with his decision."

Now Ilona laughed outright. "Oh yes, I'm well aware of how it is you assist Jorda with difficult decisions!" But the amusement died out, replaced by memory. "I may have done a reading for her husband." She described the tall, blond farmer.

Rhuan shrugged, stirring the bead-weighted fringe on the sleeves of his tunic. "I saw no one but the woman."

Ilona reflected Rhuan likely wouldn't see anyone but the woman even with the man present as well. "He came to me earlier, the husband. He blamed himself, fearing it was something in him that brought them bad fortune." She smiled faintly, recalling the farmer's diffidence commingled with conviction. "He is stronger than he believes. He's only forgotten because of the war."

Rhuan grinned. "I think she's stronger than he is. You should have heard how she told off Jorda."

Ilona grinned. "Jorda is very soft when it comes to women."

The coppery brows arched up. "Soft, is he? With women?" He paused. "With you?"

She ignored the provocation. Rhuan knew Jorda did not sleep with his hired diviners. Melior and Branca were male, which would not appeal to Jorda, but the master had also never approached her. "Is that why you have taken her part? Because she told off Jorda?" Trust the Shoia to be intrigued by such a display, especially by a woman.

"I haven't taken anyone's part," Rhuan declared. "They just didn't want to be trapped here, is all."

With everyone else, he was very good at misdirection. Ilona, however, read him better than anyone save perhaps Brodhi, who was blood-kin, and Darmuth, who was friend and partner. "Many families have been trapped here,"

Ilona remarked dryly. "That never earned your help before."

He shrugged, donning his implacable face; Rhuan was one of the more voluble men she knew, but he could become as sullen as a pen-soured horse when he decided to.

Ilona sighed. "One of these days a husband is going to kill you." She paused. "Again. And perhaps enough times, if he knows you are Shoia, to make certain you *stay* dead."

Rhuan grinned, flashing white teeth and dimples. Implacability was banished: he had found a defense. "It isn't the woman this time. Truly. Besides the husband, she has four children and another on the way."

Ilona had forgotten that. "I agree that isn't your usual preference, but . . ." She took the blown-out lantern from its iron hook. "Why else?"

Rhuan's eyes slid aside. One shoulder was lifted in a casual warning sign she knew all too well.

And chose to ignore. "Rhuan. There are no secrets between us."

That brought his head around, braid rings, clasps, and beads rattling against his shoulders. She was privy to his most intense stare, which nearly stopped the breath in her chest. And his skin had darkened. Once again she was forcibly reminded how it was so many people feared him, despite his protests that he was not in the least dangerous.

"Leave it," he said, in tones so cold her bones were chilled.

Ilona had heard it before. But never had it been directed at her.

And then he appeared to realize how he sounded and the effect it had on a woman who was his friend, who had known what he was before so many others. The intensity in eyes and skin altered, softening. "Forgive me, 'Lona."

Yet there was no explanation, merely a departure. Ilona watched Jorda's guide walk away into the darkness, contemplating the myriad facets of a man beset by many, and sharp with all of them.

Sharper than she expected.

Chapter 7

BETHID'S FELLOW COURIERS had managed to claim the table they most valued, very close to the plank bar behind which Mikal ruled. They saw her slip through the door flap and waved her over; already the dice game had recommenced, poured out across the knife-scarred surface of the table. She caught Mikal's eye, nodded, and found an untenanted stool to make her own. She dragged it to the table and sat down.

Timmon was blue-eyed and tall, with lank, light brown hair, a long jaw, and bony shoulders threatening the seams of his tunic. Doe-eyed Alorn, shorter and thicker, boasted a vibrant crop of rich brown curls that matched his eyes. Both had dented tankards next to their elbows.

As Bethid sat down, Timmon shook his head. "I don't know why you bother, Beth."

She thanked Mikal as he set a foaming tankard on the table in front of her. Bethid raised it in a two-handed grasp and drank off a goodly amount of ale before answering. "Bother what?"

Alorn gathered up the dice and rattled them in his hand. "He's a cold bastard, Beth. Always has been. He'll never change. Don't waste your time on him."

"Oh. Brodhi." She wiped foam from her upper lip. "He's not as bad as all that."

As one, Alorn and Timmon said, "Yes, he is."

Bethid sighed. "All right, so he is."

"So why bother?" Timmon asked. "Leave him to his own company."

Alorn said dryly, "Such as it is."

Bethid contemplated her tankard, tracing a line of dripping foam down the cool pewter. "I guess it's because when I joined the guild, there were those who disdained me." She raised her eyes to look at each of them. "I wasn't welcomed, you know, when I first arrived at the Guildhall in Cardatha. I was a woman. Until I was accepted, there were no women couriers."

Alorn was surprised. "Truly?"

"Truly," Bethid said, remembering how young the two were. "All men, until me. The Guildmasters refused me out of hand. They wouldn't even admit me to the trials."

Timmon frowned. "Then how *did* you get admitted?"

Bethid's smile was ironic. "A senior courier may appeal the denial. The appeal doesn't overturn the decision of the Guildmasters, but it does mean the applicant must be allowed to take part in the trials." She shrugged. "He simply said my gender would make no difference to the horses I'd ride, to the oath I'd sworn, or to the news and messages I would carry—"

"It doesn't!" Timmon declared. "Why would anyone believe it would?"

Bethid continued her interrupted sentence. "—and he was the first of all the couriers to buy me a drink when I passed each and every trial." She lifted her tankard, drank, then set it down once more. "I wouldn't be sitting here with you had it not been for Brodhi."

DAVYN DID NOT at first believe Audrun when she said there was room for them in Jorda's karavan. Oh, it was not that he thought she lied; Audrun never did. It was not that it stung his pride that she had apparently accomplished what he could not; Audrun often did.

But when she explained that they would be required to remain at the back of the karavan, behind the wagon of women euphemistically called Sisters of the Road, Davyn knew at once what kind of women she meant. *That* astonished him into disbelief.

"Mother of Moons," he muttered now. Replete after the evening meal, Davyn sat on a folded blanket with his spine against a wagon wheel, enjoying his post-dinner pipe. Not only did decent women decline to mix with such as the Sisters, but his eldest son was, after all, of an age to be intrigued by them. He wondered if Audrun had considered that, or if such thoughts were in a man's mind more often than a woman's, even if she be a mother.

He drew on his pipe, then puffed clouds of redolent redleaf smoke as he contentedly watched his family. He could afford it now, with a place in a karavan secured. Audrun, stray strands of fire-gilded hair curling at her hairline, knelt beside the ring of rocks, lifting down the kettle from the iron hook Gillan had pounded into the ground. As always, she wrapped the handle in damp cloth and deftly poured a stream of liquid into two dented pewter mugs. Ellica sat near the fire, head bent over something in her lap, while Gillan busied himself packing away the battered tin plates, pots, and iron griddle. Torvic and Megritte, having done their parts in scouring the dishes with sand and cloth sacking, were now at the far edge of the small camp arguing over something intently, but quietly enough that Davyn did not break his peace to reprimand them.

"So," Audrun said, bringing him tea and then settling down next to him to sip her own, "we are to join Jorda's people at first light. He says we won't get terribly far the first day, so there shouldn't be as much dust as we otherwise might expect." She tilted her head to direct his gaze to their oldest daughter. "I've set Ellica to making us scarves out of an old apron that we can tie over our faces."

From the darkness came a man's voice. "Wise thought, that," it said, then added the ritual phrase used when approaching a camp: "May I share your fire?"

"Come ahead," Davyn invited, and rose to offer his hand

in greeting as the visitor stepped out of darkness into the ruddy light of flames and coal. Davyn marked the coin--rings and beads, the countless complex braids twisting down the stranger's spine. The light upon his face threw carved cheekbones into relief and set shadows into the sockets of his eyes.

Audrun stood as well, setting her tea behind the wheel rim so it wouldn't be knocked over. "Davyn, this is—"

Without warning Megritte began to shriek, even as Torvic produced a sound akin to a calf's startled blat. Ellica, looking up, shot to her feet and backed away from the fire, clutching her handiwork. Gillan, standing at the wagon's tailgate, stiffened to attention. His eldest was not a coward, but he was naturally and commendably cautious. Clearly he was concerned.

In three strides Audrun reached her youngest and clamped hands upon Torvic's and Megritte's shoulders, shaking them briefly. "Stop. *Stop*. You will deafen all of us." She looked across at Davyn, attempting to restore courtesy. "As I meant to say, this is our guide."

"Demon!" Megritte announced, even as Torvic declared, "You killed that man!"

"He had *claws!*" Megritte added. "We saw them!"

Ellica nodded. "Before Mam found us."

The new arrival was clearly taken aback by the reception, as well he might be, Davyn reflected, who was as startled as the guide. But as he prepared to reprimand his youngest, he held his silence when he saw the expression on the guide's face. Surprise, first, as anyone would reflect following such an outburst, followed by comprehension and acknowledgment; and lastly, wholly unexpectedly, unfettered exasperation.

"I did *not* kill that man," the guide declared with no little vehemence, "and I am becoming *extremely annoyed* that whenever someone dies around here, I am the one who's blamed!"

That silenced them all, including the query Davyn was crafting, save for the clang of tin against wood as Gillan dropped a plate.

Davyn noted the guide seemed to realize such a response did nothing whatsoever to confirm his innocence, or provide an explanation. He made an odd, graceful gesture of apology, glanced at Davyn and Audrun briefly, then turned to address Torvic and Megritte specifically. "Let me begin again at the beginning. I killed no one, and I am not a demon. Ever. Certainly not yesterday, today, or even tonight. Not even at this particular moment. In fact, never. And while in general I do not bare my soul in public before folk who are utter strangers to me, especially before those who insist on accusing me of being a murderer or a demon—or perhaps even both—let me make an exception."

Ellica's tone was flat. "We saw you in that tent. With that man. The dead one."

Davyn, aggravated that everyone save himself appeared to be aware of what was being discussed, interjected, "*What* dead man? In *whose* tent?"

Audrun caught his eye and mouthed the words, "I'll tell you later."

But the guide, who obviously did not wish to have any such thing as a murdered man and the possibility of his own involvement discussed among strangers, looked at each of them with a single sweeping glance from his eyes.

A gesture indicated the embellishment of his clothing, the ornate patterns of his braids. "You very possibly have never seen anyone like me before. But that should not suggest I am a demon. What I am is *Shoia*. We are uncommon in Sancorra, perhaps, and her neighboring provinces, but not so rare in others. And yes, we are . . . different. In several ways. But while we may indeed enjoy the tender flesh of such livestock as sheep, cattle, game, and fowl, we do not eat humans." He looked straight at wide-eyed Megritte. "Of any age."

Gillan spoke quietly. "We did see you there, in the tent. With the dead man."

The guide absorbed that, then shook his head, grimacing. "To be absolutely certain we understand what we saw, and not what we *think* we saw, let me clarify." He made certain he had their attention before continuing. "That man came into the bonedealer's tent, collapsed, and struck his head on a block of stone. Whether he died before he fell or after he struck his head, I can't say. What I *can* say, with absolute certainty, is that I did not kill him."

Torvic announced, "He came to the wagon first. The dead man."

"But he wasn't dead then," Megritte added.

Frustrated, Davyn inquired, "Will someone please explain? *Who* came to the wagon?"

"A demon," Torvic replied.

Megritte said in her light voice, "The *other* demon. Not him." She pointed.

The guide, gritting his teeth, continued his defense rather than answering. "I sent Hezriah for the Watch, such as it is." Now he looked at Davyn, according him his place as head of the family. "We don't generally leave bodies lying around for people to trip over. We do try to find out why they died."

Davyn, still at sea, believed the guide. He knew of no guilty man who would send for the Watch.

The visitor—Shoia, he'd called himself—looked at Megritte again, studying her face as if he wished to be certain of her opinion. As if, Davyn realized, it mattered a great deal what the children thought of him. "My name is Rhuan. I am not a demon."

Davyn, who knew his daughter's stubbornness, smiled around the stem of his pipe. And Megritte did not disappoint.

Lips pursed mutinously. "You might be lying."

"But I'm not," the guide countered, seemingly unoffended. "I have given you my name. Were I truly a demon and you knew my name, you would rule me. You could order me to leap into the fire and burn myself up, and I would have to do so. You could order me never to eat again, and no food would pass my lips. You could even order me to wait on you hand and foot, and naturally I would. But of course *that* you might find pleasant, which is not what you expect of a demon."

"Roo-un," she said, trying it out.

"That is my name," he affirmed gravely. "Be careful with it, if you please. Names have power."

Megritte asked, "What if I told you to fetch me a puppy?"

"I might be inclined to do so," he answered promptly, "providing your da and mam allowed it. But I wouldn't *have* to. Only demons must do your bidding when their names are invoked, and I am not a demon."

"Rhuan," Megritte said, certain of it now.

"You may ask," the guide told her, "and I may do it. But never order. It isn't polite."

Davyn, amused, exchanged a glance with Audrun through a trickle of pipe smoke. She was very grave, but he saw the spark in her eye leap to meet his, sharing the irony: Trust a stranger's lesson to carry more weight than a parent's.

"We did see someone like you," Ellica said. "Earlier today. His hair was braided, too."

"He was mean," Megritte added.

The guide laughed without restraint, startling all of them. The expression, astonishingly, exposed long dimples. "Brodhi," he said, grinning. "Yes, he is indeed mean. I have told him so on numerous occasions, but so far it has made no difference. Brodhi doesn't much listen to me."

"Is he your brother?" Torvic asked.

"No. In your tongue, we are cousins. Blood-bound, we call it. But of course that doesn't mean the blood-bound are always in agreement."

"In point of fact," Audrun declared with some acerbity, catching Torvic's eye, "it often means they are in *dis*agreement." She looked back at the guide. "Will you take tea?"

Dimples faded as he made a gesture of polite refusal. "Thank you, but no. I came to show you the route we are taking, as you have been added so late." Rhuan indicated the beaten ground beside the fire. "Let me do this quickly, so you will have time to visit the diviners." Squatting, he smoothed the ground with one deft hand, then used his knife to draw the outline of various provinces and the roads and rivers that cut through them.

Davyn joined the others crowding around the guide's unorthodox palette. A proper map drawn by a man who knew the routes so well was invaluable.

"This is Sancorra. And we are here, beside the river." Rhuan indicated it with a finger. "This is Hecar province, abutting Sancorra to the west. And this is Atalanda, south, where you are bound." He hesitated a moment, fingers stilling, then laid in crude cross-hatching with his knife's tip. "And this area, as best we know, is Alisanos."

Torvic murmured, "The bad place."

The guide nodded solemnly. "A very bad place. It's my duty to keep you safe from the deepwood, so you may arrive in Atalanda safely."

Megritte said, "I don't want to go there. *Bad* people go there."

"Like that man," Torvic asserted. "The one with claws."

Davyn expected the guide would answer the childish fancies with casual dismissal. But he did not.

"Not everyone who ends up in Alisanos is bad," Rhuan said. "An active Alisanos doesn't care about such things. It simply *takes*."

Ellica's voice was harsh. "Like the Hecari. Like the Hecari did when they took our home. When they took our futures!"

Davyn stirred. "Ellica—"

Tears welled in her eyes. "No," she said stubbornly. "I don't want to hear this. I don't want to *do* this, any of it! I don't want to be here, and I don't want to go overmountain. I want to go home!"

"Ellica," Audrun began, "we can't—"

" 'We can't.' " The girl mimicked her, cutting her off.

"Can't do this, can't do that. I'm sick of hearing it!" She turned, took two stiff strides away, hesitated a moment to turn back briefly. "All we're doing is running away!"

And she was gone into the darkness.

Chapter 8

AUDRUN, FLUSTERED, NOTED the guide—
Rhuan—watched Ellica's retreat with startled interest. She blurted, "Gillan, would you—?" even as she caught
hold of Torvic and Megritte before they could chase after
their sister. Her eldest, rolling his eyes, said he would and
departed.

Audrun noticed Davyn's gaze on her, brow furrowed.
Then he said stiffly to Jorda's guide, clearly embarrassed
by the outburst, "My eldest daughter has not grown used
to the idea that we must go elsewhere." He gestured.
"Please continue. My son will bring her back."

It sounded uncaring, but Audrun understood Davyn's
priorities; a proper map drawn by a man who knew the
land so well was invaluable. And Gillan *would* bring Ellica
back. If they still lived at the farmstead, she wouldn't be
concerned about Ellica's sulks and tears and abrupt departures. But here, in a strange place, they could not afford to
leave her to herself.

Jorda's man hitched one shoulder in a slight shrug, then
turned back to explaining the crude map on the dirt. "We'll
cross the river—here—first thing tomorrow morning."
Long fingers moved deftly, indicating routes. "Then we go
here, along here, up to here. You turn off *here,* onto this
smaller road—do you see?"

Audrun saw Davyn's brief nod, intently focused on memorizing what the guide laid out for them.

"But if you turn off here, as you have planned to do ..." His expression was serious. "This is the shortest route. But another might promise more safety." He grimaced briefly. "If such can be found anywhere in a province newly conquered. But if you remain with the karavan a while longer there is less risk."

Davyn shook his head. Audrun noted a peculiar intensity in the guide as he squatted over his map. And his eyes, dark in the dusk, seemed to be waiting.

"I do know," her husband said finally, aware of the guide's concern. "But we must. That route is shorter, *and* less likely to attract Hecari."

Rhuan said quietly, emotion banished from his tone, "That route skirts very near Alisanos."

"Yes," Davyn agreed, nodding. "And it is because that route is used so infrequently, if at all, that I believe it offers us more safety."

"The Hecari are only one among many dangers. Better to face them than risk being overtaken by Alisanos."

Audrun looked more closely at the guide's face, then glanced at her husband, trying to keep the sudden concern from her features.

Davyn, grim-faced, saw it regardless, but did not react; he turned to the guide once more. "We have discussed it, my wife and I. We will go."

The guide held Davyn's gaze a moment, then glanced at Audrun. "It matters to me that everyone is kept safe."

She believed him; she had seen how he was with the youngest of her chicks, treating them neither as children nor as adults. As if they were merely humans, deserving of respect. And because of that, because she wanted him to think she wasn't wholly ignorant, she resorted to saying what struck her as obvious. "But a road *is* there, just as you have drawn. If it were so very dangerous, would they have put it so close to the deepwood?"

The guide's faint smile suggested he had expected the question. "They didn't." Graceful hands dangled over bent, leather-clad knees, knife clasped loosely. Beadwork adorning fringe glinted in firelight. "The road was there first. Alisanos came later." He seemed very relaxed, yet Audrun had the impression the guide was anything but. "You come from a region of Sancorra that Alisanos hasn't threatened in—"

Davyn broke in roughly, "We know what it is."

"—hundreds of years," Rhuan finished, unperturbed by the interruption. "And it has been forty years since the deepwood shifted so much as a pace. Folk have grown accustomed to it being *there,* as I have drawn it." He indicated the crosshatched area. "Generations have been born knowing precisely where Alisanos is, and how to avoid it. But too many have forgotten its greatest threat." His eyes were very steady, as was his voice. "Alisanos *moves.* It is sentient, as much as you or I, for all it is a place. And we cannot trust it."

GILLAN CAUGHT UP to Ellica before she got too far away from the wagon, though she had managed to reach the narrow footpaths winding through the tents. Dyed oilcloth, lighted from within, glowed dully in the twilight, marking his route. Gillan was irritated and impatient; the stranger, who swore he was neither demon nor murderer, seemed to have important things to tell them. But Ellica had pitched her fit—yet another in a string of them since they'd left the farmstead—and now he was missing out on the interesting things.

"Ellica. *Ell*ica." He caught her sleeved arm and swung her around. "Will you *stop*? What is wrong with you?"

Her blond hair had come loose from its binding, straggling down over narrow shoulders. She was not at that moment particularly attractive, with tear-streaked face and reddened eyes. He knew her courses had begun the year before, and her breasts had begun to grow a number of months earlier. She was, most days, inordinately proud of her burgeoning womanhood, but just now she looked thin and blotched and wretched in her dull gray tunic and skirts.

Gillan released her. "You'd best come back before Da himself comes after you."

She scrubbed tears away with both hands. "I can't go back. I don't *want* to go back. I don't want to have anything to do with this going overmountain. I just want to go home!"

"But there's no home *there*," Gillan declared in frustration; he had told her this more times than he could count. "They burned it down, Elli. You saw what was left, when we passed by on the road. The Hecari destroyed everything. Nothing's left!"

"We could rebuild." Abruptly fresh tears welled up into astonishly blue eyes. "Adric is there."

"Adric!" It shocked him. "This is about *Adric?*" Gillan stared at her, suspicions forming. "Were you and he—"

Tears spilled over.

A chill descended upon him. "Elli—you're not with child, are you?"

Her mouth fell open. "No! We never did *that*. We just—we just . . ." She was clearly at a loss, twining fingers together nervously as color rose in her face. "We talked, mostly. Sometimes he kissed me. But we knew it was meant, Gillan. It was! Just as it was meant for Mam and Da. *She* was fifteen when she and Da got married."

It remained incomprehensible to Gillan. "Adric's gone, Elli. He went to join the armies."

"But when he comes back," she said in desperation, "*we'll* be gone! How will he find me?"

Gillan opened his mouth to tell her Adric might not be coming back at all; he had overhead Da telling Mam that most men who were not trained soldiers, for all they loved their land, didn't have the same chances for survival as true soldiers did. It had shocked him to hear that, for he and Adric had pledged to meet under the oak tree on the border between their neighboring farms when the war was over; of *course* Adric would be there. But then the Hecari had overrun their lands, the oak tree had been chopped down for wood, and the farmsteads burned. Gillan, seeing the devastation, realized Da was right: Adric indeed might not be coming home.

But Gillan had told no one his fears. Not speaking them aloud meant they might not come true.

He discovered now he could say none of them to Ellica, either. He was too stunned to learn his sister and best friend had become so close without his awareness.

"If I go back," she said, "Adric can find me."

"Nothing's there, Elli."

"*I* would be there."

"But you can't go back there, not by yourself! How would you live?"

She opened her mouth to reply, but someone answered for her. "*I'll* tell you how she can live. Just let me whisper it in your ear, sweetling!"

Gillan spun around on the packed, narrow footpath between tents even as Ellica gasped and recoiled, catching herself against the guy ropes of the nearest tent. He was aware of the closeness of the man, his unsteadiness, and the reek of liquor. Behind him, Ellica was crying again.

"Hassic!" A second voice, pitched to command, cut across the footpath. "Go on your way, Hassic. Sleep it off."

It was a woman, Gillan saw in his first startled glance. In fading light and little moon, the muted glow of tent lanterns, he had the impression of smallness, of wiriness, of short-cropped hair nearly as fair as his own, and brass glinting at her ears. Flanking her were two men. They wore blue mantles slung over left shoulders, fastened with silver brooches, but the woman did not. Couriers, the men. He had seen their like before, on the road to this place.

"All I want—" the drunk began, weaving, but the two men at the woman's back smoothly slid in beside him, one on each side.

"—is to find a bed and sleep," one of them finished. "Right, Alorn? Our friend Hassic has had a bit too much, but he'll feel better in the morning." He slung a companionable but restraining arm around Hassic's shoulder even as the other man did the same from the other side. Gillan saw a look pass between the couriers and the blond woman. "Go ahead, Beth. We'll see to him."

She nodded briefly, then turned her attention to Gillan and Ellica as the drunk was led away. "All right," she said crisply, "he won't be whispering anything into anyone's ear tonight. Though likely that's all he could have managed." Her smile at Ellica was wry. "Not to suggest even that would have been enjoyable." Her assessing gaze lingered on Ellica a moment, then reverted to Gillan. "What are you doing here? It truly isn't the best place for people like you to be."

"People like us?" Gillan echoed, stung. Heat warmed his face. "Why? Who do you think we are?"

"Karavaners," the woman replied matter-of-factly, "and I'm not being rude; and yes, I can see it in your face. If you and your—sister?—want a drink, there are plenty of ale tents for you. But this particular area is where most of the—" Gillian got the impression she changed her intended words in midstride, "—'friendlier' kind of women look for men, so it really isn't surprising Hassic thought she was for sale."

He couldn't help himself. The words just came out of his mouth. "Is that why you're here? Is that why you were with those two couriers?"

She blinked, then hooted a sharp laugh. "Well, *that* is amusing! My mam always said I'd be taken for a whore, if I didn't change my ways." Her smile was unoffended. "No. I've been many things in my life, but I've never sold my favors to anyone, man or woman." The glints he had noticed were brass hoops in her ears, and she was dressed like a man in a loose, long-sleeved woven tunic, leather bracers wrapping her forearms, wide leather belt with a pouch and scroll-case attached, and trousers baggy at the thighs but leather-wrapped from knee to ankle, hiding most of the boot beneath. A necklet of charms circled her throat. "So, do you want something to drink? I can take you to Mikal's. No one will bother you there. He runs a clean tent."

"No." Gillan shook his head, embarrassed he had insulted her—even if she didn't appear to be insulted. "No, we have to go back. We're leaving in the morning."

"Who's your karavan-master?"

Gillan called up the memory. "Mam said Jorda."

"Ah." She nodded once; ear-hoops swung. "Jorda's good. Not one of the best known, mind—the wealthy folk go with others—but he's dependable, knows the roads, and has two of the best guides in the business, even if they are unpredictable. They'll get you where you're going." She lifted pale brows. "Where are you bound?"

"Atalanda province," Ellica said quietly, speaking for the first time since they had been accosted. Her voice was thickened from crying, but no more tears coursed her face.

The woman's surprise was unfeigned. "This late? You'll run into the rains."

"There's a shorter route," Gillan declared. "Da told us it will get us there sooner."

She shook her head. "I'm a courier; I know the roads. There's only one route that's shorter, but this time of year no one much uses it. Not with the rains coming. No one wants to be stuck in the mud so close to Alisanos. You'd be asking for trouble."

Defenses snapped into place. "Da wouldn't take us that way if it wasn't safe," Gillan said sharply. "Ellica, come on. We're going back." He tugged at his sister's arm. "Elli. Come on."

The woman's voice rose as they departed. "Tell your da what I said!"

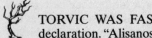 TORVIC WAS FASCINATED with the guide's declaration. "Alisanos *moves?*"

The guide's attention sharpened on the boy. A muscle jumped briefly in his jaw; Audrun wondered if he had spoken more plainly than intended with children present.

"It moves," he repeated, but added nothing more.

"How?" Megritte asked, vastly intrigued.

Audrun found the guide's eyes on her, as if he waited to hear from her before continuing. She felt abruptly self-conscious; did he think she might remonstrate with Davyn about going that way? "As you say, Alisanos has never threatened the region we've come from," she explained. "My husband and I grew up safe. Our children know that it exists, as we did, and that one wishes never to go there, but nothing more. There was no need; we lived far from the deepwood."

"There is a need now," Rhuan said flatly. "Everyone must understand what Alisanos is when they travel so close to its borders. Lack of knowledge leads to trouble."

Davyn's tone was brusque; Audrun knew he was annoyed. "We'll discuss it with the children tonight."

Megritte impatiently insisted the guide answer her question. "*How* does it move?"

"No one knows. It just does." Rhuan glanced down at the map. Thin braids depending from his temples had not been worked into the heavy plaits trailing down his spine, but swung alongside his face. Coin-rings and colorful glass beads studded the elaborate braidwork.

"Mam says demons live in Alisanos," Megritte observed.

Rhuan looked at her gravely. "Yes," he agreed. "That's where the demons are. Note, if you please—in view of our earlier conversation—that I am *here.*" He glanced briefly at Audrun, then to Davyn, and continued. "Jorda is meticulous in consulting the diviners with regard to such things, in listening to folk who understand the deepwood's habits. Some people are sensitive to aspects that suggest imminent change; I am one. And there *are* signs that Alisanos is becoming unstable. I feel it."

"Feel what?" Davyn asked sharply. "How?"

Torvic was fascinated. "Is it magic? Are *you* magic?"

For the first time the guide completely ignored the children. He looked only at Davyn, and Audrun felt a chill sheathe her bones. "If the deepwood moves again . . ." She let it trail off. Alisanos, for all she'd heard the tales, felt unreal, insubstantial. She had been threatened as a misbehaving child that she could be sent to the deepwood, but her parents clearly did not mean it, nor did they appear to believe such a thing was truly possible. And Davyn had grown up as she did, apart from the region hosting Alisanos; the idea of a *place* being able to move of its own accord struck both of them as unbelievable.

She flicked a glance at Davyn, who ground out, "I've heard the tales. We all have."

The guide was very still. His tone, despite the coiled readiness in his body, was surpassingly casual. "I saw a man today who was no longer precisely a man, not as we reckon it."

"The dead man," Torvic blurted, before anyone else could.

Megritte, following up as brightly, said, "He came to the wagon. Mam sent us away so he couldn't steal us."

Davyn's attention snapped to Audrun. "The man who died came to the wagon? Why? What did he want?"

She drew a breath. "He said he wished me to take him back home, as I had a wagon."

"He smelled bad," Megritte declared, making a face.

The guide went on, speaking to Davyn. "He was human, once. Like you. But then Alisanos took him—"

Davyn's tone was alarmed as he interrupted. "And he came back out?"

"Such as he had become, yes. *That* came back out." Rhuan hooked a dangling sidelock braid behind one ear. "You risk a great deal following the shorter route."

Audrun kept her voice steady. She had an idea what the guide would say, and what Davyn would say to her in private, but she asked it anyway. "What would *you* have us do?"

"Stay here," Rhuan replied promptly. "Wait until next season, then let Jorda take you the long way around. There are other roads to Atalanda."

"Babies do not wait for such things," Davyn said. "What if we stayed, as you suggest, and the deepwood shifted and took us anyway? What then?" He shook his head, rubbing pensively at golden stubble that caught the firelight. "This decision was not lightly made. I put much thought into it.

We consulted the diviners. We were assured it was safe, so long as we did not tarry." He glanced at Audrun. "The child will be born in four months. We must reach the lands in Atalanda where my wife's kin live."

The guide glanced down at his map, eyes shuttered behind lowered lids rimmed with coppery lashes. "Then this is the way you go," he said quietly, and continued his directions as if no one among them had ever mentioned Alisanos.

Chapter 9

*B*RODHI DOZED UNTIL his senses awakened into a
tingling awareness running like fire through his blood.
He knew at once why: Ferize was very near.

Still alone in the couriers' common tent, he hastily
pulled on boots and laced up the stamped leather gaiters.
Then paused, contemplating whether he wished to wear
the blue robe and brooch of his employment or go unknown.

He supposed it didn't matter; he was likely recognizable
to anyone who had seen him before. His clothing was much
plainer than Rhuan's, but he too wore the sacred braids
and adorned them with personal talismans and ornamentation. No one truly knew very much about Shoia, but
those who lived in the settlement were familiar with the
only two living examples they had ever seen.

Brodhi exited the tent and took the first turning of the
walkways that led away from the tent city. He stepped off
the path and into darkness, forsaking the lanterns, lamps,
and fire rings of humans. He wanted nothing to do with humans this night.

Beneath Grandmother Moon he strode away from habi-
tation to the realm of darkness, of privacy. A close-
clustered grove of high-crowned trees offered shelter.
Brodhi stepped among them, aware of the faint burring

warning of birds in the branches, the deep chirping of crickets. And then all went silent.

Stillness pervaded, until it seemed even the world paused.

He stood amid the trees, seeing what moonlight offered; little enough when the Grandmother reigned, but his vision was superior. He smiled, and waited patiently. Thinking nothing, wishing nothing, speaking no word.

Eventually, with a muted rustling in the leaves, a woman climbed out of the nearest tree. She jumped the last three feet from the lowest limb and landed lightly, bringing order to unbound hair and loose garments with an elegant motion of her hands. Tonight she had chosen to be black-haired, black-clad. Then she faced Brodhi; her eyes, too, were black.

"Well?" he inquired.

She tilted her head slightly from side to side, registering a tension in his body no one else would see. Her eyes were fixed on him as if she hungered. "No," she said. "Not yet. They expect you to complete the full term."

"No matter what?"

"No matter what," she affirmed. She circled him, examined him, touched him, *smelled* him; Brodhi stood still and permitted it, alpha male to alpha bitch. Ferize was half wild and all demon. But always when she returned from Alisanos, she brought with her an edged, feral feyness in slit-pupiled eyes, and the movements of a predator.

Halting in front of him once again, she placed the palm of one hand over his heart. "Ah. I thought so; I could smell it on you."

"I do bathe," he replied lightly. "Rather more often than humans, in fact."

"You feel it."

He relinquished prevarication. "Yes."

In the shadows, untouched by the moonlight, her eyes were masked by dark hollows above oblique, jutting cheekbones. Her other hand briefly touched the skin of his brow, tracing faint lines, then smoothing them away. "The discomfort is minor yet."

"Nothing to speak of," he agreed.

But Ferize elected to speak of it. "Will you stay here? So close?"

"The province is in turmoil," Brodhi said, "since the Hecari won it. My duty now is to serve the warlord-become-prince. But he may well choose his own couriers, rather than keeping us. Until I am sent for, or dismissed, I will remain here."

Ferize's supple mouth twisted. "In this place, this Sancorra, you are Shoia, and thus not invested in the province's defeat. He would do better, this warlord-become-prince, to keep you." She lifted her hand, then pushed back the thin braid that had found its way forward of Brodhi's left shoulder. "His men don't know the roads, the hamlets, the farmsteads." She circled him again, sliding one hand across the small of his back, his hip, his abdomen. And altered the subject. "Rhuan is here as well."

"Yes."

"How does *he* fare?"

"I have not spared the time to ask him."

Ferize's smile was faint. "Of course not. Then I must allow Darmuth to tell me—or seek Rhuan myself."

"He's not your task." Inwardly, he said, *I am.*

"My task is to do whatever the primaries tell me to do." She paused, stretched out her hand. "Here. A token; they do know you are trying."

"And failing." Brodhi took the item from her hand and studied it beneath the moon. An elegant, narrow leaf of fine silver with a loop at one end, nearly weightless. A human might see the art, the beauty, and nothing more; Brodhi recognized the leaf for what it represented: a primary's wager. He shut his hand upon it and felt the metal edges bite. "Whose?"

"Ylara," Ferize told him. "She favors you."

He offered the ornament back to her. "Will you?"

Ferize accepted the leaf. She stepped closer, selected one of his sidelock braids, and began to undo the knotted silk binding at the bottom. When the braid was loose, she ran the hair through her hands as if she tested the texture and weight of fine, costly fabric. She lifted a lock of it and, eyes meeting his, took it into her mouth.

Brodhi bit deeply into his bottom lip.

She braided the rippled hair again, this time threading the leaf into the slender plait.

"I have a tent," he told her when she finished. "But I share it with others."

"Well then." She lifted one shoulder in a slight but eloquent shrug in the mass of her hair as she moved close enough that their bodies touched. "We have the trees, do we not, here beneath the moon?"

She tasted of mist and starlight, of earth and sky and stone. Against her mouth, as he set his arms around her, Brodhi murmured all of her names one after another.

DAVYN KNEW VERY well his insistence on going the shorter route had displeased the guide. But the diviners had been consulted again and again; would the man have them ignore what the experts declared? Priests, oracles, seers, readers; the rune stones, the bones, the guts of a white goat, the drift of a black feather plucked from a living crow . . . only a fool turned his back on what had been stated so plainly. The baby must be born in Atalanda.

He glanced at Audrun. Her expression was taut, closed, even to him. A wave of uncertainty swept through; and then he cursed himself for it. Before the war, he had not been so filled with doubt. Before the war, decisions had been simple. None was easy, beyond such things as telling Torvic and Megritte they might stay up a bit later, and though he treated some decisions as less than vital, he considered all of them carefully. Before the war, he had been satisfied with his decisions. Now none satisfied him.

Now *nothing* did.

But when they reached Atalanda, when they were settled near Audrun's kin, they would begin again and find the peace they had shared in Sancorra.

Thus, a decision. The same, made again. "We'll go on."

The guide rose out of his squat. Davyn realized the man—he had named himself Shoia, a race Davyn didn't know—was not so much shorter than himself, though he lacked the mass in shoulders and chest. "Gather your children," the guide said. "Bring your wagon to those trees, where Jorda's karavan is." He indicated the grove. "You will have time for the final divination rites."

Davyn was startled. "Again?"

"Yes. Depending on the omens, you will depart with us in the morning—or not."

" 'Not'?" Audrun quoted, clearly taken aback. "But we have a place with you, yes?"

"You have a place with us, maybe."

Davyn frowned. "I don't understand. You told my wife we have a place in the karavan."

Rhuan nodded. "And so you do—unless the diviner says otherwise. If all is favorable, you will depart with us in the morning." His eyes flicked between them. "It's customary. Jorda will not have you otherwise." He tilted his head in the direction of the karavan grounds. "See Ilona," he suggested. "She is no less diligent in her rituals, and while the result may not be favorable, she is kinder than Branca or Melior."

Audrun sounded more angry than surprised. "You're saying we may still be turned away, even *after* we agreed to the terms?"

"Everyone may," the guide said gently. "This close to Alisanos, the master risks nothing. Not with lives at stake. The diviners you have consulted were for yourselves. This one is for the welfare of the karavan." He smiled warmly at them then, as if to mitigate the fears engendered by his words. "See Ilona."

Davyn well knew the tone Audrun employed. She was displeased. "We've seen *fourteen* diviners."

Rhuan laughed, oblivious to her mood; or else uncaring of it. "See another."

TWILIGHT GAVE WAY to darkness. Ellica let Gillan lead her along the shadowed pathway all of five feet before wrenching her arm out of his grasp. Startled, he swung to face her. "Elli, we need to go."

Tears were banished. Now she couldn't keep the anger out of her voice. "I know we need to go. I'm not saying different."

"Then what—"

She stopped the beginnings of his question with a silencing chop of a hand. Even as Gillan stared at her she brushed at her skirts. Her hair—well, her hair wanted a comb. In the meantime she did what she could, pushing tangles behind her ears. She scowled at her impatient brother. "That man thought I was a whore."

"Elli, that man—"

"—was in his cups; I know." She licked her fingers, smoothed them across her face, and pulled the hem of her tunic up to wipe away the grime of dust and tears. The anger remained, but it was tightly interwoven with embarrassment. "I know." She smoothed her hair against the crown of her skull. "And likely that woman did, too, and she wasn't in her cups." Ellica stopped short. "At least, I don't think she was." She yanked the hem of her tunic down. "I'm not going back to the wagon looking like a—"

"You *don't*, Elli! Mother of Moons, will you never listen? He was drunk, and likely blind with it."

She drew in a breath, released it noisily, then began to walk back the way she had come. Gillan fell in beside her. "I didn't know . . . I mean—you and Adric?"

If she thought about Adric, she'd begin to cry again. Even now tears prickled behind her lids. Best to find something else to think about, something that would deter Gillan's questions.

An idea occured. "Why do some women become whores?"

He was patently startled. "What?"

"Why do some women become whores?"

He was flummoxed. "You're asking that of me?"

"You're a man." She shrugged. "Well, almost a man."

The latter prompted a scowl. Gillan stopped. "My beard's coming in." He set two fingers against his chin. "See?"

Ellica halted, and squinted. "I don't see anything."

He pointed more deliberately. "Here. I can feel the hairs."

Though there was muted light from the tents along the footpath, Ellica could see nothing of the much-prized hairs. But she gave in on that point to remind him of her question as she began walking again. Now she was genuinely curious. "So, why do some women become whores?"

Eventually he answered. "Maybe because they have no men of their own."

She shook her head. "That can't be it. There are women aplenty in the world without men, and all of them can't be whores. That diviner isn't. The hand-reader."

After a moment Gillan shrugged a little. "She doesn't need to be a whore. She's a diviner."

"And the courier isn't a whore. She said so."

"But she might have a man," Gillan observed.

Ellica noted that his strides had lengthened. She had to make more effort to keep up with him. Maybe he *was* a man, with his voice broken, his chin sprouting, and his legs growing longer. Now that she noticed, he was indeed taller. Accordingly, she asked what to her seemed a fair enough question, in view of the topic. "Would you go with a whore?"

Gillan stopped in his tracks. His expression was a mixture of embarrassment and utter disbelief. "Why are we talking about whores?"

"I saw you looking at the Sisters of the Road. Would you have gone with one of them?"

Gillan pushed both hands through his fair hair, standing

much of it on end. "This is—this is a stupid thing to talk about!"

"I can't ask Da," she said simply. "I thought about it on the road from the settlement, but I couldn't ask him. It didn't feel right."

"But it feels right to ask me?"

"I saw you looking at the Sisters. Da didn't. Not the way you did." She thought he blushed, but she couldn't be sure in low light. "I did ask Mam."

Gillan was as astonished as she'd ever seen him. "About *whores?*"

"She's always told me I could ask her anything."

Her brother stared at her for a long perplexed moment. "I don't think she meant you should ask about whores."

Ellica nodded. "So I'm asking you."

He *was* blushing. He turned on his heel and began to walk, raising his voice to carry over his shoulder. "We're not speaking about this, Ellica."

She watched him for three strides, then hastened to catch up. She did not intend to be taken for a whore yet again this night, by a man drunk *or* sober.

And then, all unbidden, came the memory of Adric's face. The memory of hesitant kisses one summer day beneath the big old oak.

This time, when she wept, she did it silently.

Chapter 10

*I*LONA HAD PACKED away her table, cushions, rugs, lanterns, and lantern-hooks, and now sat framed in the open wagon door, spooning stew into her mouth. The night before departure her dinner was always late, as there was no knowing how many people might ask her for readings. She and the other two karavan diviners, Branca and Melior, shared the work, but which of them was consulted was up to the travelers. Some trips, she had more custom; on others, they did. This one had been evenly divided among them.

The sun was down. Grandmother Moon stood high in the heavens over the karavan grove. Only two outfits remained: Jorda's and Sennet's. All others had departed the week before.

Small fires marked where the wagons stood, casting a glow amid the trees. Wood smoke wreathed the camp with an odor Ilona found comforting in its familiarity. She had hung a single lighted lantern from the hook over her head so she could see to eat. Her booted feet were set two steps down, making a table out of her lap beneath tunic, split skirts, and the shawl thrown over them.

The last bite was in her mouth as Rhuan, coming out of darkness into light, appeared at a jog, sidelock braids swinging. His expression suggested he was very intent upon something, and Ilona had an idea what it might be.

She smiled wryly as he halted before her, forestalling his first words. "I hardly believe I am so good at making stew that you wish a meal from me. So. You want me to provide a reading for your farmsteaders." The smile turned into a grin. "And I read no hand to determine that."

Rhuan nodded, solemn. "I have told them to come." He looked away from her a moment, then met her eyes. He had made up his mind about something, but she suspected he wasn't entirely comfortable with it. " 'Lona—it needs to be a good reading."

That shocked her. "*Needs* to be! Well, I don't doubt all of us *need* good readings. But they are what they are, Rhuan. You know that." She twisted to set the empty stew plate and horn spoon behind her, then turned back to fix him with a steady gaze that belied the flinch of dismay in her belly. Did he—? Well, best to address it directly. "Don't you dare tell me you believe I manipulate my readings."

He raised a conciliatory hand. "I know you don't, 'Lona."

Still, the thought pinched. She raked him with an assessing examination but saw no humor, no irony, no affected innocence. The dismay dissipated; he was serious, then, and perhaps he truly had not intended offense. "I can't give a false reading of good that won't truly exist, Rhuan. But neither can I leave out the bad."

"I know." He had the grace to be shame-faced. "I should not have implied such a thing—"

"You didn't 'imply,' " she broke in crisply.

A gesture indicated he accepted the reprimand. "No. No. But—they do need it. Badly. I think they have been misused by other diviners."

Ilona got out another tin cup and poured tea into it from a battered kettle. "They may feel misused by what *I* read, Rhuan. Did you think of that?" She extended the guest-cup.

He accepted it, sketched a quick gesture over it—homage to his Shoia gods, he'd told her once, when she had pried out of him the admission that he was devout—then dropped into a habitual squat, forearms resting across up-ended thighs. "They understand."

She searched his oddly shuttered expression. "Do *you?*"

He drank. Then nodded, setting hair adornment aglint. But he looked into the cup, not at her. Avoiding something, she knew. She didn't believe Rhuan would ever lie outright to her, but leave parts of truths unspoken, oh, yes.

Ilona sighed. "You told them to come to me specifically, didn't you? Not to Melior or Branca."

His eyes lifted to hers. "You're kinder," he said, "when delivering bad news."

"Ah." She found that ironically amusing. "I doubt ill tidings delivered kindly affords anyone comfort."

"It might."

She gave in then, because he wasn't after all asking her to do what she could not, or what she *should* not. And he was serious, not wheedling or playful, nor employing manifold charms. "Very well. Are they coming?"

"They'll need to hitch up the wagon, and then they'll come."

She finished her tea, thinking ahead to the ritual. She would need to take out the table again; well, perhaps not. It was more comfortable to talk with people and read their hands in the proper setting—they expected it—but not required.

" 'Lona—if there is anything I can do for you, say it."

Payment offered, in his own way. She stared at him over the rim of her cup as she drank the rest of her tea. Then, smiling broadly, said, "Yes."

He nodded once, acknowledging her acceptance. "Ask."

Knowing it would shock him, she did. "Let me read *your* hand."

One blink. And then he was standing. "You know you can't."

Idly she noted, "You've never let me try."

"Why waste your time?" The tone was light, but the body held tension.

Ilona shook her head. "You go to other diviners all the time. You allow *them* to try and read your omens."

" 'Try,' " he agreed, handing her back the empty cup. "But they can't. It isn't possible. So when they *do*—when they concoct ridiculous stories about what is to come, and lecture me on the worthiness I require for a proper after-life once I've 'crossed over the river,' as your people say—I know they are false diviners." He paused, studying her. "Do you really want to risk me unmasking you as a charlatan?"

Ilona laughed. There was nothing in life she was more certain of than her ability to read the auguries. "You could attempt it, if you like. Just as I could attempt to read your hand." And had, once—or begun to—very briefly. When he had been dead.

Rhuan shook his head. "There is no diviner in the world who can read a Shoia."

"Either that," she drawled, "or there is something you don't want me to find out." Something beyond the chaos she had sensed when his hand, limp and still warm despite his death, lay in hers.

A muscle jumped in his cheek, putting the lie to the light-ness of his tone. "Ah, but you said it yourself: there are no se-crets between us."

She smiled, shrugged, set down her own now-empty cup. When she looked up, Rhuan was gone.

RHUAN DID NOT immediately go to Jorda after visiting Ilona. Instead he slipped along the perime-ter of the encampment where the firelight did not reach, and went to the horses. The horse-master, Janqeril, had picketed them for the night rather than leaving them in their small herd; the horses would be needed before dawn, as the encampment arose.

Rhuan took from the string of remounts his favorite gelding, spotted black on white, but availed himself of neither saddle nor bridle. The halter was enough. He un-tied the rope and swung it across the horse's neck, reached under and caught it, then knotted the free end to the rope loop beneath the gelding's jaw. He led him some distance from the rest of the string, then grabbed a handful of ivory mane and swung up, settling down across the spotted back.

The horse was full of snort and opinion; Janqeril's horseboys had learned not to exercise the spotted horse. Rhuan preferred to do it himself, despite the resultant displays. And one such lurked now: the spine beneath him arched, the tail whipped, the head rose up into the air, then bent at the poll with an air of annoyed impatience, ears spearing the air. Rhuan spoke to the gelding softly in a language only a very few would recognize, smoothed an eloquent hand down the long angle of shoulder, then tapped him lightly with his heels.

The journey was short. Rhuan rode only as far as a grassy bluff overlooking the river. The escarpment was neither sharp nor steep, nor was the descending angle or footing particularly dangerous, but riding down could be unpleasant if the horse missed a step in the abbreviated light offered by the moon. So he slipped off the gelding, left the loop in the rope rein across the spotted neck so the horse would not put a hoof through it while grazing on summer grass, and walked to the edge.

Below, water shone silver-black. It lazed through the shallows like a sleepy hound. Tomorrow Jorda would lead the karavan down the rutted trail to its bank, where the accomodating earth rolled out smoothly to water's edge, and all would fill their water barrels. After that, Jorda would take his people onto the road, and Rhuan and Darmuth would ride ahead to see what there was to see.

To make certain all was well with the world.

Rhuan shivered, flesh going taut on his bones. Inside, something—shifted. He felt a twinge within his viscera. A feathering along his bones. All was distinctly not well with *his* world.

He closed his eyes, hoping the sensations would pass; knowing they would not. Two days before he had awakened just before dawn, aching in every joint, queasy, with skin that wanted badly not to be touched. The worst passed within several hours, but he remained aware of a subtle pressure. A presence.

Alisanos.

After forty human years: Alisanos. Again.

He should have known the primaries would interfere. Such promises as theirs were never to be trusted.

Flesh stood up on his bones. A shudder wracked him. Rhuan's eyes snapped open; the world around him was a hazy pale red and out of focus. He gazed up at the moon, seeing the doubled stars as her acolytes burning against blackness. The moon's cycle went on no matter what he did, or what was done to him. Grandmother Moon: near to disappearing. Then no moon at all, called the Orphan Sky. Followed by Maiden Moon, tentative, growing to fertility; and Mother Moon, gravid, whelping the nights to come. And then the drift into old age again, the wisdom of the Grandmother shaping the night sky.

It was a pity, he reflected, that he could find no comfort in the cycle that ordered the lives of humans. That he was governed by something else entirely.

Beneath itching flesh, muscles spasmed. The feathery touch became demanding, wreathing itself, serpentlike, around his bones. Muscles knotted. He tried to wait it out with clenched hands and gritted teeth, but the pressure increased. Unimpressed by his petty strength, it pressed down like a hand from the heavens, unstinting with its power. That power dropped him awkwardly to his knees, body bent forward, arms braced, splayed hands flattened against the soil, breath hissing in his teeth.

A quiet voice from behind said, "It's getting worse."

Darmuth. Of course.

"You know what's coming."

Rhuan nodded. Once.

"You could leave. Distance yourself."

It took effort to speak, and more yet to speak clearly. "I won't run from it."

"If you stay here, it might take you."

The blurt of Rhuan's laughter was cut off by a sharply

indrawn breath of pain. "And is it that you want me to run from it? Or *to* it?"

Darmuth's tone was dry. "I can't ask you to do either. It was merely an observation."

Observation. What Darmuth was best at.

Rhuan felt sweat on his brow, bathing his upper lip, prickling beneath his armpits. The air was cool on the moisture, stippling rousing flesh. From aching hands and knees he moved into a seated position facing the river, legs crossed, spine to Darmuth, and sat improbably straight. A practiced toss of his head swept back the heavy plait of braids that had fallen forward so that it dangled down his spine. He wanted no impediments, no distractions, as he assimilated the discomfort.

Rhuan drew in a long breath. "I accepted the journey the primaries set before me. I accepted all potential tests and challenges, even ignorant of which are created by the primaries and which are merely happenstance. This too may be a test."

"But the primaries are fair, Rhuan. You may change your mind. You may repudiate your vow. They left you those options."

"And if I do so, I am trapped forever in a world the primaries rule, bound by their laws, made to play their games." Rhuan shook his head. "Here there are no games. Here you are born, you make your way in the world, and you die. No more."

Darmuth smiled. "Few would call it 'trapped,' to live with the primaries."

"It isn't freedom, Darmuth. Not as I desire it."

"Ah, but there are many who would say the freedom you desire is tantamount to a death sentence . . . for the soul, if not the body, for one such as you."

Rhuan smiled slightly, staring across the red-tinged darkness. "My soul is more alive among humans than it was before I came here."

"If you surmount all challenges and obtain what you desire, you'll disappoint the primaries, Rhuan. You are the first child Alario has sired in three hundred human years."

Rhuan laughed. "I would disappoint some of the primaries, but not all of them. Many of them would be pleased to see Alario's child fail. It would weaken Alario's standing among them."

Darmuth asked, "Do you suppose it is as difficult for Brodhi?"

Rhuan at last was able to turn his head. Vision was returning to normal. Over one shoulder he observed Darmuth, who sat a horse made of air and shadow, taking substance from Grandmother Moon. Darmuth could do that.

"Brodhi," Rhuan managed, "suffers daily. But it has nothing to do with—this."

"Ah. You refer to his bigotry about humans. Yes, I agree; life would be much less difficult if he rid himself of that bias." The laughter was soft. "Perhaps be more like you?"

Rhuan heaved himself to his feet, catching his balance before he staggered. The worst had passed, though the weakness afterward was never pleasant. He needed rest. He needed ritual and release so that rest was possible.

He turned to face the man on horseback. Grandmother Moon found little purchase on Darmuth's features, so that his expression was shadowed. "Oh, no doubt *that* would be Brodhi's choice. To be more like me." Rhuan moistened dry lips so his forced grin wouldn't crack them. "I think Brodhi prefers even humans to me."

"Ferize is coming tonight," Darmuth announced, changing the subject, as was his wont, without preamble. Then he paused, stilled, as if listening, as if scenting the air. "In fact, she's already here."

"Well." Rhuan tested himself inwardly, prodding for lurking pain, but it had dissipated. In its place he felt the expected nausea, the knotting of muscles at the back of his neck. He shook his head and walked to the spotted horse. Weariness descended, washed over him. He needed privacy before Jorda found him and set him to a task. "I'm sure they're aware of it, too, Darmuth. It draws nearer every day."

"I notice Brodhi came here anyway."

Rhuan scrubbed the back of his hand across his drying brow, then massaged the rigid muscle on either side of his neck with strong fingers. "He accepted the journey and the tests even as I did. I am a guide. He is a courier. We serve for five human years. Only one year remains. You know perfectly well that if either of us forsakes that final year for any reason—"

Darmuth broke in. "Yes, but if Alisanos goes active, everything changes. Perhaps even vows and journeys."

Rhuan slid gentle hands along his mount's jaw, lowering his face to share a lengthy exchange of breath, nose to nose. To draw in the warm, comforting scent of equine flesh. "I will go on as I am, Darmuth. I have a duty to the humans. And I made a vow unconnected to the one made before the primaries, but which, to me, carries as much weight." He moved, caught doubled handfuls of mane, swung himself up. "To Jorda."

Darmuth's laughter was unfettered. "He's human! And merely a karavan-master."

"Now you sound like Brodhi." He settled his weight more comfortably across the spotted back, gathering the rope rein. Even to Darmuth, he could not explain all his reasons for needing to remain. Indeed, as suggested, he could ride away now, leaving behind the karavan, the humans, and the pain that would come more often if he remained so close to an active Alisanos, pain that would increase as they neared the borderlands, but he would forsake far more than duty to the humans and a vow to the gods were he to depart.

He would also forsake his only approximation of humanity.

"So," Rhuan said, "run along, little demon. You may now report to the primaries and tell them what I have said in answer to this latest test."

"Oh, this wasn't a test," Darmuth said lightly. "This was merely me reaquainting you with your options."

"You may tell them also that I find such inquisitions by proxy wholly transparent." Rhuan, reining his mount around, sank his heels into spotted sides and set the horse to a run, leaving Darmuth and his moon-made mount behind.

Not that it mattered. Darmuth would be waiting for him when he got back to the karavan anyway, having dispensed with imaginary horses and relied strictly on himself.

Unfair, Rhuan thought, who could do no such thing. But not unexpected. Rudeness was but one of the annoying things he had discovered in riding with an Alisani demon.

Chapter 11

AUDRUN, TOLD BY DAVYN to go ahead to Jorda's diviner while he and Gillan hitched the oxen and moved the wagon, found the woman waiting at her tall, yellow-wheeled wagon. She sat casually in the open doorway of her wagon, brass-tipped boot toes peeping out from layers of colorful split skirts, chin propped in one hand. Her dark hair was a mass of long ringlets tamed only slightly by ornamented hair sticks anchoring coils against the back of her head. She wore a sleeveless knee-length overtunic belted with fawn-hued leather wrapped low on her hips. Brass studs had been hammered into the belt in myriad tangled designs, and a handful of feather-and-carved-wood charms hung from it. She was a slender, striking woman, with hazel eyes, high cheekbones, straight nose, and a wide, expressive mouth.

She rose as Audrun approached, welcoming her with a warm smile and gesturing for her to mount the steps into the tall, big-wheeled wagon. Dyed canvas sidewalls had been dropped down for privacy, and as Audrun followed the diviner into the wagon, the woman shut the door.

As with the exterior, the interior of the wagon was a panoply of colors. Even the shallow drawers built into the underside of the diviner's narrow bed were painted and adorned with brass pull knobs. A pierced-tin lantern hung from the central curved Mother Rib, and in the ocherous light Audrun saw the glint of gilt scrollwork winding around the waxed wood, the dull glow of dangling brass charm-strings. Pots, pans, mugs, and ladles hung from lesser ribs.

"Please." The diviner gestured for Audrun to seat herself on the narrow bed. Here too were myriad colors in the rich, deep dyes used on the coverlet. The fabric's woven nap was a mix of smooth and nubby. "It's informal this way, but you don't strike me as a woman in need of excess ritual."

Audrun essayed a crooked smile. "Tonight, perhaps, less even than usual. The day's events have been, well, unusual." Lower back aching, Audrun sat down upon the bed and neatened skirts that, she realized in dismay, were coated with the dust and grit of travel. She had washed her hands before preparing dinner, but now, faced with the tidiness of the diviner's wagon and clothing, not to mention the delicate texture of her warm-toned olive skin and the clarity in hazel eyes, Audrun felt the rest of her could have done with washing as well.

And a change of clothing to boot, she reflected glumly, with or without excess ritual.

The diviner sat down next to Audrun, smiling in a way that struck her as sincere, not donned for business. "My name is Ilona. My gift is to read hands, to determine whether what lies ahead for those who wish to join the karavan is auspicious. It's harsh, I do know, to realize that a journey may be ended before it begins merely because of what I see in your hand." Her expression became more serious, "but Jorda is responsible for the lives of all the people in this karavan. He would be negligent were he to accept individuals who could mean danger for everyone else."

Audrun studied the woman's expression and black-lashed eyes, seeking anything akin to guile. She found none. "My name is Audrun. We are a man, his wife, four children, and—" Her hand covered her belly, "—another yet to be born. We do not intend to travel all the way with this karavan, but to turn off and take another route to Atalanda." Desperation edged her tone; were they to be turned away after all? "Forgive my plain speech, but what danger could we cause?"

The diviner did not curb her words into a gentler truth. "Possibly the death of everyone in this karavan."

It shocked Audrun into a sharp disbelief that made her blunter yet, with skepticism undisguised. "Merely by coming with you?"

"Yes."

Audrun considered it. Though raised to respect and honor what diviners said in the practice of their art, she was not certain she believed this woman—or perhaps it was simply that she didn't wish to believe her. She had fought a war already this day and won, gaining permission for badly-needed passage from the karavan-master himself, only to have his hired guide suggest another skirmish lay ahead; and now the hired *diviner* suggested by words and expression that yet a third battle faced her. Audrun was tired and short of patience.

She smoothed back straggles of fine light brown hair, trying to maintain a self-control that felt perilously close to breaking. "What would you have me do?"

"In a moment, give me the loan of your hand. But first, you must forgive *my* plain speech." Her tone and eyes were steady. "Please understand—my concern is limited, it *must* be limited, by the nature of my employ. I will look only for images that have to do with the safety of the karavan. But there may be other things I see as well, on the edges. I will not examine those images because they aren't pertinent, but they will nonetheless exist. It's up to you, you see, whether I tell you anything of these other images."

"Oh." That thought had not occured to Audrun. "And if I said no?"

The diviner's smile was brief. "You would be one among many; few karavaners want to think beyond the journey itself. I would tell you only what I read as concerns the karavan."

Audrun drew in her breath. Fourteen diviners had said

they must go to Atalanda—would this one be the fif-teenth? "Then, yes. Tell me what you see for my chil-dren . . ." She placed both hands against her abdomen. ". . . and for this child as well."

"Then give me your hand."

After a moment's hesitation, Audrun extended her right hand palm up. Ilona took it into her own and turned it over, examining the tributaries of blood beneath the flesh on the back of her hand. Aware suddenly of broken nails and roughened cuticles, Audrun wanted to jerk her hand away and hide it in her equally dirty skirts. But the diviner, as if sensing—reading?—the impulse, firmed her grip.

Cool hands, Audrun discovered. Cool, gentle hands. Fin-gertips traced the tendons and bones hidden just beneath the flesh, the lines across her knuckles, the fit of nailbeds into her fingers. Then Ilona turned the hand over, laying bare the palm with deep and shallow creases, the calluses of work.

"Be at ease," she murmured.

Under such scrutiny, Audrun believed that impossible. Especially when she was so tired, and an aching back robbed her of forbearance.

The diviner put her own hand across Audrun's, though she did not touch it. For long moments her hand hovered, palm over palm, then was drawn away. With the long mid-dle finger of an elegant right hand, Ilona gently traced the visible lines.

Audrun did not look at her own hand or at Ilona's, but into the woman's face, searching for a reaction that could be read merely because a wife, a mother, learned to do such things with her husband, with her children. It was not a gift, merely experience. But Ilona's face was expression-less. Almost serene.

A tingle crossed Audrun's hand. She looked down sharply, thinking the diviner had done something. But Ilona merely cradled the hand palm up as before, baring it to the freckled amber light of the pierced-tin lantern.

From the creases in Audrun's palm, tingling transmuted to moisture. Sweat, she believed, though she was not over-warm. But the dampness swelled, welling up to form droplets, then, as Audrun's stiffened hand trembled, trickled slowly off the edge of her hand to spot her dusty skirts.

Startled, she opened her mouth to demand an explanation. But the diviner spoke first.

"Tears," Ilona said. "Tears for loss, for grief, for confusion. And blood." She rolled Audrun's fingers closed and released her hand with a brief pressure of her own. "There is nothing in your hand that speaks of danger for the caravan." The diviner's eyes remained guileless and forthright, offering no unspoken words or warnings in the language of the heart. "You are free to accompany us."

"But—the other images you saw." Audrun felt apprehension rising. "There is danger for my children?"

"Tears," Ilona said softly. "Grief. Blood." Her eyes were fully aware of what could be inferred from the words. "I saw no more than that."

Audrun wanted to put to the diviner any number of questions, to request a deeper reading. She was on the verge of asking when Ilona rose.

"I'm sorry, but the night is full. Now we must see what lies in your husband's hand." She opened the wagon door onto the night again.

Dismissal. Audrun stood up, pressing the damp palm against her skirts to wipe it free of moisture. She moved past the diviner and descended the few steps, thinking over what had been said. Desperation and frustration had faded somewhat with the knowledge that Ilona saw no danger in Audrun's company on the journey, but Davyn's hand might offer different news.

Audrun paused, then turned back to look at the woman. She consciously tamed her tone; she did not mean her words as a challenge, but as an appeal for explanation. "None of the other diviners we consulted said any such thing as you have."

"I read true," Ilona said, "what is shown to me. But what is shown to one diviner need not be shown to another."

Audrun could not keep the irony from her tone. "That is—convenient."

Ilona smiled. "Isn't it?"

She had expected the woman to deny it, or take offense. Instead, she was amused. Audrun didn't know if that was ill or good. "Should I be afraid of this journey?"

"There is safety in more rather than fewer," Ilona said, "and that knowledge has nothing whatsoever to do with your hand. It is merely common sense. You and your family would do better to remain with the karavan than to take the other road."

"He may have told you that," Audrun pointed out, driven to debunk. "The guide. You may not have seen that in my hand at all."

Nor did that offend the woman. Ilona merely shrugged casually as she leaned against the doorjamb. "It doesn't matter what Rhuan may have told me. I have read your hand. I saw tears, and blood. I saw loss, and grief, and confusion. But it's true a charlatan could say he saw much the same, knowing you are bound for the road near Alisanos."

"He told you that, too? The guide?"

Ilona asked, "Does it matter? My reading is never dependent on information given by others. Only on what information the hand itself offers."

Audrun nodded, once again wiping her right hand against her skirts. She was tense with frustration, but knew that the conversation was ended. "I'll send my husband."

ILONA WATCHED THE woman walk away straight-backed into darkness out of fire glow, conscious of a regret that dug more deeply than usual into her spirit. Years before, she had learned how to shield herself against the emotions of others lest she be unable to withdraw from them; the blessing *and* curse of fleshly divination, such as hand-reading, required the sublimation of one's own sense of self into awareness of the client's.

Some hands were easily read. Others required more of an investment of her art, more sublimation of herself, and left Ilona exhausted. With this woman, mother of four and bearer of a fifth, Ilona had driven herself deeply into the sense of self, the inner heart, as hand-readers called it. That sense offered up to those with the art a doorway into the future. Some doorways stood open. Some were half closed, while others yet stood barely ajar. And then there were those individuals whose doors were not only shut, but barred and bolted from the inner heart.

The farmer's wife had been open, but pregnancy complicated matters. Ilona needed to separate the woman's self from the unborn's. She had managed it, just—the baby would be a daughter—but keeping mother and daughter apart had left her own sense of self aching with the effort.

Tears to be shed, and blood. A grief so painful as to harm the heart, the soul. All interwoven with the birth of the child.

But none of it spoke of danger for the karavan, and that was her only duty: to warn Jorda should the presence of anyone threaten the safety of the journey and the welfare of the people. It was not among the terms of her employment to read beyond the journey. Jorda had been explicit. She might spend herself too profligately otherwise, and be used up when Jorda most needed her. But this woman, this wife, was deserving of more. Ilona wished what she saw had promised kindness, not fear.

She sighed, gripping the doorjamb. The day had been long and she was wrung out; she needed rest for her soul as well as her gift. But the husband, the father, was yet to come, and it was imperative that she not only find the doorway into his self, but to push it open should it be closed.

Chapter 12

*U*NLIKE JORDA OR JORDA'S diviners, Rhuan did not own a wagon. He generally slept in the open beneath the vastness of sky and the cycles of the moon, watching Maiden, Mother, and Grandmother as well as Orphan Sky. But he did own a tent for such occasions as bad weather, and strung the oiled canvas shelter amid trees, binding guy-ropes to branches. When trees did not exist, which occurred often in the grasslands, and the weather insisted he do something more than curse it, Rhuan borrowed the sideboards of Jorda's supply wagon and pitched the tent to form a simple lean-to.

This night, the final night before departure, the tent was not set up but packed. Rhuan had intended to roll up in a single blanket upon a reed mat beneath the light of Grandmother Moon and the stars. But now privacy was most definitely called for, the need for *apartness* driving him away from humans, even away from friends such as Jorda and Ilona.

The horse he returned to the picket line. Rhuan stopped briefly at the supply wagon, collected a beaded leather bag, and sought that privacy.

He walked away from the cookfires, dying now into ruddy coals; away from the painted wagons, the humans, the people whose lives would, on the morrow, reside in his hands. For all that his wish was to be *of* them, his current need demanded something other than companionship among the folk who were, no matter how much he liked and admired them, alien to his race. The reason was simplicity itself: they would not understand. *Could* not understand.

Rhuan, walking farther yet, knew Jorda, despite his ignorance of the Shoia race in all but tall tales and legends—and the example set by his senior guide—did nonetheless understand that his guide now and again required that apartness, and asked no questions. Men in these times of civil strife often kept secrets. For Melior and Branca, the two male diviners, Rhuan spared no thought; only Ilona offered empathy as well as threat. Of them all, she knew more of who and what he was. He had told her nothing of himself save the sorts of things with which anyone might be trusted, but Ilona, in one brief moment three years before when Rhuan's personal wards were down—he was dead at the time—had seen in an instant just enough of his soul to be stunned as well as curious.

This custom she would never understand, nor be given opportunity to wonder what it was, what it meant to him. And so he continued walking, leaving behind the lantern glow within dyed oiled canvas, the gray-red ash of crumbling coals, the splashes of oily, ocherous lamplight seen in open flaps of such establishments as Mikal's ale tent, and the red-hued tents belonging to such women as the one named Audrun was not: Sisters of the Night. And when in wagons bound for other places, Sisters of the Road.

In a copse of looming, wide-crowned trees some distance from the karavan grove he found suitable privacy. Kneeling, Rhuan took from the beaded bag a rolled section of thin hide. He spread it on the ground, pausing a moment to pass gentle fingertips across the slick, buttery surface. Beneath the moon the hide glimmered faintly, a rippling herringbone pattern of palest coppery scales.

As sensitized fingertips brushed it again, the thin hide warmed. He felt the loosening of his muscles in response, the answering heat in his own flesh. Hastily Rhuan drew his hand away, biting hard into his lower lip to regain self-control.

When his breathing steadied, he selected other items from the bag and assembled them in careful juxtaposition upon the gleaming scales: an ivory comb aged to watery yellow, its arched spine carved into the shape of a dragon; a series of small leather pouches, each dyed a different color; a short length of thick, jointed reed plugged with wax at either end; a pale cream gnarled root.

Rhuan settled into a cross-legged position and began to untie and unwrap silken cord, to unweave dangling side-locks. The rest of his braids remained interlaced in the complex pattern woven together into the thick main plait hanging down his spine. He also took from the sidelocks all the beads, charms, and coin-rings and set them on the hide.

When the sidelocks were loosed, Rhuan took up the ivory comb and began to work through the rippled sections of waist-length hair. It required time, that; rebraiding would take more. By dawn he must be finished with the ritual and back at the karavan to aid Jorda and his travelers. For this reason he elected to undo only the sidelock braids.

Combing tamed the loosened hair, though the ripples remained. Rhuan took up the root, cut into it with his knife, squeezed a pale, soapy liquid into his left palm, then began to apply the thin lather to the unbraided hair. Beneath the moon it shone a deep ruddy copper, verging on bloodied black.

After cleaning the hair thoroughly, Rhuan unstoppered the section of reed, poured a measure of the contents into his hand, and began to work the oil through the loose hair. When the strands of hair glistened in moonlight with a delicate sheen from scalp to tips, Rhuan began the laborious process of rebraiding the sidelocks, weaving back into them all of the beads, charms, and coin-rings he had removed. With the addition of each colored glass bead, he told over the Names of the Thousand Gods.

At the completion of the braiding and the telling, Rhuan opened the series of small leather bags set out before him. He then nicked the tip of the little finger on his right hand, the heart-hand. The bloodied fingertip was dipped carefully into each pouch, lifting out a faint smudge of colored powder. He blessed the substances with a touch of warm breath to waken them, and closed his eyes.

Rhuan touched the finger to the eleven blessing points required by the ritual, all of living flesh: the middle of his forehead, the bridge of his nose between brows, each eyelid, the faint hollow between nose and mouth, each cheekbone, upper lip, lower lip, chin, the notch beneath his throat that joined the collar bones.

He opened his eyes. The world hazed red.

"No!" The blurt of sound from his mouth was not entirely comprehensible. "Not *now*—"

Sweat burst from his pores and ran down his body in rivulets. Flesh rose up on his bones.

Speech was denied. The refrain ran only in his head: *Not now—not now—not now—*

AS DAVYN RETURNED from his visit to the hand-reader, he found Audrun waiting for him beside the wagon, spine propped up against one wheel. He marked the weariness in her posture and face, the haphazard repinning of loosened hair, the worried expression in her lean, tanned face. At least now he could offer surcease from the latter. Smiling, he nodded and spread his arms. She walked into them.

He folded her into his embrace, tucking her head beneath his chin. "All is well. We leave in the morning along with everyone else."

Audrun's sigh warmed his flesh through the thin weave of his tunic. "I think I could not have borne it had we come this far only to be told we could not go on."

"Ah, Audrun, I think you could bear anything." He

kissed the top of her head. "Are the children in bed?" She nodded. "Then come with me. Only a moment, I promise, and not far; a shorter and less eventful day would have been preferred, I do know."

He took her hand and led her away from the wagon, away from the dying fires, where no light other than that of the stars and moon illuminated the landscape.

"There." Davyn set an arm around her shoulders. "Do you see it?"

Audrun shook her head, pushing loose hair from her forehead.

"Our future," he told her. "Beyond the dark, beyond the horizon, lies Atalanda, under the Mother of Moons. Our future and our safety."

"Overmountain," she murmured.

"We will build anew. What we lost was only wood and nails, and a measure of years. We have our memories, and our children, children who will grow up without the taste of war in their mouths." Gently he placed his hand across her belly. "This fortunate one will never know it at all."

She covered his hand with hers, but did not reply.

"Come to bed," he said. "You're weary. Best to let you rest without me babbling in your ear."

"Davyn—" Her weight was set against him as he made to move. "Did she say anything else? About our future? About the children?"

The query puzzled him. "Something else? No. Should she have? She told me there was nothing in my hand that suggested trouble for the karavan."

"Or for us?"

He shook his head. "Nothing of *us* was said, other than we could accompany the karavan as far as we required. But surely that's enough. We are safe among the others."

Audrun's smile seemed forced. "Then there is nothing at all to fear."

This time she led the way to the wagon, and to the bedding on the ground beneath the floorboards. With four children sleeping within, it was all the privacy they had.

ILONA SAGGED AGAINST the wagon door-frame as the tall, fair-haired farmsteader headed back to his wife and children. She was relieved to be done with reading hands for the evening, though the realization did kindle guilt. But she was exhausted. Now free of responsibilities, Ilona sat down on the edge of her narrow cot and stared into space a moment, then let her body fall backward to sink into goosefeather mattress and colorful blankets. She closed her eyes and drifted, detaching herself from the stress of reading hands. The thought of doffing boots and crawling beneath the covers fully dressed appealed, though she knew she wouldn't do it. She did, however, pull the ornamental sticks from her hair to free her skull of weight and restraint. She blew out a huge gust of breath, then smiled crookedly. Despite telling Rhuan she would only read true, not falsify her readings for the sakes of the farmsteaders, she had been able to offer good readings because that was what she saw. At least with regard to the karavan journey. She had not read beyond their departure from the karavan, when they turned off the main route to take the shortcut to Atalanda.

Her eyes snapped open. *The woman.* The woman in her dreams. The woman even Lerin the dream-weaver had seen, in profile with tawny hair hanging loose at the sides of her face, obscuring her expression, but now, *now,* Ilona knew who she was.

"Farmsteader's wife," she murmured. She sat upright again, loose coils of hair falling down around her shoulders. "Rhuan's farmwife!"

She saw it again in her memory. A woman in profile. A woman to whom she had spoken of tears and grief and blood.

Ilona frowned thoughtfully. She read the hands of others but could not read her own. She had never sought out a dream-reader because, as she'd told Lerin, her dreams were of the mundane, the unimportant minutiae of life as a karavan diviner. She had not, for as long as she could recall, ever seen a stranger in dreams who later arrived in her presence, and in the flesh. But it was incontrovertible. The woman who had sat beside her in the wagon, the woman who had confronted Jorda and convinced him to take the family on behind the Sisters of the Road, was the woman in her dream. A woman amid crimson lightning, roaring wind, heated rain, Hecari, and . . . "—a karavan turning around."

And then from outside she heard a voice calling her name. A voice she did not at first recognize; and then she did, in marked surprise. Brodhi? Asking for *her?*

Ilona rose and stepped to the door, pushing it open.

Yes. Brodhi. Supporting a sagging-on-his-feet Rhuan.

Later, then. The woman she had dreamed, the woman for whom she had read, would have to wait.

Chapter 13

"*R*HUAN."

Sprawled across damp grass, at first he didn't recognize the name, or the voice.

"Rhuan!" Hands were on him, straightening stiffly contracted limbs into something akin to the normal fit of tendon and muscle. He smelled the elusive tang of baneflower, a scent he associated with only one woman. And if Ferize were here, that meant the man whose hands were on his body . . .

Rhuan opened his eyes. Blood ran red across his vision, but he saw beyond the fading haze to the man kneeling at his side, setting order to his body. His stiff, aching mouth—he could not yet unclench his teeth—shaped the words without thought. "Not you!"

Brodhi said sharply, "Don't speak. Rhuan, hold still—you've convulsed. Let be. *Let be.* The body will loosen of its own, if you allow it."

Baneflower. Cool, soothing hands trapped his head. Not Brodhi's, those hands. But he wanted Ferize present no more than Brodhi. "Private," he mumbled, with what small amount of self-command was left to him.

She whispered something dismissive, sibilants hissing in the darkness, and did not so much as meet his eyes.

Nor could he meet hers. He did not dare it, knowing

what he would see. Contempt from Brodhi was one thing. From Ferize was quite another, and less palatable.

Of all the people he would wish absent from the moment, Brodhi stood highest. Inwardly Rhuan cursed. He was aware now of grass and leaves beneath his body, of night-chilled ground; heard chittering in the trees and the brittle, metallic complaints of locusts. "Let me be."

Ferize knelt beside him. Long-fingered hands lifted the freshly oiled and rebraided sidelocks. Her own hair hung loose and wild about her shoulders, framing a pale face. Accusation weighted her husky, somnolent voice: "You might have let one of us aid you."

Yes, he might have. But. Rhuan's blurt of laughter was hoarse. "No, no—there is no sense in calling on a kinship Brodhi would prefer to repudiate." Bile burned at the back of his throat. "I can't let it take me. Not before my time."

"Not precisely what *I* would ask." Brodhi's tone was dry. "But whenever are we in accord on anything?" And then, "No . . . no, Rhuan. Let be. It will pass."

"I *can't*, Brodhi."

"Here." Something was pressed against his lips. "Take it. Chew it. It's kevi leaf." Brodhi's fingers pushed it between Rhuan's lips, though his teeth remained locked behind them. Brodhi's dangling beaded sidelocks brushed Rhuan's throat.

Ferize's hands slid from pulsing temples to stiff jaws. She applied pressure he could not refuse; his mouth sprang open, stretching cramped muscles.

Brodhi pushed the leaf into Rhuan's mouth and jammed his jaw closed. "Chew it. Swallow it."

He managed to do so, barely. The juice was bitter, but as it ran down his throat he felt the locked muscles in his body beginning to loosen. The haze before his eyes receded. He ached all over, but his body was his again.

Rhuan swallowed the last bit of the leaf. He lifted arms heavy as stone, set the heels of his hands against burning eyes, and noisily sucked in air. Relief, that he could do so again.

Trembling had replaced the rigidity of convulsion. With effort, he managed courtesy. "What about you? Have you more kevi?" He lowered his arms and stared at his kinsman. In the face of austere disapproval, courtesy dissipated. "Or are you so disciplined you need no such thing?"

Brodhi didn't trouble himself to answer. "Go to sleep."

"Not here." Rhuan levered himself up on one shaking elbow. "I'll return to the encampment."

"I doubt," Brodhi said with exaggerated clarity, as if to a child, "that you can walk that far under your own power."

"You could. You *would*." Rhuan rolled, gathered himself, made it to his knees with a lurching upward thrust. Indeed, the kevi did threaten to undermine what self-control he had begun to recover. Instead of the knotted tautness of overstrained muscles, he felt thinned nearly to transparency, nerves twitching with fatigue.

He began somewhat shakily to gather up the items used in the ritual and return them to the beaded bag. A glance up at his kinsman's face showed no emotion. "I have employment, Brodhi, and duties, just as you do. Jorda expects me." He pulled closed the slender thongs on the last of the pouches, knotted them, and tucked it back into the bag.

"Humans," Ferize said. The single word, said as Brodhi might, held a wealth of implication.

Rhuan inhaled deeply, seeking patience and self-control. "Yes. Humans. Whom I choose to accompany." He looked expectantly at Brodhi, brows raised. "Well? Surely you have something to say."

Brodhi barely lifted a single shoulder in a dismissive shrug, stirring braided sidelocks. "It matters less than nothing to me what you choose to do."

Rhuan slung the bag over a shoulder and dredged up a sardonic smile as he rose, expending great effort merely to remain vertical. "But it apparently matters something to you that I, a fellow Shoia, not relinquish another of my lives."

"Among humans, it matters," Brodhi agreed. "Because then I would have to haul your rotting carcass all the way home to your sire."

Ferize, in black clothing and hair, was lost in the darkness save for her husky voice and the pearlescence of her moon-illumined face. Shadowed, her eyes were blackened hollows. "Darmuth should have been with you. If you intend to do such a foolish thing as that so close to an active Alisanos, at least you might be fools together."

"It was precisely *because* we're close to an active Alisanos that I did it," Rhuan retorted. "The idea was to cleanse myself, so it couldn't scent me." He flipped his newly oiled and adorned braids behind his shoulders and examined Brodhi's expression in the moonlight. "Don't you feel it?"

"I feel it. How not? But as our goals are very different, I am less inclined to look upon discomfort or discovery as an entirely bad thing." His tone sharpened. "Do you *intend* to fall down?"

Rhuan gritted his teeth against a wave of dizziness. "I intend to walk. To the karavan. And do my duty by Jorda, and by all the families—the *human* families—whose lives are mine to guard." He took a breath. "And so long as Alisanos stays put a day or two longer—or goes active in a direction other than this one—I will be fine."

"In the meantime," Brodi moved swiftly as Rhuan wobbled and closed a hand firmly around his upper arm, "I will see to it that you retain *some* measure of decorum before the humans you are to protect, or all your fine posturing will be for naught."

Rhuan considered protesting that he could walk perfectly well without Brodhi's help, except that it was becoming increasingly clear that pride was not enough to keep him on his feet.

Ferize came up on his other side. She was far shorter and slighter than he, but stronger than either of them. And so he was propped upon trembling legs and escorted through the trees toward the firelight beyond.

"When does Jorda's karavan leave?" Brodhi asked.

"Just after first light."

Brodhi said a single markedly obscene word in the language of their home, weighted with a contempt long familiar to Rhuan. He and his kin-in-kind had been no friend-lier in childhood.

"I choose it," Rhuan said in the same language. "*I* choose it. Not you."

"Rhuan—" But Brodhi cut it off, shaking his head. "Jorda knows nothing?"

Rhuan squinted; even the distant light of dying coals hurt his eyes. "Of what we are? No, only what he should know of Shoia, with one as his guide." Fingertips itched. He curled them tightly into his palms and swore. "Stop. *Stop*, Brodhi—"

"He's ill," Ferize said sharply, even as Brodhi began to speak.

With his last measure of strength, Rhuan managed to rid himself of Brodhi's grip and turned away, to drop hastily to hands and knees as the meal he'd eaten earlier exited his belly. Decidedly *not* what he wished to do before Brodhi, but his body left him no choice.

When he had cleaned himself and found his feet again, Rhuan declared, "This is not fair."

It startled a blurt of disbelieving laughter out of Brodhi even as he again steered Rhuan toward the karavan grounds. "Whenever has Alisanos *been* 'fair,' that you could say it is not now?"

Rhuan decided to let the question be rhetorical, as he had no answer. He gestured awkwardly with the arm Ferize held. "The supply wagon is that way."

"I'm not taking you to the supply wagon," Brodhi said. "I'm taking you to the woman."

"What woman?"

"The hand-reader."

Rhuan nearly tripped. "Why?"

"Because you would do better to rest where someone may be certain you don't choke to death in your sleep, and I have no intention of being that person."

"Oh, of course not." Rhuan attempted to pull his arms away from Brodhi and Ferize, and failed. "She may have someone with her." Someone such as the woman named

Audrun, or worse: Audrun's husband. Neither of them would place their trust in a guide who couldn't walk without aid. *He* wouldn't. "Brodhi, don't."

But Brodhi did. And as Ilona opened her wagon door at his call, dark curls falling to her waist, Rhuan saw in her face sudden startlement and concern.

"He's drunk," Brodhi declared, with an undertone of satisfaction apparent only to Rhuan and Ferize.

Rhuan opened his mouth to emphatically disagree, except that Ilona's surprise and worry had already turned to wry resignation. Brodhi had purposely chosen the one explanation anyone would accept the night before departure. Anyone except Jorda, who might very well dismiss him on the spot, guide or no guide. Possibly *because* he was a guide.

"Put him on my cot," Ilona directed. "I'll bed down on the floor beside it."

Brodhi pushed Rhuan up the steps; Ferize, who would not wish the hand-reader to see her clearly with the breath of Alisanos still upon her, remained at the bottom of the folding steps.

Ilona added, "Darmuth is with Jorda."

No more explanation was required. It would be a bad idea to summon Darmuth in front of Jorda to tend his fellow guide if the karavan-master was to be kept ignorant of Rhuan's state.

Brodhi dumped him unceremoniously onto Ilona's cot and departed without a word. The only portion of relief Rhuan could find in the moment was that neither the farmsteader nor his wife was present to see it.

But Ilona was. Hitched up on a single elbow, he became aware of her standing next to the cot, examining him critically. "I'm not drunk." He attempted casual confidence, but managed only childish defensiveness.

Ilona leaned over and placed a hand against his forehead, checking the heat of his body. Hair fell against his neck. "I know that." She pushed him down against the bedclothes with a marked lack of consideration. "Did someone kill you again?"

"No!"

"Good. Then you still have several deaths left." She took his beaded bag and set it aside, dropped a blanket over him. "Unless Jorda decides to levy one when he sees you tomorrow."

Chapter 14

*D*ESPITE RHUAN'S PROTESTS that he was perfectly capable of sleeping safely in his own bed with no supervision, Ilona did not allow him to rise from the cot. She knew enough of Brodhi—*and* the arrogant Shoia's low opinion of his friendlier kinsman—to realize that if he felt Rhuan should have an eye kept on him, an eye should be kept. It had briefly occurred to her to ask Brodhi why *his* eye couldn't do the keeping, but the question died unasked when she saw the woman shrouded in the darkness at the bottom of the wagon steps.

Brodhi. With a woman.

But the courier was an intensely private man, and Ilona supposed he might well have a woman at every stop along his route with no one the wiser. She had simply never seen him with a woman here in the tent settlement, other than his fellow courier, Bethid. And Bethid, Ilona knew, preferred women in her bed.

Of the woman with Brodhi she caught a glimpse only, before she turned her attention to Rhuan. But that glimpse, with thanks to the tin lantern hanging over the door, had briefly shown Ilona black, nondescript clothing, black hair, eyes shielded by shadowed sockets. And a face so pale as to approach transluscence. When Ilona had looked for the woman again as Brodhi went down the steps, she saw nothing at all but the man exiting, walking out into darkness.

And then she turned her attention back to her "patient." Who did not in the least evoke patience in her, but rather resignation.

He wasn't drunk, no matter what Brodhi said. She smelled no spirits on him. The salty tang of male sweat, yes; also an acrid trace of several substances she did not recognize, and the faintest whisper of scented oil.

She offered to brew him tea, but he was fading before she started the question and asleep before she finished. So Ilona brewed no tea. Instead, she pulled out her extra sleeping mat, cushion, and blankets, and prepared herself a bed on the floorboards. But she did not lie down at once, nor did she extinguish the lantern. She sat down upon her bedding, settled split skirts, and contemplated the man in her bed.

Rhuan in her bed. Which, she reflected with no little measure of irony, was unmapped territory for them both.

She had met the Shoia while she grieved for a dead lover, a guide killed by a Hecari patrol as he rode ahead of the karavan. With Tansit's death rites on her mind and his ruined body in Jorda's wagon, nothing in her answered to the Shoia's charm and immense appeal as it might have otherwise, another time, another place.

And then he had been murdered within half an hour of meeting her. For his bones, he told her later, when he was alive again; Kantic diviners paid very well for Shoia bones. But though Rhuan's bones were whole, the heart warded within them had been stopped.

If temporarily.

By the time Ilona had settled her grief—Tansit, unlike the Shoia, remained dead—Rhuan had insinuated himself deeply into the workings of the karavan. Her awareness and body woke to him—Ilona thought it likely every woman's body eventually woke to Rhuan—but he himself had never indicated any interest of a sexual nature in *her*. They were friends. It was a relationship in which she found great comfort and contentment, and she would not risk that by looking for more.

Ilona studied the nearest hand showing from under the blanket. Once, she had taken that hand in her own, intending to read it as the dead flesh cooled so she might learn what final rite would be appropriate for a man she didn't know. She had nearly lost herself in that moment, in him, transfixed by something she could only describe in a single word: *maelstrom*. He was unknown, unnamed, utterly untamed.

And alive, after all.

And she never again, until now, had the opportunity to read his hand.

The Shoia slept deeply, even breaths lifting the light blanket in an unceasing, steady rhythm. Without the animation evident when awake, his face nonetheless retained the appeal of the exotic: narrow, straight nose; high, oblique cheekbones; clean arches of bone over the eyes; hollows beneath the cheeks—no incongruous dimples appearing as he slept; a well-defined jawline; and a flexible mouth that, even in repose, retained the promise of laughter.

Rhuan and Brodhi resembled one another in many ways, from a similarity of symmetry in the arrangement of their features to a shared height and weight to coppery hair worn long in ornate braids. But Brodhi never even smiled that Ilona had witnessed, let alone succumbed to the laughter that ran so freely in Rhuan.

She asked Rhuan once why Brodhi was so austere, avoiding a cruder term, but Rhuan merely shrugged and said his older kinsman had always lacked a sense of humor.

Yet Brodhi had brought Rhuan here to her wagon because of concern for his kinsman's welfare.

Rhuan was patently not drunk, no matter what Brodhi said. Ill? Perhaps. But his color was good, his lungs were clear, and his brow lacked the heat of fever. A Shoia thing, perhaps, and thus kept private from everyone. But if that, why would Brodhi not tend him? Or Brodhi's woman?

Meanwhile, Rhuan slept deeply enough that Ilona knew she probably could read his hand without his awareness, but to do so challenged the friendship, risked the trust based on mutual respect and an acceptance uncomplicated by conditions and excuses.

Ilona sighed, smiled a wry smile, and began tugging a boot from her foot. Her senses were such, even in sleep, that she would wake if Rhuan's breathing altered; there was no sense in staying up with him. She as much as he needed a good night's sleep before departure.

BRODHI, SILENT AS always, slipped into the wheat-colored couriers' common tent, lighted from within by a hanging pierced-tin lantern. Timmon and Alorn remained absent, but Bethid was present and in the midst of changing into a sleeping garment. With annoyance Brodhi recalled human courtesy required—or at least strongly suggested—that he call out before entering, but Ferize's presence and dealing with Rhuan had put the memory out of his head.

He stopped short just inside, summoning gruff words of apology; but Bethid's grin and beckoning gesture reminded him before he spoke that she didn't worry about such transgressions.

Her boots stood neatly at the foot of her pallet, along with her gaiters, scroll-case, and personal items. Trousers, tunic, belt, and cloak dangled from a roof hook. Bethid herself sat cross-legged on the pallet, half-nude as she wriggled arms and stuck her head through respective openings in her baggy sleep tunic. She tugged it down, still grinning at him. He caught a glimpse of lean, sinewy torso and small, dark-nippled breasts in the dappled glow of the lantern.

"Do I care?" Bethid asked archly. Short-cropped fair hair stood up in a tousled thicket. "No. Neither should you. Though I'm not sure you *do* care to start with—you personally, that is, since I've never seen you show the slightest interest in women *or* men—in which case it really doesn't matter, does it, what you see? Of me, that is. And I don't care."

Brodhi elected not to decipher that. He knelt and began rolling up his bedding.

Bethid tugged the tunic into place around slim hips, watching his actions with dawning surprise. "You're leaving?"

Brodhi tied bedroll thongs, caught up his courier's accoutrements and a beaded leather bag similar to Rhuan's, then lifted down the blue mantle from its hook. The change of weight distribution upon the main pole set the lantern to swinging. Candlelight guttered. "I'm leaving."

She blinked disbelief. "But why? You're not heading out, are you? At night? I mean, leaving the settlement?"

He paused, genuinely curious, absently noting the speckled play of lantern light, shaped by piercings, swaying back and forth across her face. "Why should it matter to you?"

Her mouth jerked sideways. "I suppose it doesn't. I just meant that it's not exactly safe to travel at night, with Hecari patrols around. Even if what Mikal said is true and they haven't been here for weeks. We may be sanctioned couriers, but that never stopped the Hecari from doing whatever they like."

He slung the cloak over one shoulder and reached up to still the lantern. "I'm not traveling. I'm bedding down elsewhere."

Bethid stared at him. Then her wide mouth stretched into a knowing grin. "Ah-hah! You have an assignation." Her pale brows arched up. "Anyone I know?"

"I do doubt it."

Bethid didn't give up even as he stepped to the flap, lifting her voice as he slipped out. "Male or female?"

Outside, Ferize took substance from the Grandmother's thin moonlight, gliding from the darkness as Brodhi exited. She pulled the cloak from his shoulder and swirled it around her own until the rich blue fabric enveloped her slight, black-clad body.

"You might tell her," Ferize suggested as they walked away from the tent.

A twig snapped under Brodhi's boots. "Tell her what? That I have a woman—a *wife,* as they call it—and she happens to be a demon?"

"No. That I can be either human gender." In pale light, her smile was liltingly wicked. "Or both at the same time."

"Trust me," he said, "of this I am certain: no human could ever possibly understand what you are, and what you can do. Part of the time I'm not certain *I* do."

"And so I prefer it." Ferize, mimicking humans, linked an arm through his as they walked. "Which would you like to sleep with this time?"

" 'This time'?" he echoed. "Is there to be another tonight? Should I reach deep inside and summon what little strength you left me the *first* time?"

Her throaty laugh stirred him, as it always did. "Oh, I do believe you will find it, should you wish to." She lifted a fold of his mantle and smelled it, then lightly stroked the wool against her cheek. "Which would you prefer, male or female? Or both at once?"

Brodhi found within himself a laugh no human had ever heard. It was Ferize's doing, as always, be it actual sorcery or what she provoked merely by her nearness. "All, and everything. *If* you're up to it."

Ferize's response was less a human sigh than it was a feline growl, low and languorous, and infinitely pleased.

"In fact," he began—then stopped.

Everything stopped. The words he meant to say, the movements he intended to make, even the thoughts within his mind.

Emptiness, and a fleeting sense of loneliness.

With Ferize here? How could that be possible? She filled his soul—or whatever part of him passed for such.

He saw her face, turned up in the moonlight. Saw the questions in her eyes, the beginnings of a frown as her lips parted to speak.

Brodhi fell to his knees.

She called his name. He heard it. She knelt down beside him, placing hands on either side of his face. She turned his head and made him look at her. Sweat broke out on his face, rolled down his body beneath his clothing. Breath hissed through clenched teeth as he fought to regain self-control.

Ferize's expression cleared even as she pressed the film of dampness from his face with a corner of his cloak. She smiled, nodding slightly. "So."

Expelling a vicious curse, Brodhi wrenched himself to his feet. Everything ached. "Don't," he said through his teeth, breathing hard. "Don't you dare."

Ferize, rising, laughed.

Catching his breath was easier now. "Don't you *dare* tell Rhuan."

"My poor Brodhi, whose pride won't let him admit to any weakness. Most especially not to his blood-kin." She did not sound particularly sympathetic.

"To *that* blood-kin," he elucidated. "Specifically." He stretched his back, wincing, and felt his muscles laggardly relinquish incipient cramps.

"*Do* you have more kevi, or did you give Rhuan all of it?"

Irritation sharpened his reply. "I don't need any kevi."

Ferize laid a hand against her cheek, miming startled recollection. "Oh, of course not. I was forgetting. Shame on me." She resettled his cloak around her shoulders. "Well, come along, then. Let us discover how much stamina you have left for me, after a taste of Alisanos."

Brodhi gathered the things he had dropped when he fell, rearranging them for ease of carrying. Discomfort was dissipating, but a residue remained. "You find it humorous, do you?"

Ferize was not one to shield her words for the sake of his feelings. She offered a cheerful smile. "But of course."

Brodhi scowled at her. "You spent more concern on Rhuan."

She laughed again, the sound rising on the cooling air. "And again, but of course. He is the baby of the family, after all." She twined her hand into his. "Come along, my *dioscuri*. All and everything, you said. That requires time, and the night grows short."

Chapter 15

*A*UDRUN'S SLEEP WAS filled with dreams of blood, of tears, of grief. She saw her children struck down, swept away; she saw the wagon destroyed; she smelled the odor of death. Each image carried with it the clarity of true time, not the distance of dreams. And then the faces of her children disappeared, replaced by the face of the diviner. The woman who had given them admission to the karavan by reading their hands, but who had spoken the words that now filled Audrun's dreams.

She awoke when Davyn turned over in his sleep and accidentally jabbed her with an elbow. The dreams remained clear and vivid. From beneath the floor planks of the high, huge wagon, swathed in blankets shared with her husband, Audrun did not dream of the journey, but of the unknown danger threatening her children.

She fumbled beneath the layers of blankets and found her abdomen, shielded by the cloth of her tunic and skirts. All was stillness within. The child slept.

Audrun closed her eyes. *I could ask for another reading.* Surely the diviner would not begrudge her that. Once on the way, Ilona need examine no one concerning the safety of the karavan. She could read hands and discuss other matters.

But would she?

Audrun stroked the cloth covering her abdomen. *I was a fool. I should have done as so many others do, and asked for no images other than those connected with the karavan.* But she had asked, and now she knew. She was fore-warned. Yet it gave her no guidance as to how she might halt the events that threatened her children. She felt cheated. Knowing danger existed need not always result in tragedy avoided.

Tears. Grief. Blood.

The diviner had said nothing about the importance of reaching Atalanda before the baby was born. But Audrun realized with a sense of dread that tears and grief and blood might well be her portion if they *didn't* reach Ata-landa in time.

She turned on her hip and elbow and moved closer to her husband. But even as the nearness of his body offered more warmth beneath the blankets, Audrun did not, could not, sleep.

RHUAN ROUSED TO a bitter aftertaste in his mouth, a jaw aching from clenching, and muscles that felt like water. For a long moment he lay very still with his eyes closed, evaluating his body, until he realized the scents he smelled had nothing to do with himself or his own bedroll.

Ilona? His eyes snapped open. He lay on a cot he recog-nized by the colorful blanket, which was rucked up around his waist, and the carved wagon ribs curving over his head, charms and talismans dangling. Beyond the glyph-painted canvas roof covering, the day was beginning as the sun crept slowly over horizon's edge.

Rhuan sat up, suppressing a groan. Had he and Ilona—? No. He thought not. He recalled weakness, illness, Brodhi's and Ferize's half-carrying him to Ilona's wagon, and Ilona herself dropping the blanket over him. He had been in no shape for intimacies.

Rhuan pushed the newly braided sidelocks out of his

face and leaned over the edge of the high cot. There she was on the floorboards of her own wagon, which chastened him; it couldn't be terribly comfortable. But Ilona had taken the host's part by leaving the bed to him while she slept below in a tumble of bedclothes, cushion, and sleeping mat.

He opened his mouth to speak her name, then thought better of it. Best to let her sleep as long as she could on the day of departure. He had robbed her of bed; he would not rob her of rest.

Rhuan folded the blanket aside, collected his boots, and with great care avoided stepping on Ilona as he made his way to the wagon door. He caught a glimpse of tangled dark ringlets beneath a fold of blanket, smooth olive feet, a string of brass bell-shaped charms around each ankle. Despite the bells, she slept quietly without movement or noise.

Smiling, Rhuan sketched a quick morning blessing over her, then carefully unlatched the door and climbed down the folding steps. He paused to close the door quietly, setting the latch, then turned to pull on his boots and nearly ran headlong into Darmuth. Who was, Rhuan discovered, wearing a peculiarly amused expression.

Rhuan scowled, a boot hanging from either hand. "What?"

The gemstone in Darmuth's tooth glinted as he smiled. "Reading a hand must not be difficult when the entire body is present."

"She read no part of me," Rhuan retorted, bending to don boots.

Darmuth's smile didn't waver. "None?"

Rhuan gestured sharply for Darmuth to move on, lest the conversation outside the wagon awaken Ilona. "None. Nor ever will." No matter how much he might wish her to. He walked with purpose away from the wagon. "And it was Brodhi and Ferize who brought me here after the ritual, so blame *them* that I ended up in Ilona's wagon."

Darmuth's tone altered. "It happened again, didn't it? Only worse this time. That's why I smell kevi on you."

"You smell kevi on me because Brodhi shoved it down my throat. In his zeal to help me—amazing enough in itself—he nearly choked me to death. Which, I suppose, may have been his intent." Rhuan briefly eyed the brightening eastern horizon, estimating true sunrise. "We'd best go see what Jorda wants us to do."

"Wait." Darmuth's hand on Rhuan's upper arm stopped him. "This vow you swore about not bedding the hand-reader—"

"—remains in place," Rhuan finished. "I do occasionally keep such vows."

"You have just spent the night in her wagon," Darmuth said. "And, knowing your history—and that of your sire!— I am disinclined to assume vows may not be broken no matter how sincere the maker when he swore them."

Rhuan glared. "Leave my father out of this. As for me, my vow holds. And it was not my idea to spend the night in her wagon. Blame Brodhi for that."

Darmuth said delicately, "It is not beyond Brodhi's rather diabolical sense of humor to intentionally put you in position to break that vow."

The sun passed beyond the blade of the horizon. Around them the day awoke, and with it the karavan: a multiplicity of roosters, riding in wicker crates with various harems of hens, crowed the sun into the sky.

"Of course it's not," Rhuan declared, "though I'm not certain he *has* a sense of humor. And he may well have done just that. But I know him, Darmuth. Brodhi may believe me incapable of keeping a vow, but that doesn't mean it's so. No matter how he tests me." Behind him at the nearest wagon a particularly noisy rooster roused belatedly to join the morning chorus. Rhuan winced; the sound pierced his skull, which felt markedly fragile after the experience of the night before, and set it to aching. "Are you coming?"

Darmuth smiled. "Jorda will think you drank yourself into a stupor."

"Not if no one tells him I did," Rhuan declared, thinking of Brodhi's falsehood. "Such as you."

"I won't have to. Your eyes are bloodshot, and along

with smelling like ritual oil and kevi, there's the faintest wisp of baneflower. Likely he'll think you got drunk and spent the night with a woman or three or four. Certainly such behavior is not unknown to you . . . or unknown *of* you. You have something of a reputation." Darmuth paused. "And you did spend the night with a woman."

Rhuan turned on his heel, his strides long and pronounced as he headed toward Jorda's wagon. Darmuth, unfortunately, was very likely correct in his summing up of Jorda's reaction. That was the problem with reputations, he reflected glumly: accurate or not, people tended to believe the worst. If they weren't telling tales of his various conquests, they swapped stories about killings and discussed the likelihood that the latest victim was dead by his hand.

"Not fair," Rhuan muttered.

Darmuth, laughing softly, followed.

DAVYN, TEA MUG clutched in one hand, checked the fit of the yokes across the oxen's shoulders. "Good, good," he murmured, testing rope loops and knots, then nodded across at Gillan on the other side of the tawny beasts. "As soon as the women are out, pull and stow the wheel chocks. We've no time to waste."

There was much to be done, but he and Gillan had risen at dawn and finished packing up what could not be stowed until just before departure. The narrow sideboard shelves were swollen with small kegs of nonperishables such as flour, beans, and salted meat, roped to one another as well as to the wagon. Rough sacks of herbs and dried fruits and vegetables dangled from hooks. The thick plank drop-gate next to the back door of the wagon, suspended by lengths of oiled rope, held the big iron-rimmed water barrel.

The entire karavan encampment was in motion. Dust beaten by hooves, boots, and bare feet drifted into the air above the stand of trees, mingling with threads of cookfire smoke. Children shrieked and shouted, dogs barked, mules brayed, families and friends called directions to one another amid the din.

His wife, Davyn saw, had come out of the wagon and was covering the cookfire coals with dirt. She carried the kettle in one hand and her mug in the other; a familiar lift of the kettle asked without words if he wanted his tea warmed. Davyn joined her, extending his mug.

"Nearly ready?" he asked, but shut his mouth on the observation that she looked tired.

"Once Ellica is over this latest fit of the sulks, yes." Audrun sighed. "I'm afraid I wasn't terribly sympathetic just now, but I do wish she could understand that this is difficult for everyone."

"She will come to, eventually." Davyn kissed her briefly on the top of her head, then took kettle and mug. "I'll tend these." Grinning, Davyn poured out the remains of the tea from mugs and kettle, then banged them against the sideboards. "Ellica? May I come in?"

A startled, muffled refusal and flurry of activity resulted a moment later in the appearance of his eldest daughter.

"Ah." Davyn set mugs and kettle into Ellica's hands. "Rinse these quickly, then pack them, please. We are about to move out."

Fair hair hadn't yet been tied back, tumbling over her shoulders. Ellica's face was flushed from tears hastily scrubbed away, but more threatened. She wouldn't meet his eyes as she took the kettle and mugs.

"Ellica." He spoke quietly, privately. "Your mother is very tired and needs your help. *I* need your help." What he kept to himself was that he knew Audrun was also very worried about something. "May we depend on you?"

Her eyes flickered up to his. He saw a brief tightening of her mouth, a faint creasing of her brow, and then her face smoothed. She nodded.

"Good." He dropped a big hand to her shoulder. "Thank you."

Gillan came around the back of the wagon. "Everything's ready."

Davyn squeezed Ellica's shoulder, felt a slight lessening of tension beneath his fingers, then turned to other duties.

THE MUTED CHIME of her ankle bells roused Ilona from the shallow pre-waking doze. Her body reminded her she had slept upon floorboards despite the mitigation of mat and cushions; that recollection brought her fully awake. She pushed herself upright, looked for Rhuan, and discovered her bed was empty.

Ilona felt a flicker of regret, then banished it sharply. She lay down again and attempted a stretch to release the slight stiffness in her bones. With Rhuan gone, she had only herself to tend as well as the wagon. And they were to depart as soon as the karavan was ready ... Ilona abruptly ended the stretch and got up, untangling the folds of the split skirt and tunic she had slept in.

A few quick gulps of cold tea served to quiet her thirst, then she set about changing into baggy traveling trews and the knee-length tunic she'd wear belted over them. After that came a hasty washing of her face, a check of tousled hair she would have to tend once they were on the road, and the tugging on of soft doeskin boots. Though Janqeril would bring her team and hitch them, it was her task to make certain the wagon was ready to go.

Ilona opened the back door, discovered Rhuan had neatly folded the steps away for her, and spent extra moments unfolding them. It was that or jump down, and though she was more than capable of it, she didn't relish the idea of clambering up and down repeatedly as she finished the loading.

A glance at the sky told her she was getting a late start. Ilona grimaced reflexively as she climbed down the steps, then heard the snorting of her team as Janqeril brought them.

From the other side of the wagon came Rhuan's voice. "Do you need help?"

He was already mounted, she discovered, and despite arriving at her wagon in near collapse but a handful of hours before, appeared no worse for the wear. His hair was pulled neatly back into its customary braids, ornaments glinting, and he had changed into fresh leathers. Even his smile of greeting was completely normal.

Ilona opened her mouth to suggest he might make her bed since he was the one who had mussed it, but realized before she spoke that such words might not be correctly interpreted by passers-by. Instead she said, "No."

Dimples deepened in his cheeks. "I'll stop in again on my way back."

It was his duty, when not actively scouting ahead, to mind that Jorda's people be kept on schedule prior to departure. From the front of the karavan to the rear, then back again. Darmuth did it as well, as did Jorda, helping wherever necessary. Ilona nodded and watched him ride on to the next wagon.

She touched her face. Yes, it was warm. Which meant that yes, she had blushed.

Ilona swore and turned her attention back to her own tasks.

Chapter 16

BRODHI, DRESSED FOR the day, relieved himself behind a tree, then turned back to the bed he and Ferize had made of blankets and cloaks. She stood in the midst of tumbled fabric, slender body naked. This morning her hair was red, a vivid, shining red dusted with gold, and her slanted eyes, beneath equally slanted brows, were so pale a green as to verge on translucent. The fine white flesh, dappled by leaf-born shadow, hazed bronze and green and gold in curves and contours as she greeted the morning.

She was, as always, beautiful. But to him, in any form, she would be so. Smiling, he leaned against the thick-boled tree and watched her reacquaint herself with human form, legs spread, arms upstretched above her head, flesh sliding over bone and muscle like water over stone. Her head tipped back, spilling hair down her spine, and he saw the tracery of scale pattern at the hollow of her throat.

Musingly, he said, "What do you suppose a human would think, were he to see you now?"

"Now?" Her head leveled. "Like this?"

"Like this."

She lowered her arms, but inspected the inside of her left wrist. "He would undoubtedly call me a demon," she answered, brushing a thumb across the scale pattern staining her wrist. "And so he would be correct."

"And damned?"

"Oh, undoubtedly. He would be whisked away to Alisanos immediately, I am sure." A hand touched the top of her right breast. "What about you? Am I ugly to you in human form?"

"Human form?" His grin was lazy. "Well, some might call it so. Close enough, I suppose. But the pattern is upon you, and your pupils are slitted rather than round."

"Drat." Within an instant the scale pattern was banished and pupils rounded. "Better?"

"That depends," he replied gravely, "on your intent. In human form or no, I believe any of *them* would still view you as something—other. Something more in all ways. The women would detest you at first sight, and the men . . . the men, I suspect, would very likely lose the power of speech."

"Acceptable." Ferize bent and caught up the black tunic she had worn the night before. "I rather like this power over men."

Brodhi smiled. "I would expect nothing else of you. Why should your nature be any different here? Only the form changes."

But her mind had gone elsewhere as she dressed. "Rhuan is to depart today?"

"With the karavan, yes."

She pulled the black tunic over her head. "Then we should bid him farewell."

Brodhi blinked. "Why?"

Ferize worked her arms through the sleeves, tugged fabric into place, then reached for the skirt. "Is it not what humans do, give farewell to their kin?"

"I suppose."

"Then recall that you are a human among humans, and bid your kinsman a proper farewell."

Brodhi observed her a moment, assessing the undertone in her voice that spoke of concern. "I'm Shoia," he reminded her. "Shoia are not entirely human."

"But answerable," she said, pupils slitting again briefly, "to that which has power over us all."

So they were. So *he* was.

Suppressing the sudden knot of tension pricking his belly, Brodhi shrugged elegantly. "Then we shall go and bid a proper farewell to my kinsman. Who will undoubtedly be stunned to receive it."

WITH THE MASTER and his guides sorting out the conglomeration of wagons and teams that had made up the encampment, the karavan slowly worked its way into a serpentlike line. At the back, Audrun could see nothing of the leading wagons, or even anything of the middle, the belly of the serpent. There were still many wagons before them that had not yet gotten into line. Dust clouded the air. It was difficult to believe the rains were but a week or two away.

She heard a man calling out and looked for him, found him on horseback gesturing for a wagon with a red-dyed oilcloth canopy to fall into place. It was the guide, the one who had aided her with the karavan-master. Rhuan, he had said, before drawing his map of the route in the dirt. Once the wagon was on its way, he turned the horse and rode back toward their own.

Morning sunlight glinted off the beads and rings woven into his braids. He rode a fine dun horse, bridle ornamented with bead-weighted thongs. If nothing else, Audrun reflected, the guide was a man who believed wholeheartedly in the luxury of personal adornment. The coin-rings in his hair were enough to buy their wagon ten times over—and undoubtedly twenty teams of horses.

He reined in near the oxen, looking at Davyn on the high wagon seat. "We do not expect to make many miles today; it does take time for the pace to sort itself out. So even if your oxen are slow, it will not be a burden." His glance took in Audrun and the four children, as if he had intended the last for her specifically. Then he nodded and swung his horse around, heading back up the line.

" 'Ware toes!" Davyn called.

Audrun made certain the two youngest were out of the way as he set the oxen to moving. Collar bells clanked and the wagon creaked into motion, iron-rimmed wheels turning. She had elected to walk with her children rather than to ride, and now they set out alongside the wagon, chicks following the hen.

All of them wore the cloths Ellica had torn into squares the evening before, shielding noses and mouths against the gritty dust. She did not doubt Torvic and Megritte would shed theirs as soon as possible, but for now they were masked. And, she noted, pretending to be something other than human children tasked with walking as many miles a day as possible, with respites in the wagon when necessary. Pale-lashed eyes shone above the face cloths, and giggling was slightly muffled as they ran ahead of her.

How far? she wondered. How far to the turning they would make onto the road that skirted so close to the deepwood? Would they reach it in a week? A ten-day? So much depended on such things as the weather, over which even the diviners had no control; and on the people of the karavan themselves. It was the master's duty and that of his guides to make certain all was kept in order, to sort out which teams pulled better, which did not, which drivers had better control over their animals, and which did not. Davyn she did not doubt, and Gillan had his father's skill with livestock, but the charge made by the karavan-master was true: oxen *were* slow.

Ahead, the end of the line, which for them came in the guise of a high wooden wagon crowned with crimson oil-cloth. The Sisters. Four of them. Women of loose morals. But Audrun had meant what she said when she told the master it was acceptable, such closeness. They had no latitude to request different placement, when they would travel more slowly and thus cause more effort.

More than acceptable. Necessary.

Audrun drew in a breath through the weave of the cloth mask. They traveled now in such safety as was available within a karavan, instead of risking the road alone as they had done for so many miles coming to the settlement.

She set one hand against her belly. *For you,* she said silently to the child within. *Be well. Be safe. Be free of such threat as Hecari offer.*

ILONA WAS GRATEFUL her blush had long faded when Rhuan rode up from the rear of the karavan, as promised. She sat perched atop the high bench seat, booted feet set against the slanted footboard. Her legs were slightly spread to brace against road ruts and dips, but split skirts or baggy trews lent her modesty upon the road. She had stolen a few moments to twist wayward curls into a long rope of hair, then wound it against her head. Slender glyph-carved wooden rods held the thick coil in place.

She bestowed upon him a smile as he fell in beside her team. "How fare the Sisters and our farmsteaders?"

"Cohabiting without difficulty, for the moment. When the farmsteaders have time to think, they may spend it considering how best to avoid the Sisters." He grinned briefly. "Though the woman strikes me as willing to face anything, including whores."

Ilona opened her mouth to say something more, but broke it off as she marked the sudden altering of Rhuan's expression. She turned her head, following his gaze, and saw the other Shoia, Brodhi, waiting but paces away from the road. Next to him stood a woman.

Not the woman who had been with him the night before. That one had been black-haired; this one's hair was a brilliant red-gold, markedly more flamboyant than the quieter dark copper of Rhuan's oiled and beaded braids. In the fullness of the sun, she glowed with a vibrancy that commanded the eye. The woman the night before had faded into darkness.

It crossed Ilona's mind fleetingly to be startled *and* curious that Brodhi, ordinarily so private, had allowed himself to be seen in public with two different women. But her attention returned to Rhuan. His expression was odd. "What is it?"

Clearly distracted, he glanced briefly at her but did not answer. Instead he sent his horse through the opening between Ilona's wagon and the one ahead, cutting through the karavan.

The wagons, this early in the day, this early in the journey, did not move so quickly that Ilona could not watch the meeting of Rhuan, his kinsman, and the red-haired woman. She saw him rein in, say something, and after a momentary but telling stillness, he dropped off his mount.

They were nearly of a height, Rhuan and Brodhi, and usually very alike in posture as well. From a distance, one might not be able to tell them apart; she had herself mistaken Brodhi for Rhuan recently. But Brodhi wore the bright blue courier's mantle across one shoulder, and his body was unaccountably stiff. Ilona was a *hand*-reader, but she knew enough of the language of the rest of the body to recognize that Rhuan's kinsman was not at ease. It was unusual to see them together, and wholly unheard of for Brodhi to come so near the karavan twice in as many days.

The red-haired woman shot a glance at Brodhi that Ilona could not interpret because of the distance, but she sensed something akin to impatience. And then the woman deliberately placed herself between the two Shoia and made a brief, fluent gesture. Rhuan, after a hesitation, bowed his head as if in assent.

As if, Ilona realized, he gave precedence to her.

The woman put out a hand and drew Rhuan's knife. She took his right hand, his heart-hand, into her left, turned it palm up—Ilona was reminded of her own reading rituals— and sliced the blade across his flesh.

Chapter 17

RHUAN SHUT HIS teeth with a click as the knife cut into his palm. Blood welled thick and hot—always hot, his blood—running into the lines in his hand, then spilled between his fingers to drip onto the earth. Instincts cried out to stop the flow, to keep his blood from touching anything living, but he knew better. Not when Ferize had begun the binding renewal.

He looked hard at Brodhi, expecting familiar arrogance, but Brodhi appeared no more settled than Rhuan himself. He merely watched, brown eyes hooded, as Ferize cleaned the blade on the hem of her long tunic, then returned the knife home to its sheath at Rhuan's belt.

She turned then to Brodhi and, without speaking, drew his knife and repeated the ritual, cleaning and sheathing the weapon once the cut in his hand was made. When the blood ran freely, she looked from one to the other, waiting.

Rhuan was aware the last of the wagons had passed. No one now, neither Ilona nor the farmsteaders, would be able to see what was shielded by their bodies. Only that they moved, that they clasped hands in what might appear to be friendly greetings or farewells exchanged. No one would witness that paces away from the verge of the road, where grass grew thickly, their blood dripped onto the earth. No one would see that sod crisped, burned, turned to ash.

"Do it," Ferize said.

When they did not, sharing only a hard, fixed stare of dominance challenge, she grasped their wrists tightly and slapped the palms together.

"Let be," she commanded. "For once, let be. Neither of you loses should the other win. You share the blood of your sires, but nothing more. Be what you are required to be, by the bindings of the vows."

Brodhi's teeth showed briefly, but it was not a true smile. "These vows," he said through a thickened throat, still holding Rhuan's gaze, "are more than a little taxing."

"And so they should be," Ferize agreed.

Rhuan said through a throat equally tight, "We wish different things."

"That matters so little as to be irrelevant." Ferize's arrogance, when slipped free of self-control, was far more biting than Brodhi's. "Do you think the primaries care? They have so many offspring they cannot count them all. Don't place yourselves, either one of you, so highly in their esteem that it blinds you to what is real and what is merely wished for. Yes, you may become more than you are at present, depending on your goals, but until then you are but insignificant infants mewling for food when it isn't in the least convenient to feed you."

"Well." Brodhi's tone, after a pause, lightened to something akin to his usual irony. "That does effectively underscore our value, does it not?"

Rhuan's mouth twisted in sour humor. "Somewhat."

"It's done." Ferize closed fingers around their wrists again and pulled them apart. "Darmuth and I cannot be held responsible for you every moment of the day or night. The binding is necessary, and its renewal."

Rhuan looked at his hand. The blood was gone, as was the knife cut. The touch of flesh on flesh, blood on blood, had once again replenished that which within them was kinship. And, to employ Ferize's word, it was *irrelevant* that they were as different in spirit as they were in desires, he and Brodhi. Here, in this place, among powerless humans—equally insignificant infants mewling for food, though they knew it not—shared blood mattered more than mutual dislike.

Rhuan summoned a careless smile for Brodhi, knowing it would annoy him. "Blame our sires."

The comment told in the tightening of flesh at the corners of Brodhi's eyes. For a moment, a passing moment only, a reddish haze flickered across the sclera. Then Brodhi once again donned the habitual mask he wore in place of his face.

"They were fools," he said, "guided by base lusts. I will do better. But you, I do know, are very like them."

The brief blood-forced truce was broken. Rhuan turned abruptly back to his horse and swung up. As he gathered the reins, he ignored Brodhi entirely and looked only at Ferize. "Why do you bother? Do you believe the blood-bond will make us *friends* as well as kin?"

"No," she answered. "I believe it may keep you both unharmed in a place that is dangerous to your kind."

Rhuan flicked a glance at Brodhi. He suspected his own face mirrored the rejection of that reasoning. But it was done, the binding. Neither of them could hide from one another, even were they thousands of miles apart.

But neither could they hide from the knowledge of their begetting.

EVEN AS RHUAN turned his horse to depart, Brodhi strode jerkily away from him as well as from Ferize. But he sensed her with every hair on his body as she easily caught up. Anger flared anew, tingling deep in his abdomen and kindling in his genitals. His eyes felt hot, hot enough to burst. "You intended it all along. The binding."

"Yes."

"It wasn't about wishing farewell to my kinsman."

"No. That was merely a ruse."

He could barely keep the word from exploding out of his mouth. *"Why?"*

"Because you are an utter fool when it comes to Rhuan."

"You lied."

"In this instance I merely avoided the *details* of the truth," she clarified. "Though it pleases me to lie when necessary."

"I would expect that of you, yes, when it *pleases* you. But to me?"

Striding beside him, she cast him a glance that could have burned away the grass even as his blood had. "You have your vows. I have mine."

"You are my mate."

"Here, I am your *keeper*."

Though the wound had sealed itself, Brodhi felt the flame in his hand kindle once again. Keeper, indeed. Centuries older than he, infinitely more powerful, owing service to many others before serving him. And he was, she had said, insignificant.

He stopped short. Reached out. Grabbed a handful of shining hair and pulled her around to face him. His vision grew red.

She gave up a foot in height and nearly one hundred pounds in weight. Were she human, he could break her spine, snap her neck, crush her skull. But she was not human. Her pupils, slitted now in the face of his anger, and the scale pattern awakening in her flesh were visible reminders of who, and what, she was.

She placed one hand upon his wrist. He felt the nails altering to claws, tips pressing into his skin. Saw the shape of her mouth changing as teeth elongated.

His throat was full and tight. "Go back," he managed. "Go back to Alisanos. Go back where you belong, for surely it isn't here."

She reached up, took his earlobe into her fingers, and pierced it with a thumbclaw. She grinned at him as he hissed, displaying her fangs. "I could say the same to you."

Her departure heated the air. He felt at his earlobe, wincing. Blood smeared his fingertips. He shut his eyes a moment, seeking self-control. Once regained, he allowed it

to carry him back toward the tent-city, where he thought
the foul liquor humans called whiskey might do for a meal.

THE KARAVAN WAS ahead of him now; Rhuan
hastened to catch up. But as he did so a rider fell out
of line and waited for him. Darmuth. He brought his horse
alongside Rhuan's as they met and fell in together some
distance behind the karavan. This time Darmuth rode a
horse of flesh and bone, not a mount conjured out of
moonlight.

Something flared briefly in Darmuth's pale eyes. Pupils
slitted vertically. Then he grinned, gemstone flashing in his
tooth, as his pupils regained their human roundness. "Trust
Ferize to make it happen."

Rhuan, still disgruntled by the binding ritual and not in
the least interested in discussing it with Darmuth, shot him
a scathing look.

But Darmuth merely found it amusing. His grin widened
into laughter. "I can smell it on you," he said. "What do the
humans call it . . . hellfire and brimstone?"

Knees nearly touched as they rode side by side. Rhuan
knew if he drew away, Darmuth would simply follow.
"You're the demon," he retorted. "You should know."

Darmuth inhaled a melodramatically noisy breath, then
released it on a rapturous sigh. "Oh, I do so love that smell.
Brimstone commingled with flesh. With blood for gravy."
He nodded, eyes closed, then looked intently at Rhuan.
"Would you consider cutting off a toe for me tonight? It
would be a kindness for a hungry demon."

Rhuan stared at him. "You want to eat my *toe*?"

"You have ten of them. You can afford to spare me one."

"I'm not giving you a toe!"

"If you're squeamish, I could do it myself."

"I'm not cutting off a toe, and *you're* not cutting off a
toe." He paused. "Unless it's your own."

"No, no, we don't eat of our own bodies. That would be

self-cannibalization. We may dine on others of our kind, but not ourselves." Darmuth's tone was bemused. "I've been saving you against starvation, should the need ever arise. It would be easy enough. I could kill you, then decapitate and quarter you before you resurrected. Surely there would be enough of you to last quite some time." Pupils slitted again. "The arms and legs might be a bit tough because of the muscling. But there is no bone in the abdomen, and the organs nestling there are undoubtedly sweet."

All manner of distressing images tumbled through Rhuan's mind, as no doubt Darmuth intended. In reflex he put more distance between their knees and mounts. When he could sort out his thoughts again, he managed a small victory by keeping his tone light. "I suppose that would depend on whether you kept human form or took on your own."

"That is true." Darmuth considered it. "You wouldn't make so much of a meal if I were in demon-form. I should have to keep this form." He eyed Rhuan assessively, then grinned at his expression. "But not yet."

Rhuan used a trace of Brodi's habitual irony. "I do thank you for that."

"So, Ferize forced the renewal of the blood-bond."

Memory kindled into annoyance. "She did."

"It would make life more comfortable if you and Brodhi buried the knife. It makes no sense for you to bicker so much."

"It makes perfect sense for us to bicker so much," Rhuan retorted. "We're *dioscuri*. Worse, our sires are brothers."

"But you are here together on the same journey—"

"We are *not* here together on the same journey," Rhuan snapped, cutting him off. "Our destinations are incalculably different."

"The ending of the journey, yes, should you both achieve your intentions. But not the beginning. And surely not while the journey is yet unfinished."

Rhuan twisted his mouth. "I hold no enmity toward Brodhi. He is free to choose his future any way he pleases.

But he would do better not to view *my* choice with such derision."

"Well," Darmuth said reflectively, "it is somewhat of a character flaw, to be so stubborn."

"And arrogant," Rhuan added.

"And arrogant, yes."

"And unforgiving."

"That, too."

"Rude."

"Yes."

"In fact, I believe I would run out of fingers and toes were I to count up the merest portion of Brodhi's character flaws."

Darmuth brightened. "Well, if your fingers and toes are so inadequate to the task, perhaps you could spare one for me. The smallest toe, only, I hasten to add . . . it doesn't really do much, after all."

Inside his boots, Rhuan's toes curled. With effort he straightened them. "The last time I looked," he said pointedly, "Jorda had seen to it we have plenty of food supplies for all."

"Human food, yes."

"In human form, one eats human food. Even you."

"I'd rather eat humans than human food."

"No eating!" Rhuan declared. "Not of my toes, and not of various portions of a human body!"

"Easy for you to say," Darmuth retorted. "You're not the one trying to fend off hunger an hour after eating."

"Keep fending," Rhuan suggested, and kicked his horse into a lope.

Chapter 18

OVER FIVE LONG days, Audrun had grown used to the karavan's song, the constant creaking of wheels, the subtle tympani of kettles and pots clanking against one another, the crack of oilcloth in strong wind. But now, as she walked beside the wagon beneath the midday sun, the sound of hoofbeats coming from behind caught her attention.

Her first thought was for her children, all of whom had spread out, making their own individual paths next to the dust-clouded karavan road of twinned wheel ruts cutting through turf grass and sod. Ellica and Gillan were on the other side of the wagon and old enough to tend themselves, but the small ones weren't; she turned, calling their names, and stretched out arms and spread-fingered hands to gather in Torvic and Megritte.

They came, if laggardly, scarves dropped and faces already dirty. By the time Audrun had them safely in tow close to the wagon, the rider was abreast of them. The guide, she saw; and then remembered he had ridden down the other side of the karavan some time before. He flicked a glance at the wagon with Davyn atop the seat.

Audrun pulled down the dust-scarf from her face and asked sharply, "Are we too slow?"

"No. No, you do well enough." A graceful gesture dismissed her concern. "There may come a time, as I told you, when you must press the beasts to move more quickly, but not today. They've done well."

Torvic and Megritte were trying to free their hands from her grasp. Admonishing them to stay out of the guide's way and to pull up their face cloths, Audrun let them go, then turned her attention back to him. "And if they can go no faster?" She nodded her head toward the oxen. "They have had a hard journey from our farmstead."

He studied the oxen. She knew what he saw; knew what *she* saw, suddenly, that she had not paid attention to for some time, being taken up with her children and the demands of travel. Taut flesh, the suggestion of jutting hipbones, coats without the glossy bloom of good health.

Alarm registered. *He will say we must stop. He will tell the master.* She opened her mouth to beg him not to do so, but clamped it shut again. She had fought her battle with the karavan-master with an understanding of the truths of karavan travel and stubborn insistence. She would not weaken her argument by begging now.

With an experienced eye the guide measured the distance between their wagon and the one before them, the one with its rich crimson oilcloth drawn over curving ribs, and the one before that conveyance. Judging their pace.

Audrun could no longer hold her tongue. She was in possession of yet another truth and no lessening of stubborn insistence. "I do understand you would have had us wait a season. But your female diviner gave us leave to come. You told us to trust her. Surely *she* would have seen in our hands if the oxen could not make it, yes?"

Amusement flickered across his face. "Very likely," he agreed. "When you unhitch them for the night, lead them some distance away from the wagons, and wait."

That was baffling. "Why?"

"I will have a word with them."

She blinked in startlement. A word with oxen? "But taking them away puts them in danger from predators."

He grinned. "Not so far as to risk them. But it wouldn't be wise to let everyone in the karavan see what I do, or I will spend all of my days and nights tending everyone's livestock instead of performing my own duties."

That made sense, though Audrun still could not imagine how he could make the oxen move faster. "What will you do to them?"

"I told you. Have a word."

It was perplexing, she thought, but also rude. Audrun stretched out a hand to indicate her youngest children running ahead. "I can't 'have a word' with my own children and be certain they will obey. How can you expect *oxen* to obey?"

"Oxen are somewhat more malleable than children."

She awaited additional explanation, a *real* explanation, but none came. She gave up in exasperation. "Very well. I will have Gillan take them out a little distance, and wait."

He gave her such a smile as to carve deep dimples into his face. "We will get you safely to your turn-off, that I promise."

And she believed him. Merely by looking into his eyes, by hearing the warm certainty in his tone, she believed him. Was certain of him. She found herself wishing he would do more than that, in fact, wishing he would turn onto the shortcut *with* them, to be certain they would arrive safely at their destination in Atalanda—

Suspicion kindled. Audrun forcibly stopped that line of thought and frowned up at him. "Did you just 'have a word' with me?"

The guide laughed, assumed an expression of supreme innocence, then saluted her and rode on, making his way along the winding column of trundling wagons.

After a moment, Audrun pulled the scarf up over nose and mouth, debating inwardly with herself whether she, in the company of the Shoia, was more malleable, or less, than beasts such as oxen.

"I do hope less," she murmured dryly into cloth.

 ILONA, LOST IN reverie as her wagon bumped along the track, caught the movement from the corner of her left eye. Her senses did not fail her; she knew who it was before she saw him clearly, coming up from behind. And she intended to seize the opportunity. "Rhuan!"

He had been prepared to ride past her, clearly bent on reaching the head of the column. Now he reined in and brought his mount close to her wagon.

She fixed him with a stern gaze. "If I promise not to read it while doing so, will you permit me to look at your hand?"

He was mystified. "Look at my hand?"

She held up her own, palm out. "Your hand." As he continued to stare at her blankly, she adopted the deliberate clarity of speech people used with simpletons and small children. "The one the woman cut into. Remember?"

Blankness transformed into startlement. "What did you see?"

"I saw the sun flash on the knife, and I saw her make the cut." Ilona folded her raised hand into an admonishing finger, poking it at him. "And *don't* do me the discourtesy of saying I am mistaken. You've been avoiding me, I think. But it's been five days. Past time that hand was tended, before it rots."

He raised his brows. "What makes you think I would say you are mistaken?"

"Because you have before. But I saw you *dead*, remember? And then alive again, despite being strangled and stabbed and not breathing."

His grin was easy, posture relaxed. "Depending on the circumstances, I suppose I have." He raised his hand and displayed the palm. "But I need no tending, as you can see. No rot."

Ilona steadied herself over a rut in the road, then stared at his palm. There was no sign of a cut. Not even a scar. She scowled. "Other hand."

He changed hands on reins and displayed that one to her. She stared hard at healthy, unmarked flesh, searching for some hint of injury.

Rhuan abruptly made a fist and snatched his hand close to his chest. "No fair trying to read it."

"I'm not." She frowned at him. "Am I to assume, then, that whatever allows you to come back to life, if only six times, also heals such things as knife cuts?"

He grinned. "You may."

"And I should also assume that you have no intention of explaining *why* I saw what I saw?"

Rhuan merely continued to smile at her.

Ilona gave up with a sigh. "More secrets."

"Oh, I am full of them."

"You," she said, "are being insufferably male." She waved a hand at him. "Go on, then. Take your secrets elsewhere."

Rhuan laughed at her, then set his horse into a lope that would carry him to the front of the karavan.

EVENING HAD COME upon them. The karavan-master, as he did each day, called a halt to travel as the light bled out of the sky, and the line of wagons was turned off of the road so as not to block other parties coming through. Audrun was grateful to stop for the night; her back was aching. And Davyn had apparently noticed, because he put out their sleeping mat and blankets beside the wagon, then guided her to it.

"Sit," he said. "Here, lean against the wheel; I've got a folded blanket for your back." Even as he helped get her settled, he called instructions over his shoulder to the children. This night, Audrun would rest while the others handled the dinner chores.

She was grateful beyond measure and thanked him with a smile. Davyn cupped her head briefly in calloused hands, then rose to tend the evening routine.

Audrun closed her eyes. She listened to the sounds of the karavan settling for the night: teams unhitched and hobbled to graze, dogs barking, children free to play at last continued games begun the night before, the clatter of pans and shallow plates unpacked. It wasn't long before she smelled tinder burning as cookfires were built and lighted.

She opened her eyes. Davyn had things well in hand, including Torvic and Megritte. She smiled tiredly, then opened her right hand to study the palm, which had sprouted a new blister. But her mind unexpectedly jumped elsewhere: how was it the hand-reader could see such things in her palm as grief, as tears, as blood? How could she know?

And why had the woman's face come into her dreams?

Audrun frowned. Impulse took her unexpectedly. She pushed herself upright and rose. As Davyn passed by, she reached out and caught his sleeve. "I'm going to the hand-reader," she said. "Don't wait dinner. I'll eat when I return."

ILONA HAD SET up the accoutrements of her employment beside her wagon. Crooks with lanterns hanging from them, a colorful rug, the low lacquer table, blessing-sticks, even a stack of carefully inked cards. She was passable at using both sticks and cards, but neither was her gift; there were diviners who claimed them as their art, while hers relied on living flesh. She had already read hands for three different clients. It was not unusual, once upon the road when they had monotonous hours of constant movement, for karavaners to come to her for readings unconnected to the journey. Thus she was not surprised to look up and see the farmsteader's wife walking out of twilight into the circle of lanterns.

She wore homespun skirts, scuffed boots, and a long-sleeved tunic that reached to her knees. A rough triangle of cloth hung loosely from her neck; her face above her nose was streaked with dust. Hair straggled loosely beside her face. In deference to her pregnancy she did not encircle her waist with a belt. And though five months gone was not significant compared to the girth of later months, the woman's posture had already changed. Her body knew its job.

Without preamble, the woman asked, "Why are you in my dreams?"

Ilona, prepared for a greeting or the typical query concerning her willingness to read a hand, blinked in surprise. For a moment her body stiffened into stillness. Then she looked up at the farmsteader's wife—Audrun, she recalled—and asked, "Why are you in mine?"

"Mother of Moons," the woman said softly. Then she stepped forward and sank down before the table. There was no grace in the motion; she was clearly exhausted. "How can this be?"

Ilona shook her head. "Even the dream-reader couldn't explain it all."

Audrun extended her hand. "Perhaps you can."

Ilona drew in a long, slow breath, then exhaled as slowly. She took the work-worn hand into her own. But this time, as she summoned her gift, as she studied the hand, she felt something pushing against her. She could not go in, could not sublimate, could not see. The hand was merely a hand, not a gateway to the future. A curious blankness smothered her gift.

Ilona lifted her eyes to meet those of the farmsteader's wife. Audrun. With effort she suppressed the tremble in her voice. "I see nothing."

Audrun frowned. "How can you see nothing?" She looked down at her hand still enclosed in Ilona's. "Are the tears gone? The grief?"

"I see *nothing*," Ilona repeated, with emphasis on the last word. She moistened dry lips. "Your hand is blocked from my art."

"What does that mean?"

"I don't know," Ilona told her honestly. "It's never happened before."

Audrun stared down at her hand. "Nothing?"

"Nothing," Ilona confirmed. "I don't know why . . . but something is blocking me. Something is preventing me from reading your hand." She looked into Audrun's eyes: saw weariness, worry. And fear.

"Do I die?" Audrun asked quietly.

"No," Ilona said quickly. "That is, I have seen death in other hands. It's nothing like this. That, I promise you."

After a moment, Audrun drew her hand away. She curled the fingers into her palm. "I have dreamed what you told me. Tears. Grief. Blood. I have seen my children in danger, in those dreams. Why are *you* there?"

Ilona shook her head. "I don't know—any more than I know why you are in mine."

"But you are a diviner," Audrun protested. "Isn't it your lot, to see such things? To dream such things?"

"Were I a dream-reader, yes. But I'm not. My gift is specific. I think it's why I've always dreamed about boring, routine things. I don't see people, other than as shapes and shadows." She took up the blessing-sticks almost without thought and began to turn them in her hands. It gave her something to do. "My apologies. I wish I could tell you more. But there is something in you that blocks my art."

Audrun's brow creased. "It can't be me. I have no idea how to do such a thing."

Ilona looked into her brown eyes. "Perhaps it's the child."

For a long moment Audrun only stared back. Then she shook her head slowly. "It can't be the child. How could it be the child?"

Ilona gripped the blessing sticks in her hands. "Diviners come to their gifts at all ages."

Audrun was astonished. "You're saying my *child* may be a diviner?"

"I don't know." Ilona was tired of admitting her ignorance. "I can only speak to how it came upon me. What little I know of other diviners—" She thought of Branca and Melior, "—is that in general there is an event in one's life that kindles the gift."

"This child isn't even born yet," Audrun protested. "How can it have experienced any kind of event?"

Ilona had never felt so ignorant as she did now. Audrun's questions were valid, and yet she, a hand-reader, could give her no answers that made any sense, if she had an answer at all. "I'm sorry."

Audrun was frowning. "All the diviners I saw said the

child must be born in Atalanda. None of them—none of *them!*—said anything at all about this child being a diviner."

"It's only one possibility," Ilona told her. "It may not be true."

"If it should be true . . ." Audrun thought a moment. "If it should be true that my child is to be a diviner, is there anything I must do?"

Ilona smiled. "The gift comes, or it doesn't. There is nothing *to* do."

Audrun's gaze was steady. "What did your parents think, when your gift came upon you?"

"Ah." Ilona looked down at her hands, saw that she was clenching the blessing-sticks hard enough to whiten her knuckles. "My parents considered it a curse. I was turned out."

" 'Turned out,' " Audrun echoed in astonishment. "Turned out from your home?"

"Yes."

"At what age?"

"Twelve."

"No," Audrun said, "oh, no. How could they? You were a child!"

For years, Ilona had suppressed that pain. She did so now, concentrating instead on the farmsteader's wife. "As you love your other children, love this one," she said. "In all ways but one, it will be a perfectly normal child."

Audrun nodded slowly. "You were twelve, you said, when your gift came upon you." Her hand dropped below the surface of the table; Ilona knew the woman was touching her belly. "Is it possible for this gift to be kindled in the womb?"

Ilona set down the blessing-sticks. She made her hands lie quietly on the table. "I think a gift from the gods might be kindled at any moment. But for your child?" She shook her head. "I have no answer."

"Well." Audrun smiled faintly. "I suppose we will know in four months." She rose, briefly pushing against the table to steady herself as she straightened. "I thank you for your time. I will send one of my oldest to you tomorrow, with payment."

Ilona too had risen. She made a gesture. "No. Nothing is necessary. Jorda pays me a wage."

"I wish to," Audrun said. "You have given me hope."

Ilona did not see how. But she would protest no more; many of her clients pressed something upon her. Audrun thanked her, twitched her skirts into place, and walked out of the lantern light into darkness.

RHUAN RODE THE perimeter as he did each night before seeking his sleeping mat and blankets. The cookfires had been banked, casting a quiet, ruddy glow from coals that would be brought back to flame for the morning meals. Each evening after dinner the karavaners wandered from one fire to another, making friends, exchanging stories; it was not unusual for songs to be sung. Children, wearied by the day even if they denied it, played games after the evening meal, then fell asleep while leaning against a mother or father. The occasional dog barked. Teams hobbled nearby snorted as they grazed, blowing soil from their nostrils. Overhead, Grandmother Moon had given way to the Orphan Sky, but even on a moonless night the stars lent enough light for a karavaner to see his way.

He saw movement from the corner of his eye. His attention focused sharply. There was a break at the end of the line of wagons, a pronounced distance between the red-topped wagon of the Sisters and the less-garish conveyance belonging to the farmsteaders. It was as if the oxen could go no farther and stopped in mid-stride. Rhuan didn't like the distance between the karavan and the farmsteaders' wagon. But as he formulated the right approach to giving an order, he saw the woman, the wife and mother, passing by the Sisters' wagon. It was an opportunity. Rhuan rode in close, and as she looked up, startled, he dropped off the horse and fell in beside her. Smiling, he opened his mouth to make an innocuous comment, but then saw the strained expression on her face.

"What's wrong?" he asked sharply.

She stopped walking, but did not turn to face him. Her posture bespoke weariness and worry. He could see her face clearly because of superior night vision. Coal-glow wasn't kind to her.

But she ignored her question and asked a different one. "How much farther?"

His mount pulled against the reins, seeking grass. "How much farther for what?"

"To the turnoff," she answered. "The road you've warned us against."

"Two full days, give or take," he told her, "depending on our pace."

She nodded. Her expression was one of distraction.

Rhuan knew better than to raise the topic of the family turning back. "Let me warn you that the road is little more than a track fit for goats. It has been years since anyone used it regularly."

"Perhaps that will be our protection," she said. "No bandits, no Hecari."

"Very possibly."

She looked directly at him, chin raised. "Why is it that you know so much about this road?"

"I've been on it," he replied. "Now and again, I ride it. As a guide, it's my responsibility to find safe routes. Different routes. In season, I ride with Jorda. Out of season, I ride the land."

"It strikes me," she began, "that a shortcut to Atalanda would be a good thing."

"Oh, indeed. Particularly with so many people leaving the province."

"Is there no way to make that road safe?"

Rhuan's brows shot up. "Against Alisanos?"

Even in darkness, he saw color flare in her face. "Against Alisanos."

"Well," he said, "if he were still alive, I'd suggest you ask the man who came to the settlement after escaping Alisanos. The man who had claws and scales in place of hands and flesh." He saw that register. "In the meantime," he gestured toward the wagon she shared with her family. "I wish you a restful night."

Chapter 19

MIKAL HAD TIED up the ale tent door flaps to let in light and breeze, though the latter had not yet come up. Brodhi paused in the opening, side-stepping the dangling charms and unlighted lantern hanging from the ridge pole, and discovered he was not the only one in search of liquor before the noon hour.

Kendic, titular captain of the loose confederation of men called the Watch who attempted to deal with trouble among the tents, sat at a rickety table near Mikal's crude bar, tankard at hand, pitcher in the center of the small plank table. With him, short fair hair mussed as usual, elbows planted on the tabletop, was Bethid, blue courier's cloak tossed beside her on the bench across the table from Kendic.

Two other men Brodhi didn't recognize sat at a similar table on the other side of the tent, deep in conversation over a desultory dice game. They paid his entrance brief attention, marked his presence as no concern of theirs, and turned back to their game. Kendic's hazel eyes widened as Brodhi slid by the drape of oilcloth.

Bethid turned to look. "Brodhi!" She windmilled one arm in a broad gesture for him to join them. "Sit your pretty ass down here with us, won't you?"

He desired no such thing as to sit his pretty ass down

with those two. But days later he was still unsettled by Ferize's behavior and found himself moving toward the humans regardless, shrugging out of his courier's cloak. He hooked out a stool with his foot, borrowing it from another table, then sat down and tossed his cloak to land atop Bethid's.

Brodhi caught Mikal's questioning eye. "Whiskey."

"Whiskey?" Bethid stared at him. "That's not your usual poison."

Kendic also stared at him, then shifted his gaze as Brodhi's eyes locked with his. Brodhi merely said, "What poison I choose to drink is my own affair."

Bethid scowled at him. "Of course it is. Do we care? Of course we don't care. You make it plain you want no one to assume anything about you. Which of course makes everyone do it." She drank from her tankard, then thumped it down again as she licked foam from her upper lip. "Did you hear about the murder a few days back?"

"Wait." Kendic, big and sandy-haired with a scar across his bristly chin, raised a forestalling hand. The forefinger was knobbed and crooked from an old injury. "Be fair, Beth. We don't know that it was murder."

Her smile verged on triumph. "Rhuan was involved."

That was worth some interest. Brodhi looked at Kendic for clarification.

The big man sighed and rubbed a hand across a scruff of beard. "Rhuan swore the man died when he fell and hit his head on Hezriah's anvil. Or died a moment before, and then fell. The point, Rhuan says, is that *he* didn't kill him."

Bethid's shrug was dismissive. "Rhuan's killed people before."

"Other places, maybe," Kendic replied evenly. "He says never here."

The female courier fixed Brodhi with a sharp eye. "He's your kinsman . . . what would you say to this? Is it likely? *Has* he killed people here?"

Mikal arrived with a battered pewter cup and set it down before Brodhi. The eye-watering odor of raw whiskey permeated the table. "If Rhuan's killed anyone," the ale-keep declared, "he had good reason. Enough folk have tried to kill *him*." His mouth jerked briefly. "And some have succeeded. I was here the night he first met Ilona, when two men killed him outside in the dark."

Bethid shook her head, setting her brass ear-hoops to swinging, and smiled crookedly at Brodhi. "Don't know that I'll ever get used to you and Rhuan being able to come back to life. Handy, though, I will admit."

Brodhi ignored the comment and looked at Kendic, who shrugged heavy shoulders and elaborated. "Hezriah says he didn't see what happened clearly enough to know if Rhuan did it. And in view of what the dead man was, it doesn't really matter. Dead is likely better."

Brodhi picked up the cup, brought it close, and inhaled. The odor was unimproved. He considered setting the cup back down again, but Mikal lingered, obviously waiting for Brodhi's response, dark brows raised and his mouth twisted in an expression of droll anticipation.

If he didn't drink the whiskey, he would lose face before the humans. With an inward sigh, Brodhi brought the cup to his lips and swallowed. The liquor burned through his chest and down into his belly, where a small bonfire was lighted. Mikal grinned.

When he thought he could speak normally again, Brodhi said, "Why is dead better?" It certainly was not, in his experience, a philosophy humans held.

Bethid, Mikal, and the Watch captain exchanged glances. It was Kendic who answered, in a voice carefully stripped of emotion. "He wasn't a man anymore."

"Came out of Alisanos," Bethid added pointedly.

Brodhi recalled the gaggle of children who had accosted him, talking about a demon. Something about him being at their wagon with their mother. He drank more whiskey, decided he didn't care what the humans thought and set the cup aside. "Alisanos does now and again disgorge what it takes in."

"Changed, though, aren't they?" Bethid's blue eyes were bright with fascination. "I've heard those who go in the deepwood and come out—*if* they come out, that is—aren't human anymore."

Brodhi opened his mouth to comment but was interrupted by noise from outside. One shout was joined by another, and another by a third. It was taken up tent by tent, person by person, until a chorus of voices called out one word of mutual fear and warning: *Hecari*.

Hecari in the settlement.

Kendic swore, then pushed away from the table to rise. He caught Brodhi's eye. "Will you come?" he asked abruptly. "I speak a little of their heathen tongue, but not enough as to make a difference. They say couriers have to know it."

"*I'm* a courier and *I* know it," Bethid said, annoyed by being overlooked. Then she waved a hand to indicate she understood why Kendic had looked to Brodhi. Her mouth twisted. "Go on. They'll only speak to a woman if they have no other choice."

Mikal closed a hand around the amulet he wore at his throat on a greasy leather thong, reciting a common supplication to the gods to preserve his life and business. As Brodhi and Kendic exited the ale tent, the two strangers, expressions apprehensive, slipped out the back.

That wouldn't save them, Brodhi knew. The Hecari were not so stupid as to leave escape opportunities open.

KARAVAN GUIDE DUTY was an unending plethora of tasks and responsibilities. Now, beneath the sun at its zenith, Rhuan and Darmuth rode well ahead of the wagons to find and secure the expected, such as a known watering place, or to discover and prepare for the potentially *un*expected, such as fouled water or the presence of predatory animals, possibly even bandits.

In high summer, the rolling grasslands were lush. Lone trees were scattered hither and yon like dice in an elaborate counting game bisected the horizon. Wheel ruts cut through turf to rich soil beneath, where it was exposed to the drying sun and the depredations of hooves and wheels. The rains had not yet begun so dust stirred by passage was a constant companion once morning dew dried. After the monsoon arrived, passage would be made nearly impossible by mud and thick, fast-growing grass. Jorda's final karavan of the year skirted the line between the dry season and the wet.

Rhuan, who preferred the temperate, even hot days of summer to the rains or colder seasons, relaxed nearly to bonelessness upon his spotted mount. He gloried in self-indulgent languor, smiling face turned up to the sun. Were he alone, he would strip out of every scrap of clothing so his skin could soak up the warmth. It was in him to express his pleasure with a long, insouciant purr, but he desisted lest his companion mock him.

Darmuth, riding abreast upon a dark sorrel gelding, did no such thing. Frowning, he said, "*There.* I can smell them."

Rhuan's lassitude fractured, replaced by sharp attention. "Hecari? Or bandits?"

Darmuth tilted his head slightly as his pupils slitted, then inhaled sharply. Catlike, his mouth dropped open to evaluate the scent. With a hiss underscoring the word, he said, "Hecari."

The news was not unexpected, but unwelcome all the same. Indolence and sunshine were forgotten. "How far?" Rhuan asked. "How many?"

Darmuth's pale eyes were half-lidded, almost as if he were in a trance. His tongue, narrower than was found in humans, extruded, displaying a subtle, serpentine fork as it tasted the air.

He withdrew it, retreating to the guise of a human male. "Perhaps a mile ahead. Ordinary patrol: six warriors. Moving this way."

Rhuan never asked Darmuth if he was certain of such announcements. The demon always was. Instead he nodded grimly and swung his horse around. "Wait here. Hold them for as long as you can."

Rhuan's duty now, with Darmuth posted as both lookout and delaying tactic to buy the karavan time, was to ride back to warn Jorda, to prepare the people for the meeting and the inevitable Hecari demand for "road tax." The karavan would lose hours to the patrol. Good water lay on the other side of the Hecari; they would now lack the time necessary to reach the next stop before nightfall. No water barrel in Jorda's karavans was allowed to be more than half empty if possible; the master would call for strict conservation measures until barrels could be refilled. But for all that good water was critical, it was more vital yet to receive the Hecari patrol without complaint, to pay what they asked in coin and goods so that no lives were lost.

EVEN AS BRODHI followed Kendic out of the ale tent, the winnowing had begun. Mounted Hecari warriors with warclubs rode through the mazelike pathways among the tents, sorting the men from the women, the children from youngest to eldest, ordering the designated into specific lines upon the pathways. Kendic stopped short but paces away from Mikal's ale tent, staring in shock.

Dark men on dark horses. Too many to count and all of them in motion, but their numbers clearly were well in excess of the customary six-person patrols that collected "tax" from the people. Skulls were shaven except for black scalp locks, and gleamed with pungent oil. The lower halves of broad faces were painted indigo. Heavy golden ear-spools stretched earlobes into long teardrops of flesh, and each Hecari wore slantwise across his chest a red-dyed leather baldric bearing blowpipe and feathered darts tucked into sinew loops.

Standing beside Kendic and aware of Bethid and Mikal coming up behind them, Brodhi noted that the Sancorrans' initial anger and shock had been transformed to fear, then to terror as everyone was ordered or pulled from tents, roughly inspected, sorted, and assigned a place to stand. The Hecari, directing with warclubs, counted down the winding lines and motioned specific men, women, and children to step forward.

Brodhi's emotions, trained into reflexive quietude in times of danger, stilled. He knew what was to come. "Too many," he murmured.

"One Hecari is too many," Kendic growled beneath his breath.

Brodhi shook his head. "You misunderstand me. Too many tents. Too many people all in one place. I have seen this before. It will be a decimation."

Bethid's voice was thin. "One in ten."

"One in ten?" Mikal's apprehension was clear. "What do you mean, one in ten?"

Brodhi knew Bethid, courier-trained to witness and record for dissemination, comprehended as well as he what was to come. She bit into her lip. "Mother of Moons . . ."

Kendic frowned. "I don't understand. Aren't they here for their 'tax'?"

Children forcibly separated from their parents were crying loudly, clinging to one another. If they tried to go back to their parents, the Hecari used their clubs to prod them away.

"Oh, no," Bethid blurted. "Oh, Mother, that one's coming over here."

Kendic quivered with tension. "Hold your ground," Brodhi told him. "No matter what is done, hold your ground. Make *no* complaint."

The Hecari warrior halted his roan horse in front of the four. Disease had pitted his face so badly the scars showed even beneath the dark paint. His nose, characteristic of his race, was wide and slightly flat. He had, as the others in his party, shaved his eyebrows. Ear-spools dangled in stretched lobes.

Black eyes glittered as he stared down at Brodhi. A gesture with his warclub indicated the blue mantle. The Sancorran word was guttural. "Courier?"

Brodhi did not include Bethid despite her identical mantle. In Hecari he answered, "Yes."

The warrior stared at Mikal and Kendic. He ignored Bethid altogether. Then his gaze returned to Brodhi. Still he spoke Sancorran. "With you, these?"

Again Brodhi answered, "Yes."

"Tell. Tell all." The warrior's gesture indicated the lines of frightened humans. "You know. Tell."

Brodhi drew in a long breath, then slowly released it. He adopted the emotionless detachment of his duty and raised his voice, pitching it to carry. *Do nothing! Do nothing, and you may survive!*

The Hecari gestured with his warclub. "Again. More."

"Mother," Bethid whispered.

Kendic repeated, "What does he want?"

Louder this time. *"Do nothing,"* Brodhi called again. *"Nine left alive is better than ten dead!"*

The warrior grunted and swung his horse away, returning to the winding lines of Sancorrans.

Kendic turned sharply to Brodhi. "What do you mean?"

"One in ten," Bethid murmured.

It was not the answer the Watch captain desired. "They've come for coin before, but they've never done this. Why are they doing this?"

Brodhi spoke with excessive clarity, as if to a child. "Too many in one place."

Kendic's face was blank with incomprehension. Then abruptly it drained of color as the first warclub fell, shattering a skull.

RHUAN WASTED NO time returning to the caravan and informing Jorda of the patrol ahead. A single word sufficed: *Hecari.*

Atop the high wagon seat, the red-haired man muttered a brief but eloquent curse, applied the hand brake sparingly, then eased his team of horses to a halt. "Go on, then." Grim, he nodded at Rhuan, digging beneath his shirt for a string of protective amulets. "You know what to tell them."

Wagon by wagon, Rhuan rode along the line with word of the stoppage and its cause. He had little time for details, but quietly reminded everyone to recall the procedures and suggested behaviors Jorda had explained thoroughly

before they had departed the settlement. Children fell
silent at their parents' sharpened orders while color
drained from every adult face. In place of questions were
prayers and petitions, forming a chain of low-toned voices
and frantic whispers invoking protection.

At last Rhuan reined in at the back of the column, behind the Sisters, noting that the farmsteader now walked
while his wife rode the plank seat. The youngest children
were not to be seen; Rhuan assumed they napped in the
wagon. The husband and his two eldest walked beside the
oxen.

Their clothing and hair was coated with road dust. As
they pulled down their scarves, they bared the pallor of
cleaner features. Also they bared simple curiosity; their
late arrival at the karavan had rendered them innocent of
such behavior around Hecari as Jorda had described.
Rhuan had drawn his map in the dirt and discussed the
route with them, but Jorda was always the one who spoke
of Hecari, not he. And Rhuan's concern for their nearness
to Alisanos had driven the thought of Hecari completely
out of his head.

Now came the grim and unenviable task of acquainting
them with such danger and ugliness, and no time at all for
courtesy.

"We are stopping," he told them, though as yet the easing of the wagon line from motion to stillness had not
reached the latter part of the karavan. "When the column
halts, wait quietly. There's a Hecari patrol ahead of us." Expressions were startled, then tensely speculative, and finally apprehensive. "All of you, even the youngest, must
line up beside the wagon," Rhuan continued. "Say nothing.
If we are fortunate, they'll be content with Jorda's payment; it's Hecari custom to demand a 'road tax' from the
karavan-master and Jorda carries coin for that purpose,
but occasionally the Hecari expand their demands to personal items as well. Don't try to stop them. Don't complain. Don't even speak to them." He interpreted the
questions forming in six pairs of stricken eyes but raised a
silencing hand before anyone could voice protest or ques-

tion. "Once you've assembled, hold your ground where you are. *Say* nothing, *do* nothing, and let the warriors take whatever they wish."

Shock, then anger flowed across faces formed of strikingly similar features, fair where he was copper except for the golden-haired wife. And at last, in the face of the eldest daughter, even outrage kindled, slowly but unmistakably.

Rhuan cut her off curtly before she could begin. "No."

"But—"

"Did you hear me? *No.*"

There was a wagon-length space between the Sisters' red-topped conveyance and the wagon belonging to the family. Even as Rhuan extended a hand, the oxen team was eased to a halt.

"It may cost you what you hold dear," he warned them, "but everything in your wagon can be replaced. Lives cannot." He gestured up the line. "Hold your place here. Either I, Darmuth, or Jorda himself will inform you when it's safe." He looked at them one by one, then indicated the farmsteader's wife and eldest daughter. "If the warriors come to this wagon, keep your heads bowed, and your eyes down. No matter what happens."

The wife was clearly taken aback. "Why?"

"In Hecari culture a woman never looks a warrior in the eyes."

The oldest daughter was no more inclined to accept his orders now than moments before, and challenged him. "What happens if we do?"

Her father shot her a hard glance. "Hold your tongue, Ellica."

Rhuan minced no words; best to let them know the truth if they hoped to survive. "According to the warrior's whim, a woman may be beaten, stoned, or whipped." He paused. "Occasionally even to death."

Chapter 20

*I*RONIC, BRODHI THOUGHT, that what had begun as a beautiful day should become so tragic.

Amid the settlement pathways, another man died. A woman. Then a child. Those who attempted to run were brought down by poisoned darts. The reek of death-slackened bowels and bladders was a sharp, unpleasant fug underscored by the coppery tang of blood. Yet the sun was bright, the skies clear, the breath of a breeze upon Brodhi's face temperate and pleasant.

"No!" Kendic cried in horror. *"Stop this—"*

Brodhi clamped a tensed hand upon the man's thick wrist and stepped close, so close his breath touched the other's face as he intentionally blocked Kendic's view. "Say nothing. *Do* nothing."

Kendic tried to wrench his arm free. "Do nothing? Are you mad?"

Behind them, Bethid was speaking fervently to Mikal, begging him to remain where he was, not to interfere.

Women screamed. Children shrieked. Men called out to gods as the warclubs descended and darts flew. On foot, hemmed in by mounted warriors, none of the one in ten escaped.

Brodhi's fingers bit into Kendic's twitching flesh. "You

can die. That's all. Is that what you wish? To die, and be of no help to those who survive?"

Kendic tore his wrist free. "Mother of Moons, how can you expect me to do *nothing?* They are killing women and children!"

Behind them, Mikal was weeping even as Bethid told him over and over again to hold his place. To find and hold his peace.

"I can't!" Kendic cried. "I can't do nothing! What kind of man are you, who does nothing to stop this?"

Brodhi said merely, "Nothing I *can* do will stop this."

Contempt swelled in Kendic's hazel eyes even as his lips peeled back in a rictus of disgust and disbelief.

"Wait—Kendic—" Bethid stretched out a belaying hand. "Listen to him! Listen to *me:* you must let it go!"

But Kendic could not, would not. He spat at the ground, repudiating them, then roared his challenge to the Hecari and waded into butchery.

Bethid, mouthing prayers, turned her face away.

"Fool," Brodhi murmured as the Hecari closed in.

Mikal was on his knees. His face was a tear-wetted mask of grief even as Bethid wrapped her arms around his head and turned his face against her abdomen, murmuring words meant to soothe that were nonetheless empty.

Brodhi, dispassionate, looked upon the massacre and absently counted bodies. Neither gender nor age mitigated the Hecari; the goal was to decrease the number of Sancorrans in one place and to teach by example that anyone, any*where,* could be struck down.

Even as Kendic was, smashed beneath the warclubs, feathered with darts.

In the midst of the culling, warriors dismounted to appropriate goods from the tents, then kicked over cookfires to set the oilcloth ablaze. Again, one in ten.

Bethid's words of comfort to Mikal were broken off abruptly. She stared in horror at Brodhi. "The karavan!"

Brodhi held his tongue.

"Would they track the karavan, do you think? Decimate it as well? It's only been a handful of days since they departed." He knew she expected something of him. Some word. An action. When he neither moved nor replied, she raised her voice. Its tone now was accusing. "Your kinsman is with them. Will you let *him* be a one in ten to die?"

That question he could answer in such a way as she would understand. Brodhi shrugged. "He's Shoia."

"So?"

"He may be killed, but it won't be a true death. A permanent death."

"And what if he only has *one* life left?" Bethid countered. Below her cropped cap of upstanding hair, her face was a tight, pale mask of grief and shock. "You can't be so cold, Brodhi. Not even you!"

He could. He was.

"You can do nothing here, that I know, not and live," Bethid said. "But the karavan should be warned. You can't know what this party might do once it leaves here."

Mikal's tone was frantic as he rose. "You're a courier; the Hecari will let you go. *Ride,* Brodhi! Warn them!"

He felt neither urgency nor urge to do so, even in the face of Bethid's and Mikal's stunned disbelief. But it occured to him that perhaps this was a test. Another of many tests that had passed already, with as many or more to come. In the name of a test, then—in the name of the *possibility* that this was a test—he would surrender himself to human expectations.

Ride? No need. He had other options.

But then he recalled that Ferize was gone. Brodhi believed it likely she had done as he, in his anger, commanded her to do, and returned to Alisanos. Demonkind, so long as they were kin-in-kind, had the ability to touch one another's minds; it would be a simple thing for Ferize to inform Darmuth of the Hecari actions, who would then inform Rhuan.

But she was gone, because he had dismissed her.

Even riding would be too slow if the Hecari sent a detail to follow him, and that was likely. It had happened before. As a courier, and a foreign-born courier at that, he was subject to neither decimation nor whim, inviolate because of his duty, but the Hecari did not trust him. Not yet.

Nor would they ever, if they learned what he could do.

Grimly Brodhi unsheathed his knife. Two pairs of tear-reddened eyes watched avidly, hopefully, following his movements. But puzzlement crept into their expessions and he knew what question was asked inside of their heads: Why was he not going for his horse?

Brodhi placed the tip of the knife against the ball of his left thumb, applied pressure, then broke the flesh against the point. As blood ran, he raised his hand, thumb extended, and dabbed both closed eyelids.

"What are you doing?" Bethid breathed.

A tremor ran through his body. Within, the blood-bond rose up singing.

Bethid repeated, "What are you *doing?*"

Brodhi said quietly, "Lending my eyes to a kinsman."

HIS AWARENESS OF the sun's continued kindness and his body's longing for it now displaced by duty, Rhuan rode back up the line of stopped wagons at a slow trot, marking strained looks on faces, the stiffness of bodies as the karvan-folk, following instructions, took their places along the verge of the track. From the oldest to the youngest, the fragile to the robust, Jorda's people formed a living line that stretched from Jorda himself at the head of the column to the oxen-pulled conveyance of the farm-steaders at the end.

Another man, a human man, riding along that line, might offer jovial words to bolster courage, to promise everyone safety, to dismiss the potential for danger and thus their fears. Rhuan did not. Nor would Jorda, he knew, whose responsibility now was to accede to the demands of the Hecari patrol without provoking the warriors to further action. This task was not new for the karavan-master, had not been since the Hecari invasion, but there was no sense of impatience, annoyance, or complacency about Jorda. And by such unflagging care and thorough preparations had the human karavan-master earned Rhuan's respect.

Rhuan would not lie to the people, nor dismiss their fears. But neither would he attempt to fan those fears into a conflagration of panic.

He reined in briefly at a wagon to answer a question, smiled at a young, curly-headed girl held in her worried mother's arms at another, then headed once more up the line toward Jorda's wagon. Despite Darmuth's efforts the Hecari patrol could arrive at any time, and he—

Blood.

Bodies.

His vision hazed red.

Bodies everywhere.

Bodies he recognized, faces he knew, names he had spoken.

The horse trotted three more steps, then slowed to a walk. Stopped. The taut reins were clamped in Rhuan's spasming hand.

He was no longer with the karavan, but in the tent-village instead. He was deaf to the cries, to the screams, to the begging for mercy, though he saw the moving mouths. Odor was nonexistent, as was the sense of touch and the awareness of time. But he had eyes, eyes with which to see, eyes that could not close and shut away the horror.

Not his. Not his, those eyes. *His* eyes, were they to open, to look, to see, would fill his mind with images of bright-painted wagons, halted; with the faces of anxious humans, waiting. No blood here. No bodies. Only living souls waiting for Hecari.

Hecari.

That, too, he saw; *them* he saw: painted warriors, scalp-locked warriors, black-eyed and browless men with war-clubs in their hands, with blowpipes at their lips; men of no mercy, of no compassion, merely warriors efficiently culling the old, the young, the man, the woman; the people of San-corra who, most of them, coming to the tent settlement near the border, intended to leave what once had been their homeland. To escape such depredations as found them now.

Butchery.
Blood everywhere, and broken heads.
Smoke rising in twisting columns.

Not his eyes, these. Not his, there to see, to look upon burning tents, to register burning bodies, to recognize the faces of the dead and the living. Not his eyes, though they rested in his head.

Brodhi's.

Rhuan was aware of voices, of his name being called. Aware too that he had no control of his body, no sovereignty over the physical reactions to what his eyes viewed. The spotted horse nervously sidled a step or two and Rhuan, slumping forward, slipped sideways over the gelding's sweat-slick shoulder. Another day, another moment, he would recover self-control, but not this day, and not this moment. He would fall . . .

Arms reached up, hands touched him, and he did fall; sagged against a man he did not know because he could not see him; because what he saw behind his lids was blood and bodies and burning.

"Brodhi," he murmured.

Bile rose, and saliva filled his mouth. Hands and arms attempted to help him, to hold him, to guide him to such comfort as might be found when a man lacked all control over limbs that had always served him. On his feet, if wobbling, Rhuan attempted to stop the hands and arms that held him upright, to push them away, to beg the well-intentioned humans to leave him be to sort out for himself what horrors filled his eyes. But they caged him, those arms; trapped him, those hands.

He lurched against them, twisting away, pushing against their importunities. The words he said, the words of his mouth if not of his mind, spoke a language no one knew, who was not as he was. Darmuth did. But Darmuth was absent.

Darmuth, by now, was among Hecari.

Hecari, here.

Hecari, there.

His lungs burned. "—I see . . . Brodhi—*stop*—"

Brodhi could not hear him.

Now he spoke to *them,* to those who were here: to the
voices, to the hands, to the fingers on his flesh. Bade them
let him go. Shouted at them, commanded them, to let him
go. Found enough self-control to wrench away at last and
to kneel, to slump on the verge between rut and turf, to
bend his back and dig trembling fingers into soil.

Buttocks resting on heels, Rhuan rocked forward. Held
himself upright against braced arms.

His eyes were closed, and he saw. Still he saw. If he could
sort out the images, control what he saw ... if Brodhi would
give him the time to comprehend those images and assign
them understanding ...

Brodhi looked, and Rhuan saw.

Bethid. Mikal. Kendic's body.

Kendic's *body.*

Rhuan spat. And again, convulsively emptying his
mouth of bile and flooding saliva. He released his grip in
turf to apply sleeve to mouth, then to clamp palms over his
eyes. "Brodhi ... no more."

The blood-bond of kinsmen, of kin-in-kind, renewed by
Ferize. Cuts carved, hands clasped, blood commingled.

"Let be," someone, male, said with rough authority. "Let
be, leave us room ..."

Jorda?

Hands upon him again, but this time not grasping, not insisting, not attempting to order his body. Merely hands
upon his shoulders, urging him upright.

A woman's voice said, *"Rhuan,"* then demanded, "Darmuth, thank the Mother—what's wrong with him?"

Rhuan managed, "Brodhi ..." It seemed to be the only
word he could utter.

Without insistence, a man asked, "What's happened?"

He knew that voice. Knew that name. Darmuth?

A shudder took him, violent enough that his joints ached
from it. "—sending—"

The woman again. "What can we do?"

"Rhuan ..." He was aware of movement, of the hands
withdrawing from his shoulders to cradle his head between warm palms. So warm, those palms, as if the blood

ran hot in the veins. "Rhuan, find your way. Walk the path away from Brodhi and back to yourself."

Yes. Darmuth.

It was a struggle to make his mouth form the words. "I'm not here," Rhuan blurted. Then, with greater insistence— Darmuth would understand— "—not *here.*"

"What does he mean?" the woman asked.

Darmuth's hands continued to cradle his head. "You are Rhuan, not Brodhi. You are here with the karavan. With Jorda, Ilona . . . with *me,* Rhuan."

So he was. Rhuan, not Brodhi. Not there, but here.

Coming out of a living nightmare, from the helplessness of blood-bound trance, Rhuan looked into the eyes of the demon he called companion. Their gazes remained locked until Darmuth was satisfied. He released Rhuan, who blinked himself back into his own skin and looked at those around him. Darmuth, of course. And Jorda, holding the reins of his spotted horse. But also Ilona, a crease of concern drawing dark brows together. Others gathered, too, those whom he guided, but none of them, now, stood close, or put their hands upon him. They gathered in an anxious cluster and spoke among themselves. But though they would guess, they could not know what he had done.

Seen with and through another man's eyes.

Rhuan looked at Jorda, Darmuth, Ilona. *His* eyes, now, not Brodhi's. "The settlement." He said at last what his kinsman intended them to know, the purpose for which Brodhi had used the blood-bond linking them, he who despised it. "Hecari are killing people."

BRODHI FELT A hand tentatively touch his arm. Then fingers closed. A woman's fingers. "Brodhi?" He knew that voice. Bethid. "Brodhi—come back."

He turned from the killings to look into her face. Worry shadowed her eyes. A glance at Mikal showed similar concern.

"You went away," Bethid continued. "Standing here, you went away. I could see it in your eyes. They were *empty.*"

He was vaguely aware of sobbing, of wailing, of pleas for help. He smelled the reek of urine and excrement, the thick, throat-catching odor of blood, the stench of burning oilcloth. Columns of smoke amid the tent-village rose into the air

Words came slowly. He felt detached and sluggish. "You told me to go to the karavan. To warn them."

Mikal nodded, dark brows knit. "But—you just stood here."

"Oh, no. No, I did as asked." With immense mental effort Brodhi banished the lingering disorientation of the sending. "Rhuan knows now. He'll tell Jorda. They will be prepared if the Hecari track them." He saw the mystified expression on Bethid's fine-boned face. "I told you. I lent my eyes to Rhuan. He saw . . . this." Brodhi's gesture encompassed the gruesome results of Hecari decimation.

"It's a Shoia thing, then," Bethid's tone made it as much a question as a statement.

"Shoia have many abilities." Brodhi briefly pressed a finger against his forehead as the first throb of a looming headache made itself felt. But he knew Rhuan was in worse straits; the one who received a forced sending had a significantly more difficult time coming back from the bond. "So. Rhuan knows. Jorda knows. There is nothing more we can do to prepare them." He watched Hecari warriors riding the pathways, making certain those assigned to death were in fact dead. Survivors hung back in the shadows of unburned tents, unwilling to place themselves in harm's way. "These warriors will leave," Brodhi said. "Their duty is completed. And then those people who were not chosen to die may begin to live again."

Mikal's tone was rough. "Until the next time. Because they'll come again, won't they?"

"Yes." Bethid's words sounded pinched and thin. "To see if the lesson was learned. It could be a day from now, a week from now; it might be a year."

"And if I stay, I might be chosen to die the next time they come?"

"Yes," she answered.

Mikal set his jaw. "This is my home. I choose to be here."

Brodhi nodded. "It should always be a man's choice."

"And a woman's?" Bethid's tone was bitter. "Ah, but I'm a courier. The warlord has some use for me, even if I *am* female. I'll never be a 'one in ten.' "

"They're leaving," Mikal said, surprised. "Just as you said."

Brodhi watched the warriors as they departed single-file, horse after horse after horse, paying no mind as the survivors began to come forward to find their dead and attempt to beat out flames. Women's voices rose in a keening Sancorran lament.

"Shovels," Mikal said. "And buckets. We'll need to gather shovels for the graves, and buckets of water to put the fires out." He nodded jerkily. "I have both in my tent."

As the one-eyed man walked away in rigid self-possession, Bethid looked at Brodhi. "If the Hecari go after the karavan . . . is Rhuan enough to stop them?"

"Unlikely," Brodhi replied promptly. "Probably he'll do something foolish and get himself killed."

Bethid, eyes red-rimmed from tears, looked beyond him to the people now battling flames, or searching for their dead. "Like Kendic. Except Kendic had only one life to lose."

RHUAN'S GRASP ON self-control was tenuous in the aftermath of the forced bond, and his head ached abominably. He was aware of Jorda sending those who had come to his aid back to their wagons, to their places along the road. That brought a question through the pain in his skull. "Where are they?"

Darmuth's mouth twisted in irony. "*Our* Hecari, you mean?"

Rhuan, who had recaptured his horse's reins from Jorda before the karavan-master headed back to his wagon to await the patrol, realized Ilona had not yet returned to hers. She watched him in a fixed, concentrated way, pupils contracted, that threatened to distract him. "Ours, yes. The patrol."

"Half a mile up the road, when I turned back. There was no need to delay them; they stopped along the road to eat something."

Rhuan massaged his forehead with rigid fingertips. "But they'll reach us in no time."

Darmuth agreed. "At any moment, yes."

Rhuan thought his head might burst into flame. But he turned to his horse and swung the reins up over the gelding's neck. "Then I had best go to Jorda to help him greet them."

"Rhuan, wait." Ilona's tone was imperative enough that he did not immediately mount, but turned his attention to her. "I know the look of pain," she said. "I have a tea that will help."

"I don't need tea," he returned curtly. "I need to help Jorda."

Calmly she countered, "You are bleeding from your left ear."

Rhuan put a hand up and felt the trickle of wetness. "No matter." He shrugged and turned back to his spotted horse. "It will keep."

Ilona appealed to Darmuth. "Of what help will he be if he collapses in front of the warriors?"

His lips twitched. "In truth, Rhuan unconscious is often more helpful than Rhuan awake."

The maligned subject mounted, blinking away briefly doubled vision. He hurt too much to employ courtesy. "Ilona, go stand beside your wagon. Do as the others. If Hecari are killing people at the settlement, who is to say the patrol won't do the same here?"

"You," she said.

He scowled down at her. "What?"

"*You* will prevent the patrol from doing any such thing."

He was too distracted and his head ached too much to parse out Ilona's meaning. Instead he jabbed a finger in her direction, then aimed it at the line of wagons meaningfully.

Ilona turned on her heel and walked stiff-backed toward her wagon.

"Nicely done," Darmuth murmured dryly.

Rhuan shot him a disgruntled look. "She isn't my mother."

Darmuth grinned. "Why, no, she isn't. But then, I don't think 'mothering' you is what she has ever had in mind."

Rhuan, fighting the blinding pain in his head, could dredge up no fitting reply. Instead he waved a dismissive hand in Darmuth's direction and rode away.

Chapter 21

*T*HE DAY WAS still, the skies brilliant. A good day for traveling. But now the karavan was stopped beneath the midday sun, and Audrun knew lack of movement would soon make the day seem the hotter for it.

Even if a chill did touch her spine when she thought of the Hecari patrol.

Megritte's tone verged on whining. "Why are we just standing here? Why can't we go?"

Her two youngest had been napping in the wagon when the guide issued instructions, and it would be some time yet before characteristic cheerfulness replaced interrupted-nap disgruntlement. Meanwhile, as ordered, all six of them stood in a line on the verge between road and turf four paces from the wagon: Davyn, Torvic, Audrun, Megritte, Ellica, and Gillan. It was always best to place the youngest near or next to their parents, and especially now.

"Because this is what we were told to do," Audrun answered.

Torvic, pale hair standing on end, was sullen and belligerent. "*Who* told?"

Davyn replied, "The guide who is responsible for our safety told us, Torvic—and it's not your place to question your elders."

She heard an undertone of tension in her husband's

voice and strove to keep it from hers. "This won't take long. Then we'll be on our way again."

"I don't want to just stand here," Megritte declared.

Audrun longed to say she agreed with her. Instead, she placed a hand on her daughter's head and tried to make order out of nap-tangled fair hair even as she steadied her fidgety daughter in place. "Don't whine, Meggie."

"They're but three wagons away," Davyn noted with false lightness.

Audrun followed his lead. "You see?" But increasingly it took additional effort to keep her voice casually cheerful. "It won't be much longer. Ellica—remember to keep your eyes down."

"I know, Mam."

Three wagons away. A hasty sideways glance found six mounted Hecari warriors, faces painted, eyebrows shaved, skulls oiled, warclubs at their saddles, blowpipes and darts adorning leather baldrics worn slantwise across broad chests. What Audrun could see without staring was that the patrol was not inspecting wagons, but *people*. That, she found unsettling. Hecari searching wagons for coin or goods was upsetting but understandable, in view of what they were; examining the karavaners themselves suggested a different goal. But the warriors were accompanied by both karavan guides, also mounted, from which Audrun took a measure of relief. She hoped Gillan and Ellica, old enough to be more cognizant of the dangers, might as well.

She inhaled a long, bracing breath, releasing it carefully so as not to permit her tension to show. It was just as well, she decided, that Megritte and Torvic were not currently on their best behavior; it gave her something to deal with as the moments lengthened.

"They're coming," Davyn said. "Torvic, Megritte, hold your places. Do as I say."

Audrun swallowed heavily. "Ellica—"

"I *know*, Mam."

Audrun bowed her head and fixed her eyes on the ground immediately in front of her feet. The posture did not completely obliterate her view as the patrol arrived, but neither could she be accused of looking directly at the Hecari.

She rested her left hand on Megritte's shoulder, though she wasn't certain if she offered support so much as sought it. She kept her voice very soft. "Be still, Meggie. This won't take long."

Six horses were reined in, each precisely opposite an individual, child and adult alike. Audrun wanted to look at the guides, hoping for some kind of sign, any sign, that all was under control, but that would require raising her eyes and perhaps inadvertantly meeting the gaze of a Hecari. Instead, she stared at the two horse hooves now standing within her self-limited field of vision. One hand stroked her youngest daughter's hair; the other rested atop the still-modest swelling of her belly. *This* child, at least, need not be frightened by Hecari. This child, in fact, need never even *see* a Hecari, being born and reared in the free province of Atalanda.

Audrun smelled paint, oil, horse sweat, and unwashed human bodies. One of the hooves before her stomped as the horse rid itself of flies. Despite the warmth of the day, gooseflesh pimpled her flesh. Her scalp tightened into a maddening, prickling itch, but she raised no hand to seek relief.

Rhuan's voice was pitched to soft and subtle warning. "Do nothing."

She heard the sliding of leather against woven wool, the light landing in grass as the warrior before her dismounted. It was nearly impossible not to look up.

Feet clad in sinew-laced buskins stepped into her line of vision, replacing horse hooves. Something was said to the other warriors, then to her; the rising inflection was suggestive of a question. Steadfastly, she neither looked up nor spoke. But her hand on Megritte's shoulder trembled, and she thought her knees might collapse.

The Hecari stepped closer yet. Audrun tensed, telling herself to say nothing, to *do* nothing, merely to wait the moment out. She took her bottom lip between her teeth and bit down.

Then the Hecari warrior put one hand on her belly. The other closed over and squeezed her tender left breast.

Audrun snapped her head up, blurting a shocked outcry, and met cold black eyes beneath the browless shelf of bone. She was unable to stop that immediate, reflexive reaction, nor could she halt the hands that struck out at the warrior's. Even as she knocked his away, she realized, aghast, that what she did might be all the provocation the Hecari needed for violence, precisely what Rhuan had warned against, but she could not keep herself from responding to the power of sheer physical instinct to protect her children, born or unborn.

The warrior snarled something. Davyn closed his arms around Audrun and yanked, spinning her away from the track.

Megritte was shrieking. "The children—" Audrun blurted.

Davyn's hard grip around her waist and abrupt motion triggered dizziness and nausea. Even as she fought to keep the contents of her belly in place, Audrun was aware of silver flashing in the sunlight, of shouts and outcries, a confused impression of commotion among the warriors and the guides. Megritte's shrill screaming sliced through her head.

"Run!" Davyn shouted at the children. "Gillan, Ellica— take the youngest and run!" Arms clamping even more tightly around her, he pulled Audrun aside and turned her, grunting as he stumbled, off-balance, and shoved her toward the wagon. "Go!"

Pregnancy always affected her balance. Under Davyn's rough impetus, Audrun staggered forward. At the corner of an eye she caught a glimpse of Gillan and Ellica scooping up the youngest and running, as ordered. Then she fell against the wagon, jamming an arm, and set to clanking the pots hanging underneath the floorboards.

Clinging to the wagon for support, Audrun turned. She was aware that the children were gone and thanked the Mother for it, but her attention now was on Davyn, seated on the ground cradling his right arm. Beyond him, in a tan-

gle of horses and men, she saw another wave of silver
flashes streaking through the sunlight and realized that
they were knives.

Bodies sprouting two or three knives each lay sprawled.
Two unmounted Hecari horses wheeled away as another
trotted off. A fourth warrior, still mounted, dragged his
horse's head around and kicked it into a gallop. Rhuan's
fellow guide went in pursuit.

That left four men dead from, Audrun saw in shock,
knives in eyes and throats. The last warrior, the one who
had put hands upon her, lay on his back, throat slashed
open. Trembling Hecari hands attempted to slow the gush
of blood.

Davyn, too, was bleeding.

Davyn.

Audrun hastened to him and knelt. A knife hilt stood up
from his left shoulder. He shook his head. "It's not deep,
Audrun. Throwing knives, not gutting knives. It's all right."

"It's not 'all right.' " But her attention was claimed by
movement nearby. Inititally she tensed, expecting more violence, but saw that Rhuan was going from body to body,
bending down with a bloodied, long-bladed knife in hand,
methodically making certain all the Hecari were truly dead
and retrieving short-bladed knives from flesh. As he took
time to clean each weapon, Audrun's mind told her incon-
sequentially that in times such as these, with enemies on
the roads, a man must be careful to keep and care for each
of his weapons.

The Hecari with the slashed throat, the one who had
touched her, was dead now as well. She smelled the sharp
scent of spilled blood, the odor of oil and paint now commingled with the stink of fresh urine. She watched
Rhuan pause briefly over him, expression grim. Then the
guide tucked throwing knives into the loops of his
baldric, cleaned and sheathed his long-knife, and came to
Davyn.

He knelt, inspecting without touching the knife in
Davyn's shoulder. "You need not fear for your safety. Darmuth will see to the last warrior." The tautness of his ex-

pression altered to something akin to rueful embarrassment. "My apologies. A poor throw, I fear."

Audrun stared at him. "This is *your* knife?"

But the guide ignored her, speaking to Davyn. "Hold a moment . . ." He pulled the knife free, then displayed the bloody weapon to Audrun. "You see? The blade of a throwing knife is too short to do true damage, unless—" he gestured toward the bodies, "—it goes into an eye or the throat."

Audrun was outraged. "And if it had gone into my *husband's* eye or throat?"

By now word of the killings was spreading along the karavan. People gathered at a distance, staring and speaking in low tones. Even in her anger, it struck Audrun as odd that no one came forward to help.

Rhuan cleaned the knife, nodded at Davyn's thanks, then tucked it into a baldric loop. "Oh, no—I knew when I threw the knife it wouldn't be a killing throw. I was jostled by a horse." He wadded up loose folds of Davyn's tunic, pressed it against the wound, and glanced at her. "Here. Hold this in place."

"In a moment." Audrun rose. "I need to find my children."

He reached up and caught her wrist. "Let them find *you*. For now, I need you to apply pressure to the wound."

She attempted and failed to twist her wrist free. "*I* need to make sure my children are well!"

"They are. They ran, as told." A sheen of sweat filmed the guide's face as he released her wrist. "Please . . . come and tend your husband."

Audrun wanted very much to refuse him outright, if only because of his peremptory tone, but Davyn *did* need tending and the children *had* run to safety.

Suppressing the anger, she knelt again beside her husband, replacing the guide's hand on the wadded cloth with her own. As Rhuan withdrew his hand, Audrun saw in shock why he had been so insistent that she take over the tending: a feathered Hecari dart stood out from his right forearm. "Mother of Moons," she murmured.

He plucked the dart out of arm and sleeve, mouth twisted, then held up the feathered weapon. Audrun saw that he had begun to shake. "Do exactly as I say: take this and burn it in a cookfire, then bury it. Be careful not to touch the tip, and on no account allow the children to touch it. I suspect all of the poison is in me, but do consider the dart dangerous regardless." He cast a glance at the others gathered to watch from a distance. "Ai, but too many humans refuse to involve themselves lest there be a risk to their own safety." He shook his head and extended the dart to Davyn. "I'd give this to Darmuth, if he were here, but he isn't . . . can you take it? We want no children playing with it." Abruptly graceless, he fell out of a kneeling position and sat down hard on the track. He muttered something that sounded like a curse, then pulled each throwing knife from his waistband and dropped them one by one to the earth in a chiming of steel.

Audrun felt a chill sheathe her bones as Davyn carefully wrapped and tied the dart into the hem of his shirt. The guide's color was very bad. "You're ill . . . it's the poison, isn't it?"

"Worse than ill, actually." He scrubbed the back of his trembling hand across his brow. "When the children come back, tell them not to be afraid." His glance went to the gathered spectators. "I wish this need not be so public, but there's no help for it." Rhuan caught and held her look. "I'm going to die now. But tell the children not to worry."

"What?"

Earnestly, he said, "It's not a true death. It's only temporary."

That, she found astonishing and wholly unbelievable. It robbed her of speech.

"It won't last," Rhuan continued. "As I said, it's not a true death." A grimace warped his mouth. "Which doesn't mean it is painless, unfortunately." His breath caught, and he flinched. Hollows darkened beneath his eyes. "Send someone for Jorda and Ilona. They've seen this. And Darmuth should be back soon."

Her words were made slow by the incomprehension of

Chapter 22

*I*LONA HAD NEARLY reached the crowd of karavaners when the gangly, blond boy made his way through. His eyes were wide and fearful, his movements jerky. But the moment he saw her approaching, he broke into an awkward jog.

He didn't wait to reach her before speaking. "He said you should come," he called urgently. "He said you would understand." His youthful skin was flushed, stretched taut over the still-maturing bones of his face. Ilona saw the worry and confusion in his blue eyes as he halted before her. "But—how can death be temporary?"

That was all she needed to hear. "Dead *again*," she muttered.

She didn't wait to see if the boy had more comments or questions, but, by dint of a fierce, impatient tone and no hesitation, opened a path through the crowd. When she reached the other side, she saw five Hecari bodies sprawled near the last wagon.

And one dead Shoia.

Ilona hadn't seen Rhuan dead for three years. It came as a shock, and a sadness, and the beginnings of grief to see him lying lifeless upon the track—until she recalled with a rush of relief that he would be perfectly fine within a matter of moments. One day he might reach his seventh death, the "true death" of a Shoia, but he hadn't yet.

The farmsteaders had closed around him as if shielding him from public scrutiny. The smallest girl was held in her father's arms, crying even as he told her quietly, despite the disbelief in his eyes, that she was not to fret, that the guide wasn't really dead. The oldest daughter had a death-grip on the tunic of her frustrated younger brother, holding him back from an inspection at close range. It was the woman, the pregnant wife, who knelt at Rhuan's side.

As Ilona arrived she looked up, features harrowed. "He promised. He said to tell the children not to worry. That he isn't truly dead."

"Oh, he's dead." Ilona slipped around the husband, whose right arm was bandaged with fabric torn from a tunic hem, and knelt beside Rhuan. "He's just not going to *stay* dead." She looked upon the expressive features, slack and stilled in death, lacking the dimples of a smile or laughter. The elaborate, ornamented braids of coppery hair lay spread upon the track. She saw no blood, no wound. "What killed him?"

"Hecari dart," the woman answered. "Here." She touched her own right arm to indicate the corresponding place on his. "He said it was poisoned."

Ilona nodded. "Hecari dip their darts in poison. Well, he's likely to feel terrible when he rouses, but that's better than being dead." She leaned closer. "Rhuan? Can you hear me?"

"He said you understood this," the woman told her. "So I ask you, then: how can death be *temporary?*"

"For that, I have no answer," Ilona said dryly, "despite asking him any number of times. But he is Shoia, and they can rouse from death six different times before the true death extinguishes them. Or so Rhuan told me after the first time I saw him die." She frowned, watched his face closely, then nodded, suppressing a sigh of relief. "Do you see his eyelids tremble? He'll be very much alive within a few moments." Ilona glanced around at the Hecari bodies. "What happened here?"

"He put hands on my wife." The husband gestured with a nod in the direction of a dead warrior whose head and shoulders lay in a muddied pool of blood.

Ilona's gaze flicked to the woman, whose color rose in a wave to her face. There was a tale to be told, but she didn't ask it of them yet. "Where's Darmuth?"

"The sixth warrior escaped," the farmwife answered. "The other guide went after him."

"Well, count that warrior dead, then." Ilona prodded Rhuan's shoulder with two stiffened fingers. "If you want to nap, Rhuan, borrow my wagon, or Jorda's. This is a little awkward and public, don't you think?"

His face was pale, his lips dry, his voice a husky rasp, but he spoke. "You can't expect a man to leap into the land of the living when he's already crossed the river."

"I can when he's already crossed *back*." She paused. "You're frightening the children, Rhuan. And probably a fair share of adults, to boot."

His eyes opened. He squinted into the sky. Then he brought a limp hand up to shield his eyes from the sunlight. Ilona saw the angry red streaks crossing the back of his hand. They would be gone by morning, she knew, if not before. "Have we an audience?" he asked.

"Oh, indeed. Most of the karavan. Jorda was up front talking with Branca and Melior when I came down and was met by the boy." She nodded at the elder son who had joined his father, looking no more settled by Rhuan's revival than he had by his death.

Rhuan sighed. "Well . . . I suppose I'd better get up." He rolled onto a hip and pushed himself into a sitting position, wincing. Then he saw the smallest girl in her father's arms. Rhuan paused a moment, then heaved himself to his feet with a quiet grunt of effort. Ilona saw the dimples appear as he stood and spread his arms, displaying himself to the little girl. "There. You see? Not dead."

The girl's expression was dubious. "But you *were*. Mam said so, when she tried to find the rabbit in your chest."

Rhuan's smile faded into incomprehension. "The rabbit?"

"In here." Audrun laughed and placed a flattened hand on her chest, then thumped it three times.

"Ah!" The dimples were back as he looked to the girl. "Yes, it's true the rabbit was still for a while, but now he's back and kicking away." Rhuan touched his chest. "Right here. Do you want to feel it to be sure?"

Solemnly the girl studied him, then nodded.

Rhuan stepped closed, took her hand in his, and pressed the flattened palm against his chest. "Feel it? *Thumpa-thumpa-thumpa*. A very strong rabbit. All right?" The girl nodded, and Rhuan released her hand. He reached down then, offering the same hand to the farmwife, and pulled her to her feet.

Ilona half-expected he might extend the same courtesy to her, but she was left to fend for herself as Rhuan casually informed the family that what they had witnessed was a Shoia gift and not an ability any human claimed, which meant humans were far more vulnerable and fragile and thus must be much more careful not to hurt anyone. It was for the children's benefit, she knew, but she thought it applied equally to adults.

She stood up, brushing dust from her split skirts and long tunic. There was a stirring in the cluster of onlookers, who parted and let the karavan-master through.

Jorda's expression was grim. A quick, darting glance took note of the dead bodies, and then he looked at Rhuan. "You'll explain this later." He didn't wait for the guide's answer but turned to the karavaners. "We'll stay the night here, where we are. We've bodies to bury—I'll ask for volunteers from the men in a moment—and diviners to consult. After that, I'll want the head of each family to come to my wagon so I may pay out your fares."

Ilona looked at him sharply even as gasps of astonishment rose among the karavaners.

Jorda's ruddy beard glowed brightly in the sun as he raised his voice. "We'll not be going on. We'll return to the settlement." He put up a silencing hand as additional exclamations and startled questions broke out. "I'll repay each of you in full. But we are turning back."

Stunned, Ilona stared at him. In all the years she had been in his employ, despite all the dangers and challenges to the safety of the karavans he led, Jorda had never once turned back. Except in her dream. . . .

He waited as the outcry followed his words. When it had died from disbelief and anger to quieter frustration, he continued. "I have word that many more Hecari than the six in this patrol attacked the settlement. They killed men, women, and children, and burned many tents." His bearded jaw jutted in unspoken challenge. "I've just now consulted two of my diviners, and they both said the same: Our task is to go back to the settlement and give these people—" His mouth worked as he tried to control his emotions, "—my friends, many of them!—what aid we can. We'll wait out the monsoon and get a fresh start early in the fall. Those of you who wish to go on with me then are welcome; if you'd rather go with another karavan, so be it. But those people back there deserve our help. I must do this." He glanced briefly at his guide. "Rhuan and I will welcome any who care to help us bury the bodies."

Ilona looked at Rhuan. No dimples were in evidence; no smile in place. Beyond him stood Audrun, one hand pressed against her mouth as if to lock in the words she longed to speak while the other was knotted into her loose tunic. Her face was drained of color. Briefly she closed her eyes tightly, then opened them and looked at her husband. Her expression was stricken.

And Ilona realized that by the time the monsoon was over and the roads dried enough to be passable, the baby would be born.

In Sancorra. Not Atalanda.

BRODHI WAS ANNOYED to be counted among the number of men Mikal designated for the task of sorting through the burned tents, looking for bodies or anything that might be salvagable. He had not intended to undertake any such duty, but after a moment's reflection he acquiesced. There were all manner of perils upon his journey, tests and traps he would never recognize and might fail or fall into along the way, as well as truths left unknown. The decision was uncomplicated: he accepted the task Mikal laid upon him, or refused it. He likely would never know which was the correct decision.

Grimly, Brodhi agreed to accept Mikal's task.

Bethid rounded up fellow couriers Timmon and Alorn and walked the pathways looking for children separated from their parents, either by the decimation or the confusion. The keening Sancorran wail of grief still threaded through the settlement as woman after woman took it up to mourn the dead. It broke out afresh each time the body of a loved one was found.

The work was filthy. Brodhi and the others of his detail kicked apart charred tent timbers, pulled aside burned oilcloth, cleared drifts of ash and set about making piles of salvage. With one of every ten tents burned, the landmarks Brodhi was accustomed to were missing. He claimed a stronger land sense than the humans helping him, but the lack of familiar corners, twists, and turns was nonetheless a sobering underscore to the devastation.

At a mound of collapsed and half-burned oilcloth, Brodhi uncovered the body of an old woman. She lay on a thin, straw-filled pallet, white hair lying across her shoulders in two neat braids. She was neither burned nor bloodied; Brodhi, kneeling beside her, realized that in all likelihood she had died before the Hecari attack. Someone had washed and braided the fine, white hair. Someone had carefully set a chain of charms into the old woman's gnarled hands, to see her safely across the river. Someone had, undoubtedly, begun the mourning rituals their faith required for the woman's passing. But she was alone now, clothing dusted with ash, a partially charred tent pole fallen across bare feet.

In her face was a map of years Brodhi could not count. But he knew that according to the stunted lives of humans, she had lived longer than most. Likely she had come with grown children intending to leave Sancorra, to find safety from the Hecari.

Brodhi knelt on one knee beside her. With exquisite care, he brushed ash from the aged face. Moved the fallen tent pole aside. Stroked away from closed eyes the fragile strand of white hair. "Old mother," he murmured, "where are your children? Have they crossed the river with you?"

"Brodhi. *Brodhi!*"

He glanced up and was genuinely surprised to see Darmuth astride a near-black horse, making his way through fallen tents and grieving survivors. Clear, eerily pale eyes examined the ruins, the bodies, the details working to find the dead or living amidst what remained.

Brodhi rose as Darmuth reined in. "Rhuan received the sending, then."

"Dramatically so, yes. But shortly after that we were engaged in resisting our own complement of Hecari. The scale of damage is far less at the karavan than here, however . . . five warriors dead, but no humans."

Brodhi added, "And Rhuan."

Darmuth blinked in startlement. "Was he killed *again?*"

"You didn't see? I felt it in the blood-bond. But he's back among the living now." Brodhi frowned. "What are you doing here, Darmuth?"

"I chased the sixth Hecari warrior in this direction, which is why I missed yet another of Rhuan's deaths and revivals. The warrior is dead now, of course—" Darmuth's sudden feral grin was unsettling, "—but since I am not limited to human speed in travel, I wanted to see for myself what your sending was about." The sideways jerk of his head encompassed the settlement. "Decimation?"

"Yes."

Darmuth looked at the old woman lying at Brodhi's feet. "The Hecari were uncommonly neat with her."

Brodhi shook his head. "She was dead before they arrived. But no one has returned to her since the Hecari left."

"Dead," Darmuth suggested.

"Likely."

The demon frowned thoughtfully. "She should have rites."

"She should," Brodhi agreed, "but does either of us know what would be appropriate?"

"You're *dioscuri,*" Darmuth said lightly. "Make something up."

A surge of anger rose up in Brodhi strong enough to flay the skin off a human. It took supreme effort not to unleash a torrent of verbal abuse that would achieve nothing other than to amuse Darmuth. And thus amuse Ferize, and thus any number of other demons, because of course they would be told. He *was dioscuri*, but only Darmuth and Ferize were ever inclined to mock him for it.

Even now, sly irony glinted in Darmuth's pale eyes. Brodhi buried his anger and once more knelt down on one knee beside the old woman. In the inner language, the secret language, spoken beneath his breath, he gave her spirit release verbally. Then physically, touching fingertips very lightly to the eleven blessing points: middle of forehead, the bridge of her nose, each eyelid, each cheekbone, the fingertip hollow between nose and mouth, the upper and lower lips, chin and, lastly, the notch in fragile collar bones lying beneath age-mottled skin.

Go where you will, he wished her. *Go as a human should, according to the requirements of whichever god you worship. Be well, old mother, now that the river lies behind you.*

He glanced up from the body and saw Darmuth watching him still. The expression on his face was unreadable, and yet something in his eyes suggested he was cataloging Brodhi's actions.

Brodhi rose with a marked lack of habitual grace. "I am not yours," he declared vehemently. "You will say nothing of this."

Darmuth was amused. "I may say whatever I wish."

"I am not yours," Brodhi repeated. "Leave it to Ferize. Tend Rhuan. He *is* yours."

Darmuth laughed. "You think it speaks badly of you, that you would aid humans?"

He could not trust Darmuth. Brodhi said carefully, "That is not my oath. Not the oath I swore to humans—to the courier service."

"So you remember that oath? You respect that oath?"

With vicious precision, Brodhi answered, "I remember all my oaths."

"And do you consider one less binding than another?"

The question was a trap. Brodhi knew it, and refused to let himself be led into it. "Hadn't you better ride back and make sure Rhuan hasn't been killed yet again? Possibly for the seventh time? Which, of course, would end everything. For you. And for him."

"You said you'd know if he died. Because of the blood-bond."

"Oh, indeed, I may know he has died, but that doesn't mean I will tell you about it." Brodhi made an elegant but wholly human gesture with his hand. "Shoo, demon. Ride away, run away, fly away; I leave the means of departure to you. But do absent yourself from my company."

Brodhi turned away. He neither heard nor saw Darmuth's departure, but he knew the instant the demon was gone.

Oaths. So many promises made to humans, and to his own people. He could abjure all such things and damn himself forever. That, he rejected. Therefore it remained for him to pick his way through the myriad expectations, the numberless requisites set out upon his path. He was *dioscuri*. He felt, as always, as if he were a blind man, a blind man with no sense of touch, and no understanding at all of the world around him.

A blind man whose survival depended wholly on whim, on caprice.

Upon the games of the gods.

Chapter 23

*I*N THE WAGON, alone, Audrun sat on the edge of the cot usually shared by Ellica and Megritte. She had taken the time to go apart, to let the first reaction come upon her where no one would see. Her arms and legs felt cold, strangely numb. Her hands tingled. Spots danced before her eyes.

She closed them—and saw behind her lids the painted face of the Hecari. Smelled again his stink. Felt again his hands upon her, touching breasts and belly.

Touching breasts and belly.

Audrun raised trembling hands and placed them over her eyes. She held the posture stiffly, forbidding herself the weakness of rocking that once, in childhood, had brought comfort with repetition, with the mindlessness of movement.

Oh, it was hard. Hard not to wish herself a child, innocent of the world, knowing pain and small hurts that she had learned, in adulthood, were mere precursors to what a woman faced, being both wife and mother.

Her throat cramped painfully. Audrun grabbed the front tail of her long tunic. Fabric crumpled in her hands; she pressed the wad of cloth against her face. The first keening wail of shock, of humiliation, of trembling reaction, escaped her mouth but was captured, was stifled, in the cloth.

She was wife and mother. She would let no one see her cry.

BY SUNSET, AFTER all the wagons had been moved off the road, Rhuan, Jorda, and several volunteers dug a pit. The bodies of the Hecari warriors were dumped into it, then the freshly dug earth was thrown over them. But Jorda's instructions for completion of the task were explicit: There was to be no mound marking the burial pit, nor even the look of recently disturbed soil. And so they spent hours carrying off buckets of dirt, scattering it onto the wagon ruts where it would soon dry to blend in. The top layer of sod was replaced over the pit, then tamped down flat. The grass would die, Jorda said, but for a day or two it would not be obvious that dead men lay below it. They could not afford Hecari discovering their dead brethren.

He thanked and released the burial detail, then turned to Rhuan. Both of them were grimy from fine dirt sifting into the sweaty creases of their skin. With sleeves rolled up, dust clung to the wirelike ruddy hair on Jorda's thick forearms, dulling its fire, and his loose tunic was stuck to his torso. Rhuan had removed his leather tunic to dig without its hindrance; now, as the sun went down, he felt the day cool into evening.

"Tell me," Jorda said.

Rhuan knew what was coming. He knew also he deserved it.

He sighed, rubbing dampness from his brow with the back of a hand that hours before had been scribed with the crimson streaks of poison. The heaviness of ornamented braids dragged at his scalp. He was hungry and tired; dying and subsequent revival drained him, and the chill of dusk was an affront to flesh that fed on warmth. But he knew he owed Jorda the truth first. He would eat and rest later. "They did as told, the farmsteaders. Stood quietly, and the mother and eldest daughter kept their eyes cast down."

Jorda's brows rose. He had not expected that answer. "Well?"

Rhuan drew in a breath. "One of the warriors put his hands on the wife."

Within the nest of his beard, Jorda's mouth jerked. "And so, despite instructions, the husband retaliated—"

Rhuan cut him off. "It wasn't the husband."

"The eldest son, then."

"No. Me."

"*You!*"

Rhuan kept his tone level. "She's pregnant," he said, "and the warrior touched her where no man but a husband should touch his wife, particularly a pregnant wife."

Jorda stared at him, momentarily struck dumb. Slowly he shook his head. "Of all people, you should know—"

"I do know better. I knew better even as I cut his throat."

The karavan-master remained disbelieving. "But it didn't stop you."

"No. Had you seen the look on the woman's face—"

Jorda dismissed that with a sharp, silencing gesture. "Six Hecari warriors? You saw fit to open hostilities that might have gotten the entire family killed? That might have gotten most of the karavan killed?"

Rhuan held his tongue. Experience had taught him further explanation would be fruitless.

Jorda's tone rasped. "Where's Darmuth?"

"Chasing down the sixth warrior."

"And so you might even be responsible for your partner's death."

Rhuan laughed. "Not Darmuth's!"

That was a mistake. It heated Jorda's already evident anger. Above his beard, cheeks flared red. "*You* may have lives to surrender without fear of a permanent death, but the rest of us do not. One life is all any of us has, Rhuan. You take them for granted, those lives. You risk what isn't yours *to* risk." He was angry, yes, but also perplexed. "Tell me why I should keep you on as a guide, if you are to be so irresponsible?"

It was truth in Rhuan's mouth, but also arrogance. He

knew it. But could not, in that moment, find sweeter words; Jorda had pricked his pride. "Because I *can* die for you and your people, and have. Because I *can* take risks others can't, and do. Because I may have precipitated this incident— that, I freely admit—but I also cleaned up my mess . . . and six Hecari warriors will no longer trouble the innocent folk of Sancorra. I count that a boon."

"They might have killed the woman, Rhuan. A pregnant woman."

"No."

"No?"

He could not help himself. "My reflexes are better than any Hecari's."

It cowed Jorda not in the least. "How do you know that? Can you swear to that in each and every circumstance? That you will always be faster?"

"Yes."

"How?"

Quietly he said, "Because I'm not human."

That stopped Jorda in his tracks. The karavan-master blinked, brows rising. Rhuan had seen it before in Jorda and in others: because he liked humans, because he could laugh and joke with them, humans forgot he was not truly of them.

Until they were reminded.

But it passed, did Jorda's startled recollection, and he made a reply with excessive, pointed clarity. "And. You. Died."

Rhuan laughed at him. "And I don't doubt just this moment that you wish I'd remained that way."

"You *died*, Rhuan!" Jorda wiped his face with a thick forearm, regaining control over the rumble of his bass voice. "I took it on faith, the day Ilona brought you to me, that you would put the welfare of the karavan first. I knew nothing at all of you, and she barely more. But she convinced me that with one guide dead, a Shoia might be valuable to have in my employ—"

"And so I am."

"—and you swore an oath to guard the people who put their faith in me."

"And so I have."

Jorda studied him. The anger had burned itself out. The master seemed older in that moment, and infinitely wearier. Creases deepened in the flesh around his eyes. "One day, Rhuan, you will not rise up again. You will die the last death."

"One day, yes. The true death will find me."

"And until then I should believe you will do whatever you must to protect my people?"

"Yes," Rhuan said steadily. "Judge me not by what happened today, but by all the days, all the years, I have already protected your people."

SMOKE AND ASH drifted across the ravaged tent settlement; some fires continued to burn sluggishly at sunset as men ran to fill buckets and pots with water. Brodhi, deserted by Darmuth who had departed for the karavan, could not recall that he had ever seen humans mourn, not so many as this, who struck him as weak; he supposed that yes, if a loved one died it was perhaps worth a momentary pang of regret, but nothing more. It did nothing to alter the facts, such mourning, but wasted emotions and strength that might better be spent on something else, something substantial, such as gathering up scattered belongings and setting up tents that remained mostly whole. Would they not need shelter? Or, in their grief, did they feel nothing of external reality, and thus were immune to wind, rain, and cold? And why did they not begin proper rites for their people?

He stood amid the wreckage of lives, of human lives, and felt nothing save distaste. He watched as the women keened, clutching at one another as if another's grief might aid them, but Brodhi failed to see how it could. Wouldn't shared grief double, even treble, the pain?

The men were less effusive, but he saw tears tracking channels in the grime and smears of blood that dyed faces, bearded or clean-shaven. He saw bodies bent forward as if

they suffered belly wounds; he saw trembling in the calloused, work-hardened hands. There were wounds on none
except those who had attempted to save the one in ten, and
who had paid for the interference with blows to their own
bodies. None had been killed; Hecari were meticulous in
decimation, wanting those who survived to learn the lesson, to *teach* the lesson: Too many Sancorrans banded together called for culling.

And so the settlement had lost one-tenth of its population, one-tenth of its dwelling places. Had so many not met
in the place by the trees and put up tents, there would have
been no culling. It was folly to allow so many to live as
though this were now their home. Many meant to move on
with the karavans, and many did, but too many had remained.

They brought it on themselves, Brodhi reflected. *Surely
they had learned enough of Hecari since the province was
overrun.*

And yet he stood amid the wreckage of lives, of hopes,
of dreams, and realized that even in the time he had spent
among humans, he had as yet arrived at no understanding
of them.

ON ORDERS FROM Jorda, Ilona had done with
her wagon and team as everyone else with theirs:
taken it off the road some distance away. Though they were
not left in the tight formation of a single-file karavan on
the move, neither were they halted so far away from one
another that anyone was at risk. Teams were unhitched and
hobbled or picketed for the night, allowed to graze to
heart's content on lush plains grass. The usual noise of children playing, women singing over their cookfires, and men
trading tales and laughter over pipes was absent; the
Hecari visit and resultant killings affected everyone, mut-
ing moods and actions.

Though Jorda had sought the advice of the other two
karavan diviners, Melior and Branca, Ilona was not sur-

prised when a small trickle of people one by one approached her wagon and diffidently asked if she would read their hands. The change in destination had upset everyone's plans, and now they required reassurance that Jorda's decision to return to the settlement was wise for their needs.

Outdoors beside the wagon, Ilona unrolled and spread her rug, set her low table upon it, hung lighted pierced-tin lanterns upon their hooks and set a modest fire for tea. She gathered together blessing-sticks, cards, and polished stones and lay them out upon the table in pleasing patterns. Though most came to her specifically for hand-reading, others, accustomed to different rituals, found it disconcerting that a woman might simply look into their hands and see their futures without the support of sticks, stones, bones, crystals, cards, and other such implements. Ilona told them true, but relied only on her own gift; the other items, for her, were merely props.

Three women, two men. She served tea to each, studied work-worn, sometimes blistered palms, told them what she saw in relation to Jorda's decision, and bade them sleep without worry. When the third woman, the final client, departed, Ilona set an elbow against the table and rested her brow in a spread-fingered hand, closing her eyes. She needed more tea—perhaps of willow bark, as her head had begun to ache. It took her that way sometimes, when clients were deeply worried or distraught. Certainly those of the karavan were both, following the experience with the Hecari, and with the news that they must turn back and wait another season before departing. It would be difficult; they had packed for the move, planned for the journey to take them to a destination where they would begin anew the very moment they arrived. Now they must wait again, must plan for a season in the tent settlement, where Hecari had already struck and might do so again.

Yes. Willow bark tea. Ilona rose, shook out her split skirts, tended the lanterns to make sure they wouldn't upset and spill flaming oil, then climbed up the folding steps into her wagon. A grateful client, a man who worked in wood, had paid her years before in kind, not in coin; she knelt on the floorboards next to her cot and silently thanked the man again for being so clever as to build beneath the cot a cabinet of multiple small drawers. It allowed her to organize and store various herbs, teas, spices, and oddments without taking up the precious storage space she needed for other things.

She had opened one of the shallow drawers and taken up the soft muslin bag in which the loose willow bark tea was kept when she heard a creaking step and felt the shifting of the wagon as someone mounted the steps. Still kneeling, bag in hand, she turned to see a man hesitating on the second step, head bowed to miss the lighted lantern dangling from the doorframe. Like every man in the karavan, he wore dusty, stained, and aging tunic and loose trews, belted at the waist with worn leather. His hair was brown and curly, eyes dark. Stubble shadowed his jaw.

He wanted something. Something urgent. She read no hand to discern that.

Ilona was weary and her head ached. It was with great effort she hung onto her patience and offered professional courtesy. "If you wish your hand read, please sit down at the table outside. There is tea, if you care for it. I'll join you in a moment."

He held out one closed hand. She noted his fingers were thick and scarred. "Can you look at this? It's a charm." His light voice was hesitant, yet she sensed something else underneath the tone, something tensile as wire. "I bought it from a priest who said it would rob my wife's mother of speech for a day, only a day, so I might have a little peace— only a *day*," he repeated earnestly, as if realizing that another might view such a goal as cruel. "She nags, you see ... I just can't please her." His expression was shamefaced as he looked down at his closed hand. "Maybe I was wrong ... I can see where you might think it's wrong ... but all I want is *one day* of peace. Is that so bad a thing to wish?"

Ilona supposed not. "But why bring it to me?"

His mouth jerked. "It isn't working."

She was amused and sympathetic, but also puzzled—and

she smelled spirits on his breath. Possibly that was why his wife's mother nagged him. "What do you expect me to do? I read hands. I don't make charms."

"Could you just look at it? There's a word that invokes it—maybe I'm not pronouncing it right. Here—see?" He opened his hand. Ilona saw three speckled feathers tied together with crimson thread around a sprig of some desiccated, unknown plant. "Maybe you can say the word the right way." He moistened his lips, eyes wide and fixed, and pronounced the word with great care.

Ilona could not so much as gasp as a painful tightness seized her throat. She dropped the bag of willow bark tea and closed her hands on her throat, mouth opening to cry out. But nothing issued. No sound at all, not even a shout or a whisper.

"There," the man said brightly, "it's working after all." He smiled, and in his eyes Ilona saw something more than intensity: the kindling of a predatory lust.

She lunged backward, scrabbling for a weapon of any sort, be it knife or mug or pot. But he was swifter than he appeared. He leaped up and into the wagon; she heard the clank of the lantern falling outside as he dragged the door closed behind him. He caught her, fingers digging into her shoulders. The astringency of spirits upon his breath assailed her face. The lust in his eyes now was ferocious.

Ilona tried again to find something that might buy her a moment to gain ground, but a flailing arm merely jammed itself against her cot cabinet. She mouthed profanities an upright woman shouldn't know, but still nothing issued from her mouth.

With one hard shove the man slammed her down onto the floorboards.

Ilona blessed her split skirts as he struggled one-handed with the fabric. Her headache flared into conflagration from the impact; she had put away the pallet and mat she'd slept on when Rhuan was recuperating in her cot. There was no softness beneath her, only hard wood. And something that jammed into the back of her right shoulder.

"My wife's mother wants to unman me, I think," he told her, breathing heavily as he stripped her of belt. "All her jabber about me not being good enough. Do you think a man can *do* for his wife when he can't escape her mother's nagging tongue? So I found me someone to make this charm I could use on her . . . but then I saw *you,* you see. Living alone, with no man. And it's not like you're an up-right woman with a husband to provide . . . but better than the Sisters, who want coin to couple." Frustrated by the split skirts, he yanked hard at the fabric until it tore. "There won't be another chance before we go back to the settle-ment." He saw what she knew was panic in her eyes. "Now, you won't be able to speak for a day or more—and the charm won't *ever* let you speak of what we've done; that's what the priest said—but you'll be all right." He grinned. "And so will I."

She fought as best she could, but there was no scream able to break free of her throat. He had pinned her be-tween the under-cot cabinet and the chests lining the other side of the wagon's interior. His weight and the insistence of his knees, his hands, kept her on the floorboards.

His mouth was close to hers. Spirits-laden breath gusted against her face. "A man can't *do* for his wife properly when her mother keeps saying he's not good enough, now, can he?"

Chapter 24

*T*HERE WERE THINGS to be done besides sit in the wagon and cry. Audrun set her hair to rights, drew in a deep breath, and pulled back the privacy flap. Outside her children awaited her, uncharacteristically subdued. And so in a hard-won casual manner she assigned tasks to each of them to keep their hands busy and their minds on something other than Hecari cut down in front of their eyes.

"I'll unpack what we need from the wagon," she told them, "while you go out for wood and any wild herbs and tubers you can find. See those trees there?" She pointed to a grove within shouting distance, shadowed black against the sunset. "You may go that far, but no farther. And do what Gillan and Ellica tell you." She looked at her eldest, saw the mutiny in their eyes, but knew they would do as told. Ellica and Gillan were only fifteen and sixteen, respectively, but that did not make them stupid or insensitive to her moods. "Your father and I will set up camp, and after we've eaten we'll have a family discussion."

Torvic and Megritte were both glad enough to go running off toward the trees—Audrun didn't doubt they would do more playing than gathering wood and herbs— but Ellica and Gillan did not immediately follow.

"Mam—" Ellica began.

Audrun cut her off. "Go with the young ones, Elli."

"But—"

She summoned a firm, unyielding tone. "Go."

Ellica left, cheeks flaring red. But Gillan lingered. It pierced her heart to see the worry in his eyes. "Will you be all right?"

Audrun didn't dissemble, didn't dismiss. He knew enough to look beneath her even tone to the tension beneath. "Your father is with me." She flicked a glance at Torvic, Megritte, and Ellica as they headed toward the trees. "I'm well, Gillan. Go on."

She turned back into the wagon as Gillan followed the others, blessing the Mother of Moons for allowing her to retain self-control before the children. It was a simple enough task to start retrieving from the wagon such things as were needed in camp, including iron pots, tin plates, pewter mugs, the iron tripod from which would depend the stewpot to heat its contents over the fire, foodstuffs and tea makings.

She knelt beside the modest fire ring Davyn had built with the rocks, wood, and coals they carried at all times, laying out the items she needed for starting supper. First the tea, for Davyn and herself; it was a ritual she hoped would calm her.

As she worked, Audrun kept an eye on her husband. His wounded arm had stiffened, but fresh blood no longer stained the cloth wrapped around his bicep. That it pained him, she knew, being privy through experience to her husband's moods and expressions. But he let none of it interfere with his own activities as he lay and lighted a fire, unhitched and hobbled the oxen.

She filled the loosely woven tea cloth with leaves. Her hands shook as she did so, and she spilled a drift of the costly leaves. Audrun made an inarticulate sound of dismay, then attempted to knot the tea cloth. The unsteadiness of her hands made the simple task difficult.

She recalled other hands, the hands of a warrior, of an enemy, touching her.

She recalled how his throat had gushed blood.

She recalled that not only Hecari had died, but Rhuan. Who had promised to protect them.

And so he had. But she had not envisioned, had not spent a moment on wondering or imagining *how* he would do that, nor that it would require such butchery.

As darts flew and warclubs were raised, a man forestalled Hecari butchery with a measure of his own.

Hecari hands had touched her. Owned her, if only for a moment.

"Audrun." Davyn came up to the fire. He knelt on one knee, put hands upon taut shoulders, then pulled her into his embrace. For a long moment he hugged her in silence.

She could not even control the shaking in her voice. "You might have died, Davyn. Or one of the children, or *all* of them—"

He set thick fingers gently over her mouth. "I know. I know. But let it go, Audrun. It's past. It's done. We're all of us safe."

She took a measure of comfort in his nearness, in the familiar scent of his body, in the strong arms around her. But she could not let it be. Could not accept that it was past, and done. "He made me ill. He made me want to vomit. When he touched me . . ." She shuddered, recalling that touch, but recalling also the disjointed images of the guide leaping from his horse and drawing his knife, of him slashing the Hecari's throat from ear to ear.

Davyn had yanked her out of harm's way, but she had seen that much. She had seen more.

A man who was killed had risen from the dead.

"Here. Let me." Davyn picked up the tea cloth and knotted it deftly, then put it into the kettle. She noted that his hands did not shake as he set the fire-blackened kettle onto the wood that would soon become coals, that his body didn't tremble. Was it so much easier to be a man?

But the tea kettle was not the only thing he put in the fire. Carefully he untied the knot in his shirt's hem and unwrapped the Hecari dart. It looked innocent of intent or danger, merely a slender metal tip ground to a point, and a feathered wooden shaft. She saw no stains, either of blood or poison. Such an inconsequential thing that had, nonetheless, killed a man.

Who had somehow risen from death.

Davyn set the dart into the fire. Audrun, transfixed, watched it burn.

"We will go on," he said. "I promise it."

She roused, blinking hard, and looked from the fire to her husband. She could not make herself ask the question. Had she heard aright?

"We will go on," he repeated; yes, she had heard him aright. "To Atalanda. We won't return to the settlement."

Audrun could not suppress the flicker of startled relief that kindled in her belly. Still, she had to make the effort to weigh the alternative, to let him know she didn't leap upon the offering instantly, without thought for their safety. "Should we risk it?"

Davyn said simply, "We must."

THE SUN HAD set. Cookfires flamed. The scent of meat roasting permeated the karavan campsite. But it was not the easy evening of optimistic and adventurous families on their way to a new land talking over plans and hopes. The experience with the Hecari patrol and Jorda's decision to return to the tent settlement had left them pensive, unhappy, conversing quietly with eyebrows knit together in frowns and tense expressions of worry.

Despite the sharp discussion with Jorda after the burial, it remained Rhuan's task, with Darmuth, to ride the perimeter of the encampment, then to walk among the wagons on foot patrol, but with Darmuth still absent all was left to Rhuan.

To the dead man.

To the man who *had* been dead, but inexplicably was no longer.

Outright stares and more discreet sidelong glances followed Rhuan as he rode by the wagons. People stopped what they were doing when they saw him. He heard low-voiced murmurings, the thick, almost whistling sibilance of the race's name whispered among many as they saw him: *Shoia*. Different. Alien. *Sorcerous*. How else could a man rise up from the dead?

Only one person had ever appeared to take that feat in stride, with no assumptions made; only one had witnessed a revival and then quietly accepted his explanation with no expression of shock, bafflement, or outright disbelief. But Ilona, of course, had her own measure of personal talent. Rising from the dead might be considerably more dramatic in nature than reading a man's future in his hand, but it was no more unique than any diviner's ability.

A lopsided smile twisted Rhuan's mouth. He rode with an Alisani demon, but the humans all believed *he* was the odd one, the alien one, the dangerous one. Rhuan knew quite well the kind of stories passed around concerning Shoia. That some of them were true was an exquisite irony.

He looked up into the darkness of the Orphan Sky lit only by stars. "Will I ever understand them?"

Unlike Brodhi, he wanted to.

Rhuan glanced at the nearest wagon as he rode by: Ilona's, with a small tin lantern hanging from a wagon rib to cosily illuminate the door and steps. But though her table and accoutrements were set out for divining with tea brewing over a small fire, she herself was not in evidence.

Then the door lantern fell, spilling oil and flame down the wooden steps into grass.

Rhuan was off his horse in one agile, twisting dismount and reached the wagon in three running strides. Without hesitation he yanked the rug from beneath Ilona's table, overturning it as well as upsetting her stones and sticks and tea makings, and threw it over the burning steps. On hands and knees he smothered the fire, patting the rug down so no air reached the flames. Fortunately the small lantern had used up most of its limited supply of oil, and it burned off the spilled fuel quickly enough that none soaked the rug and caused it to catch fire.

He intended not to call to Ilona until the flames were out; he didn't want her opening the door and stepping into fire. But then he heard a crash from inside the wagon and felt it shift beneath an unknown weight.

The rug smoked, but the flames had died. Still, he didn't trust the blackened steps to hold him. Blessing his height and the length of his arms, Rhuan, from the ground, reached for the latch and pulled the door open. " 'Lona?"

The images, confused as they were, stamped themselves into his mind's eye the instant he saw them. Ilona's heels digging at the floorboards, knees bucking, thighs straddled by a man's. Her skirt torn away to bare naked legs. And a man, *a man atop her,* twisting his torso to see who had pulled open the door in the midst of what could only be described as an assault.

Then the man was up, turning, lurching toward the door even as Rhuan planted a foot on the potentially precarious lowest step. He was dark-haired, dark-eyed, and his stubbled face was set in a rictus of startlement and fear, and a frustrated anger.

It was one fleeting moment, no longer, as Rhuan's mind registered movement, intent, desperation. The man, sweating, swearing, hurled himself through the door, all his weight and impetus knocking Rhuan sideways. The charred bottom step broke beneath his booted foot.

The man fled into the darkness, but Rhuan did not pursue. Instead he caught hold of the door jamb and levered himself up into the wagon.

" 'Lona!"

THE STRANGER'S WEIGHT and intensity were terrifying as he leaned down over Ilona, so close his gusting breath touched her face. But it was more than simple fear, more than panic, that seized her body even as his hands did. It was a complex layering of emotions and reactions, including foremost among them blank surprise and utter disbelief.

She tried clawing him; he imprisoned and pinned her wrists over her head with one wide hand. She tried biting him; he was quick as a snake in avoiding the attempt. And his weight and strength were such that she could make no inroads on her imprisonment. She had never known herself so helpless, so impotent in the face of physical danger. In her experience karavaners simply did no such thing as assault a woman, and a diviner at that. She had always supposed there were men in the tent settlement who might stoop to such action, but someone from the karavan, usually Tansit when the guide was still alive, accompanied her there, and Mikal allowed no improper overtures in his ale tent if she were alone, as sometimes happened.

Now she lay pinned against the floorboards in her own wagon with a stranger atop her, a man who even now tore her divided skirt from drawstring waist to hem. She smelled him now, the sharp, pungent tang of sweat and grime.

And she *could not scream.*

Could not so much as whisper.

Mute, she fought . . . her desperate movements knocked something down from one of the rune-carved wagon ribs arching overhead. Then she smelled oil and smoke overriding the man's odor. She heard the latch rattle as the door was pulled open.

And heard her name called.

She mouthed *his* name, though no sound came of it. Abruptly the stranger pushed up, pushed away, relieved her of his weight as he twisted; there was a momentary pause, and then he thrust himself forward and leaped for the door despite the person in it.

Ilona rolled onto her left side, reaching with her right hand for anything that might be used against the man should he turn back. She found nothing save spilled willow bark tea and a pot that had fallen.

" 'Lona . . ."

Hands were on her again. She tensed, teeth bared, her own hands striking out, then scrambled backward, unable to suppress the reaction until her mind recognized who it was, and recalled that he would never harm her.

Embarrassment heated her face. She had never believed herself a woman who would lose self-control.

Rhuan helped her into a sitting position. Her coiled hair had come loose of its anchoring sticks, spilling down over her shoulders. She looked into his face and saw concern in his eyes, but also a coldness in the lines of his face that shook her.

" 'Lona—are you all right?"

Her hands touched her throat.

He pulled them aside gently, searching for the expected finger marks that would bruise by morning. But Ilona shook her head and mouthed the words *I can't talk,* and *a charm,* hoping he would understand.

He did. And the anger in his eyes shocked her with its heat.

Eyes glinting *red.*

Chapter 25

*T*HE INTERIOR OF Mikal's ale tent was illuminated
by a single discolored tin lantern. Brodhi could have
seen just as well with no light at all, but the humans would
have found it strange—yet another oddity to attribute to
the Shoia courier—and so he lit the wick, placed the
lantern on the plank bar, poured a tankard of ale, and
seated himself at a table.

The tent was empty of Mikal, empty of customers.
Brodhi sat alone and drank in flickering sepia light, while
the keening laments of the women outside slowly died
away into the occasional raised, wailing voice, and the
deeper shouts of the men attempting to bring order to the
evening, order to the dead.

Brodhi had dropped the door flap for privacy. Now it
parted; a small, slender form slipped through, and the
lantern light glinted dull saffron off brass ear-hoops.

Bethid.

The bottom half of her tunic was soaked with water, and
a smear of soot stretched from nose to ear on the left side
of her face. As usual, her cropped hair stood up in haphazard spikes and tufts sculpted by a scrubbing hand, though
its fairness was now colored with a patchwork of grime and
blood and soot. An empty wooden bucket with a hempen
loop handle swung from one hand.

"What are you doing in here?" Her tone was sharp, shaded by disbelief.

He felt it self-evident and offered no answer, merely lifted the foaming tankard to his lips and drank.

"Mikal said you were here . . . I thought perhaps you'd come for a spare bucket. But you didn't come back."

Brodhi remained silent.

Her expression was incredulous. "Are you *drinking* in here? Just sitting here *drinking?*"

With delicate irony, he observed, "You have a gift for stating the obvious."

Bethid, never even when happy able to keep opinions to herself, was notably less self-contained when she was angry. She stared at him. In dim light the angles and hollows of her tired face stood out in gaunt relief. "There are people outside, people who are dead, Brodhi. Some of the tents are still smoldering!"

He asked a question with arched brows.

Bethid strode across the space between the door flap and his table and slammed her bucket down on the knife-scarred surface. "The people," she said with the kind of precision in enunciation and tone that underscored the intensity of her anger, "need your help."

Brodhi shrugged. "You asked me to aid the karavan. I did so. Mikal asked me to help search the burning tents, and I did so. For a while."

It astounded her. "There is a limit to the amount of time you're willing to help?"

Oaths, vows, and promises. Traps along the way. Brodhi said, "This is not our duty."

"It *is* our duty," she retorted. "It's the duty of any decent human being to help another in a tragedy like this."

"But I'm not," Brodhi said; and when she didn't understand, added, "not human. Remember?"

For a long moment she was speechless, staring at him. The flesh of her throat leaped as she swallowed with effort, as if on the verge of tears. Her voice was thick. "Do you know, I have always stood up for you. Always defended you when other couriers had nothing decent to say about you. And I've always reminded them that you likely have reasons for what you do and say ... but now?" She shook her head slowly, jerkily, as if dazed. "Now, I begin to believe they are right. You are a cold bastard, Brodhi."

In a swift, unthinking move he thrust himself upright, shifting the table as his thighs bumped the edge. Only the meager space of its surface divided them: providing a small but virulent battlefield.

Ordinarily he would have ignored all that she had said, but something welled up inside, something demanded to be said. To be *explained*.

"We are observers, Bethid. Oath-bound observers intended to witness incidents like this, and then to carry the news and messages unfettered by personal opinion."

"Yes, but—"

"If we allow our own emotions to unseat the neutrality of our task, then we are useless. We become nothing more than gossip-mongers. And then what we say can never be trusted as impartial, and our offices will no longer be necessary ... nor will they keep us safe from the Hecari."

"Brodhi—"

"What would you have us be, Bethid? Couriers left alive to carry word—and survive to do so again—or bodies who may well be counted a portion of the one in ten during decimation?"

She flung out one hand, pale against the dimness. "Look outside, Brodhi! Men, women, and children—*children*—who were counted out like so many kernels of corn!"

"Yes," he said sharply. "*Exactly* like kernels of corn ... because when seed corn is planted, it is expected that some will be lost. Four kernels planted per hollow, Bethid. If only one of four kernels matures into a cornstalk, a farmsteader counts himself fortunate."

She shook her head, tears of angry disappointment filling her eyes. "I don't understand you. I've tried ... I've excused your rudeness, forgiven your bad temper—"

He cut her off. "Excuse nothing of me. Forgive nothing *in* me. I am what I am, and it matters not at all what others may think of me."

She opened her mouth, closed it. Studied his face a moment, then began again. Softly, at first. Slowly, at first. "You mean it doesn't matter what *humans* think of you. Well, I don't believe that. I don't believe that at all. I think you *do* care, but for some twisted reason you want to keep us—to keep humans—at a distance. To know nothing about you, to *care* nothing about you . . . I just don't know why." She shook her head. "And maybe I never will."

"It isn't for you *to* know—"

Bethid raised her voice over his. "Maybe it's just that you're Shoia. Maybe it's that you have only one life left, and you fear to lose it, to risk yourself. Maybe it's that you can't bear to see humans die because it reminds you that you've only *got* that one death left . . . only one, the way all of *us* have only one." Her chin rose. "Rhuan was at the karavan. Had he not been, had another Shoia not been there, would you have warned them at all?"

Brodhi, startled, laughed. "If you think I predicate decisions on what becomes of Rhuan because he's another Shoia—"

"He's your kinsman."

"—*or* that he's my kinsman, then you're quite correct: You don't understand me. Not in the least."

She looked exhausted in the lantern light, worn by the events of the day and the requirements of the aftermath. But he thought perhaps something he had said, something he had said or done—or something *not* done—now deepened the shadows beneath her eyes.

Bethid picked up her bucket. He watched her turn away, watched her walk out of the tent with a spine so stiff it verged on fracturing. She was a small, slight woman, almost delicate in the way she was made, but he had on many occasions seen her display a wiry strength and enviable stamina, as well as a stubborn will to see through to completion what she set out to do.

Tonight she would put out fires and bury the dead.

Rhuan would do it.

Brodhi knew it in an unexpected flash of insight, an unanticipated thought that annoyed him: Rhuan, who inexplicably cared about humans, would work side by side with Bethid, or Mikal, or even a stranger. He wouldn't care about the oath a courier swore when he joined the service. He wouldn't care about whatever tests lay before him, what traps he might discover along the road. To Rhuan, it was the *journey,* not the destination, not the end result, that was most important.

Brodhi sat down. He picked up the tankard and lifted it to his lips. "He'll fail," he said aloud into the lantern light. And again, "He'll fail."

He drank. But the ale tasted bitter.

RHUAN SAW ILONA recoil and realized she'd seen the red flicker in his eyes. He damned himself for losing self-control, for betraying how quickly his anger, a cold and dangerous anger, could rise. It was something he and Brodhi fought, each day, apart from one another and with differing methods—and vastly different temperaments—but shared was one abiding element: they were cursed with the wilding blood of their sires.

With effort he buried that anger, plunged the kindling restlessness deep, and deeper yet; he would not become proxy for that which he detested in his father and in Brodhi's, who were brothers. Kin-in-kind. A much closer bond, a far more demanding and difficult bond than the one humans called *family.*

He sat back and raised his hands, showing her his palms in a gesture of peace. To her it would mean more than to others; she might read those palms, albeit neither was close enough for her to see in detail, to touch. And in fact the gesture had the effect Rhuan desired. Ilona relaxed, tension leaving the rigid line of her shoulders. She found one of her carved hair sticks on the floorboards, then coiled a haphazard rope of hair onto the back of her head and anchored it with the stick. She opened her mouth to say something, then recalled she had no voice.

Rhuan grinned at the expression of annoyance that crossed her face. "Oh, but we'll have heretofore unknown peace for as long as this lasts."

She scowled.

He kept his tone light, though the words were deadly serious. "Are you all right?"

The scowl didn't dissipate, but she nodded. Then nodded again. She mouthed a word he thought was *bruises*.

"Are you sure?"

Ilona nodded again, more vehemently. Her expression made it clear she in no way wanted the subject to be debated. A sharp, curt hand gesture underscored it.

Rhuan put all of the light-heartedness he could muster into his voice; he wanted nothing in his eyes to startle her again. "Well, you do know he'll have to be killed."

She went still. Immeasurably still. Then shook her head.

Rhuan found and picked up the other hair stick shed during the struggle. "Oh, I do think so—here, bow your head."

Instead, Ilona snatched the stick from him and drove it through the wiry coil of hair so hard he winced. Once more she shook her head. A gesture indicated her torn skirt, followed by a hands-up motion coupled with a shrug that suggested nothing so serious had happened that should dictate death as a means of revenge or reparation.

He grinned at her. "I rather approve of your current predicament. It means I'll win all the arguments."

She reached out and caught his wrist. Her grip was firm. With the other hand she mimed a knife being drawn across her throat, then shook her head vehemently. She mouthed a word he interpreted as *promise*.

"I don't believe I can make that promise." He lifted her hand from his wrist. "You'll have to excuse me. I have business to attend to."

As he rose, she slapped the flat of her hand against the

plank floor to gain his attention once more. Again she shook her head.

"Oh, not now," he assured her. "I mean I'm going to repair your steps."

And without using any of them, he leaped lightly down from the wagon.

GILLAN AND ELLICA, as told, walked up the low, rumpled rise to the grove of trees crowning the hilltop along the horizon. Before them, silhouetted against the sunset, ran Torvic and Megritte, playing some sort of game wherein Torvic was a hero rescuing a maiden— Megritte, of course—from the horrible Hecari. Gillan reflected that while their mam might well suggest another game entirely, he found it normal that the youngest could so quickly forget the brutal and sudden deaths they all of them had witnessed. He wished *he* could. But the images were jumbled, broken into innumerable fragments so diffuse that he couldn't possibly reassemble them in the proper order. The guide had been so fast, so quick with his throwing knives . . . and the fact that one of the blades had ended up in his father's shoulder, though an undesirable result, did not in the least lessen Gillan's admiration for the guide's prowess. Five Hecari killed within a matter of moments.

Well, and the guide himself. But he hadn't *remained* dead.

"Mam said he wasn't breathing," Gillan commented as they topped the hill. The grove of trees formed a spreading canopy over them, muffling the cries of Torvic and Megritte.

"Who wasn't breathing?" Ellica asked.

"The guide. He said he was going to die, but it wouldn't be for good. And Mam said he wasn't breathing, that his heart didn't beat."

Ellica stooped to pick up a forked branch from the ground beneath the nearest tree; her donation toward fuel for the cookfire. Pale strands of hair, coming loose from their ties, fell forward over her shoulders to mask her face. "You know what Da will say."

That puzzled him. "About the guide?"

"No, not about the guide." She bent to gather up another tree branch. "He will say we should go on. That we can't go back to the settlement." She straightened. "You saw the look on Mam's face when the karavan-master said he was turning back."

Gillan scooped up a heavier branch and whacked it against the nearest tree, knocking dry, curling bark off the smooth inner wood of the deadfall, the bone of the branch. He was aware of an uncomfortable fluttering of apprehension in his belly.

"We'll go on by ourselves," Ellica continued. She didn't look at him, but her profile, silhouetted against the setting sun, seemed sharp as cut tin. "It doesn't matter to Da what the guide said about Alisanos. Mam just wants to be in Atalanda when the baby comes."

Two trees away, Torvic mimed slashing the throat of an invisible Hecari warrior. Megritte shrilly crowed her approval.

"Because of what all the diviners told her," Gillan said, studying the branch in his hands.

"And so we'll go on by ourselves, and there won't be anyone there to save us if *more* Hecari show up." She turned her strained face to him, blue eyes shadowed with worry. "We should go back. Like all the others. Go back to that settlement, and wait. But we won't."

Gillan was certain his sister was correct. It wasn't that Da was stubborn, not stubborn for no reason; who could argue with fourteen—no, fifteen diviners; his da and mam had visited the karavan hand-reader—when *all of them* said the baby had to be born in Atalanda?

Then inspiration lurched out of the burgeoning twilight and into his mouth. "What if he came with us?" When he saw Ellica's blank look, he clarified. "The guide. Everyone's going back to the settlement. There will be no karavans to guide."

She shrugged.

"Don't you see?" Gillan continued. "There won't be any guiding jobs."

Ellica's attention sharpened as her mind jumped ahead to what he meant. "Unless he guided *us.*"

"Yes!" He nodded enthusiastically. "He can guide us to Atalanda, and protect us from Hecari. Or anything else."

"He did die," Ellica reminded him, collecting more deadfall branches. "It just didn't happen until all the Hecari were dead. If they'd killed him sooner, *we* might be dead."

It was not, Gillan felt, a convincing argument. Not when the guide had already demonstrated in a most dramatic way that he didn't remain dead. "Given a choice between going on alone, or going in the company of a Shoia who can not only kill five Hecari warriors in less than the count of ten, but come back to life if he himself is killed, which would you pick?"

Ellica grimaced. Her expression was solemn as she nodded slow agreement.

"Say after dinner that you want to go for a walk," Gillan suggested. "And I'll come with you to make sure you'll be safe. We'll go find the guide. Da and Mam don't even have to know."

Her eyes remained worried. "What if he refuses?"

"He won't."

"You don't know that, Gillan."

He hated it when she said things like that, when he was so very certain. "He won't refuse."

Now she was annoyed. "You can't be sure—"

"I can, Elli. Mam's *pregnant* . . . how many decent men would turn their backs on a pregnant woman? He's already warned us about taking a road so close to the border of the deepwood—do you think he'll just let us go on alone? He has no employment, now that the karavan's turning back. I think he'll come."

She resettled the lopsided stack of firewood in her arms. Behind her, winding around the trees and back again, Torvic chased Megritte. Apparently he had stopped being the hero saving the maiden and now acted the part of a Hecari in pursuit of his sister, whose thin-voiced shrieks of terror were clearly feigned. "We can ask," Ellica said, though doubt still shaded her tone.

"We can *beg*," Gillan corrected. "But I don't think we'll have to."

Chapter 26

*I*LONA HUNG UP the kettle that had fallen from the Mother Rib. She examined the tin door lantern for dents, found two, and inserted fingers carefully inside the housing, avoiding the oil reservoir and wick, to press the dents back out. She was not entirely successful, and it turned her fingers black, but the repairs would do. She replenished the oil, trimmed the wick, relighted the lantern and hung it up, setting the metal loop back over the horseshoe nail in the door lintel. Once again it created a welcoming pool of light over the steps, though the bottom one was burned and broken, and the middle one was blackened.

Tea leaves lay scattered across the floorboards, scenting the air with the sharp astringency of rough-ground willow bark. Tea was dear on a journey because there were never certainties as to when one might replenish stores. Ilona hand-swept the leaves into a sad little pile, intending to carefully gather up the leaves and return them to the muslin bag. But even as she recovered the bag and leaned down to begin the careful transferral from floorboards to fabric bag, she hesitated.

Diviners existed who used tea leaves in their craft. It was possible that if she saved the leaves for a diviner's service, for reciprocal professional courtesy, she might learn what was to face her in the coming days and weeks, now that the karavan would be returning to the settlement.

But did she truly wish to know?

Kneeling there upon the floorboards where so very recently her body had been thrown down by a man intent on raping her, Ilona thoughtfully removed the sticks from her hair and set them on her cot. Then she took down the haphazard coil of hair, tidied and spun it into a long rope, rewound that rope against her head with deft movements of her hands, and once again anchored it with the rune-scribed sticks.

There.

She swept the loose pile of tea into the palm of one hand, carried it to her open door, and scattered the leaves into the twilight.

There.

Ilona shut and latched her door, filled a basin with cool water, and set a washing cloth in it to soak.

There was little clothing to remove. Her belt lay on the floor, and the torn split skirt had fallen into a pile as she rose. Ilona removed the long-tailed tunic and her smallclothes, folding them neatly and setting them aside. Naked, a mosaic of bruises blossoming faintly against her olive skin, Ilona took up the soaked cloth and began to wash herself.

Face, neck, arms. Breasts. And more.

Had Rhuan not come . . .

Had he not heard the kettle fall inside the wagon . . .

Had he not seen the lantern fall . . .

But he did.

He had.

And by such subtle happenstance was a potential future averted.

She had seen the icy anger in Rhuan's eyes, in the cold sculpture of his face. Heard it, and recognized it, in his voice: *"You do know he'll have to be killed."*

And when she remonstrated, he answered: *"Oh, I do think so."*

Her memory was clear. She heard it again, the quiet in-

tonations that hid nothing of his rage despite the ease with
which he spoke, the grace of his movements; saw again in
that initial instant of anger, in that first flush of rage, eyes
that flickered red.

Other men burned hot when so angry.

Rhuan burned cold.

She wondered, as she did so often about so many other
things concerning the guide, if it was the Shoia in him.
The nonhuman in him.

Or merely the male.

RHUAN FOUND JORDA seated on his beloved
three-legged stool beside his high-wheeled wagon. He
was hunched over his writing board, the surface illuminated
by a lively, snapping fire a long pace away. Pinned to the
board was a sheet of rumpled, rough-made paper, and Jorda
was carefully marking down figures with a goose quill nib
thread-wrapped and glued onto a length of slender, whittled
sapling branch. The master lacked a fine hand, but the numbers were legible, if barely; the quality of the paper was poor
enough that if he made the figures too small, the ink would
spread and obscure them. Now and again he stopped to dip
the nib in a small pot of watery ink. He scowled in fierce concentration, chewing absently at the tuft of beard growing in
the hollow immediately below his lower lip.

Rhuan leaned against a tall wagon wheel and smiled
crookedly at a man he both liked and admired. "No wages
for the wicked, I assume."

Jorda finished the number he was scribing, then flicked
a glance at his guide from under red-gold lashes. "You'll be
paid."

Rhuan shook his head. "Save your coin rings, Jorda. If
you've paid out everything the folk paid in, you'll need
every ring to make it through to next season."

"You'll be paid," Jorda repeated. "You shirked no part
of your duty, even if you mishandled the Hecari patrol. My
people are alive."

Rhuan moved to the fire and squatted down to gather a handful of kindling piled beside the stone ring. "That's not why I've come. I suspect—I *know*—she'd rather I said nothing about it, but something should be. You're the master." With apologies to the wood, he dropped a stick into the fire. Anger flickered again, a deep, abiding anger. "Perhaps one of your people *shouldn't* be left alive."

Jorda, sighing, continued to scribe figures on the pebbly surface of the paper. "Rhuan—"

"Someone attempted to assault Ilona."

The master's voice was startled as his head whipped up. "When? Here? One of the karavaners?" As Rhuan nodded, he set down his writing board and tossed the pen upon it, smearing his careful numbers. "Is she all right?"

"Bruises, she says." Rhuan shrugged, aware of guilt that he betrayed Ilona's preference for privacy, but knowing too he was correct to tell Jorda. "She may indeed be fine save for bruises . . . but I think it's best we look in on her."

Jorda growled agreement and stood. "I'll go now."

But Rhuan, rising, stopped the master with a hand on his arm. "Not just yet. I think we should give her time to sort out how she feels. But later tonight, yes."

"I can't stay here when one of my diviners has been attacked! I couldn't stay here if *any* woman in my karavan was attacked. Mother of Moons, Rhuan, what's in your head to suggest such a thing?"

"Ilona's dignity," he answered quietly.

Firelight gilded Jorda's ruddy beard as he wiped a big hand over his tired face. His expression remained grim. "Does she need a healer? There's a moonmother in the settlement—" He caught himself. "That is, if the Hecari didn't kill her."

"I think she just wants to be alone. I have to go back there shortly anyway . . . I'm repairing her steps. I'll look in on her."

Jorda's eyes sharpened. "You said *attempted* to assault."

"Yes."

"Then . . ."

Rhuan answered the unspoken question. "No, he was not successful."

"What happened?"

Rhuan shrugged. "*I* happened. Fortunately."

"Where is he now?"

"I was more concerned with Ilona's safety than stopping him. I didn't see where he went."

"Did you see him clearly enough to recognize him if you saw him again?"

Rhuan loosed a smile he knew was not precisely friendly. "Oh, yes, I would know this man. Even were I blind."

Jorda's eyes narrowed. "*I'll* deal with him, Rhuan. It's my duty as master."

Rhuan fingered his horn-handled knife. "Yours. Mine. Does it matter?"

"It matters." Jorda turned his broad body to face him squarely. "It matters."

Rhuan was nothing if not a man who understood when to give in.

Or to appear to give in.

"Of course," he said lightly, inclining his head.

BRODHI TOSSED OFF the final swallow of ale, tipping back his head. When he brought it up, when he set the tankard down upon the table, he stilled. A child stood before him.

Even in dim light, her face was exquisite. Her skin, so fair as to verge on translucence, was unblemished. Sky-blue eyes studied him steadily, framed by thick black lashes. Black curls tumbled in disarray around her shoulders. The ankle-length homespun tunic she wore was stained with blood, and soot, hanging shapelessly from thin, narrow shoulders. Her feet were bare and filthy.

He could not ignore her. Not quite. "What do you want?"

Her voice was clear and pure, a girl-child's soprano with

no hint of whine, nor any trace of tears. "Will you come with me?"

Brodhi frowned, annoyed. "Come with you where?"

"I can't find Mam or Da."

His eyebrows arched up in startlement. "And you wish *me* to help you find them?"

Her gaze was unrelenting. "Will you come with me?"

"Have you no other kin?"

"Mam and Da."

He briefly debated reminding her that the use of the word *other* indicated those who were not mother and father. The imprecision of human speech annoyed him greatly. But he altered course. "Have you no friends? *Adult* friends," he amended hastily, imagining himself suddenly surrounded by children. "They may be with those friends." He managed to summon a moment's understanding of humans, and realized there was another possibility. "They are likely searching for you."

"Will you come with me?"

That, again. In the same tone of voice. It lacked the desperation of a frantic, frightened child, was unthickened by tears. The expectation in it transcended hope, touched on expectation. She had been taught, obviously, that adults, even strangers, would be willing to help her merely for the asking of it.

Brodhi indicated the lantern. "It's dark outside. Better to wait until morning. You may find them then, or at least someone you know who can help."

Her gaze upon him was disconcerting. "The woman said to come here. To you."

At last, more information. "What woman?" Suspicion roused. "A slight woman with pale, cropped hair and large ear-hoops?"

The child nodded.

"Ah." He smiled sourly. He desired more ale, but the tankard was empty. It would be a simple matter to rise and fetch more from behind the plank bar, thereby putting distance between himself and the girl. But he didn't rise. He matched her look for look, and said nothing. A cruel joke, he thought, that Bethid should send the child to him. "Manipulation," Brodhi said aloud, "is most unattractive." And utterly unlike Bethid.

The girl said nothing.

A lengthy hiss of frustration broke from his throat. He rose, pushing back the stool. Another man, a human man, softened by her plight, would touch her, he knew. Place a gentle hand on her head, or her shoulder, or even reach out for her hand.

He did none of those things. He merely gestured for her to turn around and walk toward the entrance.

Against his preference, he followed. The girl had won.

Or Bethid had.

HIS NAME WAS Vencik. Traveling with him in Jorda's karavan, bound for a new start elsewhere, was a wife, two children, and his wife's mother. The wife, two children, and his wife's mother were, very likely, at their wagon preparing dinner. He should be there, he knew. He should not be away from it, not with chores to do. But something inexplicable had taken hold of him, something of urgency and demand and curse-the-consequences, and instead of using the charm on his wife's mother, for whom he had purchased it with the last coin-ring in his pouch, he used it on the woman. On the hand-reader.

Away from the cookfires, away from the wagons, Vencik stumbled into darkness, fell to his knees, and vomited.

He was not, *was not* that kind of man. But what he had done—what he had so nearly done—spoke of something inside, some demon or devil that had slipped into his soul. Wanting to silence his wife's mother for a single day was not so bad a thing . . . but to assault the hand-reader? There was no other reason he could think of but a devil or demon.

He needed a priest. He needed a *different* priest, one who could cleanse him, purify him, exorcise the evil thing inside that had forced him to do such a terrible thing.

Vencik wiped his mouth on the sleeve of his tunic and sat back on his heels. And froze.

It was the time of the Orphan Sky, but there were stars. What little light existed was enough. He saw the karavan guide smiling gently down at him. "I can be a priest."

Vencik stared.

"I can cleanse you. I can purify you. I can most distinctly exorcise you."

Hope kindled. But this was a *guide*.

Could priest and guide be the same thing?

"You," the man said with every evidence of satisfaction, "are as poor an excuse for a human as I have yet seen in this land."

Vencik lowered his head to stare at the ground beneath his knees.

"And I think it's time you left it."

His head snapped up. The last thing Vencik saw, beneath the Orphan Sky, was the sudden slashing movement arcing toward him out of the darkness.

Blood. Blood. So much blood.

And no air at all, save that which whistled out of his freshly opened throat.

Chapter 27

R HUAN SQUATTED BESIDE the big supply wagon, looking through the spare plankwood Jorda always carried. He had decided it was best if both of Ilona's bottom steps were replaced, and wanted to be certain he selected the strongest planks for their construction. There were tools aplenty in the wagon as well as wood, spare ropes, harnesses, fittings, pots of axle grease, spokes; medicaments for humans, horses, draft animals; whole oilcloth canopies as well as patches, gut, and awls for stitching the heavy cloth, silk thread and needles for stitching more fragile flesh; lamp oil, lanterns, kindling; spare clothing, leather, bedding, and much more.

The light was poor, but his eyes saw better in the dark than those of humans, and his hands read tales of the wood. He had only to smooth his sensitive fingertips over the surface, brushing grain, knots, blemishes, and he knew the name of the tree that had rendered up its skin, its heart, its life. Humans wouldn't understand; they would believe he meant the name that indicated what *kind* of tree it was. Had been. But Rhuan, touching wood, learned the personal and private name of the elderling who once had lived, who had given up that life for a wholly human need.

Humans, Rhuan reflected, didn't understand all too

many things, even about their own land, their own world. About their own gods.

Light from a lantern flickered across his vision. Two people approached, movements hesitant. Rhuan looked up from greeting the wood to greet them.

He was more than a little startled to discover the arrivals were the two eldest children of the farmerfolk from the end of the karavan. "Are you looking for the master?"

The boy shook his head. "We've come to speak with you." He and his sister exchanged glances before he continued. "It's about tomorrow."

Rhuan set down the plank upon the others. A fine elderling tree, once an ancient and proud oak. Now diminished by the ax and adze of humans. "We'll head back after the morning meal. It will take a few days to reach the settlement."

The children exchanged glances again. The boy was clearly uncomfortable. A frown knitted the pale brows arching over blue eyes that would no doubt one day be as steady as his father's. "No, it's not that. We won't be going back. Da has decided we must go on as we planned, to Atalanda."

"Because of the diviners," the girl said quietly, "and the baby."

As she spoke, her face colored up. She had the fine, fair skin of youth, and pale white-blond hair that would, as she aged, turn wheat-gold. She would be very pretty, Rhuan thought. "Ah yes, the baby." He selected another plank and introduced himself in silence with the touch of his flesh. Inwardly he spoke to the tree of his regret for the death of a fine, strong elderling. Then, with carefully gauged neutrality, he spoke to the human saplings. "Your da and mam have four living, healthy children. Perhaps it might be best if they weighed those lives as heavily as that of the unborn child."

"But the diviners," the boy protested. He was, Rhuan realized, not quite so young after all, with lantern light glinting briefly off a thin crop of golden stubble along his jaw.

"Diviners," Rhuan murmured, "may not necessarily always be completely, absolutely, incontrovertibly accurate."

The girl was as taken aback as her brother. "They're *diviners.*"

Smiling, Rhuan gave in gracefully. "Alas, I am but a guide. What do I know of such things?"

The young man's tone strengthened. "You know about Alisanos."

His sister chimed in as well, no longer hesitant. "About demons, and devils."

"And how to keep a wagon safe upon the roads."

"How to save us from Hecari."

"How to *kill* Hecari."

"You're a guide," the girl declared with conviction.

Her brother, who had gained confidence as they detailed the challenges and dangers, nodded. "The karavan is turning around. It's going back to the settlement. There will be no others until next season."

"You're a guide," she repeated, more quietly now, as if she sensed the power of passion in their words. "One wagon may not be a karavan, but we need your help all the same."

Rhuan smiled, watching the plank as he once again smoothed its skin with his own. "Your parents know nothing about this, do they? That you've come to me."

In unison, they shook their fair-haired heads.

"Rhuan!" Jorda's voice. "*Rhuan*—" But he broke off as he came up on them and saw the children. Rhuan watched the karavan-master make a concerted effort to regain control of his tone. "Your pardon," Jorda said civilly, "but my guide and I have karavan business to discuss."

It was dismissal, and they took it so. Before they could turn away, Rhuan spoke. To them, not to his employer. "I will come with my answer in the morning."

The boy nodded. The girl's expression suggested she didn't believe him. Both walked away, heads bent. Indeed, they did not believe him.

It was a mark of Jorda's high-running emotions that he asked nothing about what the children wanted. Rhuan knew him well enough to realize that beneath the bristling beard, the master's broad jaw was set very tightly.

"A woman has come to me," Jorda began, "worried because her husband is missing. He missed dinner, she says; he never misses dinner. He went to relieve himself and never came back."

Rhuan said nothing. It was best to let the angry rushing river run its course.

"There seem to me to be two possibilities," Jorda continued, "as to why this man is missing. He met an animal that took him for a meal, though there has been absolutely no sign of predators—or so my expert guides have told me. Or he just might, just might *possibly,* be the man who assaulted Ilona, and met a predator of an entirely different sort out there in the darkness."

Rhuan took up another length of plank and examined it. "I suppose he might." He silently spoke his name to the elderling as he placed fingertips upon the adzed surface. "I suppose it is also possible he and his wife had an argument, and he is out walking off the anger."

"In the dark."

"Ah. Yes, it is very dark to your kind. Perhaps not."

Jorda's tone was mostly a growl. "My 'kind'?"

Rhuan paused, but did not look up from the wood. This plank would do well; it told him so as he asked it in the silent language of the trees. "Forgive me. I sometimes forget myself when learning the story of a once-proud tree who has been murdered by humans."

"I'm talking about a *man*, Rhuan, not a tree!"

A hallmark of humans, to dismiss, to diminish, what was not as themselves. And yet he liked them. Still. He grimaced. *Most of the time.* "The third possibility is, of course, that this missing man may not be the one who assaulted Ilona."

Through his teeth, Jorda said, "And what do you suppose the odds are of that?"

"I never wager on or with lives, particularly human lives, which are all too fragile as it is. But you know that." Rhuan rose and met the master eye to eye. "Are you accusing me of killing him?"

"I know you're certainly capable of it. You've done it before." Jorda made a gesture. "But no. No, I'm not accusing. I'm not even asking. Maybe I don't want to know. If he *is* the one . . ." He gestured again, but more sharply, as if silencing the direction of his private suppositions and suspicions. "You see better at night. It might bring this woman some peace if you were to search for the man."

Rhuan leaned the selected plank against the wagon. "No woman should be worried for her man's safety. But then, no woman should be worried for her *own* safety."

Jorda scowled. "Find him. Then report to me."

Rhuan understood the implication very well. He would not be asked if he were responsible for the murder, should he discover the body . . . but the body most definitely was to be discovered.

DAYLIGHT WAS BANISHED, dusk had gone. Darkness ruled. The tent settlement now was illuminated only by the stars, pierced-tin lanterns hung out on shepherd's crooks, a thin scattering of meager cookfires, and the embers of wooden tent poles transformed by fire to coals. The keening laments too had died out, replaced by low murmuring, the occasional voice raised in call or question, the quiet talk among those who even in poor light sifted through the remains of tents in search of bodies or belongings. The stench of fire remained, as well as the faint underlying odor of burned flesh, for in the destruction of the tents a few of the one in ten selected for culling were burned.

Brodhi found himself following the girl. She walked what had been narrow footpaths winding through the tent village without the hesitation of uncertainty, though many landmarks had changed. But she moved slowly, if steadily, checking at downed tents before going on. Brodhi watched her thin, straight body in its loose tunic go before him, noted the tilt of her head, the set of narrow shoulders. There was pride in her body, an unconscious grace in the economy of her movements despite her youth. Oddly, as she passed each tent, be it burned heap upon the ground or a still-standing oilcloth dwelling, she made a gesture with one hand or the other as if indicating, as if counting, the tents. Brodhi could not help himself: he looked, he counted, even as she did. And when occasionally they came across a body fallen in the culling and as yet unclaimed by kin, the girl paused and inspected each face, each body, albeit she touched no one.

When they reached a small clearing at an intersection of five footpaths, the girl stopped. She turned to him then, turned to him and lifted her exquisite face. The clarity of her eyes was unsettling.

"Did you see them?" she asked.

"See who?"

"Dardannus, the Kantic priest. Hezriah, the bonedealer. And Lavetta, the fat woman. All of them crossed the river."

Had died, she meant. "I hardly know everyone here," Brodhi told her acerbically, "dead or living. I can't be expected to, not when so many people come here and leave here nearly every day."

The curly-haired head tilted slightly as she examined his face. "They would know *you*. If you died, and your body lay here, or here, or there." She gestured to indicate the places she meant. "Anyone who saw you would know your name. Brodhi the courier. Brodhi the Shoia."

He knew, then, *her* name. "Ferize." Air hissed through his teeth as he inhaled sharply. "Ferize, what have you done? I can't sense you."

The little girl with eyes that had seen the flow of two centuries examined him mutely.

"I can't *sense* you!"

"Kendic was there, too. His body. Did you see it?"

He had seen Kendic fall beneath the warclubs of Hecari. He had not recognized him on their walk through the settlement-cum-battlefield. Just a body was Kendic. No more a man.

"Ferize—"

"I shielded," the girl said matter-of-factly.

"You can't do that with me!"

"Oh, I can. I just never did."

"Why now? Why here?"

"A test," she said simply.

Of course it was a test. Or a trick. "For what purpose?"

"To see," she said, "if you saw. With more than merely your eyes." The tilted head was incongruous in the child's semblance. He should have recognized it. "But you have as yet no comprehension of ending, of loss. Of how it is for humans who have only one life in this world to lose those they love. And what grief is."

He recalled the keening of the women. The tears on the faces of men. He recalled Bethid's anguish, and Mikal's shock. But those memories told him nothing. Nothing that was necessary. Nothing of import. Nothing that would, in any way, affect or alter his life.

"Ferize, it makes no sense."

"When it does, then perhaps you'll be ready to go on," she told him. "To move from this place, this life, to the place and life you desire so very badly."

And then the shielding was gone, and he sensed her. *Felt* her, in all places and all ways. Her loss would indeed affect and alter his life. But losing her was no risk, here; losing her would not happen, here. Because it *could* not, here.

"Look again," Ferize said in the voice of a child, in the voice of a human child, though her tone was ancient. "Best to keep looking each day, and each night, and every moment, until it makes sense. It is required, Brodhi, that it make sense. That you *understand*."

"Ferize—" But he broke it off, because he doubted she could hear him. Not when she so decisively, so suddenly, absented herself from his company.

Somewhere nearby, perhaps around the next turn, a child was crying.

"Ferize!"

The quality of her absence verged upon desertion, not mere departure.

"Ferize!"

"What are you shouting about?"

A woman's voice. He spun.

Bethid.

No one save Ferize, or possibly Darmuth, could take him unaware. But he'd been distracted, and she had. He'd been shouting, and she had.

Shouting. Where humans would hear him. Where humans would *see* him, as Bethid had and did.

"That was not necessary," he snapped. "It was wholly unnecessary."

She stared at him blankly.

"Sending the girl," he growled. "What did you hope to accomplish?"

Bethid shook her head slowly, with grave deliberation. "I have no idea what you're referring to."

And Brodhi realized that she probably didn't. That it was all too likely Ferize had lied to him. She certainly needed no directions from Bethid or anyone else to find him in Mikal's tent, either in the guise of a little girl or another entirely.

Between his teeth, he cursed.

"They've found Kendic's body," Bethid said. "They're pulling the dead aside and setting them together, so that people may have better luck in finding those they've lost. In the morning it will be easier, but the kin for now are using lanterns and torches . . . I think they don't want to wait until daylight."

Kendic's body. One of those Ferize had indicated. One of those he had seen, but not recognized. Because it hadn't mattered. And it made no sense to him that it should.

Ferize had told him it was *required* that such things matter.

He had not known by name the Kantic priest, the bonedealer, the fat woman. They served only to take up space in this settlement, in this world, if not in his life. But Kendic he had known.

Did it matter? Had Kendic, alive, mattered to him? Should Kendic, dead, matter more, or any less?

"They'll begin the rites at dawn," Bethid continued. "I'll be there with Timmon and Alorn. Will you go?"

"I imagine it's self-evident that the Kantic priest should be given Kantic rites," Brodhi replied ironically, "but how will anyone know which gods the other dead folk worshipped in order to *give* the rites?"

And then he recalled, with abrupt and unexpected clarity, how he had knelt beside an old woman, a dead human woman, and wished her well of her journey out of life into death.

"Is that what you want?" He raised his voice, turning his face to the sky. *"Is this what you want, Ferize?"*

"Brodhi. Brodhi?" And again, with more emphasis, *"Brodhi!"*

He looked from the night sky to the small woman. Irritation sharpened his words. "What is it?"

"Who are you talking to?"

Frustration bubbled up. "Why does it matter? Why should you care? Why should it possibly be any of your concern?"

She had washed her face at some point, but the overlay of shadows hollowed cheeks and eyes. Only the muted glow of ear-hoops touched by firelight lent color to her face. "Because whether you like it or not, whether you *want* it or not, I care about you. We are couriers, we two, and owe one another loyalty because of that, but we are friends, too. In general I like you, Brodhi, even though there are many times when you make it difficult. More than many times when you are insufferable."

Imprecision again. Why could no human truly grasp the details of his or her own language? Bethid in particular was difficult to follow at times, to parse through the thickets of emotion-laden words to find the heart tree. "'More than many times,'" he quoted, "would mean all of the time."

"Why, yes," she said in an ingenuous tone. "Yes, I do grasp that, Brodhi. Why do you think I said it?"

Bethid sounded, in that moment, using that tone, very like Ferize. He scowled at her, trying to see beneath the shell that was Bethid to the demon beneath, just in case she actually was Ferize in yet another form. Another *shielded* form.

"Why?" he asked cautiously. "Why does liking matter?"

She blinked. Eventually she offered, "Because it just does."

That was a Bethid answer. He relaxed. So, Ferize desired him to learn. He would learn. "Why does it matter? Why should it?"

"Brodhi!" She stared at him in perplexed. "Here we stand in the midst of a half-destroyed settlement, of a decimated people, and you want to debate why it matters that I should like you?"

"Yes."

She raised a stiff hand, palm facing him. The gesture was unmistakable. "Stop," she said. "No," she said. "There are bodies to find and identify, kin to console, rites to be conducted, belongings to be sorted. I will *not* have this conversation with you. Not here, and certainly not now. And if nothing else, you have reminded me just how *in*-human you are." Bethid shook her head as she lowered her hand. "If Rhuan were not as he is, I would begin to believe that all Shoia are like you. And then it would be a very good thing that no others have appeared."

"Rhuan?" He laughed in disbelief. "Rhuan is a fool."

"Rhuan is a good man, Brodhi. He understands us. He *likes* us. He cares about us. And for all that he can be wholly irresponsible on the one hand, on the other I have never known him to turn his back on a human when that human requires aid. And if he were here now, I know he would be carrying off and identifying the bodies, because he cares enough about us to learn our names."

"Bethid," he said curtly, with exaggerated clarity. "Timmon. Alorn. Mikal." His mouth was a grim line. "Names."

A muscle leaped in her jaw. "But *not very many.*"

He would have continued, but as she turned sharply and presented him with her back, it was abundantly clear she considered the conversation finished. Irritating, that she should take that initiative from him. Just as Ferize had. He glared after her.

When Bethid had disappeared into darkness, Brodhi looked again at the sky. He could not keep the incredulity from his tone. "Is this *really* what you want, Ferize?"

Chapter 28

"HELLO." THE WORD was hoarse, breaking in the middle. "Hello?" Not much improvement, little more than a rusty croak that tailed off into a raspy whisper. But it was sound. She was no longer mute.

Clean now of body, tea at hand as she sat upon her cot, Ilona wore a soft-woven ankle-length night tunic with a patchwork shawl cocooning shoulders and upper torso. Leather buskins lined with felt encased her feet. Her hair remained in need of washing, merely wound and anchored untidily against her head, but she planned to avail herself of the public bathing tent once they returned to the settlement, where she could wash it and let it dry in the bright daylight.

But she broke off the thought abruptly. She would do so *if* the bathing tent remained whole, and *if* the attendant hadn't been one of those culled by the Hecari.

A sharp and sudden rapping at her latched wagon door startled so her badly she jumped. "Ilona?"

Ah, Jorda. She patted her heart to reassure it and rose to go to the door.

Ilona stopped halfway there, struck by realization. She stood in the center of her wagon beneath the Mother Rib, elaborate runes invoking the protection of Sibetha, the god of hand-readers.

She could not help the flicker of resentment. *Where was Sibetha when the stranger came with his silencing charm and his lust?*

"Ilona!" Jorda was clearly worried now, pounding so hard she feared he might break the door off its leather hinges.

Which meant he knew what had happened. Which meant Rhuan had told him.

Ilona desired no visitors, not even the karavan-master whose duty it was to make certain all was well with his employees as much as with the folk who trusted—and paid—him to get them safely to their myriad destinations. She very much preferred to be left alone at least until morning.

But Jorda will break the door.

"Wait—" Barely a croak, the word failed to carry. Ilona moved hastily to the door and lifted the latch. "Jorda, wait—"

The karavan-master's anxious face and posture, fully displayed in the opening door, convinced her that had she waited one moment longer, Rhuan would be repairing more than her bottom step.

She watched Jorda's green eyes flick the length of her body, then back to her face. In the wan glow of the lantern hanging from the lintel hook, she saw color stain the skin above his beard. Ilona knew without reading his hand exactly what was in his mind: how was a man to ask a woman assaulted by another man if she were all right?

She told him she was, in her broken voice. And that broken voice, such irrefutable proof of the assault that in flesh was otherwise shielded against the naked eye by enveloping fabric, kindled Jorda's outrage. She saw it come into his face, saw it rise into his eyes; watched it make him taller, broader, *larger,* like a wild beast gone to hackles from head to tail.

"I'm all right," she repeated hastily, forcing her ragged voice because she realized what he believed. "It was a silencing charm, Jorda—he didn't try to strangle me."

His voice was thick, deepened by anger. "Just rape you."

She wanted to answer him lightly, casually, deflecting the

force of his emotion, but she had very little left, now, of what small amount of her shredded voice had returned. Instead she merely rasped, "Didn't."

"Because of Rhuan."

She nodded.

"Who is now 'in search' of a body that very likely *became* a body by his hand." Jorda shook his head. "In this case, I find it difficult to begrudge him that, though I might have preferred to do it myself. In fact, I told him so. But Rhuan is very choosy about which orders he follows and which he ignores."

She had never heard him speak so forcefully, or with such venom in his tone. But her mind moved swiftly to what else he had said regarding Rhuan: he had, apparently, killed the man. Precisely as he said he would.

Ilona closed her eyes.

Jorda's voice altered from anger into awkward compassion. "Would you rather come into another wagon for the night? Not *mine,*" he added hastily as her eyes popped open in startlement, "That is, you could stay in my wagon if you wished, but of course I would sleep outside on the ground. Or, if you like, I could sleep *here* on the ground. But surely there's a wagon with a woman or two in it who would be willing to share, if that would be more comfortable."

She realized this offer was all he could think of to ease the situation. Poor Jorda had never considered contingencies should his woman diviner be assaulted. Such a thing was incomprehensible in a world where true diviners were considered extensions of the gods.

Ilona shook her head and attempted speech again. "I'll be fine, thank you." And she would be. The incident was an aberration, not an ongoing threat. And Rhuan had killed the man. To her shame, there was less regret in the knowledge than she expected.

She heard it before she felt it. The wagon creaked. The animals of the karavan lifted voices in clear distress. Pots hanging together rubbed and clanked softly. Loose objects rattled.

And then the earth *shivered*.

Startled, Ilona caught hold of the doorjamb. Jorda actually staggered against the motion, lurching forward to grab at her wagon to steady himself. The rolling shiver passed before they could even speak, but left behind was a queasiness in her belly and a hot apprehension that prickled her flesh. The livestock quieted, but the dogs scattered throughout the karavan continued to bark.

"Mother of Moons," Jorda murmured, eyes on the residual swinging of her door lantern.

She forced her voice yet again; this time, because she had to. "What was that?" And then she saw movement in the darkness: A man walking out of shadow into the wavering glow of her lantern. Braid ornamentation glinted.

Rhuan's expression was odd, as if he too felt unsettled; rather, Ilona decided, like a cat desiring to retain innate dignity and grace yet not quite able to do so. "That," he said, "was Alisanos. A greeting, you might say." He looked at Jorda. "I've found the body."

Jorda was distracted. "Good. Now, tell me about this 'greeting' from Alisanos."

Rhuan shrugged. "It was what it was. As I've said, Alisanos is on the brink of going active. It's pulling up roots, you might say. Until that last root is pulled and Alisanos is free to change locales, these sorts of things are going to happen."

Ilona noted Jorda studied Rhuan intently, brows pulled inward to the bridge of his nose. "How is it you know such things?"

Rhuan shrugged offhandedly. "Shoia are sensitive to Alisanos. I don't know why." He grinned briefly. "Maybe we're more akin to the animals than you are. But I feel it, in here." He pressed a hand over his breast.

Despite the quick grin and the flash of dimples, there was a pinched look around his mouth. His color, Ilona noted, was not quite normal. She thought perhaps he felt Alisanos somewhere else in addition to his heart. "You look as if you might lose your dinner any moment."

His smile was crooked. "There's nothing left in my belly

to lose." He rubbed the back of his neck, looking beyond the lantern light into the darkness. "It's coming. And there's nothing any of us can do to prevent it."

The karavan-master's eyes sharpened. "If Shoia are so sensitive—do you know when?"

"No. That much even I can't tell." He changed topics abruptly, looking at Ilona. "The man is dead. Someone opened his throat."

"Someone." Jorda's tone was laden with heavy irony, but he went no farther with the implication. "Then I had better go tell his woman." His expression was strained; Ilona knew he hated this duty above all others. "Perhaps you and Darmuth might do her the courtesy of wrapping the body in oil-cloth and bringing him to her wagon. She'll want dawn rites, I'm sure, before we head back to the settlement."

"Darmuth hasn't returned yet," Rhuan said, "but yes, I can do that. I'll get the cloth from the supply wagon."

Grimly, Jorda said, "I suppose I had best come up with an explanation for his death other than murder ... a predator, I suspect, which will frighten everyone, but we're bound for the settlement anyway." He thought further. "But where were you, they'll wonder? Your job was to keep him safe."

"I," Rhuan declared, "was nowhere near him."

"A predator, then," Jorda decided. "And you were some distance away and too late to save him."

The master departed, but Rhuan lingered. Ilona met his eyes. Her voice, for the moment, steadied. "I know what Jorda believes. But I'd like to hear confirmation from you. Was he dead before you found him?"

His gaze was unwavering. "Yes."

And yet she needed a more specific answer. "Did you kill him?"

He replied without the slightest change in inflection. "No."

She could not help herself; the line of her gaze dropped to the horn hilt of his long-bladed knife, sheathed slantwise on his left hip, and marked also the line of slender throwing knives safed in loops along his baldric.

Rhuan said, "It wasn't done with a knife."

Her eyes flicked up. "You said his throat was cut."

"I said his throat was *opened*."

"But—*oh*. Rhuan—"

He overrode her failing voice. "Let be, 'Lona. No more is needed, save to know he's dead."

Perhaps in truth no more was needed. But Ilona could not avoid seeing the man's face before her, the charm in his hand, the terrible intent in his eyes. She could still hear his voice invoking the charm, still feel the closing of her own throat.

Closed. Not opened, as the man's was.

But she let it be, just as Rhuan suggested.

WITH A MOTHER'S sense of such things, Audrun became aware of furtive glances exchanged between Ellica and Gillan when they believed no one was looking. At other times, when she *was* looking, both assumed what she considered to be rather imbecilic expressions of innocence. Audrun knew better; her children were not imbeciles, and such behavior was completely alien to them. Eventually she managed to quietly call both of them to her as Davyn went off to check the oxen prior to bedtime, while the two youngest were washing plates, pots, and utensils with much slopping of water.

"All right," she said crisply, as they gathered at the back of the wagon in the glow of a battered tin lantern, "tell me."

Ellica avoided eye contact, ducking her head to study the ground. Gillan did not mimic her, but the rush of color into his face sang its own song.

"You went for a walk after dinner," Audrun said dryly, "which isn't a habit either of you have cultivated on this journey. Where was it you went, and what did you do or see?"

Her two eldest exchanged glances. Ellica chewed her bottom lip.

"I'm not giving in," Audrun warned them. "We can

stand here all night if you like, which means at some point your father is going to become suspicious, or you can tell me now."

Both children were clearly uncomfortable, but Gillan, thus prodded, finally answered. "We talked to the guide. The one with the braids." He raised his chin and his tentative voice firmed. "We asked if he'd come with us."

Audrun blinked. "Come with us?"

"We know," Ellica said quietly. "Da wants to go on to Atalanda instead of turning around like everyone else."

That took Audrun aback. She and Davyn had certainly made that decision, but all of the children had been away from the wagon when they had done so. The intention was to tell them just before bedtime. Were she and Davyn truly so easy to read?

"If the karavan goes back to the settlement, there's nothing for the guide to do," Ellica continued.

Her brother nodded. "So we asked if he'd come with us."

"He said he'd give us his answer in the morning," Ellica finished.

Audrun, struck dumb, considered several different answers, and eventually found one she felt was most appropriate. "Your father got us this far, did he not? He should be trusted to do as well for us on the rest of the journey."

Gillan averted his eyes and dug holes in the turf with the toe of his boot.

"He killed all those Hecari," Ellica declared, "and died, and came back to life. If *Da* were to be killed, he'd stay dead."

Well, yes. They had grasped the very thing that had already occurred to Audrun. If Davyn were killed, they'd be left alone on a strange road skirting the dangerous borderlands of Alisanos. Davyn had only one life to lose. The guide, who knew the route and its dangers, could possibly spare two or three.

But I'm a parent, and must act as one. "This is business for adults," she chided. "It's a decision for your da to make. You should not have gone to the guide. He isn't family."

Gillan and Ellica simultaneously opened their mouths to

speak. But in that moment every dog in the karavan began to bark frenziedly. Beneath their feet the earth rippled.

Clanking pots fell off their hooks underneath the wagon. Something inside tumbled and thumped onto the floor-boards.

Audrun grabbed the wagon to steady herself even as she called out to her children. "Into the wagon!" It seemed safest; it offered cover where the open sky did not. She lifted her voice to call the youngest. "Torvic! Megritte! Come into the wagon!"

But the earth stilled itself as abruptly as it had moved, and she found herself clinging to the wagon's tailgate sur-rounded by four big-eyed children demanding to know what had happened and *how* it had happened; what it meant, and would it happen again, loudly and all at once. But Audrun had no answer for them. Not even one of false reassurance. No such thing had ever ocurred in her life-time.

The earth had *moved.*

The guide, she thought, would know precisely what to say. He would give her children the truth, not prevarica-tion. No matter how well-intended that prevarication was.

She followed that envisioned route. "I don't know what that was." She flicked a glance at Gillan and Ellica. "But we'll ask the guide in the morning. He'll know."

That satisfied her eldest children. And she realized, with no little amount of surprise, that it satisfied her as well.

Chapter 29

*H*AVING RETRIEVED A roll of oilcloth from the supply wagon, Rhuan carried it out to the body, hidden from the karavan by distance and darkness, and dropped it to the ground. The dead man lay on his back, head puddled in congealing blood, and the gaping wound in his throat showed black in the thin light save for a pearlescent glint of vertebrae. His mouth was frozen in a rictus of terror. Open eyes stared into the sky. He stank of urine and feces.

The man had made it some distance from the wagon. At Rhuan's arrival various insects stilled, but soon began their songs again. The night was filled with chirps and buzzing.

Awareness flickered through Rhuan's body. All the hairs on his arms stood up. "All right," he said, "you made this mess. You can help me clean it up."

Darmuth, leaving behind swathing shadows as he assumed human shape, laughed. The gemstone in his tooth sparkled. "What, no questions as to whether I ate any part of the body?"

"Well?"

"No. Though not for lack of an appetite. I stole a milch cow and ate most of her. They'll assume a predator took both cow and man."

"And they would be correct, wouldn't they?" Rhuan unrolled the oilcloth with a practiced flip of his hands. "Just once, it would be nice if you accepted responsibility for the various people you murder. *I'm* the one they always blame!"

"It's best that way. With you blamed, I am in better position to keep you from harm. Were our roles reversed, I'm certain I'd end up being killed in revenge."

"You don't believe I could keep *you* from harm?"

Darmuth shrugged, leaning to take up the body's feet as Rhuan bent to its arms. "It's better if they wonder what you're capable of." They swung the body onto the oilcloth. "And anyway, I've never killed anyone who didn't deserve it. Human or otherwise."

"Did you kill that man in Hezriah's tent?"

"What man?"

Rhuan draped fabric over the dead man's feet and head, then turned to the longer portions on either side to do the same, enveloping the body. "Hezriah. The bonedealer. The one who's ever hopeful he'll come across Shoia bones to sell for exorbitant prices."

"I know who Hezriah is. What dead man are you talking about? Other than this dead man, that is."

Rhuan looked up. Darmuth's pupils were slitted, catlike. *Demon*like. "The one who somehow managed to find his way out of Alisanos."

"Ah. How much of him was still human?"

"Most of him."

"Well, I haven't killed any humans save for this one for quite some time now. I didn't kill that one."

"He looked at me," Rhuan said, "and he knew me. Or thought he did."

"And that bothers you?" Darmuth shrugged. "If Alisanos had begun its work on him, no sanity was left."

"I really would prefer not to be lumped in with demons. I'm not one." Rhuan paused, then politely added, "No insult intended."

Darmuth assumed an expression of exaggerated hurt. "We're not so bad as all that."

"You eat people."

"Only a few of them. Now and again."

"I don't."

"Oh, that's right. Your preferred main course is demon-flesh."

Rhuan winced. "Let's get this man to his wagon. Jorda's there telling the wife." And as Darmuth picked up one end of the wrapped body and he the other, he added casually, "The farmsteaders are going on to Atalanda by way of the shortcut. I've been asked to guide them, and have point-edly been reminded that I have no employment until next season."

Darmuth considered it as they carried the body between them, heading back to the wagons. "Dangerous."

"That's why they asked me to accompany them."

"Dangerous for *you*."

"Possibly."

"*Probably*. For many reasons."

"Possibly probable."

"But of course you'll do it."

Rhuan grinned. "So I will—" But then he stopped grin-ning. The night went silent. "Oh no."

Darmuth cocked his head, scented the air, and began to laugh.

Queasiness returned. Rhuan itched from head to toe, as if tiny insects crawled across his flesh. "Oh, I do hate this . . ."

The demon's laughter continued.

Rhuan's belly cramped sharply. "I'm gratified *you* find humor in the situation!"

Another rolling shiver of the earth caused Rhuan to drop his end of the body, swearing. He turned away and went down on one knee. His bones were afire as he gave way to unproductive retching. Over the sound of his own misery, he heard the karavan dogs once again barking amid the complaints of myriad livestock.

"That," Darmuth announced smugly, "should con-vince you better than I of the folly in guiding that family along the shortcut. It's too close, Rhuan. If Alisanos is affecting you this much already, going closer could be a death sentence. Or, well, worse. For you."

"A *life* sentence?" Rhuan's gust of laughter was hoarse. "Oh, by all means worse. I do know that."

"So?"

"So, they are two adults and four children—with a fifth but a matter of months away from birth."

"Oh." The demon frowned. "A human baby."

"Yes, Darmuth, a human baby. It may be a risk for me, but it's far more dangerous for them to go on alone."

The pupils of Darmuth's eyes rounded, then flickered back into vertical slits. His nostrils flared as his upper lip lifted to display slightly elongated eyeeteeth. "A *human* baby."

"Altogether innocent," Rhuan said pointedly, "of Alisanos entire, and what manner of predators live there." The painful retching had died but his belly felt fragile, and a troublesome buzzing along his bones remained. Grunting, he gathered up the oilcloth-wrapped legs of the body. "Are you certain you didn't eat any part of this man?"

"Quite certain."

"Because whatever rites his wife may desire undertaken may well require him to be stripped. I should hate for her to see bitemarks scattered throughout his flesh."

"Not even a taste."

"I'm not saying he didn't *deserve* to be eaten by a demon, mind you, but I suspect it might upset his wife a great deal."

"Of course he deserved it." Darmuth's tone was matter-of-fact. "I was back in time to see you on the way into Ilona's wagon, and him on the way out. Since you had taken charge of her, I followed him."

"And now two people I like and admire believe I'm a murderer."

"Well," he said, "you are. Just not in this instance."

Rhuan bared his teeth at Darmuth.

The demon bared his far more impressive dentition. "I win."

Darmuth always won when it came to comparing such things. Rhuan, retreating into a sulk, carried his end of the body without another word.

FERIZE HAD GONE. Bethid had gone. At what remained of the settlement, Brodhi stood alone in the darkness, listening to the nightsong of insects, the low murmuring of the men carrying out and laying down bodies in the chosen area, and the muffled sobbing of wives and husbands, mothers and children. Damp ash scented the air, with an undertone of oil and woodsmoke and meat. Human meat.

Rites at dawn, Bethid had said, for those among the decimated, the humans culled from life. It was nothing he had not seen before, or Bethid, or likely any courier, whose job it was to carry news. He supposed an argument could be made that he should return at once to Cardatha, the capital city of Sancorra province, to report to the Hecari warlord in residence there. But as the culling had been ordered by the selfsame warlord, Brodhi also supposed it wasn't necessary to bring him the news. The culling party would do it for him.

Meanwhile, if he remained, there were no announcements or messages to carry. He was free of his duties for a while.

But, alas, not free of grieving humans.

The bulk of a large man loomed out of the darkness into thin light shed by lanterns hanging on crooks. A one-eyed man whose visage was a strained combination of weariness and grief. He carried a shovel in one hand.

"We've dug the common grave. Nothing more to be done until dawn," Mikal said hoarsely. "I'm for a tankard or five of ale. Will you join me?"

Brodhi thought of the tankard he'd already downed. He owed Mikal payment for that.

He was inclined to say no, to take himself off to the couriers' common tent, but found himself nodding. Found himself accompanying Mikal to the ale tent. And found himself sitting down at a table with Mikal, once the man had poured foaming golden ale to the rim of two battered tankards.

A question issued from Brodhi's mouth of its own accord, without thought beforehand: "Will you stay, or go, now that the Hecari have found this place?"

Mikal lowered the tankard from his mouth and displayed a line of foam edging his mustache. "This place is as much a home as I've ever had. I'll stay."

"And if the Hecari return? They might, you know. To cull the numbers again."

Mikal winced and closed one big hand around his necklet of charms. "We'll pray they do not, but yes, even if they do come, I'll stay." He shrugged heavy shoulders. "I have no place else to go."

"Another settlement."

The ale-keep shook his head. "One settlement is much like another, and the very number of humans will attract culling parties. But I know people here." He shifted on his stool, wide hands cupping his head as he massaged scalp and forehead. "I just wish there were a way to fight back ... a way to break free of the Hecari ..."

Brodhi's mouth jerked briefly in an ironic smile. "Not possible."

"Just—if there were something we could *do*." Mikal raised his face and settled folded forearms on the table top. His features were a mask of grime, exhaustion, and raw appeal. "I can't help but think that if enough of us prepared in advance for a culling visit, we might overcome the Hecari."

Brodhi said again, "Not possible."

But Mikal was undeterred as he did his thinking aloud. "No one here, save Kendic, attempted to stop the warriors; we simply accepted that it was happening and tried to avoid being noticed. But perhaps if more of us attempted to stop them, we could."

"And more of you would be killed, as Kendic was."

But Mikal ignored that. His single eye took on a thoughtful, shining intensity. "Maybe that's the key,

Brodhi. Numbers. If we could gather enough of us—not just from Sancorra, but from other overrun provinces—and if we united against the Hecari, it might just *be* possible."

Brodhi, who had seen the prowess and brutality of Hecari warriors more times than he cared to count, shook his head. "They have swept across the province like an endless swarm of locusts," he said. "Do you truly believe it's possible to assemble thousands—or even mere hundreds—of Sancorrans and devise a plan without the warlord learning of it? Without risking a culling?"

Mikal wiped foam from his mustache. An idle thought had transformed itself to a cause within a matter of moments. He was afire with it. "To take back Sancorra from the Hecari is worth that risk. Worth the deaths."

"Three provinces have fallen to them."

Mikal nodded. "Yes, don't you see? That makes for three provinces of potential rebels."

"And how would you unite them?" Brodhi asked pointedly. "The warlord has thousands upon thousands of experienced and loyal warriors under his banner. Their entire culture is based on making war. And Sancorra is not so large. She has fewer men. The same can be said of Korith and Ixtapa."

Mikal's single eye was bright but steady. "The key is organization and communication, so no one acts alone. It would require couriers carrying messages from one province to another. To as many as might join us. The warlord won't be satisfied with three provinces. He has the men, the means, and the hunger to take more." He leaned forward on his stool. "Don't you see, Brodhi? You and your fellow couriers have leave to travel anywhere. Your cloak and badge buys you more freedom than any of us have under the Hecari. Bethid would do it, I know, and probably Timmon and Alorn. And there are other couriers, too. If all of you joined us, we would have a real chance at organizing a resistance!"

Brodhi shrugged. "I have no stake in this. I'm Shoia, not Sancorran, Korithi, or Ixtapan."

"And that's precisely why you'd be so effective."

Mikal's eye shone. "I'm not a fool, Brodhi—it would take time. Probably years. But I believe it could be done." He nodded. "I'll pose it to Bethid tonight. She can talk to Alorn and Timmon." He grinned slowly. "Don't you see? You could take false information to the warlord. He wouldn't know how many we are, where we are, or what we plan."

Brodhi didn't bother to explain that once the false information was uncovered, as it would be at some point, all the couriers would be executed and the invaluable method of communication would evaporate. "And are you prepared to watch an entire settlement wiped out, not just a one in ten culling? Because should any hint of this plan make its way to the warlord, that's what would happen." He drank down a fair portion of ale, then set the tankard on the table with a quiet thump of emphasis. "You've seen Kendic killed, and—" Brodhi recalled the names Ferize had mentioned, "—Hezriah, Dardannus, and Lavetta. All people known to you. Could you watch all the others known to you be killed?"

Mikal slapped the flat of one hand down upon the table with a meaty thwack. "It's because people known to me *were* killed that I'm considering this, Brodhi! The Hecari must be stopped. And if it means more of us must die, at least it's worthwhile losing a life in a fight for freedom than by being randomly executed as the unlucky one in ten." Mikal's expression was grim. "Come to the dawn rites, Brodhi, and see the people who've lost kin today. Ask everyone who lost someone if they wouldn't prefer to rise up against the Hecari than to be put into a line and counted out for culling. Then tell me it's not worth the risk."

Brodhi said, "Thousands of you could die."

Mikal nodded. "I do understand that."

But he didn't, Brodhi knew. No one here but couriers understood. No one who had not seen the cairns of skulls piled up by the Hecari across miles and miles of the plains as markers of their presence could possibly understand.

"We have to do something," Mikal declared. "Are you willing to help?"

Brodhi rose and set a coin ring on the table. "I'll attend the dawn rites." He met the ale-keep's eye. "You'll have my answer then."

Chapter 30

*T*HE CHILDREN WERE in their beds. Audrun and Davyd made theirs beside the wagon, spreading a thin mat as groundcover with folds of blankets atop it and rough, goosedown pillows. Davyn settled the oxen for the night even as Audrun settled the cookfire; then they removed shoes and crawled beneath the blankets. As always, Audrun took comfort in his nearness, in his maleness, in the certainty that he would do all within his power to keep her and the children safe.

That thought spasmed briefly in her belly as she recalled what her two eldest had done. She weighed not telling Davyn they had approached the Shoia guide against telling him the details now, on the verge of sleep. Then she put herself in his place, and knew the proper course.

"They meant well of it, Davvy," she said softly. "Keep that in your mind."

They lay facing one another no more than a handspan apart. His eyes opened. His tone was dry. "I always worry whenever you preface a statement with those words. Well, what is it?"

Audrun drew in a breath and told him what little she knew about shortcuts to Atalanda and guides now out of work, about children old enough to understand the need for help, and about the dangers facing them as they traveled the shortcut. She told him also that it would lift some of the burden of protection from him.

He was far less resigned, as she might have expected, than matter of fact. "It isn't a burden, Audrun. It's simply life. It's what must be done."

"Would it not be easier if he rode with us?"

A breath exhaled sharply informed her of a self-conscious amusement. "Very likely."

"And you told me you wanted to join a karavan for the protection of numbers."

"So I did."

"Is this so very different?"

"Of course it's different." Patience remained in his tone, but she also heard strain. "It's much more costly to hire a personal guide for one wagon. We haven't the coin rings for it. Gillan and Elli should have thought of that before they approached him, because now I have no choice but to turn him down, should he be amenable to the duty."

Audrun could smell the ash and coals of the nearby cookfire. In darkness, insects sang. Overhead the Maiden's acoloytes spread black robes rich with sparkling, star-spangled light. "They wanted to help," she said softly.

"I do know that." A smile crimped the night-shadowed lines at the corners of his eyes. One wide hand slid out from under blankets to smooth her hair against her skull. "It wasn't a *bad* thing, what they did. But they should think such things through before speaking of them to strangers."

"And if he comes in the morning and says he'll go with us?"

Davyn was quiet a long moment. "What kind of man would I be if I couldn't look after my own family?"

Audrun drew in a breath and spoke without censure, merely simple observation. "That's pride speaking."

"So it is. Yet it changes nothing. For sixteen years I have kept this family safe. I shall continue to do so."

She moistened her lips. "He killed five Hecari warriors."

"And put a knife in my shoulder."

Well, yes, but . . . "What if more Hecari come?"

He heaved a great, weary sigh. "If they come, they come.

We will behave as the guide told us to behave, and pray they will only be interested in our belongings."

Audrun could think of no additional arguments or questions that might change his mind. Part of her was relieved; she, too, felt capable of looking after her family. But another part, a smaller but distinct part, could not help but think the guide's presence might go far toward providing additional protection.

"Go to sleep," he said softly, his hand falling away from her hair, "and think about a new beginning for all of us in Atalanda."

Oh, she would do that; she *had* done that. Nearly every night. But this night, having seen Hecari warriors, having felt one warrior's touch, she could not dismiss the memories of the day, nor the realization that no matter what Davyn said, she wanted the Shoia to accompany them.

ILONA AWOKE IN the middle of the night. She could not say what—if anything—had roused her out of sleep, be it noise or movement. She was simply wide awake with no residual grogginess.

It had taken her some while to go to sleep because an unquiet mind painted all manner of pictures of the man who had assaulted her, feeding her images that hadn't actually happened but could have. She had arisen once to make more watery tea and rebraid her hair for bed. Neither task was necessary, but it took her mind from what caused the lack of sleep.

Now she was wide awake, and annoyed because of it.

Tea was not the answer; she had no wish to use the nightcrock more than was necessary. She pushed back the covers and sat up, listening closely for the sort of noise that might account for her sudden wakefulness. But all she heard was the tinny buzzing and chirps of various insects, the occasional dog barking, the whuffling and stirring of livestock. That, she was accustomed to.

Ilona reached down to the floorboards next to her cot. She

had placed there one of the shepherd's crook lantern hooks. Never before had she considered the need for a weapon of any sort, and while the hook was unwieldy, it remained a good weight in her hand. She believed it might do some damage.

But Rhuan had killed the man. Come dawn, rites for his passage across the river would be held. Ghosts and spirits did not exist despite the tales told to children, so she held no fear of incorporeal visitation.

Which meant, of course, that a human was outside.

Fear rose, startling her with its intensity. She had latched and locked her door before climbing into bed. It went against habit to do so, but, if nothing else, the assault had taught her to put no trust in a blithe assumption of personal safety. Now she was grateful for such meager protection.

Kneeling on her cot, Ilona set the lantern hook beside her and turned to the oilcloth side curtains. Very carefully she slipped her fingers between the side of the wagon and the lowered shadecloth. Even more carefully she began to lift the heavy fabric, hunching down so she might surreptitiously peer out the slanting slit between wagon side and oilcloth.

What she saw took her aback entirely. There was Rhuan, settling a bed made of blankets atop a woven mat. Whereas Jorda had asked if she wished him to sleep outside her wagon, Rhuan simply did so. Ilona wasn't certain which she preferred: a man who acquiesced to her wishes, or one who simply did as he intended regardless of her preferences.

Nonetheless, she felt the safer for his presence. Relief swamped her fear and dissipated it. Ilona smiled and let the oilcloth drop down again. She leaned over the cot edge to return the lantern hook to its place, and burrowed beneath her blankets. The knowledge that Rhuan was so close, so prepared to defend her, let sleep return in a rush. She fell into it with a word of grateful welcome in her mind.

 WITH FERIZE GONE, there was no reason not to seek a roof somewhat more waterproof than trees.

Brodhi returned to the couriers' common tent. Bethid, Timmon, and Alorn had not moved any of their belongings, so he claimed the pallet he'd used before. His cloak went up on one of the long hooks dangling from the Mother Rib, and the rest of his meager belongings he arranged neatly by his bed. Though he could see well in low light, he nonetheless lighted the lantern depending from the roof rib. It smoked and guttered, casting unsteady saffron light.

For the first time in more months than he cared to count, Brodhi felt at loose ends. That he should return to Cardatha to report to the Hecari warlord went without saying, but there was no one to know he dawdled save his fellow couriers, and they clearly were in no more of a hurry to return than he was.

Brodhi removed his boots and stretched out on the pallet, arms thrust beneath his head. He contemplated the oilcloth roof, letting tension seep out of his body. He could feel it going, could feel the muscles loosening one by one. It was bothersome that the concerns of humans could become his own. He longed for the heat and indolence of a high summer's day, yearned to strip down, strip away every shred of human clothing, and stand beneath the light of the sun, letting *it* clothe his flesh. Wanted nothing more than to take the light and heat into himself to run through his veins, with no thought at all about humans or patrons or tests.

He closed his eyes and began in silence, lips moving, to tell over the Names of the Thousand Gods, following the strands of mnemonic memory in order to forget no one. They took time, such devotions; he had learned that among humans, the best he could hope for was fits and starts.

He had not gotten very far when a hand pulled back the door flap and a body slipped in.

"Oh." Her tone was startled.

He stopped telling over the Names. He stopped even thinking about them.

Bethid went to her pallet, dropping her cloak in a pool of

rich blue fabric at the foot of the bedding. "I didn't expect to see you here."

He saw no reason to reply.

"I had a talk with Mikal." She sat down and began to pull her boots off. "He said he'd spoken with you." Shed, the boots were set at the foot of her pallet. Stocking-footed, she crossed her legs and looked at him. She waited for a comment; when none was forthcoming she continued. "It could work, Brodhi. Couriers can go far more places than others can, and we're trusted. Do you realize what an advantage that is?"

He gave up ignoring her. "It's an advantage only as long as we can prevent the Hecari from finding out."

"Well, *that's* a brilliant observation."

Brodhi opened his eyes. Sarcasm was not Bethid's usual weapon. "When planning something of this magnitude, something with so much danger attached, only a fool dismisses all probabilities."

"Of course it will be dangerous, Brodhi! We're *not* dismissing that." She ran a coal-grimed hand through up-standing hair, scratching at her scalp. "Timmon and Alorn are still there with Mikal, discussing things. But we all of us believe it could work. It will take time, of course—"

"Years," he put in.

"—but it's still a worthwhile task," Bethid finished pointedly. "And yes, you're undoubtedly correct: years. But we must begin sometime, somewhere, and this place, so lately the victim of more Hecari atrocities, will serve very well."

He hitched himself up on one elbow and stared at her. "You intend to make this settlement the breeding ground of a newly hatched rebellion?"

Bethid nodded. Brass ear-hoops glinted. "Everything that makes it a good place for the karavans to gather makes it a good place to stage a rebellion."

He could not mask his incredulity. "One decimation was not enough to prove this place is known to the Hecari? It will be watched, Bethid! Another culling party—or even the same one—might return tomorrow. In fact, they'd be wise to do so; how better to convince everyone that the warlord won't countenance Sancorrans gathering in numbers?"

She shrugged narrow shoulders. "Then this will be the first battleground."

"They could very well decide to kill more than one in ten."

"All of us," Bethid said promptly, nodding. "We do know that. Which is why it's imperative that we prepare the people here for an effective resistance, in case the Hecari come again."

"This place hosts people who have only today lost kin to a decimation," he declared. "Do you truly believe they will agree to fight against the Hecari should they return? These people know what will happen. I can't believe they would attempt to resist."

Bethid smiled grimly. "That's because you're not human. You don't understand us. When faced with a true test, most humans rise to it. These folk will, too." There was neither amusement nor fear in her eyes, only conviction and a powerful commitment. "It's time, Brodhi. They've beaten us down too often. Sancorra loses more people every day, either to a Hecari culling or to those in karavans who leave the province to begin again elsewhere." She drew in a breath. "Are you with us?"

"To do what?"

"Initially, only to carry word throughout Sancorra that resistance, though dangerous, is not impossible. Actual organization will come later."

"Three couriers."

"Four, if you join us."

"And you believe this is enough?"

"No. We believe informing as many couriers as possible is the first order of business."

Instinct prompted a sharp response. "Be wary of that."

Bethid blinked. "Why?"

He was surprised she did not see it for herself. "It may well be that not every courier will join with you, and then secrecy is diminished, if not lost outright. Or that a courier might be *seen* to join, only to carry the news to the warlord in hopes of reward."

"We all swore an oath! You know that!"

"But not an oath to rebel," he pointed out. "In any resistance, any organized rebellion, there are factions. If they cannot be brought together and bound by an oath all of them will honor, there will always exist a risk of someone betraying you to the warlord."

She was vehement. "But we *must* get word to the people of Sancorra that there is hope. The only way we can do that without the Hecari finding out is for couriers to carry word."

Brodhi lay down again. "We're not untouchable, Bethid. We're allowed to carry out our tasks because the warlord permits it, for now. He sees value in our duty and neutrality. One day he may not. We as couriers are as vulnerable to his whim as anyone else."

"Then there's no time to waste, is there?"

"Are you proposing to leave in the morning on this fool's quest?"

"No. There's much more to be discussed." She paused. "We would be grateful if you discussed it with us, even if you elected not to join us."

"And why is that?"

"*Because* you'll tell us we're fools. That this can never work. That the Hecari are impossible to defeat. That all of us could be killed."

It was baffling. "And you find that of value?"

Bethid laughed, ear-hoops flashing. "You'll make us think, Brodhi! You'll make us devise better plans. You will keep us from letting emotion carry us when what we need to succeed is to be as cold-hearted and calculating as they say the warlord is." She paused. "And of us all here in this place, you have that capacity."

Brodhi, rather than taking offense, agreed with the assessment. It indicated strength, not weakness. And humans were weak.

He closed his eyes. "I told Mikal he'll have my answer in

the morning. You might as well be there to hear it." He turned on his side then, giving her his back; an eloquent and final way to end the conversation.

Bethid, for once, did not attempt to continue.

Chapter 31

*J*ORDA WAS NOTHING if not discreet; all everyone in the karavan knew, save for himself, Ilona, and his guides, was that the man named Vencik had been killed the night before by a beast of some sort. Said beast had also eaten most of a milch cow that had somehow broken her tether and wandered into jeopardy. And so the dawn rites were attended by karavaners respectful of the wife's grief, and, in their ignorance, of her husband's memory.

Rhuan, standing with Ilona at an edge of the gathering, heard no hint of irony in the voices of Branca and Melior, the two male diviners who performed the rites; clearly, they didn't know the truth. And while custom dictated that all three karavan diviners should take part in the proceedings, Jorda, pointedly avoiding eye contact with Rhuan and Ilona, briefly explained to all that Ilona had come down with a malady that affected her voice and would not be able to participate.

Rhuan glanced at her sidelong. Nothing in her hazel eyes gave away her thoughts, but her lean face was taut. He had suggested she not attend, but she insisted in a voice that by morning was nearly normal. He wondered if now she wished she had decided otherwise.

He had seen human death rituals several times because now and again people died on a karavan journey. The night before, Vencik's wife and her mother, with help from Branca and Melior, would have accorded him the ritual cleansing, washing his body carefully with a costly priest-blessed soap kept against such need. Next would come the head-to-toe oiling, followed by the careful wrapping of the body in clean, gauzy muslin. The swathed body that resembled, Rhuan decided, prey spun into spider silk, now lay upon matting to keep it from touching the earth; after the rituals were completed, the wrapped body would be placed into the hole Rhuan and Darmuth had dug the night before and covered with soil as the diviners once again invoked the blessing of Vencik's god. The activity put Rhuan in mind of the same service done for the Hecari warriors he had killed, save there had been no ritual; privately, he thought it would be fitting if Vencik were thrown into the pit containing the dead Hecari. But he held his peace, and kept his place beside Ilona.

Branca was a tall, excessively thin man of nondescript features, lackluster ash-blond hair, and somewhat protruding pale blue eyes. His counterpart, Melior, was of medium height with brown hair and eyes, his face overshadowed by a prominent nose. They wore clean, undyed robes of fine-carded wool, unpacked for the purpose, exuding the scent of herbs. Neither man was a priest, but diviners, in lieu of a priest's presence, were fully empowered to conduct such services.

Melior stood at the wrapped body's head, while Branca stationed himself at the foot. One at a time, using a call-and-response format involving attendees, they blessed the dead man and appealed to the god his wife said he worshipped to grant him an easy voyage across the river. During pauses in the invocation, only the quiet sobbing of his wife, standing shawl-wrapped with her mother, was audible, and the occasional fretting child.

Rhuan frowned. No, the sobbing and fretting were *not* the only things audible. There was a faint humming, a thrumming vibration in the air. The pitch was such that it seemed to work its way through the outer surface of his flesh, through the muscle, and into the bones below.

He looked first at Melior and Branca. They appeared to notice nothing unusual, nothing that might affect the rites. They took turns speaking quietly the words intended to guide the dead man on his final journey. A quick glance at Ilona elicited no response that marked her awareness of anything untoward.

Then he looked at Darmuth, standing beside Jorda. The demon's eyes were fixed on Rhuan's. There. *He* felt something, or sensed it. Or even, knowing Darmuth, scented it, like a hound upon a trail.

Carefully, Rhuan lifted his chin and brows in subtle inquiry. Darmuth's response was just as subtle, and left no doubt.

The rites for the dead man were attracting the attention of something best left blind to such prey as humans.

No, Rhuan said inwardly. *No, not now. Leave them be. Leave all of us be.*

But his bones were invaded, muscles frayed, ears annoyed by the vibration. No sound existed; at least, no sound humans could hear. But Rhuan heard it. It set his teeth on edge. Imprisoned by flesh, his muscles jumped and twitched. He could not stay still, could not stand there a moment longer. He had to *move;* to walk, to jog, to run. To do anything other than stand in one place.

Rhuan knew he should be self-disciplined enough to govern his own body, but he was incapable of it. His bones seemed to vibrate in time with the humming. Even his teeth resonated with it, no matter how hard he clenched them. Deep inside, his ears itched.

He turned abruptly and walked away from Ilona, away from the karavaners, away from the rites. He moved without haste, but purposefully, closing his hand over the hilt of his knife. And as he rounded Jorda's wagon at the head of the fractured karavan column, he drew the weapon and bared the long blade.

Hidden from all, he lifted his left hand, fingers spread. With a deft twist of the knife he cut into his flesh, opening a deep slice from the ball of his thumb to the outer heel of his left hand. Then he turned the hand palm down over the earth.

"Not now," he said aloud. "Let them be."

Blood fell from his hand to the soil beneath. The lush sod crisped into twisted, charred scraps.

He let the blood run. He let the sod burn.

HE MADE NO sound, no movement, but Ilona felt it, felt *something* take hold of Rhuan, something that stripped him of habitual grace and good humor. He was like a startled dog frozen in place, hackles rising slowly from the nape of his neck to the root of his tail. She sensed it so strongly that she could not keep her head from snapping around to look at him, could not keep her mouth from opening to ask him sharply what was wrong. But before she completed either motion he had left her side, had *retreated,* though she had never thought to couple that word with Rhuan. He flowed away with grace regained, but it was grace with a precision and purposefulness in his movements that spoke of sheer instinct, not rational decision making. Rhuan could be impulsive, but he was not a man who disrespected the rites and rituals of others. She could not fathom what would drive him away from a burial ceremony when it was custom, when it was *required* in karavan employee covenants, that everyone would attend dawn rites for a man killed on Jorda's watch.

Or was it on Rhuan's watch?

That might send him away. *That* might drive him away, to know he had failed in protecting the man.

And another alternative presented itself, despite his disavowals: Would it drive Rhuan away if he had murdered the man?

Ilona considered following. Every muscle in her body tensed to do so. But with effort she held herself back; Rhuan did nothing without purpose, even if what kindled that purpose was unknown to others. She had learned that much of him. Had learned, too, that there were gaps in their friendship, personal interstices that disallowed her presence.

She trusted herself to know when he needed someone to ask of him how he fared. She had done so before, and only rarely had he rebuffed her. But this time, now, she thought he might again.

Ilona held her place. She did not go. She put her mind on Branca and Melior and continued witnessing the ritual for a man who had assaulted her. She supposed his god might understand if she did not add her voice to requests for peace in death.

It mattered less than nothing to her if his god did not.

THEY WERE ONE family among many, gathered at the rites. When Torvic had protested getting up so early just to witness some old dead man getting buried, Audrun and Davyn simultanously chided him for disrespect, nearly word for word. That was enough to silence the sleep-sullen boy, and his attention was further distracted by his younger sister's glee at his chastisement. Megritte made certain he saw how quickly she was washed, dressed, and ready, whereupon she grinned at him in triumph. That prodded him into accelerated motion, and Audrun directed their little troop out of the wagon and up the slight hill to a lone tree, where everyone else gathered to witness the rites.

There, in hushed tones, Audrun directed her two youngest children to watch closely so they might understand the gravity of what had happened, and how absolutely vital it was that they stay close to the wagon rather than wandering away. But even as she said it, Audrun found her own recalcitrant gaze wandering away from the two diviners conducting the rites to the other karavaners. Though seeing off the dead was not the sort of activity that elicited happiness, she nonetheless noted that expressions were far more strained than sorrowful. Audrun supposed the dead man might have been a stranger to most of them, depending on when he and his family had joined the karavan, but the strain in every face was profound.

But then all of them, those folk, were to turn back when the rites were done. The plans painstakingly arrived at over weeks and months of careful thought were now as dead, as wasted, as the cleansed and oiled body wrapped in cloth.

It crossed Audrun's mind that if Davyn approached some of the other men, those most upset by the change in plan, perhaps they might yet gather up a makeshift caravan even without a master, for safety on the road. She allowed herself hope for a moment, and extrapolation, until she recalled with an anxious, painful pinching in her burdened belly that none of Jorda's people were bound for Atalanda. None but her family were to take the shortcut that ran so close to Alisanos.

In the background of her thoughts, she heard the murmuring of the diviners carrying out the rite. She was aware of spare dawn light, of coolness, of the rising of the sun out of darkness into day. But she was aware, too, of tension seeping into her muscles.

She could not escape the acknowledgment that their family, too, had the opportunity to turn back to the settlement. There they could wait out the season, as Jorda suggested; it would not be impossible. There were crops to plant and to till, gardens to tend, water in plenty, and fodder. And other adults with whom to share the days while the children made new friends.

They could start anew at the settlement. Remain in Sancorra, remain *of* Sancorra, despite the depredations of Hecari.

What does it make of us, to run from the enemy?

Well, not run . . . she wasn't sure the oxen could manage such a gait.

But. They weren't turning back.

She felt Davyn's hand on her shoulder and looked up, becoming aware that everyone at the gravesite was taking part in the call-and-response led by the diviners. Even Davyn's mouth moved to shape the words, but his eyes were concerned. Questioning.

He deserves better.

With effort Audrun threw off the thoughts of such things

as crops and gardens and friends, and joined her husband
in the portion of the rite they all were a part of.

But a stray thought implanted itself nonetheless: *Let the
guide decide to come with us.*

Even as she thought it, even as she mouthed the responses, Audrun looked for the guide. But he was no
longer with the hand-reader. No longer among the group.
He was absent from a ritual all were required to view.

Chapter 32

*H*E WAS NOT, Brodhi knew, truly among enemies, but he supposed the others might consider him one. At the very least they undoubtedly wondered if they could trust him, and for the first time since he had sworn himself into the courier service, he realized that it mattered.

Dawn had broken, but as yet sunlight did not reach to all the corners of the world. It also did not reach into Mikal's ale tent even as Brodhi slipped through the entrance flap, so that a pierced-tin lantern upon the plank bar had been lighted. With the oilcloth side panels let down and thus no freshening morning air to dissipate the odors of the night before, those inside shared a musty miasma of strong ale, smoke, lamp oil, of customers in need of washing, the memory of blood.

One-eyed Mikal, broad and battered. Slight, almost delicate Bethid, ear-hoops glinting. Timmon, blue-eyed and tall, with lank, light brown hair, a long jaw, his bony shoulders threatening the seams of his tunic. And Alorn, curls straying from a damp, cursory taming. Four people, four *humans,* whose intent was to change the world. Four disparate individuals who wore commitment like a cloak, and were thus identical. A powerful number, four; Brodhi in silence told over the Names he knew in their lesser incarnation: Earth. Air. Water. Fire.

And me? Perhaps I am the Trickster.

But surely not. That was Ferize's role.

They shared a table and, by the crumb- and crust-laden wooden platter, had broken bread supplied by Mikal from the morning's first baking, had drunk deeply of new ale. Brodhi knew too little of humans, and even less of these four—despite sharing a common courier tent with three of them now and again—to dare to make assumptions about whatever rites they may have undertaken before his arrival. They all wore cords of dangling charms around their necks—beads, feathers, bones, and other items—representative of their particular beliefs. Brodhi had never been interested in asking his fellow couriers what their beliefs were.

He wore no such string of charms, and that possibly, in their view, made him more untrustworthy. He did not pray as they did, nor visit diviners, nor invoke his gods in laughter, fear, admiration, or anger. In ordinary days, uneventful days, he was to them a cipher, and all were content to leave it so. But no longer. These days were neither ordinary nor uneventful. Not when four folk met to discuss taking the first tentative steps toward what might become, were they successful, a full-blown rebellion.

Under their eyes, Brodhi pulled free the heavy brooch of his office, as effective a protection as anything else a man might wear while the Hecari warlord made use of Sancorran couriers, and slipped the mantle from his shoulders. He added it to the pile of other courier mantles, identical in color, in weave, in weight, dropped across the nearest table. The ornate badges had been set upon the table the others inhabited, placed in front of Timmon, Alorn, and Bethid. Bright silver against dark wood. There was not, he noted, a fifth stool pulled up to their table.

With a faint smile, Brodhi hooked out a stool from a neighboring table and sat down. He did not join them. He put distance between himself and the others so they might take ease in it, stilled his movements, and even schooled his expression into bland neutrality.

He placed his badge upon his table. Quietly he said,

"They will kill every single courier if so much as *one* breathes word of rebellion."

Timmon was affronted. "Who would, of us? We swore oaths. Each of us, even you."

Brodhi shrugged lightly. "Those oaths, when weighed against the brutality of the Hecari, mean less than nothing."

Timmon and Alorn exchanged startled, outraged glances.

"*Every* courier," Brodhi emphasized. "Not one in ten, intended as a lesson in numbering. All will be killed. The warlord uses us now because his attention is more firmly fixed on subjugating a province, and because it is always easier to leave in place such infrastructure as a courier service, men and women who know the roads and settlements better than he. We are of use to him, so long as we do not upset that infrastructure."

Bethid's eyes narrowed. "Then tell us another way. A *better* way."

"Leave," he said simply.

That baffled all, but Bethid found her voice before the others. "Leave?"

"Leave Sancorra," Brodhi elucidated. He looked at Mikal. "You as well. Pack up this tent and your supplies, and go across the border. Get out of Sancorra."

The one-eyed man was stunned. "You're suggesting we run away?"

Brodhi suppressed a sigh of disgusted impatience. "Is it running away to go to a safe place? No. It's expediency. If all of you persist in believing that you can successfully rebel against the Hecari warlord, you might consider moving across the border to another province." He paused, noting an array of expressions running the gamut from shock to anger. Invoking extreme patience, he said, "The warlord would not necessarily expect a *Sancorran* rebellion to germinate in another province. And he is so busy now establishing his hold on Sancorra that he can't afford to deal with another province . . . at least not yet. In time he'll take them all, if he isn't stopped."

"That's the *point*," Bethid said sharply.

"Of course it's the point," he agreed. "In the meantime, consider taking yourselves elsewhere. We are not so far from the Atalandan border, and there is a shortcut."

"What, do you mean the road that runs beside Alisanos?" Mikal shook his head. "Only a fool would take it. I realize these three couriers, being but children in their twenties, have no memory of the last time Alisanos moved, but I do." His mouth jerked. "I was not so very old, but I recall it. For more than a year my family lived in fear that we would all be swallowed up."

"And therein lies the choice," Brodhi said. "Remain here and risk another culling; or go to Atalanda and risk Alisanos."

"An ugly choice," Bethid declared. She flicked a glance at Mikal. "It's true I wasn't born the last time Alisanos moved, but I have heard the tales. I find it far safer to stay here in Sancorra, even if the Hecari return with another culling party. We are couriers, Brodhi . . . that buys us time. Provides opportunity. For now, the warlord doesn't bother us—but Alisanos might."

Brodhi inclined his head in graceful concession; he would not maintain a debate when his points were ignored. "Do as you will."

"We would work better from here," Mikal persisted. "This place exists because people *are* leaving Sancorra. People who are fleeing one place are not expected to rebel. Only to run."

"Do as you will," Brodhi repeated. "I merely offered an alternative."

Bethid's expression was hard. "Last night, when I spoke of this plan, you told me I was a fool."

"No. I said it was a fool's quest. And so it is." He let that settle a moment, noting simmering anger, annoyance, and frustration among the others before he continued. "But without fools undertaking such quests, many things in the world would not exist."

Timmon's brows met over the blade of his nose. Straight light-brown hair brushed thin shoulders as he leaned forward. Sharpness shaped his tone, lent intensity to blue eyes. "Be very clear with us, Brodhi—is this some sort of Shoia jest?"

Brodhi raised his brows. "I think it would be fair to say that among you all I am never inclined to jest."

At that, Alorn laughed softly. "Among other things."

"The warlord would not expect couriers to be the heart of the matter," Brodhi continued. "He knows us merely as servants. We own no dwellings or farmsteads, nor the horses we ride—" he gestured, indicating the table with its weight of blue wool, "—nor even the cloaks on our backs. All belongs to the Guildhall in Cardatha. Even all but a few coins are kept for us at the Guildhall, because we are fed on the road by those who hear our news." He glanced at Mikal, who was nodding in agreement; no courier was required to pay for food or the drink accompanying it, only when he or she drank for pleasure after duty was discharged. "It would be far more likely that couriers might turn rebel if dismissed from the service and left to fend for themselves. When we are fed, clothed, horsed, and housed at no cost to us?" Brodhi shook his head. "The risk lies not in the warlord suddenly assuming couriers have turned rebel, but in a courier who thinks he—or she—may be well-rewarded for betraying our confidence *to* the warlord."

"So?" Bethid said. "How would you have us begin?"

"Sow your seed," Brodhi answered. "As we four have shared a common tent here, you also share courier tents in other settlements. Or in the cities, when we share rooms in the lesser Guildhalls." He nodded at Bethid. "You said it last night, that we as couriers are in a better position than anyone to learn without prejudice what others across the province feel. But you must not put your trust in a person simply because he or she is a courier. First, you must learn their hearts. *Earn* their hearts. Any courier may say a thing simply because of the moment, but when put to the question, does he mean what he says? Truly? Enough that he will risk his life? Put your trust only in those whom you know without question would never take money to sell your names to the Hecari."

Alorn's damp hair had dried into its customary wiry, dark curls. "No courier would do such a thing!"

Brodhi looked at him. "What convinces you that *I* never would?"

Bethid frowned. "What do you mean?"

"You know my name and my race," Brodhi answered. "Nothing more. Is it enough to convince you, to make you believe in your heart of hearts that, offered something I wanted badly—and, suffice it to say, you have absolutely no idea what I might want so badly—I would not betray you?"

Timmon's expression was unsettled as, in deep thought, he repeatedly traced with a fingertip a crude, cross-hatched pattern carved into the tabletop. "I see."

"In fact," Brodhi continued, "as I now know your intentions while you know so little of mine, you would be wise to kill me."

Bethid's tone was exquisitely dry. "How many times?"

He ignored the pointed sally. "Would you do it? Could you? None of you are killers. I'd wager what fighting skills you have are with words, not knives, not garrotes. Nor even hands naked of weapon. You must be certain—sure that every courier you speak to of your plans will make the same commitment you have, even to being willing to kill one of his own." Brodhi looked into three troubled faces. "You may argue that you are couriers, and so you are; that you have sworn an oath to the service, and so you have. But that oath binds you always to be truthful with the news you give or receive, to remain neutral and dispassionate, and to carry, word for word, the messages others entrust to us. That is an oath we must honor to remain in the service, and so we do. But is it worth *dying* for?"

"We wouldn't be dying for the service," Bethid answered. "We'd die for Sancorra. Just like the lord did."

"He was a lord," Brodhi said matter-of-factly, "and it was known from the moment the Hecari crossed over Sancorran borders that, if captured, his life was forfeit. But we are merely couriers carrying word of his death; we are not expected to do more than that."

Bethid stared at him a long moment. Then she took up the courier's brooch she had placed on the table before her, and set it down decisively in the center. "My pledge," she declared.

Timmon and Alorn, following her lead, tossed their brooches to clink against hers. Mikal, with a wry hook to his mouth, slipped off his eye patch and dropped it atop the pile of brooches, baring the puckered, twisted lid of his missing eye.

Brodhi rose then, gathering up his courier's mantle and brooch; the humans would wish to discuss his words without his presence. "Anyone you doubt, anyone at all, once you have spoken of your intentions, cannot be allowed to live."

Alorn's expression was outraged. "We're not assassins!"

"Then would you have yourselves be martyrs?" Brodhi shifted his gaze briefly at Mikal, then at each of his fellow couriers. "This is not what you were meant for, this rebellion. You have not the training that soldiers or mercenaries do, let alone the Hecari. But if you believe it worth the doing, then see it through." He looked at Alorn. "And remember, when you speak of your plans to another courier, when you commit yourselves to a course that could end in your deaths . . . it is easier to die than it is to kill."

 DARMUTH SAID, "YOU can bleed yourself dry, but it changes nothing."

Rhuan didn't question how the demon could have come upon him unaware as he stood behind the wagon, absenting himself from the karavaner's death rites. Darmuth did that with great regularity, even if no one else could. And at the moment, his body afire with the humming vibration, he doubted he would hear anyone's arrival. Not a safe thing, but for now there was no surcease.

"Not to change," he said tightly. "Delay. Misdirect."

"Stop it, Rhuan." But there was no urgency, no censure in Darmuth's tone as he leaned a casual shoulder against

Jorda's wagon, bare tattooed arms crossed. Merely resignation. "If you're not careful you'll bring down Brodhi on us; you and he renewed the blood-bond, remember? And I suspect he will have far fewer polite words for you than I do when he finds out what you're trying to do."

"This has nothing to do with Brodhi." But even as he said it, Rhuan knew Darmuth was correct. He flipped his left hand palm up, then curled fingers and thumb into a fist. After a moment the blood stopped flowing. The cut closed. "When they invoke the gods in this kind of ritual, they tempt Alisanos."

"A man died. It's the human thing to do, is it not, to see him across the river?"

"They're ignorant of what such rituals can do at this particular time," Rhuan insisted. "They're opening the door to an enemy far worse than Hecari warriors."

"Yes," Darmuth said, "but you are not to interfere."

Rhuan closed his eyes before the red haze slid across his vision. Blind, he nonetheless still retained a voice—and an opinion. "It's not your place to command me."

"And so I didn't. I merely reminded you. It is my place to do that. If you like, I'll remind you again: *You are not to interfere.*"

"I'm not." But an inward wince underscored his awareness that such words sounded childish. "These are innocent people."

"So innocent that one of them attempted to rape Ilona."

The haze faded. Now Rhuan contemplated his healed hand. "I suspect perhaps he, too, was innocent. Oh, he did indeed attempt to rape her, but it's entirely possible that Alisanos, as it wakes, is beginning to affect people as it prepares to move elsewhere. That it's warping how they think."

"As it affects and warps any human who winds up *in* Alisanos."

Rhuan nodded. "Exactly." He cleaned the blade of his knife and returned it to its sheath at his belt. "I have but a few human months left to me. Can't it wait that long?"

"Alisanos waking has nothing to do with you," Darmuth

declared flatly. "It's simply grown bored with its current location after forty years—forty *human* years—and is taking itself elsewhere."

He gritted his teeth. "And it kills people, Darmuth—or, perhaps worse, takes them into itself. Makes them *of* itself."

"It does what it does. Opening your flesh changes nothing. Letting blood changes nothing. Alisanos, for the moment, has no awareness of you whatsoever."

Rhuan glared at him.

Darmuth remained unperturbed. "What you're feeling isn't sent to afflict you personally. It's simply a side-effect of the waking process. As you have told the humans many times, you're sensitive to such things. So is Brodhi. But to assume you are being specifically targeted is to claim yourself *important*. To claim yourself *worthy of attention*."

Bitterly, Rhuan said, "And I am neither, is that it?"

Darmuth laughed. "Oh, very much neither!"

"And if I go closer? If I accompany the farmerfolk on their journey via shortcut to Atalanda?"

The demon's laughter died. "Then you would be as a mouse walking very near the rousing cat. And the cat, upon waking after a forty-year nap, will undoubtedly be hungry."

Rhuan stared into the distance a moment, then lifted one shoulder in a slight, lopsided shrug. "I'd be a tough morsel to swallow. Too much gristle."

"For Alisanos?" Darmuth's toothy, gem-sparked grin faded into incredulity. "Rhuan, you can't seriously be considering this!"

"I can. I am." Rhuan met the demon's pale eyes. His own, with effort, held steady. "You are not the arbiter of the tests I face. You've not even been told what is and isn't related to my journey. How can you know this is not another test? You overstep your bounds to counsel me against accepting the task."

"Because too much risk is involved," Darmuth replied promptly, "and it may be sheer whimsy, not a test. Yes, you may face several options at any given point in time, but this one? I think this option is entirely of your devising, not necessarily a true part of your quest."

"You should remain at the settlement," Rhuan told him abruptly. "This doesn't require your presence or assistance."

"Don't be childish," the demon snapped.

A joyous laugh bubbled up from deep inside. Rhuan gave way to it, mouth falling open, and was pleased to see the concern in Darmuth's face. It wasn't often he could so deeply discombobulate the demon, and it gave him intense pleasure.

"Don't do this," Darmuth said. "You have invested too much of yourself . . . your time here is nearly done."

"But you don't *know*," Rhuan said plainly, "that this decision isn't part of the quest. One of the tests. Do you?" He loosed a lazy grin. "You are, in accordance with the terms of engagement, an observer. Nothing more. You have no insight as to what tests I face."

Darmuth's eyes flickered between the rounded human pupil and the vertical slit of demonhood. For the barest moment, the tracery of a ruddy-colored scale pattern stained the flesh of his throat.

"It's too large," Darmuth said. "Too much for you."

"It is what it is," Rhuan retorted. "A choice. And the comment you applied to me earlier applies equally to you: You are not to interfere."

"I guide."

"You *accompany*. There's a difference."

The merest tip of Darmuth's split tongue slid between his lips. The sibilants in his speech acquired a hiss. "Human wordsssss. Human meaningsssss."

"And that," Rhuan said with triumphant finality, "is precisely the point."

For a brief moment fangs glinted in Darmuth's mouth. "You are *dioscuri*."

"Through no choosing of my own."

Darmuth's pupils slitted. The blood came up in his flesh. "Why?" he asked. "Why would a *dioscuri* wish to become human?"

Rhuan saw the sheen of scales flash at Darmuth's throat. Such loss of self-control was rare. Were any of Jorda's karavaners to see the demon now, they would know precisely what he was.

"Do you suppose," he began lightly, "that Ferize asks Brodhi why he wishes *not* to become human?"

Darmuth inhaled a hissing breath.

"Precisely," Rhuan said. "Observers ask no such thing. It's for Brodhi to choose, and me . . . and neither you nor Ferize are to attempt to influence our decisions in any way." Laughter was banished. No trace of amusement remained. "You are on your own quest, Darmuth. It's not my place to interfere with that journey, any more than it's your place to interfere with mine." He lifted his left hand and displayed his unblemished palm to the demon. "Let me choose, Darmuth. Let me *choose* what I will be."

Darmuth's reply began as a hiss, but resolved itself into human speech. "I am somewhat fond of you, little *dioscuri*. You aren't my get, but that changes nothing. I have no wish to lose you. Not to death, certainly, but not to the humans, either."

Rhuan gentled his tone from anger into serenity. "We have time, Darmuth. No choice can yet be made."

"But it can. It can! If you tempt Alisanos, if you tease Alisanos, you choose an ending. *Your* ending."

"Let us hope not," Rhuan said lightly, "but should it come to that, I would hope for some sort of ritual to mark my passing. Perhaps even a human one."

"Rhuan—"

But he overrode the demon. "I want you to stay in the settlement. Help Ilona, if she needs it. And Jorda. As for me, it's time I found the farmsteaders and gave them my answer."

Chapter 33

A SENSE OF RELIEF trickled into Audrun as the death ritual for a man she didn't know drew to a close. The two male diviners she knew no better completed a final blessing, arms outstretched over the wrapped body, and as the keening wail of grief from the widow rose again into the brightening day, the gathering of karavaners began to turn and depart the hilltop, including her own family.

Considering fidgeting Torvic had only been held in place by his mother's hand clamped on one shoulder—Megritte, as was her habit, had sought a release from boredom by climbing into her father's arms—Audrun felt her children had gotten through the lengthy ritual with a fair portion of self-control and parental equanimity.

"Yes," she said before Torvic even asked, "you may go." Freed of her confining hand, he dashed away. Megritte, with better manners—always, in her father's presence— *asked* to go; she was put down and raced after her brother, though Ellica and Gillan lingered, exchanging privately anxious glances. Raising her voice, Audrun called after her youngest to assert renewed authority, "Go straight back to the wagon! We're leaving as soon as we can!"

Davyn's hand settled on her shoulder, then briefly massaged her neck with casual affection. "By the time the new baby is as old as Torvic and Megritte, they will be of an age to help you, not add to your burdens."

Head bent back into his strong fingers, Audrun managed a weak smile, aware of Ellica and Gillan glancing sidelong at her. She did her best to suppress her anxiety. It would not do to allow anyone, husband or children, to see how truly worried she was. *Or how much my back aches.* Even as she thought it, she pressed a hand against her lower spine.

"If it would please you," Davyn said, "we could wait another night and go on tomorrow."

It pricked her pride; apparently husband and older children knew after all how worried and weary she was. But Audrun understood the intent of the offer. Rather than turning their backs on the rest of the karavan as it made its way toward the settlement they had left but a few days before, they could allow the youngest to play, the oldest to help, and Audrun herself to rest. It was not in a man's ken to truly grasp the physical requirements of pregnancy, and in that Davyn was no different than most, but he wasn't utterly blind to her heightened emotions and lessened physical stamina.

"Thank you," she said, "but it's best we go on as soon as we may. Babies do not always count the days properly."

"Ellica, Gillan, go ahead to the wagon." Davyn's voice rumbled pleasantly; though he would have done as offered, he was nonetheless relieved not to delay. "The oxen need hitching. We'll leave once all is—" But he broke off. The hand on her shoulder tightened as his tone lilted into surprise. "He's coming *here.*"

Audrun had been watching her steps down the grassy hill. Now she looked up, following the direction of Davyn's gaze, and saw the Shoia guide.

Blessed Mother of Moons, he *was* coming here.

ILONA WAS STARTLED, as she returned to her wagon from the dawn rites, to discover that Darmuth was present, replacing the charred steps with the new wood planks and pegs Rhuan had laid out the evening before. It was not out of the ordinary for Darmuth to undertake such efforts, but it was a task Rhuan had promised to do; despite a certain fecklessness of nature, he mostly completed what he'd begun. And Darmuth's expression was nothing at all akin to the casual friendliness he generally bestowed upon her. She did not know him well, even though he had joined Jorda's karavan a matter of months after Rhuan had done so, but she was accustomed to being at ease in his presence. Darmuth's droll comments often made her laugh.

At this moment, as he tested the pegs fastening the new steps into the slotted folding mechanism, she sensed nothing remotely droll, but a thrumming ferocity in posture, in movement, and an expression that robbed her of the innocuous question forming in her mind.

He glanced up briefly, and she saw water-pale eyes hard as ice. Darmuth was a compactly built, strong man who very likely was not as old as his single silver-haired braid, wrapped with a crimson leather thong, suggested. His skin was smooth as butter, the tones rich as honey beneath the tribal tattoos he wore on both arms, bared by the chopped off sleeves of his black leather tunic. The rich purple sash doubled around his waist, and the gemstone set in one tooth had always lent him, in her view, a hint of rakish abandon.

It did not do so now.

Ilona summoned her wits and said, *"Oh."* Which was not at all what she had intended to say, and left her feeling the fool.

Darmuth's movements were quick, efficient, and tinged with a simmering, tensile anger she'd never seen in him. "I have been told," he said, with a certain formality to his anger, "to help you."

The words were stiff, as was his posture. Most unlike Darmuth.

She managed another word. No, two: "Thank you."

"I have been *told* to help you. And so of course I will."

That freed her mind and tongue. Now she understood. "Don't tell me he's leaving!"

"He is." Darmuth tapped the new-made pegs with the wooden mallet to anchor them in their holes. "And *I* am told to remain in the settlement."

The chill of his tone as much as realization unfurled pain in the pit of her stomach. "Why is he leaving? Where is he going?"

Darmuth folded and unfolded the steps to test their operation. They were whole again, functional, and nakedly new when viewed beside the others, weathered and stained, roughened by hard usage.

He rose. They were almost exactly the same height. He was short for a man, she tall for a woman. "Why is he leaving? Because the farmsteaders have asked him to guide them to Atalanda. Where is he going? Along the track skirting Alisanos." Something flared in his pale eyes, something almost red, or cat-green. His pupils, not shrunken in response to the bright morning sun, seemed almost to elongate.

Except, of course, human pupils did no such thing. "You're afraid," Ilona blurted, shocked to hear those words issuing from her mouth with regard to Darmuth, but knowing them nonetheless for truth. "You believe the deepwood will take him."

"It will," he said. "Oh, it will. He is too tempting a morsel." Darmuth's gem-glinting smile was a blade newly honed, slicing into her flesh. "I am told to remain at the settlement. And so he lacks the first and best measure of his protection."

Ilona felt oddly empty. Somehow, with three years of Rhuan's company, difficult as he might occasionally be, had come the belief, the conviction, that he would always be there.

She was startled out of that thought by a hand clamping down on her forearm. Through the rich green shawl swathing her torso and the sleeves of her cream-colored woven tunic, she knew nonetheless she would bruise. Darmuth's fingers seemed to burn.

"You might," he said. "*You* might."

Ilona felt completely disoriented, jerked out of assumptions she had no right to make. "Might what?"

"Go to him. Ask him to stay."

Her startled laugh was short and sharp. "If Rhuan's made up his mind—"

"Rhuan is a child. He has a child's mind."

It was a simpler matter to focus on physical pain as opposed to the emotional. Steadily, she said, "You're hurting my arm."

He unclamped his fingers instantly, eyes flickering, cold and cutting, behind briefly lowered lids. "Your pardon."

"If he has made up his mind, and *you* can't change it—" Ilona looked for and saw the brief grimace that told her she was correct in believing Darmuth had indeed tried, "—then there's nothing I can say to dissuade him." She rewrapped her shawl around her shoulders—tightly, very tightly, letting the yarn form a shield—wincing from the soreness in her forearm. "He's a man full-grown, and he has the right to make his own decisions."

"He's a child," Darmuth repeated. "His line is slow to mature. Why do you think I'm here?"

Behind the simmering anger, Ilona sensed a suppressed but growing fear in him, and a thread of desperation. She was tempted to grasp his wrist as he had grasped her arm, to turn the hand palm up so she could see into it.

At this moment, faced with the subtle ferocity of his feelings, even the thought of doing so filled her with fear.

She had never been afraid of Darmuth.

He saw it in her, she realized, saw the fear, the unease, the discovery that he might be something other than what she had always taken him for. For a moment, one sliver of a moment in a day full of them, Darmuth knew that she saw beyond the calm competence of Jorda's second guide, saw deeper than ever she had before. That now she found him intimidating, and decidedly dangerous.

And yet he did nothing to dissuade her of that impression, to dismiss that certainty. Darmuth permitted her, by his unshielded emotions, to understand that Rhuan's decision was somehow vital to him.

She wrenched her thoughts from the newborn curiosity that was Darmuth. It hurt to say it, but she did so. "I am not enough to sway him. You know that."

A muscle along his jaw leaped. "You might be. You *should* be."

That, somehow, was even more painful. "If I were, if I meant that to him and used it as leverage, I would lose him. This way we have at least something that goes a little beyond friendship, for all it lacks intimacy." She did not know why she said such to Darmuth. He was not a man who encouraged confidences, by word or deed. "He makes his own choices, Darmuth. And he lives by them."

"Or dies." His tone was oddly tight.

She felt a great need to step back emotionally, to recover distance and raise it, like a shield, between them. With effort she approximated a sardonic tone. "But he'll only resurrect himself again."

It was enough after all. Darmuth hadn't moved, but there was the knowledge in them both that the time for speech unencumbered by self-consciousness had been extinguished. All that existed between them now was the casualness of acquaintances.

NOT FAR FROM Mikal's ale tent, Brodhi paused. Under the newborn sun the scent of charred poles and oilcloth lingered on the morning air as warmth crept into the day. Worse was the odor of death. Bodies had been gathered, rites were underway, but the dead were dead. Certain processes rendered them far less than they had been alive, and unfortunately pungent. If the bodies were not burned or buried soon, the settlement would, within a matter of days, become unlivable.

Behind him, a matter of paces away within a tent where men—mostly men—gathered to gulp spirits, three men and a woman, three couriers and an ale-keep, discussed his words. Discussed, no doubt, *him,* and whether they could trust him.

Brodhi smiled wryly. A moment later it bloomed into a grin. A tooth-bearing, self-mocking grin. *I gave them the key, then I offered myself as the one to turn it.*

He had not intended that. He intended merely to introduce them to realities that all too often went unsaid or worse, went unthought. And yet he had placed himself amid the plan. *He* had. No one asked him to. No one expected him to. He most significantly less than the others.

Three men, one woman. And thus a rebellion was born.

Three men, one woman, and a Shoia warrior. And more: *dioscuri*, as Ferize herself from time to time reminded him. Was it test? Was it quest? Or was it human folly?

"Mine," he said aloud. "My folly."

As Ferize undoubtedly would tell him.

Summerweight blue mantle draped over one arm, silver brooch closed within a hand, Brodhi glanced back. The door flap to Mikal's tent remain dropped. Privacy behind a flimsy shell of oilcloth. And yet he thought that perhaps it made more sense to shield themselves with nothing more than fabric. Behind wood, behind metal, such plottings were expected. But who would ever think an ale tent would harbor rebellion?

Brodhi opened the hand in which the brooch lay. Silver glinted.

Who might think an ale tent would harbor rebellion?

Hecari might.

Or Hecari might not, but burn it for the doing. Kill them for the counting.

DAVYN TENSED AS the guide walked slowly up the hill. His hand fell away from Audrun's neck. He felt awkward, ungainly, and altogether inept. Something in him, from their first meeting, had recognized, had answered, if unspoken, to the guide, and the question he had ignored then arose now: *Is he more competent than me? More of a man than me?*

That he was alien, no doubt. Pure-blooded Shoia, a race so distant and far-flung they were nearly unheard of in Sancorra, with ritually braided multiple plaits aglint with ornamentation even as the hems of his clothing were, a long-knife sheathed at his hip, and a baldric of shining throwing knives strung slantwise across his chest. Nothing about the guide bespoke modesty, in dress or demeanor. And yet Davyn knew, Davyn felt, that the man was some-how—*more*. More than him.

Audrun? Oh yes, she saw it. Felt it. Even if she remained unaware of her response; but of that, Davyn could not be certain. She was not a woman who looked after other men, who yearned for what another man might offer; she had fixed her future upon his when they were no more than El-lica's and Gillan's ages. But he was all too aware that a woman grown might nonetheless be attracted, might respond to a man, even if that response was neither recognized nor acknowledged by her.

Davyn stopped halfway down the hilltop. The two eldest of his children halted. And, at last, his wife. But only because the guide had reached them.

The smooth, youthful features were blandly ignorant of Davyn's self-doubts. Rhuan smiled, and dimples appeared. The cider-brown eyes were warm and, Davyn felt, altogether too attentive.

Because of that, Davyn took the offense. "My children spoke out of turn."

He heard Audrun's sharp, indrawn breath, and realized his abrupt words insulted Gillan and Ellica, who had meant only the best. But Davyn refused to look at either. Hurt feelings could be set to rights later; for now, everything in him cried out to deny the guide what Davyn believed he himself could offer: safety along the road.

Even if it did skirt Alisanos.

The guide's eyebrows arched slightly. "Did they?"

Davyn made a deprecating gesture. "It was done out of care, out of a sense of responsibility; a father does not take his children to task for that." He hoped it was enough to assuage the hurt his eldest felt, but did not have the time to look for himself to be certain of it. He merely locked eyes with the guide, giving no ground to a man who, he felt, was used to taking it. "But nonetheless it was done without my knowledge. And so I am left with the duty of telling you that we will not be needing your services after all."

The voice was very quiet. "*I* think we do."

Audrun. It was *Audrun*. And it hurt.

He overrode her, still looking only at the guide. "Thank you, but we will do well enough unaided. I understand your concerns and warnings about Alisanos, and I dismiss none of them, but it must be acknowledged that no one knows what the deepwood may do. You say it has grown active and intends to shift—"

The guide said, "I do. And it does."

"—but no one can predict where Alisanos will go," Davyn continued steadily. "There is no certainty of safety *anywhere*. Were we to return to the settlement and remain there until Jorda led karavans out again, we might be taken regardless. So? We shall continue on our way and put our trust in the gods." He managed a slight, tight smile. "The diviners have told us to go, and so we go. There is no room for discussion with strangers, no matter how well-intentioned."

The guide looked at him for a long moment, expression oddly blank, and then he looked, from one to the other, in order, at Gillan, Ellica, and Audrun. "I see," he said. And then grinned. "But the roads are open to all, and if I elect to travel the shortcut skirting Alisanos, there is no one to keep me from it."

Defeat. Davyn felt it. *Knew* it. And the knowledge was bitter.

"Of course." It took effort to keep his expression neutral, to maintain control of his voice. "I wish you safe journey."

Chapter 34

RHUAN WAS NOT blind to the tension in the father, but neither was he unaware of the same in the wife and the elder children, who very much disagreed with the decision. Family conflict was a familiar thing to him—and one reason he had taken service with Jorda—but he had no experience of such things among humans. He didn't blame the father for *wishing* to protect his family unaided. He did blame him for being stubborn enough to refuse that aid when the lives of his family depended on it.

Rhuan recognized the cause. Pride. Excessively male pride. He knew the latter well; he was too acquainted with the urgings of his own pride to say one thing or another, to *do* one thing or another. That pride had, in fact, been the bane of his kin for generations.

So Rhuan smiled, infused his voice with light-heartedness and acceptance, and simply informed the father of his plans to travel the same direction upon the same road.

He saw relief in the faces of the children and the wife. He saw anger and resentment flare in the farmer's eyes; saw too, and appreciated, as the man applied self-control to keep from permitting the disagreement to kindle into true and lengthy argument.

"Safe journey," the father said courteously, if through

stiffened jaw. The wife glanced up at him, fully cognizant of the tension between two men, and so Rhuan purposely diffused the moment.

"My thanks," he said warmly, "and to you. If you'll excuse me, I must return to my duties. I will see the karavan to the settlement, then begin my own journey."

As he turned away, he glimpsed the startled and dismayed faces of the wife and the two elder children. They had expected him at the very least to depart at the same time they did, thus placing himself near them upon the road. His return to the settlement with the karavan would put more than a week between them. But on the face of the farmsteader, Rhuan saw a relaxing of the features from stoniness into relief, and an easing into cheerfulness. Just as he expected.

He smiled again, made the graceful gesture of departure required in his own kin, and strode back down the hill toward Jorda's wagon. Behind him, he heard the father firmly directing the oldest son to see to hitching the oxen.

The thorn of anger pricked as he walked. Rhuan flattened it instantly with a wave of rejection. Anger he knew as well as pride; it rose quickly when teased into life or beckoned on purpose. Usually it was Brodhi who brought it roaring to the surface, heated and strong, which was one of the reasons Rhuan preferred to keep his distance from his kin-in-kind. No good, and quite a lot of bad, might come of it were they to enter into kin-feud. Such things killed among his people, including the innocent.

Then, of course, there was Darmuth, who ridiculed him in an entirely different way for entirely different reasons.

And now it was anger encouraged by a human. Rhuan shook his head briefly in denial and dismay. He knew better. Humans were very young, and very emotional. Those older were held to be wiser, and thus responsible for guiding the young *with* that wisdom.

Guiding. As Darmuth guided him? As Ferize did Brodhi?

He thought not. He thought most decisively not.

"Rhuan."

Lost in musings, he had been watching only his direction of travel, unaware of others as he neared the wagons. With the rites completed, families were busy packing belongings and hitching teams, calling to one another. But this voice was quiet, pitched to privacy. This person waited specifically for him.

There was pain in hazel eyes. There was a rigidity in slim posture. There was pride, female pride, every bit as strong as that claimed by males, as she stood waiting, swathed in a rich green shawl. Dark hair was wound in untidy coils against the back of her head, anchored in place by rune-carved sticks, but had loosened around her face so that wavy tendrils framed her features. He had stood beside her throughout the dawn rites held for a man who had assaulted her, and had seen nothing in her of the emotions she tried to suppress now.

He halted, aware of warmth rising in his face. He owed this woman honesty, and so he answered before she could ask. "Yes. It's true."

She did not look away. She met his eyes levelly, and a slight twitch moved the corner of her mouth. "For all your wilding ways, you have always offered to help those most in need of it."

He had expected something entirely different. He stumbled with a reply. "They shouldn't . . . it's . . . they are going into danger."

"Extreme danger." Ilona nodded. "While the karavan is returning to a safety that is somewhat more evident, if not wholly assured in a province overrun by Hecari."

Floundering—he had not thought ahead to envision what it would cost to wish farewell to those he treasured—he sought to offer reassurance. "I'll return, Ilona." He grimaced. "If Jorda will have me."

"He doesn't keep guides in his employ out of season; how can he consider this desertion? If you survive to return for the next season, he'll have you."

"If I *survive!*" He began to laugh, halted it before it could gust from his mouth, insulting her concern, and tamed it to a crooked smile. "How could I not? I have several lives left to me."

The single word reply was an odd mixture of emotions. "Several."

And so he lied, to give her ease. "Six."

She sought the truth in his eyes. She found something there, but he could not tell what it might be. "Six."

He glanced beyond her, seeing Jorda in the background. He owed the man news of his decision sooner rather than later. "I will return," he repeated.

She made no move to detain him as his body and thoughts inclined toward the karavan-master. She merely said, "If Alisanos allows it."

That came as a shock. He fastened all of his attention once again upon the hand-reader, and accusation. "You've been talking to Darmuth."

"Not intentionally. He was mending my steps."

"Oh Mother, I forgot." Rhuan put out a hand in an apologetic appeal, then withdrew it. "I forgot, 'Lona."

"But yes, I've been talking to Darmuth. And he has been most frank."

Warily he said, "Darmuth, frank, is often dangerous."

"Yes," she agreed. "That I have seen. But I have never seen him afraid."

Rhuan swore. The flicker of anger deep in his belly threatened to grow, to rise, to redden his gaze. And she would see it, and wonder. More than she already did. "He is a consummate manipulator. Don't allow him to sway you. Darmuth—"

"This wasn't manipulation."

"Darmuth's version of the truth is often manipulation. I know it well, Ilona. I've been its victim all too often."

"He believes if you go so close to Alisanos, you invite it to take you."

She was pale. Her face was carved of bone. Beneath dark, level brows, her eyes were unflinching.

Darmuth's truths could be most discomfiting when used on fragile humans. And yet that was not how Rhuan had ever viewed Ilona. This moment in particular, she was strength incarnate.

He owed her much. But not this. "I'm going, 'Lona."

"I know that." Her mouth curved slightly. "I came only to say farewell, and to wish you well on your journey."

She could not possibly know the costs of his journey, the requirements of a highly personal journey so different from the one he now embarked upon. But Rhuan nonetheless very much appreciated the sentiments from the only human who knew him half so well.

"In the name of the Mother of Moons—" But no, that was a human oath. Rhuan wanted to give her something more. He raised his hand. He turned it to her, displaying his palm. Displaying what he had kept hidden from her for three years. It was not true disclosure; that he kept shielded. But it was more than he had ever offered before. "On this," he said, "I promise. I will survive. I will return."

He did not lower his hand.

And she did not look at it.

"Be certain of it," she said, and turned away.

Rhuan watched Ilona go. He was aware of a pinch of guilt, of regret, of wishing life might be different. That he could explain to her why it was necessary she not truly read his hand; that he could show her what it held. But of them all, Ilona was most dangerous to him. And so he let her go despite a twitch of his body that nearly sent him after her. He restrained that which was goading him to fol- low, to catch up, to place a hand on her shoulder and turn her toward him. To look into her face and see no disbelief, no fear, no alarm, as he told her the truth.

They were friends. Nothing more. And so it had to remain.

In other women, he found physical release. He had loved none of them, nor had they expected it. He chose carefully, and as carefully exercised self-restraint in the bedding so that he would impregnate none of them. He would risk no child of his having to make the choices he did, nor to un- dertake the tests he faced every day. And so he did no more as Ilona departed than to watch her as she walked away, straight and tall and slim, until she was lost among the wagons.

KNEELING INSIDE THEIR wagon, Audrun tucked away various items more properly than her children had. She appreciated their efforts, but when a family of six lived out of a wagon—a large one, to be sure, but not so large as the home of sod and wood Davyn had built at the beginning of their marriage—every bit of space was important. Anything left out of its place, anything put away haphazardly, affected everything else in the wagon.

On the road to the tent settlement as they made their way through steep hills on a difficult track, they had seen an array of furniture, of things once beloved of a woman, built with care by a man, left at the side of the track. Audrun was stunned by the waste until Davyn grimly explained that packing a wagon with too many unnecessary things burdened the draft animals required to pull it. Lives, he'd said, were far more important; a man could build another table, had he the skill, or buy another bureau mirror for his wife, had he the money.

But it was the woman-high harp standing beside the road that took her breath. She knew nothing of the instrument save that she had heard about harps, heard that a person who could play it conjured the music of the gods. The sweeping belly wood had cracked, destroying the symmetry of the carvings that once had been silver-gilt. The strings were a snarled ruin. One, only one, remained as it had been, taut top to bottom, glinting in the sunlight.

No, she had said when the children walking beside the wagon wanted to explore the abandoned things. No, she told herself inwardly, when her own heart wanted to touch the single harp string, to hear a whisper of the magic.

No, Davyn said, asking the oxen to move out more smartly as he called his children back to the wagon, back to the barren track to raise dust with their footsteps.

Now, the wagon shifted and creaked beneath the weight

of her husband climbing in from the back. Some idea, some concern, set vertical creases between his brows. He smelled of oxen and labor and grime, the salty tang of perspiration.

She noticed suddenly what she undoubtedly should have marked before: his hair was receding.

She wanted to touch that hair, to smooth away the cares. But even as she lifted her hand, he spoke. "I have done my best. All the years of our lives." His tone was lowered for privacy, but nonetheless thrummed with emotion. "I always will, Audrun."

Instead of touching fine blond hair, she placed her hand over the calloused one of her husband. "There is nothing, and no one, who could possibly make me doubt it."

His eyes sought hers. "The guide."

In her mind's eye, she saw the Shoia. His attire, so alien to her; the deft motions of his hands when set to a task; the kindness, the humor, in his eyes. The unexpected dimples carved deeply in his face as he smiled, or laughed. And how he understood her children.

The father of those children now doubted himself.

"No," she said. "*No*, Davyn."

He looked away from her, lips working as if he chewed the interior of his mouth.

"I was blessed," she told him, "when the Mother made you and set you into my path. *We* were blessed when she gave us healthy children growing straight and strong. Guide or no guide, Davyn, you are not alone in this."

After a moment he nodded. He turned his hand beneath hers so that it faced up, and interlaced his fingers with hers. "*I* was blessed," he said hoarsely.

She smiled, leaned forward, brushed a light kiss across his stubbled chin. "If we're bound for Atalanda, we'd best be going."

He squeezed her hand, then backed out of the wagon, ducking his head so as not to brush the string of charms hanging from the white-painted Mother Rib.

Audrun stared at the dangling leather thong, the tarnished silver charms, the fragility of feathers, the carved stone and wooden beads. At her throat hung something similar. She closed one hand around the necklace.

"Mother of Moons," she whispered, "see us there safely."

 IT WAS AS she climbed the steps into her wagon that Ilona realized what Rhuan had told her.

Six deaths left.

Six.

He had meant it as comfort, to assure her that he had other deaths left to him. And despite the wonder that still, even after three years, teased her mind as she remembered the first death and resurrection she had witnessed, she had grown complacent with the knowledge. He had died again only two days before, and resurrected. And now he told her six deaths remained to him of the seven.

Her hands holding onto the doorjamb, one foot poised for the top step, Ilona stilled.

Six deaths. *Six.*

But she had witnessed two.

Surely Rhuan could count.

She could.

A man who died twice, who had, supposedly, six deaths left to him out of seven, was one death wrong.

Her muscles tensed to turn, to descend the steps in haste, to go to him, to confront him, to explain that lies to her were not necessary. But she held her body in check.

Ilona had known liars in her life, men and women who, for whatever reason, almost never told the truth. Her own father had lied to her time and time again, until she learned, as a girl, to believe nothing he said; except those promises made to punish her if her chores were not done on time. She had seen the satisfaction in his eyes, sensed an inner amusement that was pleasure. She had never looked into his hand with the eyes and senses of a hand-reader because in those days she didn't know what she was, but there had been no need. He lied. That was all, and it was enough.

Rhuan was not a habitual liar, but she had known him to lie. Always it had to do with a question from a worried, exhausted karavaner on the verge of breaking down for one reason or another; or with his own health. He lied to mislead people from frightening truths.

She knew then that he had *not* killed her assailant. She had allowed herself to believe he might have, but now, removed from the emotions of that time, she knew.

But this time, she knew he lied. Six deaths, he said, and Shoia only died for good on the seventh.

She had witnessed two.

So. Six deaths left were more likely only one.

Ilona climbed the top step and stood inside her wagon, staring at the rune-carved Mother Rib and the dangling string of charms. Absently she removed the sticks from her hair, let down that hair, shook it out, then slowly began to twist it upon itself once more. When it was more neatly wound against the back of her head, she thrust the sticks through again to hold the coils in place.

Her own ritual, to busy her hands as she prayed to the Mother. A simple prayer, withal: *Let him live.*

Chapter 35

AT JORDA'S BEHEST, the karavan made haste to return to the tent settlement. Rhuan spent the journey riding up one side of the column and down the other, calmly but firmly urging those driving the wagons to get quicker gaits out of the draft animals. He knew Jorda's mind was on discovering the magnitude of the damage done to the settlement where he had many friends; his own attention was split between wondering if he also had lost any friends in the Hecari decimation and concern about how the farmsteaders were faring as they struck out on their own. Practically speaking, though the settlement decimation was a brutal thing, it nonetheless left survivors who could help one another, while the farmsteaders numbered only two adults, and one of them was pregnant. With Alisanos preparing to go active, they were, Rhuan felt, in a far more perilous position.

And yet as he at last rode ahead to the outskirts of the settlement, Rhuan revised his opinion. The odor of burned oilcloth, timber framing, lamp oil, and human hair and flesh clothed the remaining tents like a miasma. He saw charcoal-smeared inhabitants dragging forth the remains of their property from burned tents, while others piled up wagons with charred and useless tent poles and destroyed belongings, preparing to haul the loads away for burial or burning some distance from the settlement. Others were raking the pathways through the narrow, winding routes throughout the settlement, mixing ash and wet coals with dirt so it might pack down somewhat. He saw grieving families piecing through the ruins of their tents frantically as others tried to gather up and take away that which was no longer of use. And he saw a place amid the copse of trees usually reserved for the karavans that now, seated or lying on blankets, was filled with the wounded. Many of them had burns from fighting the fires, while others had sustained injuries from the Hecari in the midst of the culling.

The sight stunned him into halting his horse abruptly, staring mutely at the destruction. Away from the settlement, merely hearing news of the culling, the magnitude of the destruction had not registered. He had been busy with Hecari incursions upon the karavan, including his own death, and had allowed other matters to remain in the forefront of his mind.

"Mother of Moons," he murmured as Darmuth rode up beside him.

The demon made a hissing sound of derision as he reined in his mount. "You know very well what gods were responsible for this. Not the humans' puny 'Mother.' "

Rhuan ignored that, shaking himself out of shock and into action. "Ride back to Jorda and tell him he'd do best to put his karavan on the other side of the settlement for now. We can use the spare oilcloth for putting up temporary tents, and I daresay break down some of the wagons for their wood." He saw Darmuth's raised brows. "Yes, I know it won't please those of the karavan, but until new supplies can be brought in, there's little choice. They're going nowhere this season, so they may as well help rebuild the settlement."

"And bring the Hecari down upon this place for a second culling?"

Rhuan bared his teeth at Darmuth in a humorless smile. "Which is why it's *your* task to speak with the Watch and any other men people will listen to, to sort out how to prepare for another Hecari party. Sentries, for one, to report back if an approaching party is seen. Jorda's karavan increases the population the Hecari just reduced; the most obvious plan should be a way to hide them." Rhuan glanced around. "For a start, save as much of the burned tenting as can be salvaged, and the wood. It's time the inhabitants learned to transform themselves to ground rats."

"Ground rats?"

"Have them dig holes," Rhuan replied succinctly. "Holes large enough to hold several people. But no mounds to mark the burrows; place wood or oilcloth over the top, and dirt over that; air shafts can be kept small and covered with brush." He pointed with his chin toward the karavan grounds. "If each burrow hole has a wagon over the top, the Hecari may not even think to search. They come only to kill."

"Rhuan." Darmuth said it sharply enough that it stopped Rhuan's thoughts. "This is not a village. It's not a city. It's just a transient place where people meet the karavans. It counts for nothing. Why not tell them all simply to go elsewhere? Nothing ties them here."

Rhuan reined in his temper, replacing it with clipped conciseness. "Have you ever thought about how villages and cities are born, Darmuth?"

The demon frowned. "Why waste my thoughts on such a thing?"

"For you, perhaps it is a waste. But not for me." Rhuan's gesture encompassed the settlement with its gaping holes of lost tents. "This *is* a village. There are people who came here, thinking to move on elsewhere, who remained. There are diviners, and whores, and ale-keepers. A Watch, men who have taken responsibility for keeping people safe. A bathing tent. A common tent for couriers. Cook tents. As karavans come through, usually one or two people remain here. Babies are born. Old folk die and are buried or burned, according to their rites. Sickness can be treated by two different moonmothers. What more do you ask of a village, Darmuth?"

The demon watched Rhuan in evident puzzlement. "But why do you *care?*"

Rhuan sighed deeply, shrugging as he looked across the denuded settlement. "It appears to be my nature." He glanced over a shoulder, then lifted the reins of his horse. "I'd best go tell Jorda to lead the wagons to a different place."

"Wait, Rhuan."

He briefly halted his mount. "What?"

Darmuth searched his eyes and face. Slowly the pupils of the demon's eyes elongated. His upper lip lifted, displaying the tips of his teeth. Nostrils flared. After a moment, the face Darmuth showed the world again resembled that of a normal man. "Your nature," he said, "is polluted by humans."

Rhuan laughed outright, then tamed it to a grin.

Darmuth did not find the reaction amusing. "You are *dioscuri,*" he said tightly. "You can choose."

"Oh, I will choose," Rhuan said, "when all the tests are completed. When *I* am completed."

EVEN SEVERAL DAYS after the Hecari decimation, custom remained slow in Mikal's ale tent. Now and again a man would come in and ask for spirits, but there was no lingering, no loud, laughing parties inhabiting battered tables, passing early evening before retiring to tents. They came, they drank quickly, they left, as if looking for strength, or relief, or escape in the liquor and gaining none. They brought with them the odor of death on their flesh and in their clothing.

Mikal tenanted the area behind the plank bar as usual, greeting each customer, but the words of welcome lacked sincerity. There was no life in Mikal's tone, no spark in his eye. Bethid, slouching once again upon a bench at a table near the bar, watched as the big man made every attempt to be himself, and failed.

We none of us can be ourselves, after witnessing the culling.

It had been Bethid's first, to watch from start to finish.

Once before she had come upon a smaller settlement where the Hecari had culled, but it was as the warriors rode away, as the grieving began, not during the killings. The painted warriors had eyed her openly as they departed, fingering bloodied warclubs, but the rich blue courier's mantle hanging off her shoulders bought her freedom.

The freedom to see what had been done.

And it was that memory, coupled now with everything she had witnessed the day before and today, that had brought Bethid back to Mikal's tent. Once again she sat with a platter of bread before her and a tall tankard of dark, pungent ale. As countless others had done before her, Bethid used her meat knife to carve a design in the wooden tabletop, a series of sharp, jagged angles, as if she carved her emotions into the wood. She had seen Mikal put a stop to it when others did it, but he said nothing as she cut, nothing as she flicked splinters away with the edge of her knife hand. The sun now was down, and Mikal lighted the tin lanterns, setting them out on the tables. Bethid found the scent of lamp oil and tallow candles more bearable than the odor of burned bodies.

Mikal set a lamp before her. He noticed but did not comment on the mess she had made of the bread loaf, the pelleted crumbs crushed and rolled in clamping fingers, the piles of shredded crust. That destruction had come before Bethid had taken her knife to the table, but nothing soothed the ache of despair in her soul, the fear that accompanied the anger, the conviction that organizing a rebellion was necessary. She knew Brodhi was correct about the risks. She understood and acknowledged that the couriers must be willing to kill to keep their plans safe. But that was the portion of her that burned as fiercely as the fires consuming the ruins of tents, of bodies. There was another portion of her that was ice cold.

Like Brodhi? But she broke off the thought abruptly. *Speak of the demon.* Brodhi was slipping through the door flap.

Lantern light played across his face, gilding his skin,

glinting off ornamentation, bathing the sheen of his hair. And then with a start she realized it wasn't Brodhi at all. Shoia, yes. But Rhuan.

He was unaccountably grim—and then she remembered that all men would be grim, coming through the tent settlement. Rhuan had not been present for the decimation, but the stench of death and desolation, the odor of desperation would lead him to ask what had happened the moment he arrived. He didn't come to Mikal's to find out; he knew.

Then Bethid remembered *how* he knew: Brodhi had somehow, some way, communicated with Rhuan without leaving the settlement.

Bethid heard the faint clinks and muted chiming of glass and gold as Rhuan walked toward the bar, the quiet tone as he asked for ale. It was not often that she saw the two Shoia together, and less often that she noted the differences between them because there were so many obvious similarities in the long, ornately woven braids, the color of skin and hair, the likeness in build and posture. Rhuan was alone, but his expression now echoed what she witnessed so often on Brodhi's face. She saw no dimples, no light of laughter in Rhuan's eyes, no easy grace in his movements.

He turned as Mikal handed him a tankard, saw her, and took the two paces that placed him at her table. She saw the question in his eyes and nodded, gesturing invitation with her knife. Rhuan kicked a stool over and sat down. Long, slender fingers wrapped around the dented pewter tankard, sliding through the curved handle. Foam spilled over the rim and dribbled down to wet his flesh. It painted channels in the dust coating his hand.

She said, "Brodhi reached you."

Rhuan nodded, lifted the tankard. He drank at least half of the contents before setting it down to foam ale onto the table.

"Will *you* tell me how he did it?" she asked. "He said it had something to do with being Shoia."

Rhuan wiped his lips free of foam against the back of his

wrist, then nodded. "It's a Shoia thing, yes. But mostly because we're kin-in-kind." He paused. "Cousins."

Bethid realized his gaze was doing more than looking at her. It was an evaluation. "Yes," she said flatly, "I'm all right."

The corner of his mouth jerked in a brief smile, but faded back into thinned grimness. "Jorda turned the karavan around when he heard."

She had believed he returned on his own because of Brodhi's message. Now, startled, she sat up straight on her stool. "The *whole* karavan?"

"There was no choice," he told her. "Jorda has friends here."

"What about all of the karavaners? It's end of season . . . there are no more karavan-masters readying to go out."

"They'll stay," Rhuan said. "They'll help rebuild."

"With what? No supply trains will be here for months."

"The karavan itself will be the supply train. Each wagon carries the means to begin homes elsewhere, so instead they'll do it here. There is seed. Livestock. Oilcloth. Wood. People to do the planting and harvesting. People to *help*, Bethid. Come next season they can restock and go on with Jorda, when he's ready. Since he returned their fees, it won't be a hardship."

"They can't be happy about it, Rhuan! To lose a whole season because of strangers?"

"Perhaps not," he agreed, "but they were given a choice: to go on alone or to turn back. All but one family came here when Jorda explained what had happened, especially on the heels of our *own* encounter with Hecari. But in our case, the warriors were culled. Every one of them."

She knew better than to ask if he had done the killing. One had only to look at his eyes to know the truth. "Did the Hecari kill anyone there?"

"Only me." Dimples flashed, framing a white-toothed grin. "But I recovered."

Bethid shook her head. She could not grasp how it was that a man might die and come back to life. She had asked Brodhi about it more than once, but remained ignorant be-

cause he refused to address how it was done. It just *was,*
he'd said.

But for the moment she didn't care. One in ten people
had been killed a few days before, and none of them
would recover from it.

"Have you talked to Brodhi?" she asked abruptly.
"Here, I mean. Did he tell you what we plan?"

Rhuan shook his head. "I haven't seen him." He drank
more ale, the motion of swallowing visible beneath the
smooth, sunbrowned skin of his throat.

With her knifetip, Bethid traced the design she had cut
into the table, thinking hard. The jagged, sharp, angry design.

After a moment she lifted her eyes to meet his. "Then let *me*
tell you."

He wasn't a courier. But he was Brodhi's kin, and a man
who could survive death. Such an individual might come in
handy during a rebellion.

Chapter 36

*B*RODHI, ALONE IN the couriers' common tent as the sun dropped below the horizon, was at his personal devotions, telling over the Names of the Thousand Gods. He sat on his bedding with legs crossed, flattened palms upturned, eyes closed, murmuring syllables no human had ever heard, and likely could not pronounce. He was on the four hundred and thirty-sixth name when a noise at the drooping door flap interrupted.

Laughter.

Quiet, more of a gust of breath, but laughter all the same.

He opened his eyes, expecting Timmon or Alorn, who, like Bethid, had gone to drink, to think, to discuss if they had the belly for rebellion. They were not in the habit of laughing at him—all men and women had one deity or another they served—but Brodhi supposed if they were drunk they might find it amusing to discover him in such a vulnerable position. He did not worship in front of anyone.

But it wasn't Timmon or Alorn, or even Bethid, who was far less likely to laugh at him anyway.

Rhuan. Of course.

The door flap was only partially pulled back, so that half of Rhuan was obscured by drooping oilcloth. With the darkness behind him and the single hanging lantern in the tent sputtering for want of fuel, he was in flickering chiaroscuro, painted black and ocher.

The grin was wide and white in his pale copper face, dimples deeply shadowed. "You," Rhuan said. "*You.* Aiding humans? Planning a rebellion against the Hecari? Guiding the well-intentioned but untrained couriers in revolt? Why Brodhi, if I weren't so certain they would be killed, I'd say you had changed your colors and are taking an interest in the welfare of humans."

"They are fools," Brodhi agreed, resolving to begin anew with his devotions once Rhuan was gone, "but not stupid. They are thinking things through."

"With your advice?" Dimples flashed again. "You'll get them killed more quickly than they would themselves." Rhuan shook his head. "Bethid told me—"

From behind, from the darkness, Rhuan's head was abruptly jerked back. Brodhi saw the knife blade flash, saw the cut in Rhuan's throat, saw the drenching gout of blood.

He was on his feet then, his own knife drawn. He grabbed a handful of Rhuan's tunic as his kinsman sagged and yanked him aside, cursing the impediment; one step outside the door flap and he saw the two men, one with bloodied knife in hand.

Brodhi bloodied his own knife by shoving the blade up under the nearest man's breastbone. The stranger fell, wrenching the handle from Brodhi's hand. The second man, mouth agape—they had likely neither of them counted on *two* Shoia present—turned to run.

Brodhi spun back, took three paces, knelt briefly at Rhuan's body and yanked from baldric loops two of his knives. At the door flap he threw. One knife. Another. The retreating man fell.

That man's partner, the one in whose body Brodhi's knife still resided, wasn't quite dead.

"Why?" Brodhi asked, leaning over him.

The man's life was ebbing, but fear stood paramount in blue eyes. "B-bones . . ."

Of course. Shoia bones.

Brodhi reached out and closed a hand around the horn

grip of his knife, jerking the blade free. With a brutal efficiency he slit the dying man's throat from ear to ear, then went to the body lying facedown upon the ground with Rhuan's throwing knifes in his spine.

Brodhi flipped him over, driving the short-bladed knives deeper. He bent, once again slashed throat flesh, cleaned his knife on the dead man's tunic, then turned. Four long strides brought him back to his tent, and to the lake of blood flowing across the packed dirt floor. To the slack, tumbled limbs, the fanning out of multiple braids. Rhuan's face was obscured by the woven plaits.

Brodhi sighed. "You're making a proper mess of things. That's Bethid's pallet; I suppose I'll have to give her mine." With a booted foot he scraped a film of dirt from the packed earth and tried to dam the blood flow before it reached his pallet. "One of your more dramatic deaths, I believe."

Rhuan's limbs jerked. He coughed weakly, groaned, then rolled over onto his back. Braids fell aside, baring a pale, blood-spattered face and the slowly healing flesh of a riven throat. He clamped a hand to the wound, then swore in the same tongue Brodhi had used to name off the Thousand Gods. After a moment he levered himself up to a seated position. Bloodied hands pushed braids behind his shoulder; then he saw the cascade of blood staining the front of his tunic.

Rhuan made an inarticulate sound of annoyance, frustration, and disgust, then lifted his eyes to Brodhi's. "That's twice!" he said aggrievedly. "Twice in a matter of days!"

"Apparently you make enemies more often than friends." Brodhi wiped at his own face, realizing that it also was splattered with Rhuan's blood. He gestured. "Get up. You can be useful by cleaning up after your own mess; bring in some loose soil to cover all this blood."

Rhuan, face twisted, was feeling at his scalp. "He almost ripped the hair out of my head."

"It wasn't your hair he wanted." Brodhi made a more definitive gesture. "Get up, Rhuan. The others don't need to come back and find a lake of blood in their tent."

"Oh. Bones." Rhuan rose, though he was as yet not quite steady on his feet. He stepped to the door flap and pulled it open. "Ah. Two of them. Well, let Hezriah have their bones, not mine."

"Hezriah's dead. Culled." Brodhi picked up Bethid's pallet by the soggy end and dragged it toward the opening. "And don't bother with the Watch, because Kendic's dead, too."

Rhuan moved out of the way as Brodhi pulled the blood-soaked pallet out of the tent. A hand on the door flap found dampness; he looked and saw blood. A generous spray had spurted across the tent and stained the oil-cloth walls.

Brodhi reappeared. "You're wobbling," he noted. "Lie down on my pallet for a moment. I'm going to drag these bodies and Bethid's bloodied pallet away from the tent, so they don't draw predators too close." He paused. "There's a waterskin there, and a washing cloth there, by my bed. Clean yourself up. If Timmon, Alorn, or Bethid come back any time soon, they're likely to drop dead of shock, and then I'll have *more* bodies to deal with."

He waited as Rhuan once again frowned down at his ruined tunic, brushing ineffectively at the still-wet stains. Muttering imprecations against men who ruined his clothing as well as killing him, he managed to sit down without falling over.

Considering he and Rhuan had as little to do with one another as possible, Brodhi realized he had of late done more than his fair share of looking after his kin-in-kind. Shaking his head in disgust, he departed the tent to tend to men, human men, who lived only once, and remained dead when killed.

ILONA, PERCHED ATOP the high bench seat of her wagon with wide leather reins in her hands, wearily applied the hand brake as the karavan ground to a halt. There had been some slight confusion when the column was turned away from its usual camping ground, but Ilona knew to trust Jorda. Going elsewhere to camp near the tent settlement was utterly unfamiliar, but she had no doubt there was a good reason. Jorda did manage to lead them to a scattering of trees so there was some daytime shade—and trees, for some reason, always made a campsite feel friendlier to Ilona, more private and personal—so she guided her team to a thick-trunked, wide-crowned tree and halted them under its leafy branches. Janqeril would come and unhitch the horses, leading them away for grooming and feeding—it was a boon allowed the karavan diviners that they need not spend themselves on their animals—but in the meantime she would begin to unpack the things used in her art. She expected to be busy this night, with so many lives and plans thrown into upheaval.

As she climbed down off the high, spring-mounted seat, she saw Darmuth riding the line. She hailed him, calling his name; he slowed, then turned back as he recognized her. He knew very well what her question was, and answered it before she could even ask.

"The usual grove hosts the sick and injured and homeless left over from the Hecari culling," he explained. "You'll be camping here instead."

"How bad is it?"

Darmuth's face was grim. "As bad as I've seen." He eased his restive mount with a hand upon its neck. "I suspect you would be as needed at changing dressings as reading hands."

"Then I'll go," she said immediately.

But Darmuth put up a hand and shook his head. "Stay here. If you go there, everyone will be thrusting their hands into your face even as you wrap a burn that is sure to rot otherwise. There are other women in the karavan who can help. Stay here and tend your business. Diviners can do as much as caregivers in times like these."

"Only if I give them good readings," she reminded him. "That isn't always the case, Darmuth."

His mouth twitched in a smile banished before it was

born. "But hope can do much to strengthen a despairing soul."

He was right, she knew. Countless times those whose hands she read merely wanted company, someone to listen. Someone to reassure them.

A strange expression crossed Darmuth's face. "He's not gone yet. He's at Mikal's, if you wish to find him."

It was a knife in her gut, and wholly unexpected. But she ignored the pain. "I've already said my farewells. I'll see him when he returns."

Darmuth fixed her with a penetrating gaze. Then he smiled faintly, inclined his head, and rode on.

Ilona stood beside the steps of her wagon, hands full of silks she would spread over the low table. She *had* said farewell. She *had* wished him well of his journey. She *did* know he was gone.

For all that he was here, and so was she.

BY THE TIME Brodhi returned, Rhuan had washed himself of all but the faintest traces of blood caught beneath fingernails and drying in his braids. He had stripped out of the soaked tunic and rolled it up, setting it aside with the bloodied washing cloth. In its place he wore one of Brodhi's tunics, a green one, found by digging through his belongings. Once again he wore his belt, his long knife, and the baldric of throwing knives, minus two. He fingered the empty loops, his memory a blank from the moment after his throat had been opened to resurrection. He had lost part of himself, just as when the poisoned Hecari dart killed him. Fortunately this time no one but Brodhi witnessed his death.

With time to think about it, it came as no surprise that he would be attacked for his bones. The tent settlement was in disarray, its people grieving and terrified the Hecari might return. One cure for fear was to know what was coming, and Shoia bones, burned, could tell them, provided there was a diviner left alive who could read them. Hezriah the bonedealer was dead, Brodhi had said; Rhuan briefly wondered about Dardannus, who was always prepared to pay well for Shoia bones.

He was tired and slow, weak from blood loss and shock. Revival did not put lost blood back into his body; it did not restore him to perfect health. It brought him out of death and healed such things as had killed him. But there was always a price to be paid as his body recovered, and because of it he would not be riding out to follow the farmsteaders this evening, as planned. The best he could do was start fresh at dawn, and ride at speed.

Brodhi appeared in the door of the tent. He grimaced as he marked the tunic Rhuan wore. "I stopped by the karavan—I see I should have picked up spare clothes when I dug out your bedroll." He held out a hand. "Here."

Two throwing knives, cleaned. Rhuan tucked them back into their loops, pleased to have a full complement once more.

Brodhi motioned with his head. "Come. We're going to spend the night in the trees."

That was startling news. "Why the trees?"

Brodhi stepped all the way into the tent and knelt down, gathering up his beaded bag and blankets. "You can't stay here; courier tents are reserved for couriers alone. And all the undamaged tents are full of survivors, many of them still in shock while others are grieving. Loudly." He grabbed up his leather courier's pouch and scroll case, slung both over a shoulder. "I suppose Mikal might let you sleep on his bartop, except more and more men who've been burying and burning bodies are gathering there to drink themselves insensible, and that will probably go on until dawn."

Rhuan frowned in perplexity, shrugging. "I'll just go back to the karavan."

"To let the hand-reader look after you again?"

Unexpected warmth rose in his face as he heard the trace of contempt in Brodhi's tone. "No. She doesn't need to know I died again." Especially since he wasn't certain how many deaths she knew about. He had a vague, uneasy memory that he had told her the last one was sixth, which meant this one should have been a permanent death. "I'll sleep elsewhere."

"Just as well." Brodhi rose, staring down at his kinsman. "I had a brief but enlightening talk with Darmuth. It seems that you have not been fulfilling a portion of your responsibilities. Darmuth is most displeased by it, since it places him in a precarious position."

Heat rushed to Rhuan's face. A brief flicker of red crossed his vision. "That is not your concern."

"How long has it been since you allowed Darmuth to Hear you?"

Ordinarily Brodhi's probing questions would have amused him, even as he ignored them, or replied with a quip. But he was tired in body and soul, and reaction to the latest death was likely to set in at any moment. "I don't have the same relationship with Darmuth that you do with Ferize. I'm the prodigal, remember?"

Brodhi arranged his bag and blankets under one arm, then reached down and caught Rhuan's elbow, exerting upward pressure. "Come with me. We have a long night ahead of us."

Rhuan stood up because he had no other choice. But once on his feet, he twisted free of Brodhi's grip. "Let be. This is not your concern."

Brodhi said something very succinct in their milk-tongue, the language all male babies learned first and spoke until their voices broke, at which time they were allowed to begin speaking the tongue of adults. It was an intentional insult in and of itself, but from Brodhi, for whom arrogance was an art, it fired Rhuan's blood and turned his vision crimson.

"If you behave as a child, you shall be treated as a child," Brodhi declared, seeing the reaction. "And if you wish to challenge me here and now, be certain I shall win. You haven't the strength to defeat me." Once again he clasped a hand around Rhuan's elbow, intentionally tweaking a nerve so that Rhuan hissed in discomfort. "We are going away from here for the night. But before you sleep, I will Hear you. In every detail. I insist upon it."

"What, so you can tell Ferize? She's hardly my advocate."

"She's hardly *mine,* most of the time," Brodhi countered dryly. "Would you rather have me fetch Darmuth?"

Rhuan considered the last time he and Darmuth had spoken. "We're not on good terms at the moment."

"Neither are Ferize and I. So, that leaves me. Not your choice, perhaps, but in this world I *am* a trained courier; I know how to carry messages exactly as they have been given to me. But if you like, I will spill blood for the oath."

Rhuan winced, feeling at his throat. "I think there's been more than enough blood spilled tonight."

Brodhi's gaze was steady. "We *will* do this. It is a part of the journey, as you well know, and weighs a great deal in the final outcome. You have made it abundantly clear to me and to our sires what you want, so I suggest you fulfill all the oaths you made if you expect to have your wish granted."

Another time, Rhuan would have challenged Brodhi. Another time, he would have freed himself of Brodhi's grip and walked away, secure in his own strength to do so. But not tonight. Not after a death that had bled him nearly dry.

"All right," he said, "but let go."

Brodhi's grip remained firm on Rhuan's elbow. He waited.

Rhuan sighed. "*Dioscuri* to *dioscuri.*"

It was pledge enough. Brodhi released him.

Rhuan swore in the tongue of the humans, but he accompanied his kinsman away from the settlement.

Chapter 37

*T*HE OXEN, WHO had preferred traveling with the karavan and objected to being turned away, were slow and recalcitrant. Davyn told everyone to walk in hopes the lighter wagon might improve the animals' attitudes, but it made no difference. And nothing he did hastened them, either. The best distance the family made by dusk was a day or two away from the turnoff that would take them to Atalanda more swiftly. Come morning the oxen should have forgotten what it was like to be in a karavan, and they could make better time.

Davyn was walking a handful of long paces ahead of the wagon. "Here," he called to Gillan, who was guiding the oxen. "We'll pull off . . . not too far. Head for the trees." There was a modest grove of trees not far off the track, and Gillan waved a hand to indicate his understanding.

His family was scattered on either side of the road, avoiding the dust raised by oxen and wagon, though they had left off face scarves now that they were no longer at the end of a long karavan. Torvic and Megritte were, as usual, challenging one another to games and dares made up on the spot—he tried to remember when he had such energy, and failed—while Ellica walked near her mother. His daughter had at some point undone her hair, so that it hung down her back like a fall of rippled pale silk. She was growing into the promise of a prettiness, not obvious, not astounding, but evident in her complexion, the curve of cheekbones, the long eyelids, the under defined browbone, and the well-molded shapes of her jaw and nose. She was tall, taller than her mother, with a body just beginning to lose the angles of girlhood, to soften and mature into womanhood.

She did not, Davyn thought, resemble her mother as much as in childhood. She had his coloring, with nearly white-blond hair, blue eyes, and extremely fair skin, though his skin was much weathered now. Audrun's hair was the color of a dun horse, though the sun had bleached streaks of gold into it, and her eyes were brown. After four births and a fifth child on the way, she lacked the bloom of youth her elder daughter claimed, but retained a refinement in the features of her lean, tanned face. Audrun was gold and bronze; Ellica, rose and white.

It was well they were going to Atalanda, Davyn thought; there were few available young men in Sancorra because of the war. Ellica would have a much better, and much safer, opportunity to find a husband in Atalanda.

And that made him smile as he headed toward the grove. Audrun had been Ellica's age when they married. Often it felt like yesterday, and it seemed impossible that their own oldest girl might well be marrying and starting her own family within a year or two.

Davyn nodded, content with the life he and Audrun had made. He gave thanks to the gods, to the Mother of Moons, and asked them to grant the same health to the unborn one, a baby who would never see the face of war, of loss, of tragedy. A baby who would never see a Hecari, but only hear about the painted, brutal warriors who had overrun Sancorra as they had overrun two other provinces, a flood tide of killers. Atalanda lay on the far side of Alisanos; Davyn believed not even the Hecari would attempt the deepwood.

Not far from the grove Gillan halted the oxen. With Gillan's aid, Davyn chocked the wagon wheels and un-hitched the oxen, directing his son to lead them off for forage in the lush prairie grass. They would be hobbled against wandering too far, but with plenty of succulent grass at hand Davyn doubted they would take more than two or three steps even left free.

Already Audrun had sent the two youngest, with Ellica's help, to round up rocks suitable for building a fire ring even as she began to gather the makings for stew. Meatless stew; it had been a week or more since they had eaten fresh meat, and Davyn resolved that tomorrow would be a half-day on the road so that he and Gillan could set snares and hope for a hare or two. Cooked and packed in salt, the meat would last them a day or three; more, if they were lucky with their snares.

They carried a store of kindling and firewood at all times, and though they had the makings to start a fire, they also carried a small cloth-wrapped iron coal pot. It was Gillan's task to keep the coals inside alive, to monitor how many hardwood chips were needed to preserve the coals. With this pot and dried kindling they need not worry about the challenges of starting a cookfire in wet weather; beneath a wide section of oilcloth stretched out from the wagon and attached with cloth torn into strips to poles planted upright in the earth, they could cook even in rain, huddling together under the cloth.

But the skies, though darkening at dusk, were clear, with the first exuberantly bright stars starting to appear. Days before, Grandmother Moon had turned her face away, giving way to the Orphan Sky, the time when the elderly often died, crossing the river to a land where there was no darkness, no cessation of light. It was a time when diviners experienced better custom, when people handled their necklets of charms and prayed for a return to light, to the Maiden Moon's mercies, a sliver that slowly, as the Maiden gained confidence, bloomed into the full round face of gravid motherhood. The Orphan Sky had passed. Maiden Moon rose now, easing toward the welcome light of the Mother.

Davyn's necklet of charms had fallen inside his tunic. Pausing to give thanks skyward, he pulled the thong out

and felt the individual charms, distinct in shape, with cal-
lused fingers. Pewter, brass, carved wood, even two
costly glass beads, both a streaky red. And lumpy knots
scattered along the length of leather, tied into the thong
by the moonmother who had spoken ritual chants over
the necklets asking the gods to look kindly on the
wearer, to bring him to worthiness before he crossed the
river.

He heard high-pitched voices and saw his two youngest
sharing the load of an oilcloth bucket. It sagged between
them as they came down the freshly cut wagon ruts, briefly
scraping up soil as they carried it toward their mother.
They were mired in an argument over who had found the
largest rock and were negligent in their care for the
bucket, dragging it in the dirt time and time again.

Not far behind them was Ellica with another oilcloth
bucket. She caught his eyes, mouth twisted as she set down
her load beside the place Audrun had selected for the fire
ring. "I don't recall Gillan and I arguing this much."

Davyn shook his head in negation. "More." Grinning at
her immediate protest, he rescued the bucket from the
ministrations of his two youngest and carried it to Audrun,
already busily spading up thickly-rooted grass in preparation for the cookfire. The routine of preparing dinner was
well-known, and there was little more to do save oversee
Torvic and Megritte so that they didn't neglect their responsibilities.

Gillan came back from the oxen. "No stream that I could
find, so I've watered them from the barrel. They're eating
well."

Davyn nodded. "Good. Perhaps this slower pace will put
flesh back on them." He noted Gillan's faded blue tunic for
the first time. "Isn't that mine?"

Gillan nodded, somewhat shamefacedly.

"I gave it to him," Audrun said from where she super-
vised construction of the fire ring with Torvic's and
Megritte's haphazard building skills. "Your son has out-
grown his own in the shoulders; the seams need to be let
out. Ellica can begin that task tomorrow." She glanced up,

offering a private smile for him. "I think he'll be taller than you once he's grown."

"Can't he let out his own seams?" Ellica asked acerbically.

Her older brother stared at her, startled. "That's woman's work!"

"I'll trade," she offered. "I'll tend the oxen tomorrow morning, and you can let out the seams of your tunics."

Audrun raised her voice slightly. "I don't think you want to see what will become of the tunics if your brother lets out the seams." She paused a beat. "Or your father, for that matter. Not with their big hands."

Davyn and Gillan, simultaneously, looked at their hands. Davyn nodded ruefully; they were broad, calloused hands, fingers scarred from years of work. He dared not take up Audrun's precious silver needle, or it would be lost certain-sure.

Broad hands, broad shoulders; Davyn smiled as it dawned on Gillan that he was being accorded a man's place, not a boy's. At the farmstead, it had been easy to see Gillan merely as a boy as the years passed by. But this jour-ney had made a man of him even as it guided Ellica across the threshhold of womanhood.

"Well done," Audrun said of the fire ring. "Hands?" Tor-vic and Megritte displayed their palms and fingers. Their mother nodded, gesturing to the water barrel on the back of the wagon. "Wash up. And *try* not to get them dirty again before we eat!"

They would, Davyn knew. He grinned to see Audrun quickly change out several rocks to strengthen the lop-sided affair Torvic and Megritte had built. Then he sur-veyed the heavens critically. "Tomorrow, then. Not enough light left." He glanced at Gillan. "Snares. First thing tomor-row morning. We'll delay our start until after midday and hope for fat hares."

"*I* could set out snares," Ellica announced.

"Man's work," Gillan said briskly.

Davyn, smiling to himself, turned back to the wagon to dig out the snares even as Ellica protested that she was as capable as any *man* at doing such work. He supposed it was true, but there were other tasks Ellica was needed for. She had been young enough at Megritte's birth that there was little she could do then to assist her mother, but this time, in this pregnancy, Audrun could rely on Ellica for real help.

He grinned, climbing up into the wagon. Ellica might complain about being relegated to woman's work, but she would undoubtedly sing a different tune when it was her turn to bear her own children. That was the sort of work no man could do.

RHUAN STILL FELT shaky from the attack and subsequent death as he walked with Brodhi away from the courier tent and into the trees. And he discovered it was difficult to maintain anger when he wasn't fully recovered from dying. Flickers of it rose now and again, but they faded quickly, quenched by sheer physical exhaustion and the need for sleep. By morning he would be fine, but in the meantime he felt feeble as a man ready, in the parlance of humans, to cross the river.

That thought kindled a twitch of droll amusement. He *had* crossed the river. Several times.

"Here." Brodhi stopped walking. "This will do."

The night had been loud with the song of locusts. Now the sound abated. A flutter of wings against leaves spoke of birds departing the Shoia's unwanted presence. But after a moment the nightsingers began again, locusts come above ground after months entombed to shed their skins, live a handful of days, and die.

Rhuan watched his kinsman indicate the place he meant, the foot of a wide-bolled tree with lower branches so heavy with leaves they curved over in a leafy arc, forming a very private pocket between trunk and limbs. Brodhi pulled branches back and ducked through, motioning Rhuan to join him. As he did, grasping springing limbs just as Brodhi released them, he saw his kinsman place a palm

against the tree, quietly asking permission to conduct a ritual at its very feet.

After a moment Brodhi nodded, murmured his thanks,
and began preparations for the Hearing, unrolling and
spreading oilcloth as a shield against moisture, then two
blankets atop it. Brodhi settled down on one side of the
blankets with legs crossed and began to pull items from his
beaded bag, setting them out in a precise line. A sharp gesture commanded Rhuan to sit down as well, placing himself in identical position across the blanket from Brodhi. It
was more difficult to comply than he expected, with trembling limbs that wanted merely to sprawl any which way.

The sun was down and the newborn Maiden Moon took
precedence in the sky; Rhuan felt the preliminary seepage
of chill making its way up through the trebled fabric beneath him as he settled, crossing his legs. With night so
near, a human would need lamp or candle to see in the
leaf-shielded pocket, but he and Brodhi required nothing
save the eyes in their heads.

Attempting to take his mind off of the upcoming Hearing, he asked, "Have you ever died from a throat-cutting?"

Brodhi shook his head, attention focused on what he
took from the beaded bag.

Rhuan felt at his throat. "Well, avoid it if you can. It's uncomfortable at best." The skin seemed whole and firm as
ever, but some wounds did leave scars.

"I try to avoid dying as a matter of course." Brodhi set
the leather bag aside and began unrolling a section of thin
hide. "You, on the other hand, seem to attract it." With exquisite care, Brodhi spread the hide between them, fingertips lingering to stroke the surface. The color of the hide, as
Rhuan looked upon it, almost blended into the dark blankets, a dusky twilight blue with the barest sheen of silver,
tiny scallops of interlocking scales. He saw Brodhi's fingers
tremble slightly and looked up to see that his eyes were
closed, his lips moving. Brodhi's cheekbones, Rhuan noted,
were flushed, and a sheen of perspiration lent glinting
highlights to his kinsman's angular face.

It felt—wrong. It made Rhuan feel awkward and un-

comfortable to witness that private inner communion,
even if it did have something to do with himself. He
wanted nothing more than to get up and walk briskly
away, refusing even to glance back, but Brodhi was undertaking this night's journey for Rhuan's sake, not his own,
and for Rhuan to turn his back on that sacrifice would not
endear him to those who judged his worthiness, who
weighed the information Darmuth provided in making
their decision.

Or, in this case, information Brodhi would Hear and
later transfer to Ferize, when next he saw her.

Rhuan fidgeted. He drummed his fingers on his knees,
shifted position several times, gnawed first on his bottom
lip and then the insides of his cheeks.

He hated Hearings. It was why he avoided them.

Brodhi's eyes were now unshielded by lids, open but
lost in shadowed sockets. He smiled faintly, acknowledging Rhuan's discomfiture, then drew his knife. "To give
you peace, I will do it anyway." And before Rhuan could
protest, Brodhi cut into the ball of of his left-hand thumb.
Quietly he shook out blood in each of the four cardinal
points of the earth, murmuring Names, then looked again
at Rhuan. "The blood is spilled. I swear to tell only what
I Hear."

Rhuan instinctively sought to delay the moment with
carefully casual lightness. "What, no opinions?" he asked.
"No irony? No . . . superiority?"

Brodhi's reply was to flick blood droplets at Rhuan.
"The oath is made." After cleaning his knife, he touched
the bleeding thumb to the section of thin hide. When he
lifted it, there was no more blood to be seen, nor the mark
of the knife. He then took up a section of reed and turned
it on end. With care he worked the wax plug free, then
cupped the reed upright in both hands and presented it,
waiting mutely.

Rhuan hesitated, staring at the open reed. The scent of
the contents was so sharp his nostrils prickled in response.
It would be horribly disrespectful to sneeze, so he rubbed
his nose violently to kill the impulse.

"It's for you to do," Brodhi said. "I can't take it from you. You must offer it."

"I know that." Annoyed, Rhuan reached out, set a fingertip into the reed opening, and felt the heat of the contents, though cool to the touch, burn a line up to his wrist. He gritted his teeth. "I'm going to hate this . . ."

"Had you lived up to your responsibilities, this would not be necessary."

Rhuan grimaced. "Do we have to trade words even on the brink of this?"

"Had you lived up to your responsibilities, 'this' would not be necessary."

Trust Brodhi to maintain arrogance even now, humbled by nothing. Rhuan scowled at him in the darkness, then closed his eyes. He touched the oil-laden fingertip to the eleven blessing points: the center of his brow, the bridge of nose, both eyelids, the hollow between nose and mouth, the arch of cheekbones, upper and lower lips, his chin, and lastly his throat.

What irony, in view of his earlier death to an opened throat.

It began in each place his fingertip had touched. A lattice of fire blossomed across his face, running from one blessing point to the next. Every hair on his body, save for the heavy braids, stood on end, prickling abrasively.

With Darmuth it was a simple and painless process handled much differently. But this was Brodhi. This was kin-in-kind. This was a *dioscuri* even as he was, and what they made between them this night would never be forgotten. Oh, the words would be, but not the emotions. This ritual would bind them to one another even more than the ritual that allowed them to communicate with one another over great distances.

"Let go," Brodhi said. "Open to it, and the pain will subside."

The lines of pain felt like they were sinking through flesh. Through clenched teeth, he asked, "Have you ever done it this way?"

"Never," Brodhi answered. "But then, I accept my responsibilities. I understand what the term 'regularly' means when it comes to Hearings."

Reprimand. Arrogance. Supreme self-confidence. As always.

Rhuan's skin crawled, rising on his bones. He felt doors opening inside him. He sensed the vastness of the world, the maelstrom that defined his mind, his personality, the essence of who and what he was. That laid bare his soul.

The words burst out of Rhuan's mouth, slurred together on a note of pure, primal fear, of abrupt appeal in the midst of an interior pain, of a mental rearrangement, that threatened to burst his skull. *"LetmegofindDarmuth . . ."*

Brodhi said, "Too late."

Chapter 38

*I*N THE DARKNESS of night, Audrun awoke abruptly with the echoes of a scream, her scream, inside her head. Her heart pounded so so hard she feared it might burst her chest. Something, *something* in a dream had terrified her, driving her into wakefulness. But she realized she had not truly screamed, for neither Davyn nor the children reacted. All was quiet, save for her own ragged breathing.

Beneath the wagon, she lay curled in blankets next to her husband, spooning to share his warmth, to place the unborn baby safely between them. He slept deeply, not stirring. She envied him his peace. Sleep always eluded her after a bad dream.

As her heart slowed to its normal rhythm, as perspiration dried and her breathing settled, Audrun tried to recall the nightmare and could not; the images were fleeting, unrecognizable, fleeing memory's grasp now that she was awake. Frowning, she brushed hair back from her face, then, as cool night air crept into openings, pulled the blankets more closely around her neck. She did not suffer nightmares often, but when they occurred they were terrifying.

A moment later she gritted her teeth against whispering an unkind word of annoyance. Her bladder had awakened as well. After giving birth to four children, her body was much quicker to reach the characteristics of late pregnancy. And ignoring it would not work. She had learned that years before.

The knowledge of the nightmare still teased her. Bladder pressure or no, she wanted nothing at all to do with crawling out of her blankets and walking off into the darkness. But the urge would merely increase to true discomfort if she remained where she was, and she would never get back to sleep.

Moving slowly so as not to awaken Davyn, Audrun got to her hands and knees and crawled from under the wagon. She took the top blanket with her, wrapping it around herself as she moved, and put on felted buskins over stockinged feet. Audrun reached for the small pierced-tin lantern hanging off the side of the wagon. The rock-rimmed cookfire, with some coals still alive, was a matter of a pace away.

She rose, took that pace, and knelt once again. She felt for and found the kindling twigs, selected one, and poked an end into the coals. When the twig caught and flared, she carefully touched it to the wick inside the small lantern. As the wick took flame she quickly closed the vented door and latched it. She tossed the half-burned twig onto the coals and raised the lantern high as she climbed to her feet, shedding freckled illumination.

Such times as these were when she regretted leaving the night-crock in the wagon with the children. But she and Davyn had decided it was far better for adults to go wandering in the darkness to find an appropriate tree or shrub than to permit the children to do so. So she and Davyn always slept clothed, save for shoes and boots.

Ordinarily it didn't bother her at all to seek relief in darkness, but the nightmare had left her jumpy. She couldn't remember what it was she had dreamed, but its effects remained vivid and unsettling. Fortunately the small lantern was enough to light her way to the nearest tree. It was a gnarled old oak, an odd juxtaposition in a stand of immature trees with as yet fragile limbs and branches. Its thick roots had broken through the soil in places, forming pockets and hummocks and hollows. Audrun stepped carefully to the other side of the tree, set the lantern down, and began to gather up long skirts and blanket.

The lantern winked out.

This time, Audrun did swear. But very softly.

Her approach had stilled the nightsingers, but the lantern drew moths. Now, with the lantern out, the moths were gone. The nightsingers remained mute. As Audrun's eyes adjusted to the darkness, she was aware of how very quiet it was in the little grove of trees.

Beneath tunic sleeves, beneath blanket, the hairs rose up on her arms. Audrun remained standing next to the big oak, frozen in place with skirts and blanket clasped in knotted hands. She felt vulnerable because of it; Audrun opened her fingers slowly and let the fabric drop, falling again to her ankles. She drew slow, silent breaths, released them as slowly and silently. Still there was no sound.

She bent down, bracing herself with one hand against the tree while the other felt around for her lantern. She found it sitting upright just as she had left it. The pierced tin was cool to the touch, but then the wick had not been lighted for long. Audrun closed her hand around the handle and stood up again with care, listening for some sound, any sound, that would mark the night as ordinary.

A twig snapped behind her. Audrun swung around, raising the lantern for use as a weapon, searching for something, anything, that she might see.

Eyes shone in the darkness.

RHUAN'S VOICE DIED out. Brodhi waited in case there was something more, but nothing else was said. In place of the voice of his kinsman he heard the chittering rasp of the nightsingers, intermittent noise from the settlement, the whisper of leaves fluttering in response to a rising breeze.

Brodhi studied Rhuan. His eyes were closed; he was lost in the reverie of completion, the mental blankness that occurred when one has poured oneself out. A Hearing was precisely that: An opportunity for the speaker to open himself, to explain himself and his thought processes, his decisions, the ramifications of his actions, regrets or satisfaction, the emptying of his heart and, finally, the restatement of his goals. Ordinarily there was no drama attached; Brodhi told Ferize what he had done during the interval since she had last Heard him, explained how it might affect his goal, and declared how he felt and what he wanted. His goal had never changed. He told Ferize with great regularity, within the confines of a Hearing or simple conversation, what he felt, what he wanted, and what he had done. His Hearings were routine and painless.

But it had been months since Rhuan availed himself of the ritual, ignoring the needs of his own journey even as he put off Darmuth's needs. Rhuan was alone on his journey no more than Brodhi. But Rhuan hated the entire concept of the Hearing. Backwards, Brodhi thought: he himself was a very private individual, but had no difficulty in participating in a Hearing, in communicating his thoughts and opinions. Rhuan, who was far more open when among the humans, wanted nothing to do with the ritual.

Perspiration was drying on Rhuan's skin. That the pain had ceased, Brodhi knew, for there was no more tension in Rhuan's face. Just emptiness, the enervation of completion. The next step was Brodhi's.

But he put it off. He stared at his kinsman, his kin-in-kind, and wondered what made them so different. Their sires were brothers and shared likenesses physical and emotional. But he and Rhuan had been different for as long as he could remember. They had never seen the worth in one another's thoughts or desires as long as they had lived. So little time separated them in human terms, and even less in the terms of their people. But they might as well be strangers born on opposite ends of forever.

"Fool." It was little more than a whisper.

Rhuan did not hear, did not respond. He sat a matter of feet away, drained. Yet Brodhi was full. It took time to assimilate what he had been told, to wall it off in his mind, into the self-containment of a courier. Carrying the words

of humans, Hecari or Sancorran, meant nothing to Brodhi.
But now he was to carry the words of his kin-in-kind.

Carrying poison.

It took effort to speak, to bring Rhuan fully out of his
post-Hearing reverie. "I have Heard you," he said quietly,
"and the vows hold. What I tell Ferize will be free of opinion, of emotion. I will say what you have said, in the way
that you have said it." He waited until Rhuan opened his
eyes. "But now I may say what is in *my* mind." Brodhi replaced all objects he had removed from the beaded bag,
carefully rerolled the section of hide and tied it off with a
silken cord. That too went into the bag. A glance at
Rhuan's expression showed brows arched in faint curiosity as he came back into awareness. "Now," Brodhi said, "I
speak for myself. I have wanted to say this for a very long
time. Now, I do it." Again he waited, making certain he
had all of Rhuan's attention. He tucked the beaded bag
under one arm and said, with exquisite clarity, "You are a
monster."

AFTER SAYING A VARIETY of prayers and petitions in her mind that she would be kept safe from
whatever was behind the eyes, Audrun, still gripping the
extinguished lantern, began very slowly to back away. With
buskinned feet she felt for exposed roots, placing her feet
carefully. A fall would be disastrous, laying her wide open
to attack as well as risking the welfare of the unborn baby.

She would not call for Davyn. She would not turn and
run. Four children slept in the wagon, and all of her instincts screamed out that she must first protect them. If she
awakened the entire family, she could very well get them
all injured or killed.

She stayed close to the tree, hoping it would at least
shield her right side. But as she negotiated the tangle of
roots and emerged onto level grassland once more, that
protection ended. She was now surrounded by open air, by
nothingness but the night.

Audrun did not turn. She refused to expose her back to the eyes. Still she carried the lantern away from her side, her fingers clamped upon the handle. A few more backward steps put her close to the wagon; she spun then, dropping the lantern, and fell onto her knees beside one of the big wheels. A scramble under the floorboards put her close to Davyn; she burrowed a hand through blankets to find and shake his shoulder.

"Davyn!" She kept her voice low. "Davyn!" When he did not waken, Audrun leaned close to his ear, putting command into the strident whisper. *"Davyn, wake up!"* And as he responded, coming fully awake, she said before he could ask, "There's something out there."

He rolled to his belly, stripping away blankets. He too kept his voice low. "Where?"

"In the trees."

"Can you see it now?"

Audrun crawled out from under the wagon even as he did. "No. But it was back in the trees."

Davyn rose. In the Maiden's moonlight, Audrun saw the brief sheen of naked knife blade. "Guide me."

She hesitated. "Should we go back there?"

He looked down at her. "Well, either we go see if whatever it is has departed, or we spend the rest of the night huddling under the wagon, too frightened to sleep."

His point was well taken. Audrun sighed and moved beside him, remaining on his left so as not to impede his knife-arm. "This way."

"Lantern?"

Quickly Audrun found and relighted it, hoping this time it would remain alight. Davyn nodded and stepped out.

She was no happier going toward the place where she had seen the eyes than when she backed away. But Davyn had always been a man who went *to* potential trouble, who resolved things rather than ignoring the problems and hoping they would go away.

Audrun stopped him at the big oak. Both of them kept their voices low. "I was here." She searched the darkness. "The lantern went out; it looks different, now." She opened the small door to provide more illumination and raised the lantern. She heard the quiet breath expelled abruptly from Davyn's mouth. "Are you *laughing?*"

"Audrun, you saw the oxen." He gestured with the knife. "See?"

The flame guttered slightly as she turned the lantern so the open door faced the direction Davyn indicated. She saw the shadowed bulk of two fawn-colored bodies and the glint of huge bovine eyes as they looked toward the light.

But she was certain. "It wasn't the oxen."

"Audrun—"

"It *wasn't the oxen.* I know oxen, Davyn! And besides, the lantern went out; how am I to see the reflection of the oxen's eyes in the darkness without a lantern? Under the trees, there isn't enough moon for light." She pointed to her left, away from the oxen. "It was there, Davyn. Over there." Before he could respond, she added, "The oxen are hobbled. I would have heard them had they moved from there to here. They're not quiet beasts." It struck her as ludicrous that they would be arguing in whispers over draft animals in the middle of the night, but she stood firm. "What I saw came from *there.*"

"And is it there now?"

She clenched her teeth, hearing the note in his tone that divulged his continuing doubt. "No."

Davyn said nothing for long moments, as if sorting through responses that wouldn't hurt her feelings. "Well, it's gone now. I guess we can go back to bed. Tomorrow we should reach the turnoff."

Audrun didn't budge. "I did see something, Davyn. Something that was indisputably not oxen."

"All right. I believe you. Let's go back."

But he didn't believe her, she knew. He still thought she had seen the oxen. And either they could continue to argue out here in the darkness or they could return to the wagon and attempt to salvage the remainder of their sleep.

"Here." Audrun thrust the lantern toward him. "Hold this." As he received the lantern, she began to gather up blanket and skirt folds.

"What are you doing?"

"I came out here to relieve myself," she said sharply, "and I'm going to finish the task. The least you can do is stand guard, in case the oxen with glowing eyes decide to come trample me."

Davyn's laughter this time wasn't so suppressed.

Chapter 39

RHUAN CAME BACK to himself, aware of Brodhi speaking. The first few words meant nothing because of passing disorientation, but as Brodhi assured him the vow would hold, that he would give Ferize the Hearing with no opinions expressed, he felt a sense of relief. Brodhi was one who highly valued the rituals of their people; if he swore a vow, he maintained it. And now the Hearing was completed, and he felt an overwhelming peacefulness in his spirit coupled with the weariness of a long-ignored duty discharged.

He opened his eyes, smiling, just as Brodhi said, "You are a monster."

Smile, relief, and peacefulness fled.

"*What*—" But his kinsman was ducking under branches to vacate the space between trunk and low branches. "Brodhi!" Rhuan thrust a hand against the blankets and pushed himself upright, ripping aside the swaying branches. "Brodhi, wait—" Free of tangled branches at last, he saw his kinsman's back, held very straight, as Brodhi strode away.

A monster?

You are a monster.

Rhuan broke into a ragged run. As he reached Brodhi he put out a hand, clamped down on a forearm and yanked his kinsman partway around. It was the best he could do.

Brodhi shed the grasping hand easily, jerking his arm away, but he did stop and turn to face Rhuan fully. The campfires in the tent settlement were behind him, outlining his shoulders, glinting off braid ornamentation. They were nearly clear of the trees. "Oh, did you not hear me?" Brodhi asked with exquisite scorn.

Rhuan, nearly swaying with exhaustion, kept to his feet by sheer nerves and strength of will. "I heard you."

"And you want to know why I would call you such a thing?" The tone remained delicately contemptuous.

"Brodhi—"

But Brodhi raised a silencing hand. "Let me ask this: How can you claim yourself the get of your sire? He is a lord over lesser lords . . . a *primary,* Rhuan! Yet you dismiss his blood and heritage as if they had no meaning, no weight in the world. Our world, Rhuan! This one is not. It belongs to the humans, given to them thousands of years ago, as the humans count time. This world is not for us. We are of different blood. We are of better blood. We are made to rule—"

Rhuan cut him off. "I don't wish to rule."

"And that's part of it," Brodhi declared, habitual self-control falling away. "You wish to be a servant. A plaything. A gamepiece on the board, instead of a primary working the board."

"Not a servant," Rhuan answered. "Precisely otherwise, in fact. I want freedom, Brodhi—"

"The kind the humans know?" Brodhi turned his head aside and spat. "I am ashamed of you. Shamed *by* you—"

Exhaustion dissipated in the rush of anger. "What I want has less than nothing to do with you, Brodhi! There is no shame when a man makes his own choices."

"A *dioscuri,*" Brodhi stated. "The moment your sire's seed took root, you were a *dioscuri. More* than man."

"Not my choice," Rhuan said evenly. "But I am given a choice now—or will be, when my journey is completed. In the confines of the Hearing, you know what that choice is."

"Monster."

"No, Brodhi—"

But Brodhi, ablaze with righteous fury, overrode him. "You shame your sire, you shame me, you shame *my* sire! You shame every one of our people!"

"I do no such thing! I make a choice, nothing more. Do you think I am the first to do so? To make such a choice?"

"Millennia!" Brodhi used the human term. "Not in millennia has such a choice been made."

"But the point of the journey is to make that choice, Brodhi. To know fully what one wishes. To understand what one is. To select a future." Rhuan barely managed a casual half-shrug. "It shouldn't matter to you what my choice is. Our sires have many children."

"But not *dioscuri*," Brodhi said. "You know that. We were born to be what our sires are, not what the other children are. They are as nothing." He made a dismissive gesture. "Let them remain as they are. Servants. Unblooded. Impure. But we *have* the blood, Rhuan! There is only one choice for *dioscuri*. And you throw it away!"

"While you throw away the value of the choice," Rhuan retorted. "You devalue the journey, the meaning of the word. We are sent on this journey so that we can be certain of our futures, of our self-worth."

"I was certain of my future and my self-worth from the time I was a youngling," Brodhi declared. "I told the primaries that. I told them there was no need."

"And perhaps that's why they set you *on* the journey." Rhuan grinned reflexively, though it held little humor. "They don't want you swearing yourself to them, to *be* one of them, when you know nothing else."

"From the cradle I've known what I am meant to be."

"What you think you're meant to be," Rhuan corrected. "Your arrogance blinds you to anything else."

Brodhi expelled a blurt of incredulous laughter. "Arrogance? I'm *dioscuri*."

"And thus superior to everyone else in the world save the primaries. Save your own sire."

"Yes," Brodhi said.

Rhuan sighed. Weariness threatened his ability to think, to speak clearly. "Take comfort, then, in your conviction.

Know before completion what choice you will make. Be certain that you will one day be a primary yourself."

"I do. I will be."

"And I will complete an honest journey, so that when the day comes to tell the primaries what I wish for my future they will know I make that choice out of experience, out of understanding, not out of self-delusion."

Brodhi shook his head. "You shame me."

"Ah." Rhuan nodded. "Well, be pleased, then, that we will not share status—nor one another's presence—when we have achieved completion. Your path leads one way, mine another."

Brodhi's tone was clipped. "As it does now."

Rhuan watched him spin and walk away. He let him go, making no more attempt to hold him back. Brodhi at his most stubborn was impossible.

Monster.

"No," he said aloud in the wake of Brodhi's departure. "My worth is not measured by you. My decision is not to be questioned by you. There is no shame attached to the choice I will make at the end of the journey. There is no shame."

Rhuan pressed the heels of his hands against his eyes. He could barely think straight.

Well, Brodhi had taken himself and his ritual objects away, but the blankets and oilcloth remained. Rhuan made his way back to the tree and pulled branches aside, ducking down into the womblike area between limbs and trunk.

He knelt down with care upon the blankets, facing the tree trunk. With equal care he set both hands and his brow against the trunk in supplication.

Rhuan closed his eyes. *So weary . . .* "Elderling," he said shakily in the tongue of his people, "bear watch over me this night. Share with me your tranquility."

 A HORRIFIC HOWLING startled Audrun out of the light doze she had eventually achieved following the incident with the eyes. She started to sit bolt upright and very nearly smacked her head against the floorboards of the wagon before recalling there wasn't enough headroom. Davyn too was awake, attempting to untangle himself from blankets.

The howl climbed in pitch until it was very nearly a screech, similar to the almost humanlike shriek of a hare caught by a predator, but markedly louder, stronger, and of greater duration. Yet as she and Davyn both crawled out from under the wagon, the noise stopped as if cut off. Now Audrun could hear Megritte inside the wagon crying in fear, Ellica's unsuccessful attempts to quiet her, and Torvic's immature voice asking over and over again what the noise was.

"What is it?" Audrun whispered tensely to Davyn.

"Some kind of animal. Not human."

Audrun's outstretched hand on the sideboards guided her to the rear of the wagon, where she peeled aside folds of oilcloth and climbed up into the high, huge conveyance, yanking skirts out of her way. "Meggie, it's all right. I'm here. Gillan, go ahead and light the lantern. Meggie—I'm right here." The floorboards were a nest of thin pallets and blankets. She found her youngest daughter curled into a ball in her bedding. Audrun knelt and folded back the shielding blankets, then pulled Megritte up so she could wrap arms around her. "It's all right, Meggie. We're here. *Shhhhhh.*"

Gillan struck sparks with flint and steel and lighted the lantern hanging from the Mother Rib. All the faces were visible now, showing fear and apprehension.

Davyn stood outside at the back of the wagon, holding oilcloth aside. "It's just an animal," he said reassuringly. "And it's not even that close—"

He was interrupted as the howling began again, once more ranging up into an ear-piercing shriek. Ellica clapped her hands over her ears as Gillan winced. Torvic, silenced, was wide-eyed and staring. Megritte, predictably, held onto her mother more tightly than ever, adding a thin wail to the cacophony. Fortunately most of her contribution was muffled against Audrun's shoulder.

Ellica lifted her voice over the unearthly shriek. "It's going to deafen me!"

The noise broke off as abruptly as before. Audrun somehow found a smile and offered it to Torvic. "It sounds rather like you used to, when you didn't get your way. Last week, I think it was, wasn't it?"

He blinked at her, most of his mind on the noise, but then natural defensiveness reasserted itself. "It does not!"

She glanced at Davyn, still standing at the back of the wagon. She opened her mouth to say something more when the night was broken a third time by the wailing howl. Davyn grimaced, then climbed up, wagon planks creaking. Pitching his voice to carry over the noise, he said, "Well, if this continues we're none of us going to get any more sleep. So, shall we tell stories?" He settled down next to Audrun, setting his spine against one of the traveling trunks. "Meggie?"

She lifted a tear-stained face, voice still choked. "I don't want to!"

As the shriek died out again, Audrun sighed and stroked Megritte's sleep-tangled pale hair, exchanging a rueful glance with her husband. But she couldn't blame Megritte; if she didn't have to be brave for her children, she might prefer curling into a ball with the blankets pulled over her head as well.

"Meggie?" Davyn reached out to touch his daughter's head. "All will be well," he told her in his deep, soothing voice. "It's just noise. It doesn't concern us."

Gillan, who looked no more pleased than his youngest sister, said forcefully, "I've never heard anything like *that!*"

Audrun could feel Davyn's shrug against her. "Well, we haven't seen every animal in the world," he said reasonably. "Different kinds live in different areas."

The intentional lightness in his tone did not fool Audrun. He was attempting to put them all at ease, but she knew he was concerned about the very thing that had leaped to the forefront of *her* mind.

Each revolution of the wagon wheels, each step forward, brought them closer to Alisanos.

Or brought Alisanos closer to them.

AS HE NEARED the fringe of the tents, Brodhi had to stop. His anger at Rhuan had not cooled, and he dared not permit any humans to see him. His vision had hazed so that he saw the world in reddish hues, and his flesh, including his scalp, stung and tingled unpleasantly. He needed his self-control back in place before he returned to the couriers' tent.

It crossed his mind that ale might help, but that would require him to walk into Mikal's tent where others drank. Unwise, in his present state. Best he just go to the couriers' tent and try to get some sleep.

He closed his eyes and attempted to will away the anger, but it remained very near the surface of his emotions. He almost never lost his temper or self-control, but Rhuan had managed to kindle both. And every time Brodhi listened to the exchange in his mind, the anger heated again. At this rate he'd never be able to return to the tent.

Brodhi swore inventively in the human tongue, switched to his own, then at last ran out of invective. To replace it, he began to tell over the Names of the Thousand Gods. If nothing else restored his sense of self and cooled his anger, that should.

By the time he reached the twenty-first Name, he felt better. At thirty-two the worst of the anger was banished. By thirty-six he felt much more himself, so he set off for the tent. He continued the Naming as he followed the familiar pathway through the remaining tents, and as he reached the courier tent he ended the ritual on the forty-second Name. The anger was buried, though not the contempt.

As Brodhi pulled back the loosened door flap, he found Bethid standing in the center with her back to the entrance. Startled, she spun around. Eyes widened as she identified him. "I thought you were dead!"

She had lighted the lantern. He could see her expression clearly, the residue of horror. "No."

Bethid gestured. "All this blood . . ."

He looked where she indicated. Yes, there was blood splattered across the oilcloth sidewalls. "Not mine. Rhuan's."

"Is *he* dead?"

Brodhi found himself regretting his answer. "No."

"What in the name of the Mother happened here?"

He was disinclined to enter into a lengthy conversation, but Bethid was due some explanation. It was her pallet that had taken the brunt of Rhuan's blood, even if he had replaced it with his own. "Two men thought they would kill Rhuan for his bones."

Bethid blinked at him, brass ear-hoops glinting in the lamplight. "Did you kill *them?*"

"Of course."

"Both?"

"Of course." He set his beaded bag at the foot of the space where his pallet had been, recalling with annoyance that his blankets remained at the tree. Well, he had his mantle, even if it was summerweight.

"'Of course,'" Bethid echoed blankly. Then she shook herself out of startlement. "Is he all right now? Did he revive?"

"He revived." Brodhi took his mantle down from its hook. The Hearing had tired him and he wished to sleep, pallet or no. He draped the cloak over a shoulder and sat down on packed dirt, preparing to pull off his boots. He could use his beaded bag and a doubled arm as a pillow.

After a moment Bethid sat down on what was now her pallet, beginning the effort to take her boots off as well and arrange them at the foot of her pallet. "We told Rhuan about our plans," she said in a subdued tone. "He was less than enthusiastic."

Boots shed, Brodhi settled his bag at the place where his head would rest. "What do you expect of a man who refuses to accept responsibility?"

"He laughed at us."

The corner of his mouth hooked down in irony. "That comes as no surprise."

"But I'd have thought Rhuan would approve." From the sound of it, Bethid was having trouble with her boots. "*He's* always taking risks."

Brodhi lay down, arranging the mantle over his body. "He is a feckless fool with no understanding of consequences, and no acknowledgment of undertakings requiring commitment. And it will get him killed one day."

Bethid laughed lightly, yanking a boot from her stockinged foot. "Only to revive later. A handy gift."

Brodhi thrust a doubled arm beneath the bag his head rested on. "Rhuan will die, Bethid. And he will remain dead. I don't doubt it will be sooner rather than later." He turned over, facing the sidewall next to his nonexistent pallet.

There was an odd note in her tone. "Did you two have some kind of argument?"

Brodhi frowned into the dimness. "Why would you ask that?"

"Because you sound for all the world like you're wishing he was dead. That he stayed dead."

Brodhi's frown faded. "He is a . . . *difficult* . . . individual."

Bethid's tone was tentative. "He won't betray us, will he? Our plans?"

He resettled the hip against the packed floor of the tent. "Put no trust in him."

Brodhi could tell by the sound that Bethid was stripping out of her tunic. "But he's your kinsman."

He grimaced. "You may be certain I wish it were otherwise."

"But—"

He cut her off. "Go to sleep, Bethid. Or at the very least stop talking."

After a moment of heavy silence, she said, "You can be very rude, Brodhi."

He did not deign to answer.

Chapter 40

*A*S HER LAST client departed, Ilona set elbows on the low lacquered table and rested her face in her hands. It was well past time for the evening meal, and she was very hungry. But she was so weary she wasn't certain she had enough strength left for eating. She had lost count of how many karavaners visited to find out if waiting in the settlement until the next karavan season was the best plan for them. No one faulted Jorda's decision to her face—they were aware she was in his employ—but she knew how to read what wasn't said. It showed in their eyes, in their faces, in their hands.

She had a dull headache, likely from hunger, and her eyes were gritty with exhaustion. She was relieved that all of her readings had promised folk that the decision to stay was a good one, but it was tiring nonetheless to look into so many palms, to experience, no matter how distant, the worries and concerns of others. But circumstances were not normal. The karavaners were full of memories of what the Hecari raiding party had done at the karavan, and fresher memories of their shock and fear as they saw what the decimation had wrought at the settlement.

Ilona smiled faintly. She was in an identical situation to the karavaners; she too would wait here at the settlement for the new karavan season, petitioning all the gods for assurances that no Hecari would return.

"Ilona?"

The gravelly voice was Jorda's. She looked up, lifting her face from her hands.

Meager lamplight glowed in the karavan-master's luxurious red beard. "You could use a drink," he said. "Come with me to Mikal's."

Jorda meant well, she knew. But Ilona wasn't certain spirits was what she needed. Perhaps a cup of hot tea, followed by bed . . . "Yes," she heard herself say. "I would like that."

Jorda didn't smile much, and what she had of him this time was fleeting at best. Ilona backed out of her position behind the table, then stood. Every joint from her waist down cracked. She smiled as Jorda's ruddy brows jerked skywards. Within a matter of moments she had blown out all of the glowing lanterns hung on their iron crooks, settled her skirts, and wrapped around her shoulders the soft green shawl.

"Custom has been good?" Jorda asked as she fell into step beside him.

"Better than good. Fortunately, all that I read suggested staying here was the best course."

"And if it were not?" He glanced at her sidelong. "If the readings suggested it was better to go on?"

Ilona slid her right arm through his left. "But none did. Don't borrow trouble, Jorda. You're doing the best you can. There was no other choice. Could you have borne it, wondering every day upon the road who was killed here, and who survived, as we traveled farther and farther away?"

"No," he replied in a subdued tone.

"Of course not. Naturally some folk are unhappy with your decision, but I saw no ill tidings in their hands."

He was silent for a long moment as they walked the pathways of the settlement. Finally he said, "You do know he's leaving."

Ilona suppressed an aggravated sigh; how many more would ask her that? "Yes, of course."

"Will you be all right?"

She tightened her grasp on his arm. "We are no more than friends, Jorda. I will miss him as friends do, but that is all."

"Oh. I thought—"

She overrode him. "I know what you thought. Apparently everyone thinks it. But there has been no man for me since Tansit." It brought but a twinge now; Rhuan had found work with Jorda only because Tansit, Jorda's guide and Ilona's lover, had been killed by Hecari. "I will do well enough. And he swears he'll be back in time for the new season, so you won't have lost a guide."

They threaded their way through the denuded settlement, Jorda taking pains to find the smoothest footing for her. "Have you read his hand, to know if he will be?"

"Rhuan's hand?" She could not keep the note of surprise from her tone. "Oh, no. Rhuan won't allow me to read his hand."

Jorda's startlement was palpable. "Won't allow?" he echoed.

"No. He never has."

"Then he's seen Branca or Melior."

Ilona smiled crookedly. She knew Rhuan disdained the other two diviners as weak in the art, but she said nothing of it to Jorda. "Rhuan believes he makes his own future without such aids."

The karavan-master made a sound akin to a growl. "It is a term of employment, that all new hires see one of my diviners. I assumed you had read his hand before recommending him to me."

She kept her voice steady. "Tansit was dead, Jorda, his butchered body still in your wagon awaiting rites and burial. You needed a new guide to take over his duties as soon as possible."

"So you knew nothing about him." Jorda shook his head, scowling at the ground. "I don't like to scold, Ilona, but it's imperative I be able to trust my guides. I believed you had read his hand."

She didn't duck the mild rebuke, nodding her understanding. "Yes, I recommended him without reading his hand; he is Shoia, and I felt it appropriate, in view of Tansit's death, that the karavan have a guide who could revive if he was killed."

Jorda mulled that over as they walked, finally growling acquiescence as they reached Mikal's tent. "He's been trustworthy enough, I'll agree—but in the future, do as I ask and read the hands of all potential hires. Men do tell lies ... I depend on you to find the truths in their hands."

Ilona promised him she would do so, but did not divulge her fear that hiring a new guide might occur sooner rather than later, if Rhuan did not return from escorting the farmerfolk to Atalanda along the road so close to Alisanos.

Jorda stepped aside and motioned for Ilona to precede him into the tent. The door flap was tied back. Lantern light, voices, and the tang of pungent ale spilled out into the darkness.

Ilona's stomach growled noisily. She clapped a hand to it as warmth suffused her cheeks. But it elicited a brief chuckle from Jorda, and if it played any role in easing his concerns, the embarrassment was worth it.

"Come." Jorda, grinning, guided her inside. "We'll find a table and I'll ask Mikal for food as well as ale."

She would be glad of food. But she was not glad to have misled Jorda.

Once, she had looked into Rhuan's hand. She had believed him dead, not yet knowing he was Shoia and would revive; she wanted only to discover what manner of death ritual he might prefer. But what she had seen, that fleeting glimpse of Rhuan's soul, had left her with no knowledge of anything substantive. Only an awareness of *maelstrom,* the violent, drowning whirlpool of his spirit.

BRODHI AWOKE ABRUPTLY to a hot hand on his cheek. It was a woman, a black-haired woman leaning over him, her lips but an inch away from his own. As they brushed his mouth, he felt the familiar pull of arousal, the helplessness to resist. But he and she had parted in anger; a portion of him remained angry and did not want to submit to her kisses.

And yet he did. He always did. And did so now.

When he finally broke the kiss, she sat back from him, feet folded neatly beneath her. Brodhi heard the steady breathing of Timmon, Alorn, and Bethid, all lost to sleep, ignorant of Ferize's presence. She smiled at him, tossing back the curtain of tumbled, waist-length hair. Black-haired tonight—or perhaps for only a moment—and black-eyed, with fine, fair, translucent skin begging him to touch it.

Her smile broadened as he reached to trace the outline of her face. Even as his palm cupped her chin she twisted her head, sinking teeth into his hand.

No. Sinking *fangs*.

Blood ran. He tried to jerk his hand away but Ferize gripped it in her own. She turned his bleeding palm up, studied it, then kissed it. He felt the fangs transform themselves into human teeth. He felt her lips burn. The blood stopped flowing.

A lesson, she said within his mind, *to teach you to treat me better.*

He answered in kind. *I treat you as you deserve.*

Ah, but you don't. You treat me as you believe *I deserve. But since you have only such knowledge of me as I choose to give you, you are ignorant of what I deserve.* Black eyes sparked. *But I forgive you. This time.*

Ferize could drive him mad with her beauty in any form, her heat, her mercurical and unreliable emotions. Just now she sat demurely at his side, hands and feet folded, lips curving in a slight smile. She knew very well how he reacted to her; it pleased her to use him as her instrument.

She reached out and took one of his sidelock braids into her hands. Still smiling, she began to untie the thong that held the hair and the ornaments in place.

Brodhi closed a hand over hers. *Not now. Not here.*

Ferize displayed a complement of very fine teeth. Human teeth, though the look in her eye was nothing approaching human. *Yes, now. Yes, here.*

Ferize—

I want it, she said simply, *and I shall have it.*

It was its own ritual, this unbraiding of the hair, undertaken only by the one who wore the braids and the one he or she took as a sworn lover. Ferize was his wife, in the parlance of the humans. She had the right. Humans wouldn't understand, but to his people this marked them bound, that she had the right and exercised it.

Under her breath, Ferize began to sing very softly as her slender, long-nailed fingers deftly unwove the sidelock and began to strip it of ornamentation.

Brodi felt the welling up of an unaccustomed desperation. He clamped his hands around her wrists and stopped the unbraiding. Saying nothing, still imprisoning her wrists, he rose to his feet. Ferize was clearly startled, but then she began to smile.

He took her outside the courier tent, took her into the deeper darkness of the treeline but paces from the tent. He heard the occasional impact of hair ornaments striking the earth, falling from the loosening sidelock. But he did not pause for them.

At the verge of trees, he stopped. Her wrists remained trapped in his hands. Ferize was laughing at him.

"No," he said. "*I* say when. *I* say where. And just now, there is something else more urgent."

Her voice was husky. "I think not."

"Rhuan's Hearing."

She stopped laughing. "That's Darmuth's business. What does it matter to us?"

He released her wrists. "It matters because it was I who Heard him earlier this evening. Not Darmuth."

Ferize frowned. "Why?"

"Darmuth told me Rhuan has been avoiding it. Earlier this evening he was killed, so I took advantage of it." Brodhi shrugged. "He had no strength to refuse me."

She looked thoughtful, studying his face. "You feel polluted, yes?"

He bared his teeth in a violent grimace. "I feel *poisoned.*"

"Well, then," she took him by the hand. "We'll see that you are purged, and then I will finish what I began." She captured the loosening sidelock, tugged it lightly, then led him deeper into the darkness, where humans would not see.

BY DAWN, AUDRUN was exhausted. She had not slept again, and her eyes felt full of sand. The children, trusting to their parents, managed to fall asleep; Megritte, who had refused to return to her little nest of bedding, now slept slumped against Audrun's left shoulder. It pinned her in place, for she had no wish to disturb her youngest, but her body was unhappy. Now and again she moved a limb in search of a more comfortable position, taking care to do so quietly and slowly, but she ached with the need to stand, to stretch.

To sleep.

Even Davyn, spine set against the trunk, had drifted off. He didn't look particularly comfortable with his head drooping sideways toward his left shoulder, but his breathing was deep and even. She had no doubts he would complain of a stiff neck and old bones come true morning, but he would be more rested than she.

Outside, as the lightening of the sky presaged dawn, nightsingers fell silent. In their place came early birdsong from the tree canopies. Despite the drama of the night, morning, though barely broken, was perfectly normal. And, as Davyn had promised the children, all seemed much improved now that the moon was replaced by the sun.

If she were not to sleep, then it was time to begin morning chores. Audrun eased Megritte off her shoulder and carefully tipped her down toward the bedding on the floorboards, settling slack limbs even as Meggie roused just enough to briefly complain before falling asleep again. Audrun pulled a blanket up to her daughter's chin, then began the careful process of untangling herself from hummocks of bedclothes and stepping over Davyn without waking him as she made her way to the rear of the wagon. She pulled back the loose oilcloth, noted that it was cool enough for a shawl, and liberated it from the tangle of bedding. She climbed down, glad to move at last, stretched prodigously, then made her way to the remains of the cookfire, skirt hems heavily dampened by dew. Kneeling, she scraped ash away with a stick, uncovered live embers, and began to add bits of kindling. As she blew on the remains, they came sluggishly to life. Within a matter of moments she teased flame from the coals, and the fire renewed itself with the aid of chips and twigs.

Audrun sat back. The rim of the sun began its climb above the black blade of the horizon. It seemed impossible now that the night before had engendered such fear and apprehension. She pulled the string of charms from beneath her tunic, clasped it in both hands, and gave thanks to the Mother of Moons, in her guise as the Maiden, for seeing her through the long night, for blessing the day again with light. That accomplished, Audrun reached for the kettle. The routine of morning tea would blunt any remaining concern about such things as glowing eyes and ear-piercing, howling shrieks.

Then she remembered that the karavan guide would be upon the road, intent on catching them up, and that knowledge lit within her an overwhelming sense of relief. By the time Davyn climbed down from the wagon, cracking his back with one hand as he scratched stubble with the other, Audrun was able to offer him a bright smile and a cup of hot tea, her weariness forgotten. A new day birthed new hope. Atalanda no longer seemed so distant.

Chapter 41

*T*HE TREE RHUAN slept under was a haven for a multiplicity of birds, and it was the noise of competing morning songs that woke him. He lay flat on his back, right arm stretched out into cool, damp soil; the left, he discovered, was bound by something. He opened his eyes and rolled his head toward the enormous tree trunk and discovered that at some point during the night, the elderling had sent out a questing root. The thin, immature rootling had wrapped itself around his left arm in a spiral from armpit to wrist.

He smiled, sleepily patted the woody root, then remembered that he was near the human encampment, not elsewhere. Certainly not anywhere that a tree should be able to bind his arm. And that served to startle him into complete wakefulness. It shouldn't be possible here, not in the human world. Other places, yes. But he lay quietly, not moving to free himself. To do so would be rude, when the tree was merely being supportive in response to his petition the night before.

Rhuan again touched the root wrapped around his arm. "Elderling, I thank you." He had specifically asked for tranquility, and the tree had made certain he slept without cares, without unsettling dreams. "But I must go now. Thank you for your kindness."

For a long moment there was no response. Then the root gently squeezed his arm and began to unwrap itself. When his arm was entirely free, Rhuan sat up. The rootling nosed through the rich soil beneath the tree canopy, then plunged, snakelike, into the earth, leaving only a ruffle of soil to mark its passing.

Rhuan suppressed the concern the tree's action engendered; there would be time to consider it later. He assumed a kneeling position as he had the night before, and once more pressed palms and brow against the rough wood. He spoke his appreciation again in his own tongue, not that of the humans, then hastily set about shaking out and rolling up his blankets and oilcloth groundcover.

He had recovered from the killing the evening before, and the Hearing. No more delays existed. It was time now for him to pack onto his horse the things he needed for a solo journey, and to set out at a good gait. He had lost more time than intended, but he traveled light and his horse was capable of sustaining a goodly pace, while the oxen hauling the farmsteaders' big wagon could not travel quickly.

He hoped he could catch up to them soon. The tree's action, though sanguine, nonetheless was yet another signal that Alisanos was preparing to go active. No magic existed in the human world save it was wielded by those in whose blood and bone the power resided. For an elderling to exhibit sentience in the human world meant Alisanos was beginning to bleed through. There was very little time left before the deepwood uprooted itself and moved elsewhere.

Rhuan tied the bedding and ducked through the low branches, trying not to harm any leaves with his exit. He spooked a few birds from their perches with his haste, striding quickly toward the karavan encampment. He had made his farewells to those who mattered; now he need merely prepare his horse, mount, and go.

"Dioscuri."

It was a whipcrack of tone. Rhuan, startled, stopped dead in his tracks. From the trees came a woman—ah, but no, she was more than that, far more. And he knew exactly what and who she was the moment he looked at her, though she wore no form he had ever seen.

He inclined his head briefly. "Ferize."

She wore white, pure white, and a long girdle of gold and onyx. Her hair too was white, hanging heavily to her waist. He had never seen her when she was not beautiful, but it was an alien beauty, an unsettling beauty. In green eyes her pupils were slitted, like a cat's—but she was all demon.

On bare feet she came to him, leaving no whisper of movement in the lush grass, gaining no weight of heavy dew on the hem of her skirts. Now she was close enough that he could see the faint mottling at her throat, the barest trace of a multihued scale pattern. When she smiled, it had nothing of kindness in it. Only anger, and fangs.

"How dare you?" Ice and fire, in voice and eyes. "How *dare* you?"

"Ferize—"

"We have tasks, Darmuth and I, journeys to complete even as you and Brodhi do. How dare you keep us from them? How dare you risk our futures?" She had never, in all of her guises, been particularly tall, but at this moment, afire with anger, her slender frame contained enough power to dwarf him. "Be not so selfish that you harm Darmuth, *dioscuri*. We are kin-in-kind, he and I, as much if not more than you and Brodhi. I will not have him endangered." Slender hands reached up, caught sidelocks, and began to wind them around her palms. He was so shocked by that presumption he could not speak. Ferize tugged, and was not gentle in the doing of it. "*You* have tasks," she continued. "You have responsibilities. Are you such a child that it does not matter to you what may become of Darmuth?" She tugged again, hard, gripping sidelocks in unkind hands. "I will not have you risk his fate."

He finally managed to speak. "And what would you do, should it come to that?"

She took another bight in his braids. "You ask that of a demon? You ask that of *me*?"

His smile was no kinder than hers. "I ask."

The scale pattern crawled from throat up to chin, bled

into cheekbones. The flicker in slit-pupiled eyes was oddly yellow. Her hands, wrapped in braided, ornamented hair, rested at his temples. But she moved them slightly, enough that long thumbnails rested on the delicate skin of his eyelids just beneath the arch of bone. With her strength, it would take very little effort to punch through flesh and into the eyes beneath.

Ferize smiled. "Ask again, *dioscuri*."

Rhuan kept a firm rein on his own emotions. "All of this anger and threat because I postponed a Hearing?" He closed his hands around her wrists. His strength could not match hers, but he was fairly certain she would not do as her thumbs implied. "Let be, Ferize. You have made your point."

She stepped close against him, so close her breasts touched his chest, then jerked his head down to hers. Her tongue, in its demon form, flicked out and stung his bottom lip, leaving fire in its wake.

As she released his braids Rhuan jerked away, cursing, and pressed the back of one hand against his mouth.

"I cannot kill a *dioscuri*, or I risk being sentenced to the worst of all the hells," she said, "but be certain I can make his life most inventively miserable."

He swore at her, lip afire.

The scale pattern faded from her face. Ferize smiled. With a final flick of her forked tongue, she turned in a swirl of pristine skirts and glided away from him, white hair swaying.

Rhuan spat once, twice, then swore again. Nothing but time would mitigate the poison she had injected. The dose was not enough to kill him, but for at least half a day he would indeed be miserable.

He grabbed the bedroll from the ground and strode jerkily away, attempting to think up the most effective reprisal, and knowing with glum acknowledgment such a response would merely mire him in more trouble. Ferize had the right of it: His neglect of the required Hearings could indeed jeopardize Darmuth's fate. It was that admission coupled with guilt that lent Ferize's sting more heat.

"Point taken," he muttered as he walked. "Point very much taken."

But he felt no better for saying it, for confessing his shortcoming. He felt young, and small, and punished.

BY LATE MORNING, Davyn declared they had given the snares enough time to possibly provide fresh meat, and he and Gillan set out to see if they had had any luck. Part of him knew it was a retreat; Audrun clearly was short on sleep, which made her short of temper. She had suggested with some acerbity that they simply pack up and go not long after the sun crept into the sky, setting snares elsewhere along the road, but Davyn overruled her. He wanted fresh meat, and felt this grove of trees and lush vegetation might well provide it. He had learned through hard experience that if one put off a task in favor of another day, the task often was all the more difficult to accomplish later on. And so with quiet insistence he took up the snares, nodded at his eldest son to accompany him, and went out as the dawn brightened to day to set the snares amid the trees. They could afford no more than a few hours, but it would give time to the hares as well as to Audrun, who might relax as the lack of haste permitted her time to rest.

He and Gillan had found active burrows in the grove and hoped for luck. But the first snare was empty. Gillan took it up and tucked it into his belt.

The second and third snares were also empty. The fourth contained a partially eaten hare. Someone had beaten them to their meal. Davyn sighed as Gillan disposed of the remains and cleaned off the snare. They went on to the fifth and final snare with no real optimism. It was with a twinge of surprise and relief that Davyn saw the snare had done its job.

"I'll get it." Gillan went on ahead, pushing through the undergrowth. But as he bent, he made an abrupt, startled sound and recoiled. "This is no hare, Da!"

The note in his son's voice spurred Davyn into a jog. When he reached Gillan he saw that indeed, it was no hare. It was nothing he'd ever seen before. The thing was approximately the size of a hare, but all resemblence ended there. In place of fur it had scales, dark spiky scales, and each front paw boasted three long curving claws.

"I think it's dead," Gillan said.

The thing did appear to be dead. It lay on its side, one hind leg twisted as if it had fought the snare. Already the belly had begun to bloat.

"Da," Gillan began, "you said different kinds of animals live in different places . . . what *is* that?"

Frowning, Davyn found a tree branch and used it to flip the thing over. This view was no more informative, but every bit as worrying. The scaled hide was like no other flesh Davyn had ever heard of, let alone seen. Its muzzle was drawn back in a rictus, displaying a mouth full of serrated teeth. Filmed-over black eyes bulged in their sockets.

Davyn tossed the branch aside. "We'll head back. I don't want either of us touching that thing."

"What about the snare?"

"Leave it," Davyn said briefly. And then, out of no thought he had considered, "Don't tell your mother."

"What do you think it is?"

Davyn shook his head, turning to follow the trail through the tall grasses that their passage had beaten down. "I've never even heard of anything like that."

Gillan followed closely behind him. "Why don't you want me telling Mam about it?"

"Because she came out here last night to relieve herself, and doesn't need to know she shared the grove with something like that thing." The corner of his mouth jerked wryly. "I don't think I'd want to know it, either."

He wondered briefly if after all Audrun *had* seen eyes during her sojourn the night before; if this thing could in fact be what she'd seen in the darkness. He wondered also if this was what had emitted the horrible howling that had awakened them all. Lastly, he wondered how it had died. Snares trapped, they did not kill. Clearly some predator had found the hare in the fourth snare and dined well until interrupted. But there had been no sign that a predator had killed the thing in the last snare. Davyn had heard that some animals would chew a leg off to get free of a trap, but that was a spring-trap, not a snare. There was no sign of struggle, no sign of violence. Just a dead—thing.

Davyn suppressed a shudder. "Let's go," he said. "Time to get back on the road."

Chapter 42

*T*ORVIC NATURALLY WANTED to accompany his father and brother to check the snares, but Audrun was adamant that he stay near the wagon. Lack of sleep and the experience the night before with glowing eyes and shrieking animals left her feeling dull and out of sorts, even though morning tea improved her mood for a bit, and she had no patience for overactive children. She assigned cleanup chores to Torvic and Megritte to keep them busy, and kept one eye on them as they sloppily scoured the tin plates in a big pan of water heated in the fire. Already the fronts of their tunics were sopping. With strict orders to herself to overlook it so she need not think about one more thing, Audrun climbed up into the wagon to help Ellica finish folding up the bedding and tucking it away.

Ellica, seated on the floorboards, glanced up as she entered. Once again Audrun was struck by the realization that her eldest daughter was growing into a beauty. Audrun smiled inwardly. Gillan's voice had broken, and Ellica's courses had begun. Neither of them were children anymore. They would settle in Atalanda as a family of seven, once the babe was born, but Ellica might very well marry before the year was out, and Gillan could be courting a girl for himself by this time next season.

She knelt down beside her daughter and helped her

pack away the bedding. Audrun remembered very clearly her own transition to womanhood. At Ellica's age she was being courted by Davyn, the boy from the next farmstead over. She hadn't understood then the smiles her parents exchanged, the knowing glances shared, but she certainly grasped both now. Audrun opened her mouth to tell her daughter how proud she was of her, but the impulse was cut off as shrieks emanated from outside. Meggie . . . and now Torvic was shouting for his mother.

Audrun scrambled out of the wagon with Ellica close behind. She found her two youngest standing rigidly beside the fire, staring at something in the grass. "Stay still!" she shouted. It was pure instinct: Hold still until you could see the danger clearly. "Meggie, Torvic—stay still." Very slowly and carefully Audrun climbed out of the wagon, motioning for Ellica to remain inside. "I'm here," she told the youngest quietly. "Remain still."

Megritte was crying, but she did as told. The tension of fear in Torvic's body had lessened; he struck her now as a pointing dog watching the prey for his master. Audrun reached up slowly and took from the side of the wagon the long-handled spade she used in the garden. Davyn had made it for her when she was pregnant with Gillan so she wouldn't have to kneel as her belly grew.

She kept her tone calm and conversational. "Torvic, can you hold very, very still? I'm going to ask Meggie to move away . . . can you stay where you are as she does that?" He nodded, still intent on whatever was in the grass. "Meggie, I'm coming to get you. Will you wait for me?"

With her mother now present, Megritte's tears had stopped. Audrun took careful, quiet steps, raising the spade in both hands. Over the years she had killed any number of vermin and snakes with the spade, and she didn't fear to do so now. But Torvic and Megritte had grown up in her garden and in the fields with their father; even snakes didn't engender this kind of reaction. It had to be something more, something unknown.

Audrun reached her son and daughter. On the other side of the fire ring she saw something dark but tall; dense grass shielded most of it from her view. Carefully she put a hand on Megritte's shoulder. "Meggie, I want you to back away slowly. Don't run. Just back away very slowly. Torvic, stay where you are. I'm right here. Meggie—*slowly.*" She pressed her daughter's shoulder and carefully guided her backward. "Count to ten, Meggie. One count for each step. When you reach ten, stop. All right?"

Megritte's blond hair was, as usual, in disarray. Her braids were constantly falling out of confinement. Even as she guided Meggie back, Audrun couldn't help but be momentarily amused by the knowledge that the mind thought about any number of inconsequential things even in the midst of unknown danger.

"Ten steps. How many have you taken?"

"Four." Meggie still sounded frightened, but she no longer cried and clearly believed she was safe now that her mother was present.

"Six more." Megritte was now past her, and Audrun released her hold. "Torvic, I want you—"

But something moved, and Meggie shrieked, and Torvic ran even as Audrun brought up the spade as a shield.

It was brown. Brown and blunt-nosed. In shock, Audrun watched it stand up on its hind legs, balanced on a long, whippy tail. Down its spine ran a line of flat, serrated spikes. The belly it now displayed was yellow-green, blending into a scarlet throat.

Audrun's mind registered details even as she stared at the thing. It was, her mind decided, a snake with legs. It simply could not grasp anything else. Part snake, part lizard.

It stood up before her, blood-red eyes staring, and hissed at her.

"Get in the wagon," she said. "All of you."

The thing before her began weaving from side to side in an odd, unearthly dance. She saw a pouch at its exposed throat pulse, skin folds moving, and then it abruptly expanded the pouch and screamed at her.

It was reflex, no more. The scream startled her badly; she blocked the thing's leap with the flat of the spade without conscious effort. The snake-lizard fell back, still hissing. A sideways scuttle through the grass put it clear of the fire ring. Audrun turned as it moved, keeping it in front of her. She was aware of Megritte's shriek but could not spare a glance for her children; she prayed to the Mother that they had obeyed her and climbed up into the wagon.

The thing rose up again onto its hind legs, balancing on its tail. Audrun focused sharply, recognizing its preparation prior to striking. The dance began, the throat-pouch filled, the scream was emitted even as it leaped.

Once again she blocked the strike with the spade. But this time, as the thing fell back, Audrun followed up with two more blows. She had done damage, she knew, and the tail whipped frantically. Three more blows with the flat of the spade stilled it, and then she raised the spade into the air and brought the edge down on it, cutting into and through the scaly neck. It took three tries to completely sever the head from the body.

She was aware then that Davyn was there, and Gillan. They were speaking at once, and Torvic and Megritte piled out of the wagon. "Don't touch it!" she cried as the youngest ran up. She caught at Torvic's arm even as Davyn grabbed Megritte. "We don't know what it is . . . don't touch it."

Davyn took the spade from her. "Here," he said, "we'll bury it. That way no one can mistake where it is as we prepare to go on. Gillan, why don't you fetch the oxen and hitch them?" He planted the spade in soil and grass and brought up both. "Torvic, Meggie, why don't you help him? It's time you learned how. Ellica, can you see to things inside the wagon?" And quietly, as the children disappeared, he asked, "Are you all right?"

Audrun couldn't help herself: She was shaking. "Yes. Yes, I'm fine." And she was, though her trembling continued. It exasperated her, that she could not control it.

Several more spadefuls built a mound over the thing. Davyn patted the soil down, then draped an arm around Audrun's shoulders, turning her toward the wagon. "We're ready to leave anyway. And no meat, I'm afraid; the snares were empty."

Mostly meaningless talk. But by the time Davyn had returned the spade to its rope loops along the side of the wagon, her trembling had abated. She looked at her children waiting at the back of the wagon. Audrun forced a smile. "I think for a while we'll all of us ride. We can walk later." And she shooed all of them up into the wagon as Davyn nodded approval.

IT WAS AS Rhuan packed the spotted horse—little enough to take: bedroll, beaded bag, a packet of flatbread and a few hanks of meat dried and seasoned for preservation along the road—that he felt the shiver down his spine. Hair stood up on his arms. The horse, as clearly sensing something, sidled against the rope reins, tautening them. But Rhuan stood perfectly still, making no effort to curb the horse.

It came up from the earth beneath the soles of his boots. No sound accompanied it, merely a rippling vibration, an almost tentative probe of what lay above the surface. Like the rootling sent out from the elderling tree, something quested. There was no disturbance in the soil, no movement in the tall grass, nothing at all that he could see. But he *knew* it.

He knew it.

For a moment Rhuan stood very still. Every portion of his body clamored alarm. Like the horse, his first instinct was to run, to run until he dropped, until he was well beyond the reach of the thing that quested after him.

Then, as the horse's ears speared forward and his nostrils expanded in a concussive snort, Rhuan knelt upon the earth. One hand remained clamped on the reins, the other dug down through the grass and into the rich, black soil below. He brought up a handful, shut it within his hand, and let it speak to him.

Swearing, Rhuan surged to his feet and threw the clods

of dirt aside. In one smoothly interconnected series of motions he turned, took a long stride to the uneasy horse, grabbed a double handful of mane and reins, and swung up into the saddle. He gave the horse neither time nor rein to protest, merely wheeled it toward the tent settlement. He longed to gallop, but there were always children and adults clogging the footpaths between tents, and now, still not far removed from the Hecari culling, survivors continued to sort through the remains of charred belongings. The best he could do was a long-trot, but it was better at least than a walk. With so many of the tents destroyed by flames he could thread his way through swiftly enough, and reined in at Mikal's big tent. Dismounting, he quickly looped the reins around one of the anchoring ropes and yanked aside the drooping door flap.

He saw faces he knew, and faces he didn't, all startled by the abruptness of his entrance. Mikal was present, of course; but also Jorda, Bethid, and Ilona. Mikal had joined them at their table.

Rhuan strode over to the table hosting those he called friends and knelt on one knee, speaking quietly but urgently. "I don't have time for questions . . . go through the tents and tell everyone to leave. Now. They need to get as far from here as they can. *Now.*" He drew breath and continued. "It's Alisanos . . ." He was conscious of the stunned and incredulous expressions, and how improbable his words sounded. "I don't know exactly where it will appear again, but I'm sensing the settlement may be in danger. Jorda and Ilona, gather up your karavaners and send them east. Mikal and Bethid, you can sort out those of the settlement. Gather everyone and go east. I can't tell you how I know, but trust me. Tell everyone to get out of here."

"But—the Hecari." Mikal's brows met as he frowned. "These folk have lost loved ones and shelter, all of their possessions—and now you expect them to leave everything else?"

"I have no time," Rhuan said bluntly. "Tell as many as you can. Go east. *East.*" He looked straight at Ilona. "Trust me." He looked at Jorda. "Trust me."

They asked, of course. Humans always asked. All he could do, as he rose and strode swiftly out of the tent to his horse, was to hope Ilona and Jorda, who knew him best, would understand his urgency, his plea for trust, and act.

He unlooped the reins from the tent rope and mounted. Part of him wanted to remain, to help with convincing the inhabitants to depart, but there was no time.

Rhuan set the spotted horse upon the track leading away from the karavan, away from the tent settlement, and asked of it a gallop. The horse was more than willing to provide the gait; he wanted free of the unsettling questing as much as Rhuan did. He wanted away from Alisanos.

Except that Rhuan now rode *toward* the deepwood, not away. Not to escape. Not to safety.

To a family upon a road leading directly into danger.

Chapter 43

"HE CAN'T BE serious," Mikal protested as the Shoia exited the tent. "Rhuan is known for his jests."

Ilona rose from her stool, scraping wooden legs across hard-packed earth. "He doesn't jest about people's lives. If he says there's danger, there is." She nodded in Jorda's direction to include him in her reference. "We both know to trust Rhuan in something like this. There's no time to waste."

Bethid rose, too, but her thin face was worried. "But Mikal has a point. I don't think anyone will want to leave when they've lost so much already."

Ilona hung onto patience with supreme effort. "Will mothers risk their children? Will men risk their wives?" She drew in a steadying breath. "I dreamed this, Bethid. What's coming. A killing wind, rain . . . everyone needs to *go*."

Jorda was standing as well. "I have a karavan to protect. I indeed trust Rhuan in this kind of warning, and I intend to tell my people so. And if Ilona has seen this in her dreams . . ." He rubbed at his scalp. "This settlement is yours, Mikal, if it can be said to belong to anyone; tell your people to go. Tell them to *run*." He closed a hand on Ilona's elbow and escorted her swiftly out of the big tent. "Now it's time for you to run, 'Lona. Go east, he said."

She shook her head and gently disengaged her elbow. "I have a task as much as you do: I will urge the women to gather their children while you talk to the men. With both of us insisting they go—and I am a diviner, after all—they may heed the message better." She was outpacing Jorda with her long-legged stride. The karavan-master was a large, bulky man and she could always outrun him. "Forgive me," she said, then hiked up her skirts as she broke into a run toward the grove that was temporary housing for the karavan wagons.

But even running, she was aware of a terrible fear chilling her bones. Go east, he had said; run. But how far, and for how long, had not been part of his warning. *Too slow,* she fretted as she ran toward the grove. *Mother of Moons, let me be in time . . . O Mother, let them run far enough, let them run fast enough!*

In the midst of a bright, cloudless sky, lightning split the air.

BY MID-AFTERNOON THEY found the turnoff and set the oxen upon it. Audrun and the children ventured out of the wagon and onto the track, which gradually transformed from an obvious roadway into overgrown, rock-strewn ruts nearly invisible to the eye. Davyn guided the oxen as carefully as he could, but the jarring of the wagon was constant. Wheels creaked a protest; floorboards loosened into chatters and squeaks. Audrun, walking next to the wagon, winced every time the wheels struck a particularly large rock. Davyn attempted to miss them, but oxen were not as responsive as horses or mules, and the overgrowth hid many of the rocks until it was too late to avoid them.

The children walked immediately ahead of the wagon. Initially Audrun carried the long-handled spade in case any other strange creatures appeared, but it grew awkward after a while and she returned it to its loops on the sideboard. Pots hanging from the floorboards clanked as the wagon rolled onward, and the bunghole in the big water barrel began to leak. Audrun did her best to tighten the spigot, but it simply worked its way loose within another revolution of the wheels. She tied a rag around the spigot in hopes of stemming the leak, but once the rag was soaked it began to drip. There was no help for it. They left a trail of splashes along the narrow ruts.

Just as she gave up on the leak, the wagon lurched over a pile of rocks, then slammed down. Audrun heard an ominous creaking, the noisy clatter of pots crashing together, and then a popping crack. The left rear wheel canted at an odd angle for one haphazard revolution, and then the axle gave way, dropping the corner of the wagon to the ground even as she shouted to Davyn. The collapse was so abrupt that the lid to the water barrel came loose and a wave of water slopped over the edge, drenching the front of Audrun's skirts. Stunned, all she could do was stand there in the middle of the track as water dripped from sodden fabric.

"Gillan!" Davyn called. "Come unhitch the oxen. Ellica, watch the others." He went to the rear of the wagon to inspect the damage. When he saw Audrun's state he missed a step, then worked hard to contain a smile. "Are you drowned?"

"Nearly!" She twisted wet skirts to force the worst of the water out.

Davyn squatted to inspect the wheel. When he rose, his expression had become grim. "It's split lengthwise." He ran both hands through fair hair in a gesture of frustration. "Well, there's no help for it. We'll need to unload the heavy things, then prop up the wagon so I can mount a new axle." Like all karavaners, they carried extra wheels and a spare axle lashed to the sideboards. But Davyn did not immediately return his attention to repairs. He rubbed his arms and frowned, glancing into the sky. "The light has changed. Do you see it? And all the hair on my skin is standing on end. I think we've got a storm on the way."

Even as he spoke, the ground beneath their feet shuddered.

RHUAN, RIDING AT a gallop the third day out of the settlement, felt the tremors in the earth, felt the wind come up. It began as a breeze, moved into a series of flirtatious gusts, then settled in for an unceasing hard howling, the kind of wind that stripped tree limbs, knocked down and shredded tents, hurled birds to their deaths, drove humans to despair. He knew it as a killing wind, the kind that, unabated, did much more than cursory damage. It came from his left side, slamming his mount broadside with enough force that the horse stumbled and nearly went down. Rhuan yanked the horse's head up, let him regain his balance, and went on once more at a gallop.

His scalp prickled. The hair on his arms, though shielded by a long-sleeved tunic, stood up. A cold frisson ran down his spine, stronger now than when he had dug into the earth near the tent settlement. His body was answering the wind, responding to its song. There was power in that wind, a crackling, sizzling power that touched him, knew him, tempted him. Though squinted against the flying dust and debris, his eyes grew red as a membrane slid over them. The world colored around him, the horizon bathed in a ruddy halo of fractured light.

But Rhuan had no time for himself. A family he had sworn to protect was on the same road, accosted by the same terrible wind, but lacked any kind of power to withstand the storm. Rhuan was stubborn enough to put it out of his mind, to focus only on going forward, on reaching the wagon, on doing what was necessary to save the children and parents.

The sky now took on a faint greenish light. Tree branches and debris spun through the air. Rhuan could feel the effort it took his horse to continue onward without faltering as the ground quivered beneath him; his gait was uneven, lacking the smooth consistency of motion that made him Rhuan's favorite of all the karavan remuda. He leaned down and patted the spotted neck, promising the horse he would be rewarded in good time.

Peering through flying dirt and debris, he came upon the family in the midst of disarray. The wagon canted in the unmistakable angle of a broken wheel or axle. Even in the screaming wind, the father and his eldest son labored to prop up the wagon so repairs could be made; the wife, head and face screened by a shawl, stood by. The eldest daughter and the two youngest children, wrapped in blankets, huddled on the other side of the wagon, using its bulk to shield them from the worst of the wind. Chests and heavier belongings had been set out upon the road to lighten the wagon, putting Rhuan in mind of a sad, untended burial ground.

Until he reined his horse to an abrupt sliding stop next to the wagon, no one knew he was there. He saw surprise on the father's face, and the flaring of profound relief in the mother's eyes.

Rhuan wasted no time. He pitched his voice to carry over the wailing of the wind. "You can't remain here! You have to leave!" He gestured. "Give me the two youngest. Put the smallest girl here, in front of me, and the boy behind. The rest of you will have to run as best you can. As far and as fast as you can."

"Run?" the husband shouted, incredulous. "You want us to leave the wagon, the only shelter we have?"

Beneath their feet, the ground shuddered. Grasslands undulated. The wife went to her knees even as her husband grabbed the wagon to steady himself. "This is only the beginning!" Rhuan shouted as his horse snorted and danced. "Put the youngest ones up on my horse. *Now.* Waste no time." There was startlement and doubt in the father's eyes, even as another tremor rattled pots and pans. "It's Alisanos," Rhuan explained in curt impatience. He smelled the unmistakable sharpness of lightning in the air. "I have land-sense. Do as I say. Or do you wish to be taken by the deepwood?"

The wife, skirts flapping in the wind as she climbed to

her feet, said something to her husband and then made her way to the other side of the wagon where her children waited. She lost her grip on her shawl, which was ripped out of her hands and carried away; now her hair was whipped free of its braid. Rhuan rode close, steadying the horse as best he could in the midst of the storm. He was un-surprised when the wagon's battered oilcloth tore, then shredded. Within moments it was ripped from the curving ribs of the wagon, spun away through the air. The end of one flapping portion slapped his horse across the face.

Cursing, Rhuan barely managed to remain in the saddle as the horse spooked in a scrambling, panicked retreat. He regained tenuous control and urged the horse beside the wagon once again, though it took effort to convince the horse to do so in the wake of torn oilcloth. "Give me the little girl!"

By now the father and eldest son had joined the rest of the family. With the oilcloth gone from the wagon, there was less to shield them from the storm's fury. "Do it!" the wife shouted. "Davyn, we must! The rest of us can manage, but Torvic and Megritte can't!"

Rhuan saw grim acquiescence in the father's face. Then he scooped up the youngest girl and lifted her.

She was frightened and crying, wanting nothing to do with Rhuan. He caught her around her slender, fragile rib cage and tucked her between himself and the pommel of the saddle, a shield against the wind. "Now the boy!" He reached down again as the boy was guided to him by the father. He closed his hand on the boy's wrist and swung him up and back so that he landed on the horse's rump. "Hold onto me! Don't let go!" He bent over the girl in front of him so he could speak without shouting. "We're going to gallop. This horse loves to gallop. And I'll wrap one arm around you. Are you ready?" He heard no reply, but felt the rubbing of the girl's head against his chest as if she nodded. "Good."

Crimson lightning streaked across the sky, leaving a too-brilliant white in its place. Thunder greater than anything heard before nearly deafened them. Leaves, debris, and tree limbs wheeled through the air. He blamed no one for their fear, for their hesitation.

"The rest of you, run!" Rhuan told them, pointing. "That way, as hard and as fast as you can." He saw fear in the eyes of the older children, but there was nothing he could do for anyone else. Even the two smallest would slow his horse. *"Run."* He wrapped his left arm around the youngest girl. He turned his head so the boy behind him could hear. "Hold on. Grab my tunic and don't let go." Hands worked themselves into his tunic. "We're going to race the wind," Rhuan told his two human burdens. As red lighting split the air yet again, he looked down at the parents, at the older children. "Run. For your lives, *run.*" And with a final admonition to "hold on" to the girl in front of him and the boy behind, he urged his mount once again into a gallop.

THE FEAR IN the faces of her two youngest as they were taken up onto the guide's horse nearly broke Audrun's heart. But she had no time to permit worry to govern every action; incredibly, the wind intensified. In the wake of deafening thunder she turned to Gillan and Ellica, urging them with shouts even though she knew they couldn't hear her above the wind and in the aftermath of the thunder. She made sweeping motions with her arms, directing them to go after the guide. Gillan grabbed his sister's hand and ran.

Davyn moved close to Audrun as she attempted to control her hair so it wouldn't blind her, gesturing for her to follow the oldest children. She knew he intended to gather needful things from the wagon. She shook her head, grabbed a handful of his tunic and yanked, trying to guide him toward the direction the guide had indicated.

She saw refusal in his eyes. She didn't blame him for it; all they had left in the world was in the wagon. "Davyn!" She nearly tore her throat with the force of her shout, but couldn't hear herself in the wind. "Davyn, *we all go!*" She caught her breath, spitting out grit. *"We can come back when the storm is over!"*

He hesitated a moment longer, then nodded resignation. Audrun grabbed up a handful of her skirts, let him take her hand in his, and ran after the children she could no longer see.

Chapter 44

*I*LONA WENT TO JANQERIL, the horse-master. She told him her idea for aiding the karavaners; at his nod of understanding, she hurried to the nearest wagon. The four women she recognized as something quite different from the farmstead wives; they were the Sisters of the Road.

"Listen to me," Ilona said. "There is no time—I must tell as many as possible. We are to go east. All of us. Immediately."

The women had laid and lighted a cookfire, and a tea kettle whistled. They wore clothing of a finer cut than the other women, and their tunic belts were of fine leather studded with silver. Four pairs of startled eyes fixed upon her. "Go east?" one of the Sisters repeated. "Why should we go east?"

"Alisanos," Ilona answered succinctly. "The karavan guide, Rhuan—the Shoia, with all the braids—has land-sense. He swears Alisanos is on the verge of moving, and that it's coming this way. If we go east, we may escape it." She raised a silencing hand as all four women began to speak at once. "Waste no time. Believe in me, as I believe in Rhuan. Take your horses, but leave the wagon; there is no time to hitch up." She nodded at the two draft horses picketed near the wagon. "They are large enough to carry two each. Just mount and go. *Now.*"

Ilona left them still asking questions and went on to the next wagon, repeating the warning. She knew that somewhere in the grove Jorda was doing the same. But the wagons had been scattered any which way; in the wake of cancellation, drivers were no longer required to follow directions as to how they should arrange themselves.

"If you lack for horses," she told a family of five, "go to Janqeril, the horse-master. He will give you a mount. But hurry!"

She heard the echo of Jorda's voice in the grove, bellowing orders. Mount and ride east, mount and ride east. She said it. He said it. But the people were slow, too slow. Urgency filled Ilona's chest near to bursting.

Mount and ride east, she said over and over again. *Go east, go east, go east.*

As she reached another wagon, a sudden rising wind hissed amid the trees. Ilona felt a prickling in her scalp. The palms of both hands began to itch.

She was aware of eyes fixed upon her. Had she spoken? Had she told this family what she had told the others?

"Go east," she said. The wind keened through branches. "Waste no time!"

Her palms now burned. Some unknown instinct told her to kneel, to spread her hands against the earth. She did so, and felt the thrumming power rising up through leaf mold and soil.

Was this Rhuan's land-sense? Or Alisanos awakening? Did Branca and Melior feel the same thing?

Ilona pulled her hands from the earth and displayed them to the family. The still-rising wind blew her hair out of its confining rods so that the wild, dark curls fell down her back. "I say—*I* say, as a hand-reader—that we must all go. Now!"

Then Jorda was with her, helping her to her feet. He settled a large, calloused hand on each of her shoulders. "You as well," he said. "Go, Ilona."

Leaves were torn from limbs, wheeling away on the wind. Ilona felt the tug against her scalp as her hair was whipped into tangles. "I can't, Jorda. There are children in the settlement."

"That task is for Mikal to do, and Bethid. We've done what we can for our people." He squinted as dirt and debris were thrown into his bearded face. "It's time for you to go."

Her skirts flapped in the wind. Ilona caught handfuls of blowing hair and tamed it by winding one hand in it. "You as well." It took effort, now, to be heard above the wind. "You also, Jorda!"

"There is one more wagon," he told her. "Then I'll come."

She thought he might not, that his pride would keep him among the wagons he had sworn to lead overland in safety. But she knew how to convince him to leave. "Then I will come with you, and we'll go east together."

A flicker in green eyes told her he knew what she intended. His mouth jerked briefly in annoyance, and then he nodded. "One wagon. And then we'll go."

BETHID FELT HAMPERED by a lack of information. How many people still mourning loved ones killed by the Hecari would heed her words? Yes, she could tell them Rhuan had specifically ordered the settlement residents to leave immediately, but Rhuan's reputation among those who had stayed in the tent-village long enough to hear the stories was of a mysterious Shoia more than willing to kill if crossed. She and Mikal, hastening along the footpaths, told everyone they saw to leave, to go east, and to carry word to others, but she saw the doubt in their eyes. They had lost too much; leaving what little they still claimed was an impossibility.

"If Rhuan's right," she told Mikal as they walked hurriedly, "the people who stay will die."

The ale-keep adjusted the patch covering one eye. "They may not die. They may end up in Alisanos, and lost to the world. That's worse than death."

"Do you believe him?"

"I believe Jorda and Ilona. If they trust Rhuan to be telling the truth, that's enough for me."

"Do you have any doubt at all?"

"More doubt than I care to think about," he replied gruffly. "But if Rhuan is correct and we do nothing, could we live with ourselves?"

It took no time to consider. "No," Bethid declared.

"And so we warn everyone and tell them to go east, knowing many of them, perhaps even most, will not do so."

A gust of wind swirled between the two nearest tents. It gathered ash from the ground and blew it into their faces. Bethid stopped walking as grit lodged in one eye. It watered prodigiously. Even as she struggled to remove the grit, Mikal was coughing.

The wind continued to rise. Bethid attempted to turn her back on it as she worked on her eye, but it seemed to come from every direction. She swore as the grit scored a line of pain across her eye.

"Here." Mikal's voice was hoarse from coughing. "Let me." He stepped in front of her, blocking the wind with his big body, and pulled down her lower lid. "My fingers are too large," he said, "but I can tell you when you've got it—there, you're on it."

Bethid worked carefully, her eye still tearing. At last she felt the blessed relief of an eye freed of impediment. It still burned and watered, but the eye no longer hosted grit. She kept it closed and viewed the world through one.

"Now you are like me," Mikal said lightly, "one-eyed."

Bethid wiped her face with the sleeve of her tunic. "The wind is still rising."

"Well, perhaps that will convince them when we may not." Mikal's arm at her back gently urged her onward.

The thought was sudden and startling. "This would be Kendic's task." She remembered other times when the head of the Watch had carried warning to the settlement of one thing or another.

"So it would be, if Kendic were alive," Mikal agreed. "But the Hecari have seen to it that now we do his work."

That was enough for Bethid. Newly inspired, she went on through the remains of the settlement, crying Rhuan's warning and instructions in a voice ringing with conviction. And as the wind increased, as it lifted ash and debris from the burned tents and hurled it through the air, she found the people somewhat more attentive.

"Alisanos!" she called. "Alisanos is coming!"

BRODHI STOOD WITH Ferize at the jagged border between trees and settlement. He could not help it: he smiled.

"Yes," Ferize said. "Oh yes, it's nearly time." She looked into his eyes. "This is what you want, isn't it?"

His smile became a grin. "I do not fear Alisanos."

Ferize laughed. "Nor do I, of a certainty! But all will be changed. Even you."

"Yes, but my journey will be ended." He turned to her abruptly, clamping hands upon her upper arms. "Ended, Ferize! No more petty humans in their petty world—"

She didn't let him finish. "*Will* it be ended? I wonder." Her pupils flickered between round and elongated. "Do you believe the primaries will accept you if the journey ends too soon?"

He hissed displeasure. "Through no fault of my own."

Ferize's laughter rang out. "Do you think that will matter? To them? Only a fool might believe so."

Brodhi felt an unaccustomed emotion: apprehension. "They wouldn't ask it of me again. They wouldn't ask me to *begin* again!"

Ferize turned her face to the sky as the wind came up. "They may. They may not."

"But—"

She cut him off by placing a hand across his mouth. "No more. Not now. Don't you feel it?" Her grin widened as fangs replaced human teeth. "It's coming."

Ferize had banished his hope that his journey might be over. Now he feared what might become of him. Would the primaries require him to begin again?

He growled frustration. But it died away in surprise. "Where are those people going? Ferize, look . . ."

She did so. Then shrugged. "As *you* might say: humans. Who can explain them?"

He continued watching. It began as a straggling line of people exiting the settlement. Men, women, children. Some carried belongings while others were empty-handed. Then came the horses—big draft horses, not smaller everyday mounts, carrying two humans at a time and occasionally three, if the burden were children. Karavaners.

"They're leaving the settlement." Frowning, he knelt and dug a hand through turf and into the dark soil. He felt it, felt the power leaping upward, wrapping tendrils around his fingers.

And he knew.

"Rhuan." Brodi pulled his hand free and rose. "Rhuan has done this. He's warned the settlement."

A hint of scale pattern mottled Ferize's pale throat as she smiled. "Your kin-in-kind is not prepared to end *his* journey too soon." Rising wind lifted waist-length black hair. "Clever *dioscuri*. That will please the primaries."

AUDRUN'S WORLD WAS full of raging wind and flying debris. Flapping skirts hampered her as she tried to run with Davyn, the fabric tangling around her legs. Eventually she gave up holding her hair with one free hand and snatched at her skirts, yanking them up around her thighs. But there was so much fabric that still she was impeded. Without Davyn's strong hand pulling her onward, she feared she would be unable to continue simply because the strength of the wind was so overpowering.

Her children were somewhere ahead of her. The youngest were with the guide, and though she worried about them she knew they stood a better chance with Rhuan. Ellica and Gillan had disappeared into the flying dirt and debris. The sun, so bright at dawn, was now blotted out. The world was swallowed by a light brown curtain.

She clung to Davyn's hand. He did his best to guide her, but Audrun knew he could see no better than she. All they could do was continue on, taking care not to turn in one direction or the other lest they go off course and lose all the children.

Davyn was coughing. Though her hair would be a tangled mess by the end of the storm, it still offered her face shielding of a sort. Davyn's was naked and taking punishment.

Mother of Moons, she whispered inside her head, *guard my children. Keep them safe.* She put her hand over her belly. *Even this small one, if you please.*

The ground fell out from beneath her feet. Audrun lost Davyn's hand as she was thrown down hard. She lay half-stunned, aware of trembling in the earth in concert with that of her body. "Davyn!" She yanked hair away from her mouth. "Davyn!"

She heard nothing but the keening of the wind.

"Davyn!" Audrun rose to her hands and knees. *Mother, let me find him . . .* "Davyn!"

Beneath her, the ground rumbled. She braced herself against it, braced herself against the wind. From behind she was struck by a large tree branch, its leaves stripped away. Even as Audrun tried to catch it, the branch spun into her hair, was caught, then blew free and wheeled onward with a hank of torn-out hair tangled in its branches.

The day somehow grew blacker. Audrun remained on hands and knees. "Davyn!" He did not answer; or, if he did, she was unable to hear him over the roaring of the wind. *"Davyn!"*

But he must be ahead of her. If she searched to right or left, she might easily become disoriented. She dared not lose her sense of direction. If she were to recover her children, she must remain on the path taken by the guide.

She felt for hoofprints in the turf. But the ground was a place she no longer knew. Beneath her hands the thick grasses lay down, obscuring foot- and hoofprints. *Mother, O Mother, where is he? Where are my children?* Her scalp felt lacerated. Grit and debris had been driven into it as the wind blew it into tangled flags.

Audrun stopped crawling as desperation overwhelmed

her. She attempted to catch her breath, but there was so little air. Everything was a mass of flying dirt, grass, leaves, and the Mother knew what else. When her eyes teared, the wind whipped them away. There was grit in her eyes, in her mouth, even in her nose. She could see nothing. No husband, children, or guide. She could hear only the wind.

Panting, Audrun tried to tear a strip of skirt fabric to use as a face shield, as she had done at the end of the karavan. But when a sizzling streak of crimson lightning lanced groundward from the storm-darkened skies, she forgot all about tearing fabric. The lightning was close, so close it was accompanied by a crack of thunder so loud she felt it deep inside her head and chest. Audrun clapped her hands over her ears and flattened against the earth.

Her world now was an odd reddish hue. All around her thin bolts of lightning struck but paces apart, over and over, like rain. She smelled the power, smelled the smoke of fired grass. Even as the thunder rolled across the land, the land itself rumbled and shuddered.

She could run. She could crawl. She could remain where she was. Audrun knew it didn't matter what her choice might be. In such a storm as this, there was no escape. She would survive, or not.

She tried a last time. *"Davyn!"*

But it was lost in thunder, in the rumbling of the land, in the roaring of the wind.

Chapter 45

*T*HE STORM SWEPT down upon the tent settlement. What wasn't anchored in the earth blew over immediately. Small items, light items, were carried off like wingless birds, tumbled over and over, and eventually dashed to the ground. Ash from the fires coupled with soil and grit shrouded the settlement in a haze of gray and ocher. Those who had refused the suggestions to leave, those who had disbelieved the news of Alisanos, now ran to catch up to those who had wisely fled.

The grove hosting the remains of Jorda's karavan was stripped of leaves and smaller branches. There was little grass in the shade of broad tree canopies, so the wind lifted the soil and hurled it into Ilona's face. She heard Jorda cursing and spitting.

Then his rumbling voice rose above the storm. "One horse. It will have to carry us both."

Ilona saw the lone horse then, one of Jorda's own draft horses. Janqeril had put two halters on the animal in case one wouldn't hold, with accompanying lead ropes. The big bay was clearly frightened by the storm, ears pinned back, nostrils flaring, eyes rolling in their sockets so that the whites showed. The horse had been tied to Jorda's wagon, and the karavan-master lost time trying to soothe the animal as he untied the lead ropes.

Ilona kept out of his way. She spent the time rebraiding her hair, stuffing it down the collar of her tunic. But the wind merely snatched it loose again, even as it yanked at her skirts.

Jorda used a wagon wheel as a mounting block. Bareback, with only halters and lead ropes fashioned into reins, he had reduced control of the draft horse. Clamping his legs around the horse's deep barrel, he leaned down and reached out a thick arm. "Jump," he shouted. "I'll swing you on behind me."

It was an awkward, ungainly mounting, but with Jorda's help Ilona was able to scramble onto the broad bay rump. She put her arms around the karavan-master, locking hands into his belt. "Go!"

RHUAN FELT HIS MOUNT'S distress as they passed from grasslands into stands of trees and out again into the wide, wild land. The girl and boy were small, but the spotted horse nonetheless carried three in the midst of lightning and thunder and shuddering earth beneath his hooves. He galloped on, as Rhuan urged, but his strides flagged and his gait grew rough.

The outer fringe of a forest rose out of the dusty, reddish gloom, highlighted by streaky lightning. At the border between trees and grasslands, Rhuan eased the horse into a ragged trot, a stumbling walk, and at last reined him to a halt. The spotted head drooped. Sweat ran down his shoulders and flanks.

Rhuan twisted in the saddle so the boy might hear him. "I'm going to set you down," he said. "Take my hand and slide off." But when the boy's hands remained locked into his tunic, Rhuan was forced to peel the fingers loose. "We'll find cover in the forest—get down, boy. Take my hand. Then I'll put your sister down."

The boy, disentangled, clung tightly to Rhuan's hand. Rhuan swung him over the horse's right hip and leaned down to dangle the boy as close to the ground as he could.

He let go and turned his attention to the younger sister, her spine pressed against his ribs.

"All right," he said evenly, keeping concern from his voice, "your turn, little one. I'll set you down with your brother." He encircled her chest with one arm and shifted her over. He steadied her with his free hand and carefully let her down, shifting his hold to grasp her arms as she slid groundwards. She dropped the final foot to the ground and sat down hard. Her face was dampened by tears, filmed with dust and grit. "Follow me." Rhuan dismounted. "Hold hands, and follow behind the horse. We need to find you cover." It would make more sense were they to walk before him where he could see them, but he felt they'd be safer if he put himself and the horse ahead of them as a shield going into an unknown forest.

Lightning streaked over their heads, shearing through trees. Even as the girl screamed in terror, thunder drowned her out.

"Follow me," Rhuan repeated, and led the horse across the ragged line between rolling grasslands and thick, over-grown forest.

BETHID SHOUTED, "GO! Run! Run east!"
She heard Mikal's bellow, the thin wailing of crying children. It was next to impossible to see her own way in the storm, let alone mark where other people were. But even as she jogged along a footpath, dodging debris, more and more people gave up trying to save their tents, shouting for news, for a promise of safety. They had ignored all warnings and now realized their folly.

"Go east!" Bethid yelled at them indiscriminately. "Run!"

The dust in the air took on an eerie reddish tinge. A moment later crimson lightning streaked across her vision with thunder in its wake. A second, then a third bolt followed the first.

A shiver took her from head to toe. "Close," she murmured. "Too close—"

Lightning sizzled just overhead. Bethid threw herself flat, hands clamped over her ears. Even then her head ached with the magnitude of accompanying thunder. The world around her was red now, dyed crimson by the lightning. Thin, bright streaks of that lightning came down like arrows, striking everywhere at ground level.

"Bethid—" It was Mikal, reaching to pull her up from the footpath. "We can't stay any longer! We've done what we could—it's up to the people now to make their own decisions."

She was willing enough to leave, especially now that she was no longer alone. The ale-keep grabbed her hand with his own and they ran, ran and ran, passing tents in the process of being ripped and shredded, stakes uprooted, poles thrown down. What the Hecari had not burned now was lost to the storm.

East, Rhuan had said. But how far? When could they halt? When would they be safe from Alisanos?

Beside her, Mikal labored. She was markedly smaller than he, and much swifter. It was a simple matter for her to run on and on, but not for him. He was a large man, a sedentary man who was two decades, possibly more, older than she.

They carried no water. No food. Nothing but themselves.

"Keep on," Bethid shouted. "Keep on, Mikal!" But inside her head she said something entirely different. *Mother of Moons, when is it safe to stop?*

With lightning all around them and thunder in their ears, as the earth beneath them trembled, they ran and ran and ran.

AT FIRST DAVYN blessed the rain. It would knock down the worst of the dust and debris and allow him to see again, to find his wife. Audrun had disappeared just as his children had, any cries for help were swallowed by the fury of the wind. He shouted for Audrun time and time again; he searched, on hands and knees, the area immediately surrounding him, but he found nothing. His family was simply gone.

Davyn's sense of direction had always been good. He considered backtracking to find Audrun, but realized that this storm, the pressure in his ears from unceasing thunder, played havoc with his ability. He knew which way the guide had gone with Ellica and Gillan in his wake; it was best now, he felt, to continue on in that direction, and pray Audrun did the same.

When the rain came, he rejoiced.

Until it turned hot.

Hot rain? He had never heard of such a thing. Rain was simply rain, sometimes very cold, sometimes less so. But this rain, these drops striking him, was decidedly hot.

Davyn heaved himself to his feet. The wind had not died; in fact, it blew the rain sideways. Ducking his head did little to keep his face shielded from rain that blew horizontally. He was soaked in a matter of moments . . . and the rain only grew hotter.

Scarlet lightning danced upon the earth as Davyn began to run.

THE WIND BUFFETED Audrun unceasingly. It was almost impossible to walk. So she staggered, tangled hair trapped against her chest by tightly folded arms, head down, shoulders hunched, eyes slitted. Her torn skirts flapped and cracked, tugging her first one way and then another so that her strides were ragged. She considered removing the skirt so there was less for the wind to grab, but her smallclothes were of finer fabric and she feared she would give up a measure of protection, slight though it was. So she walked on, doing her best to hold a straight line in the direction the guide had indicated.

She had given up shouting for Davyn, Gillan, and Ellica. The roar of the wind was too fierce, the thunder too constant. She flinched each time lightning shot over her head; flinched again as thunder boomed behind it.

When the ground shook beneath her, Audrun stumbled and fell, instinctively turning in midair to protect the unborn child. Her shoulder and hip took the brunt of the impact. She lay against the earth on her side, gasping for breath, pulling arms and legs close against her body so the child would be sheltered. Even with eyes closed, even with one hand spread over her eyes, she could see the flashes of crimson lightning.

Despite the stillness of her body, her thoughts ran on. *What if I stayed here? What if I waited out the storm here?* Could she? It had to stop at some point. What if she let it pass on while she lay huddled in the wind-flattened, tattered grass?

If it passed. If it stopped.

Was this Alisanos? Unceasing wind, lightning, and thunder? Shuddering earth?

Something struck her. And again. She believed it debris; she had been battered by all manner of twigs, leaves, branches, even small stones mixed in with grit and dirt.

But this was *wet*.

"Rain!" She levered herself up on one elbow, turning her face to the heavens. Indeed, rain.

Audrun laughed in relief. Rain would wash away the dust in the air. She would be able to see again, to find husband and guide and children.

Raindrops fell faster, harder, smacking against her face and scalp. Audrun sat up, hands outstretched to the heavens as she grinned widely, joyfully. She prayed to the gods she favored, thanking them for the blessing of their rain.

But the wind still raged, and the sharp, stinging impact of large drops blown hard against her body kept Audrun from realizing the truth of the rain for several long moments. When those drops began to burn, she was stunned. Hot rain? *Hot* rain?

And hotter yet.

Hot as fire.

This rain was not a blessing bestowed by gods.

Sheer instinct pushed Audrun to her feet. Rain continued to fall, a hard, hot, slanting rain, burning her skin. She gathered up damp, tattered skirts into fisted hands and ran as hard, as fast, as she could.

Chapter 46

R HUAN LED THE HORSE and thus the children into the shelter of the forest. The wide tree canopies offered some protection against the storm, though even the greater trees had limbs tossed by the wind. There was no path save for the one he broke, and it was a difficult passage even for him.

He came across a tumble of boulders, massive boulders the size of karavan wagons. He tied the reins to a tree branch and turned back to the children. He squatted and kept his voice calm. "What are your names? I do you dishonor, I know, to forget them, but I have." His smile was crooked and felt forced. "I'm Rhuan. And I'm here to help you as best I may."

They told him as a flicker of lightning illuminated their dirty, tear-streaked faces. Thunder crashed overhead.

"I want Mam!" the little girl cried. Very likely she had been saying it for some time, but in the storm no one could hear her. Here, the forest muffled the worst of the wind and thunder.

"They'll come," Rhuan said. "The horse couldn't carry everyone, so I chose the most important folk."

The boy slanted him a disbelieving glance. "*Da's* the most important."

Rhuan elected not to argue it with them, even as a device to distract them. "There is a crevice here where these two boulders meet. See it? It's not large, but I think it will do for a brother and sister." Rising, he untied his bedroll from the back of the saddle. "Here is oilcloth, and a blanket for each of you. Climb up in there and wrap everything around you, even over your heads."

"What about you?" Megritte asked.

Rhuan began to drape a blanket around her shoulders, bundling her up. "I," he said, "am going to ride back a way and look for the rest of your folk . . . can you hold this? Good." He pulled a portion of the blanket over her tangled hair, turned her, and gave her a gentle push toward the crevice. "Go on up there, and leave room for your brother."

Torvic was struggling with his own blanket, but Rhuan didn't want to injure childish dignity by treating him as mostly helpless. He waited until Torvic had climbed up tumbled fragments of shattered stone and sat down next to his sister, then swept the oilcloth around both.

Lightning sliced diagonally into trees some distance away, shredding leaves, exploding trunks. The children flinched. Tears rolled down Megritte's cheeks.

"I'll be back," he told them. "I swear it."

"With Mam and Da?" Megritte asked.

"What about Gillan and Ellica?" Torvic demanded.

"Gillan and Ellica, too," Rhuan declared. "But maybe not all at once." He smiled at them, then untied the horse. "I know you're probably hungry and thirsty, and when the storm dies we can go back to the wagon for water and food. But for now you must remain here, tucked up in your stone cocoon. Will you do this for me?" Both nodded. "Good. I will see you as soon as may be."

It was far more difficult walking away from them than he expected. But there was nothing else he could do. While the storm raged, blotting out visibility, smothering shouts for help within the cracking and crashing of thunder, he believed it unlikely the rest of the family might find one another. He saw better than they in the gloom and was not intimidated by the first tentative awakening of Alisanos. He was the only one who *could* find the family.

Rhuan led the horse back along the way they had come, following broken stems and crushed vegetation. But when he was clear of the forest, walking out of the depths into the thinner verge, he realized he had far less time than he'd expected. The rain had turned hot, much too hot for humans.

Swearing, Rhuan tossed his reins over the horse's head and swung up into the saddle. With a mental apology, he asked the spotted horse for a gallop once again and headed back the way he had come, ignoring lightning, thunder, quivering earth, and burning rain.

AS BETHID AND Mikal ran, debris from the settlement blew past them, tumbling along the ground, carried on the wind. From time to time something struck them; Bethid reflected that she'd be bruised by morning, provided morning ever came. Mikal now was laboring, but she knew by the look in his eye that he was committed to continuing on no matter how difficult. But the wind's strength was greater than his, the wind's speed faster. Bethid finally pulled him to a stop, but let him believe it was she who needed it.

"Wait," she gasped breathlessly; the word, the plea, was snatched out of her mouth so quickly she didn't know if Mikal even heard it.

He tugged at her hand. "Come on!"

Bethid, bent over for breath, looked back toward the settlement. It was invisible in the shroud of ash and dirt—or else it no longer existed.

Could the wind be so strong as to erase an entire tent settlement? Or was it all Alisanos?

Mikal tugged again. "Beth, come on!"

Even as she straightened to continue, she wondered how Timmon and Alorn were. She wondered *where* Timmon and Alorn were. Ahead of them? Behind? Possibly even dead? Her courier's oath required her to help fellow couriers in need; she felt surviving this storm qualified. But all she could offer were prayers that both would be safe.

ILONA, CLINGING TO the security of Jorda's belt as they rode his draft horse through the storm, thought she might be chafed before they completed the ride. Draft horses were never meant to be ridden; they were huge, ungainly horses prized for their strength, their stolid temperaments, not their gaits. She had already discovered that this one favored one side more than the other, and was large enough, powerful enough, that any human upon its back for any length of time would end up sore. She fully expected her spine to be bent like wire by morning.

But she was infinitely grateful to *have* a horse to ride. She and Jorda passed many people straggling unhappily from the settlement, wives clearly commanded by husbands; husbands obviously begged by wives. And there were those who did not straggle, but ran; jogged when they could not run; walked when they could not jog. As an exodus, it was something; as actual escape, Ilona could not say. But she was safer than all of the others, save those who were also on horseback.

She had no idea how far they should ride. For all she knew, that entailed riding through the night. A deeper night; the day, at the moment, looked more like twilight because of flying ash and dust.

They and others who were mounted were glared at by those on foot as they rode by. It was true that the urging by Bethid and Mikal strongly suggested all settlement dwellers leave at once, forgoing horses if they had them, and now, clearly, folk regretted their hasty departures. In fact, Ilona saw a few families stopped along the way, arguing over whether to continue on or turn back. So once again she played the part of Rhuan's proxy.

"Keep going!" she shouted into the wind. "There are no

tents left! Keep going!" She didn't know for certain that no tents survived, but she believed it likely. Too often the wind carried items past them that had clearly come from the settlement.

Jorda turned his head so she might hear him. "How far?"

Ilona raised her voice. "Rhuan just said to go east!"

She sat close enough to his broad back that she could feel his grunt. "Trust him to give us only half the information."

It was true Rhuan had said nothing at all about how far they should go, or when they might stop. But she knew him well enough that she felt it likely they would know when to stop, that something would happen to provide the information.

For now, the wind still raged, debris still blew, the east yet lay before them.

And rain began to fall.

IN THE MIDST of a modest clearing, surrounded by elderling oaks, Ferize danced in the rain. Her skirts flared out as she spun, arms outstretched, black hair flying. She laughed as she danced, as she twisted and spun, as the wind slid through the grove, tossing branches and fluttering leaves. Brodhi, leaning against a wide trunk with arms crossed against his chest, allowed a smile to reshape his mouth, to let his face shed its usual solemnity and relax into appreciation of Ferize's dance. It was not solely for him, he knew; the wind sang of Alisanos, of deeper woods than this, of sulfur pools and sweetwater, of crags and heat and ice, of a land that, as easily as Ferize, shifted its shape from day to day, from moment to moment. Ferize was born of Alisanos; it lived within her body. And that body, now, rejoiced in the process that would set her homeland free.

She danced her joy in Alisanos, laughed aloud as she whirled, gestured for him to join her. But though he heard the same song she did, he was not moved to dance. His joy was not of the deepwood and its imminent move, but of her, only her, dancing for Alisanos in the midst of wind-ruffled elderling oaks and rain.

TWO HUMAN SHAPES, holding hands as they ran, hove out of the gloom as lightning streaked overhead and sheets of rain fell from the skies. Rhuan slowed his horse so he wouldn't overrun them. He recalled their names: Ellica and Gillan, the eldest of the children.

That they had been hard-used by the storm was obvious. Ellica had gotten the worst of it, with torn and tattered skirts and hair so tangled she would need to cut it off. Their faces were browned by dust, eyes reddened from irritation. The rain, burning hot, flattened their hair against their scalps and soaked the shoulders of their tunics. They flinched as droplets struck them.

Rhuan reined in for only a moment, long enough to give them explicit directions to the boulders in the forest where the youngest took shelter. "Keep running," he told them as they slowed. They were young, with more strength than even they knew inhabiting their bodies. They might think they could run no more, but what he said next would as-sure they could. "It will only get hotter."

A muted wail of exhaustion and fear issued from Ellica's mouth. Gillan, face taut with fear, reached for her hand and closed it in his own. "Let's go, Elli."

Rhuan nodded approval and went on. Riding west as they ran east.

DAVYN REALIZED THE rain, hot as it was, had begun to settle the dust. It was easier to see now than when the wind was whipping dry dirt into the air. Ahead of him he saw a distant fringe of tree canopies along the horizon. His children were there somewhere, but Audrun was not.

The wind still blew, thunder still crashed in the wake of

lightning, the rain, hot rain, still fell. But he stopped and turned around, hoping to see his wife. Instead, he saw only the grasslands, flattened into submission beneath the continuing storm. Wind stripped his hair back from his face so that raindrops, unhindered, burned against his skin.

Davyn placed cupped hands over his eyes as a shield against rain and wind, squinting. "Audrun!" As before, the wind caught his shout. He tried again and again with no result.

Standing still gave the rain carte blanche to hammer at him, drenching hair and clothing. His flesh quivered, flinching from the heat.

Now he cupped hands around his mouth. "Audrun!"

Could he have gone astray? The storm had destroyed his sense of direction. It was possible he—or even she—had run the wrong way. All were blinded by the storm; it was a simple matter to take the first wrong step, then more and more and more. He could be anywhere, lost amid the grasslands. Or she could.

"Audrun!"

Nothing. Nothing. The only thing he could see, the only thing he could recognize, was the distant fringe of trees along the horizon, little more than a smudge of darkness. That, he could use as orientation. He prayed Audrun would, if she saw it. If she were not going in the wrong direction.

In despair, as the rain grew hotter yet, Davyn once again faced the horizon with its rim of trees. And ran.

AUDRUN GASPED AUDIBLY as she walked, unable to breathe normally. She was exhausted, empty of all save the conviction that, for the sake of the child, she had to keep going. One step, followed by another, and another, and all the additional anothers she needed to arrive at what safety the guide had promised when he told them all to go east. Told them to run.

But she couldn't run anymore. Her body's compre-

hension of the movements required to run had dissipated moments, or even hours ago. Walking, she could
manage. Walking, she maintained despite the lashing of
burning rain. It was all she could offer the child in her
belly.

Chapter 47

MIKAL FELL TO HIS KNEES. He gripped his chest, panting. Sweat sprang onto his brow. His face was gray.

"Mikal!" To see him, Bethid had to turn into the wind. "Mikal, we have to go on!"

He shook his head, breathing heavily. "I can't."

"Mikal—"

"I *can't* . . . but you go on. Go, Beth!"

She knelt before him. "What's wrong?"

"My chest . . . pain." He patted his broad chest with one hand, gasping for breath. "Pain inside." He gazed at her out of his one good eye. "Go on, Beth."

She shook her head. "I won't!"

". . . lie down . . ." Mikal slumped to the side, collapsing onto his back. ". . . must . . ."

Bethid was paralyzed, staring down at the man so obviously in pain. *What do I do? What do I do?* Her world was full of wind and lightning and thunder, of fear and desperation. A portion of her wanted to get up and run again, to leave Mikal in the dirt. And on the heels of that realization came shame. *What I can do is help this man.*

Kneeling in the midst of the storm, Bethid looked around. Most of her world was blotted out by dust, by blinding crimson lightning, but she could see dark shapes within the dust and debris, people from the settlement going east, as she, and Mikal, had told them. If a man would stop, or even two, they could lift Mikal up and carry him east.

Bethid shouted for help. No help came.

Mikal, she knew, was dying. She knew also that she could not leave him.

She moved around the ale-keep until she could block some wind with her back, take his head into her lap. She leaned over him, closing her eyes against the storm.

The ground beneath her trembled as hot rain fell.

"Alisanos," she murmured. *Alisanos is coming.*

THE GROUND SHUDDERED. Rain was not enough, wind was not enough, lightning was not enough. Now the very earth beneath the hooves of Rhuan's horse rebelled.

Oh, it was close, so close, Alisanos. Rhuan gritted his teeth, baring them in a rictus of frustration, of pain. He felt the deepwood as a thrumming in his bones. His skin itched. Rain bathed his body with welcomed warmth, but the wind howled on.

He was *dioscuri*. Could he control the storm? Could he placate the earth?

Ah, but this was of Alisanos. And Alisanos wanted, it very badly wanted, to move to new environs.

The spotted horse flagged. Rhuan leaned forward, patted the soaked neck, and promised, in his milk-tongue, that the horse would receive the finest of care when they were free of the storm, when they had time to rest, to drink, to eat.

But the earth shuddered and abruptly split asunder. The horse, too weary to change his direction even as Rhuan tried to rein him aside, went down, front legs collapsing into the widening rent in grass and soil. The horse screamed and floundered, trying to scramble up, but the earth was unforgiving. It crumbled away into chasm, soil and grass falling out from under hooves.

As his mount went down, Rhuan threw himself sideways, striking the ground and rolling aside, then scrambled up to lunge away from the chasm that had opened immediately in front of his horse. Raw earth boiled up, was hurled away by the wind. The horse's face was caked with dirt, his eyes rolling in terror. As he fought to pull his front legs free, the chasm widened beneath his belly. It was now too wide for Rhuan to reach the reins without falling in himself.

He felt the shivering of the ground. It squirmed, writhed, broke apart in a rumble far deeper than the thunder's song. Only moments remained.

The terrified gelding screamed. Lather coated him, foam dripped from his mouth. But there was nothing Rhuan could do. The earth had every intention of eating the horse.

Rhuan strung together a twisted, tangled skein of curses, exhorting the horse to break free, damning the chasm. Already it was beginning to close. The horse, when swallowed whole, would suffocate.

Rhuan hissed between his teeth. He had only two choices. The first was untenable; he owed far more to the horse than to walk away from his terror. The second was a mercy, albeit one he hated to render. It was also dangerous.

But nonetheless worth the doing. Rhuan knew that.

The wind was too strong for throwing knives. He drew his bone-handled, long-bladed knife. He ran two long paces, then sprang.

He landed crouched atop the saddle with his legs doubled up, swung forward under the horse's neck as he clung to mane with his left hand; with his right, he stabbed deeply with the knife. Once. Twice.

As the horse floundered and screamed, gouts of blood spraying, Rhuan used the impetus to leap free, to leap far, to land crouched again, legs doubled again, one hand pressed against the earth to steady himself while the other, still gripping the knife, he kept away from his flesh.

He thrust himself upright and turned to see the horse. So much blood. The white patches of hair between the black spots became red.

After a moment, the horse stopped screaming. The spotted head bowed slackly.

In the rain, in the wind, in the midst of crimson lightning, Rhuan paid tribute with the only thing he had: words of sorrow, words of thanks.

The earth opened. It took the horse down. It swallowed him utterly.

Rhuan cleaned and sheathed his knife. Then he turned west—and heard the woman's shout carried upon the wind.

ILONA HUNG ON to Jorda's belt. She felt shaken nearly to death and her head was aching. The uneven lumbering gait of the draft horse was worse now than it had been when their ride began, and since they rode bareback there was no security in their seats. They clung to the horse with their legs, and Ilona clung to Jorda, who kept up a steady stream of invective, all of which concerned the parentage of the horse as well as the gelding himself.

They still rode east, she thought. Though in the midst of the storm she wasn't certain which direction was which. She was no more certain which end was up or down.

They had lost track of the exodus from the settlement. For all she could tell, in the midst of the storm, they were the last surviving humans in the world. One man, one woman . . . one incredibly uncomfortable horse.

And then the uncomfortable horse took it into his head to stumble badly.

Jorda went off, and Ilona went with him.

She landed hard, and alone. At some point she had lost her grip on Jorda's belt. Blinded by the storm, she could see nothing of the ground. She fell hard, facedown, left arm doubled under her body. Her left hip struck stone. She sprawled flat upon the earth.

The pain in her arm was immense. She could not restrain her outcry. And she could not restrain her body's impulse to seek relief; she rolled over onto her back, cradling her left arm against her chest.

Hot rain struck her face, fell into her open mouth. She lay gasping on her back like a landed fish. Long strands of dark hair stuck to her face and neck. Sweat broke out. Tears ran from the corners of her eyes to the earth she couldn't see.

Jorda.

She said his name. She said it twice. It took immense effort to speak his name at all, with an arm screaming at her. Broken, she thought. No; broken, she *knew*.

"Jorda."

The rain was *hot*.

"Jorda!"

When no answer came, Ilona gritted her teeth and rolled onto her right side. The arm continued to scream at her; she pressed it firmly against her chest, levered herself with her good right arm onto her right hip, and drew her legs up. She took a breath and heaved herself upward, face set in a grimace. She managed to get her legs under her so she had support, then used her right arm to brace herself against collapse.

The world around her spun. She thought it might be the storm. She thought it might be the pain.

She had no time for pain.

"Jorda?"

No answer came.

ELLICA TRIPPED AND FELL. She landed on hands and knees and bit into her lip. Blood welled up. She spat. Her tangled mass of soaked hair hung down on either side of her face. "Gillan?"

"Ellica!"

She spat blood again. "Where are you?" Her grip on his hand had broken when she fell. Her eyes were gritty, lashes crusted with dirt. Wind whirled around her. "Gillan!" She stood up, shielding her face with her hands. "Where are you?"

Through the roaring of the wind she heard him calling for her. His voice sounded more distant.

Panic swept through her body. "Gillan?" She ran three steps, then stopped. What if she was moving away from him? What if he was going in another direction as he looked for her? *"Where are you?"*

This time she heard nothing.

In her head she said: *MotherMotherMother . . . O, Mother of Moons . . .*

She was alone.

Ellica grabbed up her skirts and began to run.

IT OCCURRED TO Audrun to doubt herself when she saw the human-shaped form. Was it the guide? Could it *be* the guide? Or was it a hallucination, a wish wished so hard, a prayer prayed with all the conviction of her body, with such an investment in belief and hope that she fooled herself?

It was him. It had to be; she wanted it too badly.

His features were indistinct. The only thing recognizable in the rain now beating down was the shape of his body and the telltail swinging, as he turned, of multiple braids.

It was. It *was.*

She shouted his name. And took such sheer joy in relief that weariness dissipated. She could run again, and did, even as he, echoing her movements, came running in her direction. She registered braids, the gloom-dulled shine of ornamentation, the shape of his body, so lean and fit, and the burgeoning of a grin, as he arrived, that displayed white teeth and deep dimples.

And then she saw the grin fade, saw horror reshape his features. Saw a helplessness in his eyes.

Fear replaced relief even as she gasped for breath. "What is it?"

He didn't answer. He drew his knife and cut into his left wrist. Before she could speak, he sheathed the knife and took the single stride necessary to stand very close.

With one hand he cupped the back of her skull, holding it still; he pressed his left wrist, his bleeding wrist, against her mouth. "Drink."

Audrun recoiled, stunned, but his right hand held her in place. She jerked her face aside hard, feeling the warmth of blood on her face. Mother of Moons, what *was* this? His blood? "What are you doing!"

"Drink it." Grim determination and an unshielded desperation shaded his tone. "I know—I do know it sickens you . . . but you must. I swear it. You must."

She struggled to break free, but now his right hand gripped hair as well as her skull. Her lips pulled away from her teeth. "Are you mad?"

He turned her then with both hands, blood still flowing freely from his left wrist. "Look. See it?" Fingers bit into her shoulders. "This is to keep you safe—to keep you as you are. Do you wish to be changed? Be certain of this: Alisanos will do it."

He was close to her, so close, right arm around her ribs, the left wrist once again pressed against her mouth. But now she didn't move. She didn't protest. She stared across his forearm, transfixed.

Blackness crawled across the ground. It was flood tide, it was wildfire; it was consumption of everything. It crept forward inexorably, swallowing earth and air.

IN THE SHELTER of the boulders, shielded by close-grown trees, wrapped in blankets and oilcloth, Torvic scooted closer to his sister. "Meggie, don't cry. They'll come find us. The guide said so."

But she cried all the harder.

"Meggie, stop."

Sobs wracked her words. "I want Da . . . I want Mam and Da!"

"He went to find them. He went to find all of them. They'll come, Meggie. Don't cry."

Lightning sliced through the trees. Accompanying thunder crashed over their heads.

"We have to wait," Torvic said. "He told us to wait. He'll bring them. He said so."

Megritte cried.

Torvic wormed an arm behind her back. It wasn't long enough to curl around her ribs the way Da did it. "They're coming, Meggie. He promised. Don't cry."

But as Torvic hugged his sister as best he could, tears ran down his face.

FERIZE SHED HER clothing. Brodhi, still smiling into the storm, watched her dance, shared her joy, understood the exuberance of her spirits.

Nude, she thrust her arms into the air over her head as the wind whipped at her hair. She spun and spun, and with each revolution color came into her flesh. He watched as the scale pattern asserted itself, climbing from naked toes up toward her knees, slipping earthward from her neck. Bit by bit she was clothed in scales, in the complex latticework of multihued opalescence. When all of her flesh was colored she stopped her spinning, stopped her dance. Her eyes, as she looked at him, were green. The pupils were no longer round. Her tongue, as she opened her mouth, was forked.

Despite the human-shaped body, what looked at him now had no humanity in her.

"Go ahead," Brodhi said indulgently. "You know you want to."

Ferize laughed at him. Then she leaped into the air and exploded in a shower of crystalline flakes as she sought to ride the wind.

He grinned. She was nothing now but a blot in the sky, stretching wings and claws and tail.

Heated rain, crimson lightning, unceasing thunder. Earth that shuddered.

Brodhi fell to his knees. He stretched out his arms, arched his spine, tipped his head backward, turning his face to the heavens. He laughed for the joy of it.

Alisanos was coming.

 PAIN WAS A KNOT in Audrun's chest. "My children!"

"Drink," the guide directed.

But she could not. It sickened her.

"We can't escape," he said, "not anymore. But if you take my blood into you, there may be some protection."

She knew exactly what it was, the devouring blackness. He had warned all of them. He had tried to keep them from placing themselves at risk. He had tried to see them to safety after risk became reality. She trusted him.

But to drink his blood?

Once again he pressed his bleeding arm against her face. *"Please."*

Her gorge rose. She wrenched free, spinning in place, turning her back on the black tide consuming the grasslands. She caught one glimpse of the knowledge in his face, of the fear so like her own, though she knew, without knowing how she knew, that his fear was for her. Not for himself.

Because Alisanos would change her.

Panic put her to flight. He leaped, and caught her. Dragged her close. "We have to stay togeth—" But the world went black around them, smothering her scream, stealing the air in her lungs. It took her into itself and slammed the door shut behind her.

As consciousness waned, Audrun was visited with a vision: an old, filthy man with claws in place of hands, begging her to take him back to Alisanos.

To take him home.

And then the guide was torn from her, or she from him, as her presence in the human world was erased.

Chapter 48

*T*HE EARTH BENEATH ILONA SHUDDERED. A bolt of crimson lightning hissed across the heavens with thunder on its tail, thunder loud enough, strong enough, to threaten her hearing. Ilona hunched shoulders against it and ducked her head, flinching. And the reflex hurt. Badly.

She cradled her injured arm against her breasts and gasped in pain, clamping teeth shut on a moan. She could see nothing; the day itself had been swallowed by a frightful dance of harrowing wind, blinding lightning, and burning rain; of dirt and debris and the turgid blackness of roiling clouds. Her hair hung loose and heavy, tangled and wet, straggling down into her lap as she sat upon the trembling earth.

She drew in a breath—and held it. For a moment she believed she was imagining it, but no. The rain *had* slackened. It had been a hard, painful rain, scalding against her scalp, unlike any rain she had endured. This was a rain created by Alisanos.

But now it ceased. Ilona released her breath on a murmured prayer to Sibetha.

The quality of light changed. She looked up into the sky. Black clouds were thinning. Lightning had ceased, and thus the thunder. Even the wind was losing strength, fading to a breeze that was also dying out. And the sun, occluded for so long, burned through the thready remains of dissipating clouds. Day dawned again.

But Ilona closed her eyes.

Day dawned—but was it over Sancorra province? Or did she live now within the confines of Alisanos?

IT TOOK HIM. It tasted him. It spat him out. Rhuan, rousing, could only laugh hoarsely.

No more wind. No more lightning. No more thunder. No more rain. No more world as he had known it, living among the humans.

He lay upon rock, arms and legs sprawled, face upturned. The primary sun was very white in a pale sepia sky, while the small secondary sun burned yellow. The double suns of Alisanos heated the stone beneath him. His body answered the comfort, aches and pains fading. He found himself disinclined to leap up, or even to sit up. Upon stone humans would find hot, he lay and reveled in the heat. He was a creature of such warmth, was a child craving it.

The membrane in his eyes covered them against the brilliance of two suns, turning the world red. But as he came back to himself, the membrane lifted. It slid away, banishing the haze, and he saw clearly again.

Sepia sky, not blue. White sun, yellow sun. Trees grew up from the earth twisted, not straight, rose from the tangle of roots serpenting upon the earth from tree to tree to tree; rose from the heavy underbrush of thorns, briars, and needles. Blackened trunks knotted, branches latticed, bearing wide, sharp leaves and twining purple vines. Vines that reached to other trees like humans holding hands.

Humans.

Rhuan sat upright. But Alisanos was never gentle; he groaned as a headache took possession of his skull. He crossed his legs, planted elbows atop them, and leaned his head into his hands, willing the pain to go. But his will was not answered.

His tongue was not hindered by the headache. He spat out invective. But gently.

Then he remembered he had cut his wrist. A glance showed him the purplish line of scar. He no longer bled. Alisanos had sealed the wound. By morning, such as it was in Alisanos, the scar would turn pink; by nightfall, white. Healed. That much Alisanos would do for him.

Someone groaned.

Memory, sharp as a knife, sliced through the pain in his head.

The woman.

He recalled now that he had clung to her as Alisanos took them; that he had tried, without success, to offer her assistance, the kind that would shield her in the deepwood: his blood. But she had refused, refused again and again. And Alisanos, scenting prey, had taken advantage of those refusals.

She groaned again. This time Rhuan rose. All around him lay stone, a massive rounded platter striated rose and white and green, a huge shallow hollow with a rim of tumbled, ruddy rock circling it and a border of thin-limbed, knotted trees bowing down over the platter. Not natural, this; it was built for something. A purpose he didn't know. Perhaps it was a womb. Or perhaps a crucible.

He had survived his birth, though it killed his mother. He wasn't sure that he could survive the crucible. Alisanos had taken him before he was ready.

Audrun. Audrun was her name.

She had not drunk his blood. Thus she was prey.

A third groan rose, was transformed into a choked-off sound of extremity. Rhuan heard rustlings in the thorny underbrush surrounding the womb of stone. He heard the noise of those who wanted the prey. Who wanted to feast upon her.

He saw faces, then. Open to them now, letting his senses come alive, he felt them as well. Heat from bodies, from panting mouths. Elongated yellow eyes. A wide nostril here, scales there, a tail writhing briefly. He felt the low thrumming hum of predators drawn by the human, the female, the woman carrying young.

No. *No.*

Yet again he ran. He left behind him the massive stone platter, the rim of stone, tore through the bowing, twisted trees and ruthless underbrush.

AS THE STORM died out, so did Mikal's chest pain. Bethid, who had positioned herself by him as a windbreak, opened her eyes as he stirred. She saw instantly that his color was improving. The horrible grayness of his flesh was gone, and the bluish tinge to his lips had been replaced by a healthy pink. She was no moonmother or healer to know what to do, but she had eyes to see. Mikal was better.

Still on his back, the ale-keep rubbed at his chest. Bethid could see lucidity return to the eye not covered by a patch. "It's gone," he said on a profound note of relief.

"The pain?"

"Gone," he repeated. He levered himself up onto one meaty elbow, looking at her in something akin to wariness. "It just—stopped."

"Thank the Mother for that!"

Mikal pulled from the neckline of his tunic the charms and fetishes on a leather thong. He closed his broad hand around it. "I do thank the Mother." He pushed himself up into a sitting position. He spat out grit from his mouth, taking care not to do it in Bethid's direction. He blinked at her. "Your face is filthy."

"Probably no worse than yours." But Bethid was too relieved to speak tartly. She grabbed the hem of her long tunic, turned it inside out and bent to wipe at her face. "I suspect a dunking in the river would be more effective," she muttered. "That is, if the river still exists." She raised her head, looking around. "It looks the same," she observed. "The world. Soggy and wind-scoured, but the same." She squinted up at the sun, visible again now that the clouds and blinding dust were gone. "Doesn't it?"

Mikal hung his head and brushed at wet, dark hair, trying to rid himself of sand. As Bethid spoke, he looked up, attempting to peel the grit from his gummy eyelashes. "No trees," he said, blinking his one eye as it watered. The tear carved a route through the dust on his face. "The grove is down. The karavaner grove."

"Are you sure?" She twisted to look. "I thought we'd gone far enough beyond that we couldn't see it anyway."

Mikal readjusted the patch over his missing eye. "We didn't get that far."

Bethid stood up. She saw what he meant. Indeed, the grove of wide-crowned trees that had become the place where all the karavans gathered was down. She saw twisted, broken roots rising high against a horizon that had always been clothed by trees at the tent settlement. The leaves that soon would dry and die were wind-tattered, many stripped away so that the branches were naked. Tall prairie grass had been blown flat, forming an untidy rug of stems over mud.

"We're still here." Relief mixed with astonishment. "We're safe." She turned back to Mikal. "We're still here!"

Mikal nodded. "The Shoia was right."

She had left. And she had lived. She owed the Shoia her thanks.

Bethid felt at her ears. The wind had not torn the big brass hoops free of her lobes. Then she put both hands into her short-cropped fair hair and scrubbed as hard as she could, attempting to rid it of sand and soil. But it was wet, and debris clung to the strands.

It occurred to her then to think of Brodhi, of Timmon and Alorn. They too had been in the tent settlement as the wind roared down, as the heated rain fell from blackened skies torn apart by crimson lightning. Were they safe? Were they whole?

Bethid turned back. "We have to go. Mikal, we have to go back to the settlement. They'll need our help." She paused, remembering laggardly that the ale-keep had been on the verge of death. "I'm sorry—you need to rest, of course."

He shook his head, pushing to his feet with a grunt. He

seemed steady enough. His color remained good. "I'm well, Beth . . ." He broke off as he saw her expression. "What is it?"

She frowned, squinting eastward beyond him. "Who is—oh! It's Jorda and Ilona!" She spared a glance for Mikal, but his color reassured her. Bethid broke into a swift jog.

Eastward again. But this time toward people she knew. People she valued.

DAVYN WAS NUMB from the wind, the pounding of the rain, the ear-shattering thunder. When all ceased, it took him long moments to realize it. He lay still, face down, arms wrapped over his head where his fingers interlaced. He kept his eyes closed tightly. He waited, anticipating the rise of the wind again, the burning of the rain, the crashing of thunder on the tail of crimson lightning. But nothing rose. No sound, no wind, no rain.

There was no part of his body that did not ache. Carefully he loosened his fingers, then scraped his arms across sodden grass. He doubled them, pressed his palms flat, and pushed.

All of him was wet. Hair was plastered against his skull, dripping into his face. Gasping, he pulled knees under himself. As he rose up, as he made his battered body do his bidding, he realized the skies were clear again. Gone were the boiling clouds turgid with rain. The sun shone as usual. But he had only to look out across the prairie to see miles of flattened grass. The soil ran with rain that could not be taken into already-soaked earth.

"Aud—" But his voice cracked. Davyn swallowed, moistened his lips, and shouted his wife's name.

There came no answer. In a haphazard upward lunge, Davyn pushed to his feet. He caught his balance with care. Rainwater ran from his scalp, trickled down his temples. The clothing Audrun had woven him with habitual care was heavy with the weight of water.

"Audrun!"

Still, there came no answer. The skies were blue, the day was bright as if nothing untoward had occurred, but one need only look at the surface of the earth to see the storm's effects. Davyn slicked wet hair out of his face, slowly turning to look in every direction. And again, repeating it, when his eyes found nothing.

"Gillan! Ellica!"

But he was alone upon the land.

He cried out in pain, the inner pain that tightened a throat and weighted a chest. He found himself mumbling a litany of phrases, of prayers, of promises he meant entire if they resulted in his wife's well-being and the safety of his children.

All of them, gone.

"Audrunnnnn . . ."

Mother of Moons, don't let him be left alone.

The wagon. He would go to the wagon. It was where his wife and oldest children would go to find one another. Then they all of them could search for the youngest.

For Torvic, and Megritte. Torvic and sweet Meggie.

He knew the direction. He knew his way. He prayed his family did.

But when he found the wagon, he saw that they had not.

Davyn fell to his knees, his throat clogged with pain. Arms hung slackly at his sides; his head was tipped back, so that the light of the sun warmed his face. Dried away the rain, but not the tears.

Next to the remains of the storm-stripped wagon, both oxen lay dead, skin scoured away by the winds of Alisanos.

Chapter 49

"*I*LONA!"

Her eyes snapped open. Some four body-lengths away, pushing himself into a sitting position, was Jorda. His wet homespun tunic was plastered against his broad chest and shoulders, and he stared at her, startled and disbelieving, even as she returned his look. Then his expression, muddied into a mask of grime and rainwater, changed to joy and relief, white teeth parting his beard. Jorda was a big man, but he managed to make his body scramble to her side.

His green eyes were bright. "Thank the Mother. Are you all right?"

Ilona could not contain the laughter that bubbled up. It was an unexpected sound, birthed by emotions she only now could release. "Yes," she said, grinning, "I'm all right." She held her right hand out and saw the familiar olive tint of her flesh. She remained herself.

His gaze went to her injured arm. "Broken?"

She grimaced. "I think so."

"Then you're not all right."

"Oh yes," she said, "I am. Most certainly. I'm *alive*." He knelt beside her, concern etching deeper lines into his weary, dirt-grimed face. "I'm alive," she repeated, giddy with relief. The memory of the lumbering draft horse they rode was clear, as was the fall both of them had taken when it stumbled and went down. Jorda had an impressive knot on his forehead. The horse was nowhere to be seen.

He noted the line of her gaze and touched the prodigious lump with thick fingers. "The fall stunned me, or I would have searched for you."

She had called for him again and again, fearing for his life. But the storm had hidden all from her except its violence.

Ilona looked around. "Is this—safe? Are we still in Sancorra?"

Blue skies, now; a sun where it should be; scents she recognized; the stillness of dawn, though it was afternoon. Dust blown by the wind had turned the weave of her clothes the color of mud. Discolored droplets slid sullenly down the wet, wind-tangled ringlets of her hair.

This couldn't be Alisanos. It looked, felt, and smelled as the world had prior to the storm.

She heard Rhuan's voice again in her memory. *Gather everyone and go east. I can't tell you how I know, but trust me.* There had been no further order. *Go east,* was all he said. And so they had gone east, as others had; where were those others?

"Safe," Jorda confirmed, answering her question even as he scraped a damp-sleeved arm across his face, smearing dirt and grime. "As anyone might be, that is, after such a storm."

The day was temperate. Despite wet clothing, she felt neither warm nor cold.

Jorda gestured. "The settlement's behind us." He paused, ruddy brows meeting over the bridge of his nose. "If anything's left of it."

Ilona climbed unsteadily to her feet, wincing against the pain of her arm. Standing there, cradling her arm, she turned in a slow circle. Everywhere she looked, the world was as it had been.

But no. It was not. It seemed so in the absence of rain and wind and lightning, but when she looked beyond relief, she saw desolation. The grass beneath her feet lay flattened against the earth, smashed down into soil become mud, with scorched and still-smoking holes where the lightning had struck, bleeding splattered clots of earth. Trees had been uprooted and thrown down, branches broken, leaves stripped away, roots ripped apart. The plains, the horizon, naked now of forests, was an uninterrupted line against the sky. She heard no birds, no insects. Only silence. Only stillness.

Fear bloomed. The world *was* changed. But it tantalized her with seemingly familiar scents, a familiar sun.

"Tell me we're not," she blurted. Jorda, standing next to her, turned to read her expression. His own was grim. "Tell me this isn't Alisanos."

"It isn't."

She turned in a circle again, seeking something known. "How can you tell where the settlement is?" she asked sharply. "All the landmarks are gone."

His mouth crooked in a faint smile as he pointed to the sky. "That landmark is enough."

Of course. The sun. Ilona released a breath of renewed relief, tucking tangled, muddied hair behind an ear. Of the tales she'd heard of Alisanos, anything was possible. The deepwood, stories said, was a living being, unutterably alien, with a will of its own. She had been raised on those tales, of horrific punishments there promised by parents if she didn't do as told.

Now, she realized, her parents had threatened her with the truth. Like a field of corn scythed down, Alisanos had taken what stood before it and swept it away.

But not her. Not Jorda.

"Where is everyone?" Surely she and Jorda could not be the only ones left. The only ones alive. They had passed straggling groups of people heading east, as they had been told to. Had she and Jorda, on horseback while refugees from the tent settlement walked, gone astray from the fleeing inhabitants?

"Your arm needs tending," Jorda declared. "We'll go back to the karavan and find wood and cloth for a splint."

She looked at her battered arm. It was swollen between her wrist and elbow, with a knob of shiny skin stretched taut over what she knew was bone turned askew. It had not torn through the flesh, thank the Mother, but was ugly nonetheless, promising trouble.

Jorda slid a careful hand under her right elbow. "Come, Ilona."

Hair hung in tangles to her waist. Her skirts were tattered, and the seams of her tunic had torn. Jorda was no better with soaked, soiled clothing and hair ripped loose from his braid framing his broad face. He looked concerned.

"I'm well," she told him, wanting to wash away that concern.

"Are you?" His faint smile was grim. "You risk fever with that arm. Do you want to survive Alisanos only to die from a broken bone?"

She felt distant, dreamy. "Jorda . . ."

"Yes?"

"We survived *Alisanos.*" If she said it, said it aloud, she made it a true thing. "It went elsewhere—I think." Frowning, she turned in a circle again. "Jorda, this is where we were, yes? Sancorra province? The settlement? Going east, as Rhuan said?" A knot of tension and apprehension took possession of her belly. *O Mother, let this not be Alisanos making fools of us.*

"Come along," he told her patiently, easing her into movement. "You're fretting because of your arm. We'll see to it, then do what we can for others."

She turned abruptly to the karavan-master. "Give me your hand."

His brows rose in surprise. "My hand?"

"I can't read my own." No hand-reader could. "If you'll allow me to read yours, I may be able to see a little of your future. Enough to know whether we are in Alisanos, waiting with its traps; or if we are east of the settlement, east of all things familiar."

"Ilona—"

"Please."

Jorda extended his hand palm up. She could not use both her hands in the reading, but one should be enough.

AUDRUN LAY ON her side, curled upon herself to safeguard her belly. But it cramped. She felt the pain roll through her, rise up, crest, then recede too slowly.

Was she to lose the child?

She cramped again and curled herself more tightly yet upon her side, breathing noisily through an open mouth. The flesh of her abdomen felt overstretched. Felt on fire.

With her eyes closed, Audrun could not see. She wished not to see. That Alisanos had taken her, she knew. But she was ignorant of such details as where in the deepwood she was, what it might do to her, when the changes might begin, and whether she could escape.

The old man had escaped.

And begged to go back.

The ground beneath her was pocked with stone and wood. Sharp-edged leaves scraped her skin. Grass poked, like needles. A shadow of branches bent low over her, shading her, but beyond was light, too-bright light.

Audrun bit into her lip as she cramped again. She tasted blood. As a deeper cramp took her, as her belly skin burned, she could not hold her silence. A groan escaped, and another. Her world, her human world, was absent. Husband. Children. All absent.

Except for the unborn in her belly.

"Audrun."

Her eyes snapped open as she rolled her head to look upward. In that first moment the sky visible between branches and leaves wheeled above her. Brownish sky, not blue. Much too bright. And numberless trees surrounding her; twisted, gnarled trees linked together by thorny vines and interlocking branches bearing wide, flat leaves, bluish leaves, speckled with the rust of disease.

Or merely of Alisanos.

Pain took her again and she bit once more into her bloodied lip.

"Audrun, I'm here."

He knelt beside her. She heard the chime and click of hair ornaments, sensed his nearness even with eyes shut again against the brightness, the worst of it screened by low-hanging branches dangling large, sharp-edged leaves.

Her breathing came now in gasps broken time and time again as she caught her breath on a foreshortened grunt of pain. Blood ran into her mouth from her bitten lip. She coughed and gagged. She had refused to drink his blood; now she swallowed her own.

His hands were on her. "Let me see, Audrun." Gently he urged her to turn from side to back. He slid a hand beneath her skull and lifted it, then resettled it on earth, not stone.

The sky above was *not blue.*

Cramping, again. Audrun could barely speak. "I'm losing . . . losing it. The baby . . ."

The quality of his silence, the sudden stillness of his hands as he eased her over, frightened her badly. Audrun opened her eyes. She lay now in the shade from the nearest tree, in the shade he made, blocking sunlight.

"No," he said. "You are not."

How could he say that? How could he know?

Cramping seized her again. This time she cried out. "How am I not losing this baby?"

He took her hands in his own. He guided them to her belly and flattened them there, pressing them against her abdomen.

Roundness. Pronounced roundness. It was not the belly of a woman at five months, but of a woman nearing term. And she felt it, *felt* it grow beneath her hands. Her skin stretched, but not enough. She thought she might split open.

Sweat ran into her hair. She stared in horror at the man beside her. "How is this happening?"

For a moment he said nothing. She could not read his expression. Then he spoke a single word, very quietly: "Alisanos."

Realization sent a wave of fear through her. She was not losing the child. She was *bearing* the child.

In Alisanos.

Her belly spasmed again. She felt it heave beneath her hands. "It's too soon!"

"No." His hands were gentle upon her, stroking hair back from her sweat-filmed face. "No, it's at term."

Cramps transformed into contractions. Her belly now was huge, tight. It writhed beneath her trembling hands. "Why is this happening? *How* is this happening?"

He wore no mask now. His expression was grim. "Alisanos wants it."

The words stunned her. "Alisanos wants my *baby?*"

"Hush now," he said. "Save your strength."

Audrun ignored the instructions. "Why? *Why does it want my baby?*"

She saw a kind of grief in his eyes. But his tone was curiously flat. "Your baby is human."

The contractions now were harder, closer together. She reached out for his hand, clung as she found it. A question occurred. "Why," she began on a caught breath, "did you want me to drink your blood?"

Something flinched in his eyes. She saw grief again, briefly, and surrender. "I believed it might offer some protection."

"Your blood would offer me protection?" She tasted her own in the back of her throat. "How?"

"Alisanos recognizes its own."

"Its own," she echoed. Another contraction took her. She forced the question between her teeth. "You're not Shoia, are you?"

"No."

"Then what are you?" She squeezed her eyes closed as the contractions worsened, coming much more quickly. It was time to push, time to use all her strength for bearing the child. But she had to know. "What are you?" Audrun repeated. She recalled her youngest daughter's accusation. "A demon?"

His mouth twitched in a brief ironic hook. "No."

"Then what?"

"Half-human. But I was born here."

The contractions now came very hard. "And what is the other half?"

"You need to concentrate on bearing the child."

A cry of pain was wrenched out of her. She bore down upon the baby that wanted to be born well before its time, but was, inexplicably, at full term. Audrun bared her teeth at Rhuan. "I'm trusting you to help me deliver this baby . . . tell me who you are. Tell me *what* you are."

"Dioscuri," he said quietly. And before she could ask what that was, "My father is a god."

Pain gripped her. Pain tore her asunder. And on that pain, on a rush of blood, she bore the full-term child that was not due for another four months.

The child, he had said, that Alisanos wanted.

In the depths of the trees, howling began.

THE TREES BEHIND Brodhi quieted. Thunder dissipated. The sun crept out and began, albeit slowly, to dry his hair and clothing even as it shed light upon the wasteland. He heard silence, nothing more.

Brodhi's arms fell to his sides. He remained upright on his knees, but the joy of anticipation was usurped by a dawning awareness he refused to acknowledge. He felt his body begin to tense, muscle by muscle, fiber by fiber, until he ached with it. An unrestrained howl of fury broke from his throat, banishing silence. Hands curled tightly into fists as he bared his teeth. The world, free of storm, nonetheless turned red. He broke into a lengthy litany of curses heaped upon the heads of the primaries of Alisanos, the gods who had the ordering of that world.

One thousand of them. And not one of those thousand had seen fit to release him from the journey he despised with all of his being.

They left him here, the gods. Left him among the humans.

The message was plain: He was not one of them yet. Not *worthy* of them yet.

He heard the snap of a twig from the forest just behind him. "They would believe you mad, the humans," Darmuth observed, gliding out of cracked, upended, and leaf-stripped trees. "A moon-touched man shouting nonsense to the sky in words they can't understand."

Brodhi lunged to his feet, spinning to face the demon who wore human form. "I care less than nothing what humans believe."

"Yes, you've made that rather plain." Darmuth folded muscled arms across his chest and cocked a hip, looking wholly at ease. "And that may be the very reason Alisanos left you behind."

"I belong there."

"That's yet to be determined." Darmuth's winter-gray eyes lacked the irony that so often glinted in them. Black pupils elongated into slits. "Your time among the humans isn't completed."

It was all he could do not to shout it. "Alisanos *moved.*"

Darmuth shrugged lazily. "That matters less than nothing. Human time, Brodhi. The land may be different, but the time, and the counting of it, remains unchanged."

"Why are you here?" With effort Brodhi cleared his vision of the red haze. "Why not go to Rhuan? *He's* your task, not me."

Something flickered in Darmuth's eyes. "Rhuan's not available."

Brodhi shook his head in disgust. "He went with those foolish farmsteaders, didn't he?"

"Rhuan's in Alisanos."

For long moments Brodhi could only stare silently at Darmuth. When he could speak again, the words issued from his mouth in heat and raw pain. "The primaries took him back? How by all of their names could they take him? He's not worthy! He's repudiated them. He wants to be *human.*"

"The greatest test Rhuan can face now is the knowledge that he *is* in Alisanos. Before his journey is done. Your greatest test?" Darmuth shrugged again. "I think you know."

"To remain," Brodhi said tightly. He spat onto the earth. "To remain here, knowing Rhuan is there."

"I rather think so." Darmuth's tone was light, but his eyes remained frigid. "It's as well for you I have no vote in your final disposition. Your arrogance and unflagging hatred of humans bodes ill for your ascension."

"The primaries are arrogant beyond bounds," Brodhi retorted, "as they should be; they're gods. And thus I am like them. You know it. I do. I belong among them."

"Until the human year is done, you belong *here*."

"I could go," Brodhi declared. "I could go across the border and into Alisanos. I am *of* it; it can't deny me entrance."

"Of course you may go," Darmuth agreed. "And of course it can't deny you entrance. But to return to Alisanos now negates the vows you made to the primaries. Negates the time spent here. You would either be required to begin again, which would prolong your misery, or be refused outright. Which might be worse. *Would* be worse." The demon paused. "They could do that, you realize. Refuse you altogether. And then you would no longer be *dioscuri,* but trapped between the godhood you desire and the humanness you despise. A neuter."

Brodhi opened his mouth to roar in rage at the demon, but Darmuth abruptly was standing in front of him, immediately in front of him, so close Brodhi smelled the musk of his scales, though he wore human flesh. Brodhi jerked his head back as the sinuous forked tongue flicked between Darmuth's lips, tasting his anger.

"This is why," Darmuth said, sibilants harsh. "*This* is why Ferize and I were sent to be your watchdogs." Human teeth shifted shape and size, forming curving points. A ripple of scale pattern stippled Darmuth's skin. "You prove yourself unworthy by behavior such as this."

For once Brodhi wished he had demons' teeth. His own, bared, lacked the impact he sought. "Ferize is more than my watchdog."

"That you are bound in the way humans call marriage has no bearing on this, and you know it, Brodhi. She owes her bones and blood to the primaries. That takes precedence over whatever you may share with her in copulation."

He could not win this battle, Brodhi knew. He, who had

the wit and words, the delicacy of tone both subtle and telling, and the knowledge of when and how to wield them all to crush a human soul—or, he reflected with grim satisfaction, to provoke Rhuan into anger—could not use any of those weapons against the demon. Because the demon was correct.

But even as Brodhi, helpless, howled his fury again, Darmuth took his leave and did not hear it.

Epilogue

AUDRUN WAS BREATHLESS from pain, from pushing; from the shock of the realization that in a matter of moments her body could be changed from a five-month pregnancy to full term. That was Alisanos. He had told her so.

Alisanos.

Howling filled her ears. Inhuman howling; an inharmonious melody that raised the skin on her bones. "What is that?"

Rhuan wore a mask now, an expression that gave nothing away of his thoughts. "They give welcome to the child."

Her body was wracked with weakness, even as the afterbirth followed the child. She could not control her tears, her gasping; could not stop her trembling. "*Who* gives welcome to my child?"

"The denizens of Alisanos."

In her exhaustion, Audrun could barely open her eyes. But when she did, when she saw again the sepia sky, the double suns, the gnarled, twisted trees unlike any she knew bowing low over her where she lay upon grass and ground, a flicker of anger kindled. Small, so very small and fragile, but slowly gaining strength. "Why? Why does it matter to these—*denizens*—that I've borne a human baby?"

"That answer," Rhuan said, "is complicated. Perhaps for

now we would do best to make certain you and the child are well."

Nearly lost in the howling, she heard the baby squall. A mother's ears, even amid wholly alien noise, recognized its own.

As Alisanos did. He had told her so.

Oh, but she was weary. Her body ached, muscles overstretched from the effort of bearing the child, from the abruptness of her belly's change from five months gone to nine. She made a sound, and his eyes flicked to meet hers. Cider-brown eyes, not red; but she had seen them turn red.

"She is strong," he said.

She. A daughter. The child intended to be born in Atalanda, among the kinfolk who had not emigrated to Sancorra province as her parents had. Where she had married a good man and borne him four children.

And now this fifth.

Fourteen diviners told her to bear the child in Atalanda. She had not. The karavan diviner had seen tears, grief, and loss in her hand; and she had lost her family. She grieved for them. Cried for them. Had bled in childbirth upon the soil of Alisanos.

Audrun moistened dry, cracked lips as fear threatened to swamp her. "Is she human? Is she whole?"

Dimples flickered briefly in his face. "She is."

That much she had, despite the fact four months of pregnancy had flown by in a matter of moments. She lifted a trembling hand. "Let me see her. Let me *see* her."

Audrun yet lay on her back. Rhuan settled the baby face down against her breasts, lifted and crossed her arms over the child. Without thought the left hand swaddled the tiny spine, elbow hooked under the baby's bottom; her right hand cradled the fuzzed head.

Human. Whole.

But even in the moment of bliss as she met the infant, fear blossomed. Human, and whole. Yes. But this was Alisanos.

Audrun closed her eyes. When she opened them once more, her voice was steady. She looked up into the warm, kind eyes of the man she had known as guide, as Shoia, but who was after all something entirely different. Something entirely *more*.

She stroked the downy fluff upon the infant's head. "We have to find them," she said. "My husband. My children."

There were no dimples in evidence. "It may be difficult."

"That doesn't matter."

He shook his head. "We don't know where they are."

"That doesn't matter, either."

"They may be in the grasslands still, and safe, or here in Alisanos."

"Then we'll look in both places."

"Audrun—"

She was adamant. "We'll look in both places."

The warmth in his eyes was gone. In its place was the chill of bleakness. "We can't leave here, Audrun. *Look* here, yes. That much I can give you. But for how long, I can't say."

Desperation was a tangible ache in her chest. "Why can't you say?"

He took a breath, then released it slowly. "Because Alisanos will change you. It changes every human unfortunate enough to be taken. There may come a time when you no longer remember you had a husband. That you had four other children. Or even that you ever lived in a place other than here."

Audrun tightened her grip on the infant. "And my baby as well? She will be changed?"

After a moment's hesitation, he nodded.

Tears. Grief. Loss. Danger for her children. The karavan diviner had seen it all in the landscape of her hand.

Audrun drew in a trembling breath. "We have to look. We must."

Rhuan reached out and covered her hand as it cradled the infant's head. "We will look."

"For as long as it takes."

His emphasis was delicate. "For as long as we can."

About the Author

Jennifer Roberson wrote her first novel at the age of fourteen, and shortly afterward received her first rejection slip. Fifteen years and several manuscripts later, *Shapechangers* was purchased by DAW Books and a career—and a fantasy series—was born. In addition to the eight-volume "Chronicles of the Cheysuli," Jennifer also concocted the *Sword-Dancer* saga, featuring swords-for-hire Tiger and Del and employing a desert setting she is quite familiar with after residing in Arizona for nearly fifty years. In a departure from her primary genre, Jennifer has also published: three historical novels, two a retelling of the Robin Hood legend, and one set in the seventeenth-century Scottish Highlands, based on an actual incident; and several other titles in various genres. She has also edited fantasy anthologies, and has published nearly thirty short stories.

In 2000 she left the desert behind and moved to Northern Arizona, where she lives on acreage in the shadows of a dormant volcano and the largest ponderosa pine forest in the world. Her primary hobby is the breeding and exhibition of Cardigan Welsh Corgis (the corgi with the tail) and currently shares her household with seven Cardis, one elderly Labrador, and two cats. In 2004 Jennifer embarked on a secondary hobby when she began creating mosaic artwork, which threatens to take over the house.

In the 1990s, Jennifer Roberson collaborated with Melanie Rawn and Kate Elliott on *The Golden Key,* a finalist for the World Fantasy Award. *Karavans* marks the beginning of her first new (solo) fantasy universe since the "Sword-Dancer" series first appeared in 1984. Her website resides at *www.cheysuli.com*.